CORSICAN HONOR

Books by William Heffernan

BRODERICK
CAGING THE RAVEN
THE CORSICAN
ACTS OF CONTRITION
RITUAL
BLOOD ROSE

WILLIAM HEFFERNAN
CORSICAN HONOR

A DUTTON BOOK

DUTTON
Published by the Penguin Group
Penguin Books USA Inc., 375 Hudson Street,
New York, New York 10014, U.S.A.
Penguin Books Ltd, 27 Wrights Lane,
London W8 5TZ, England
Penguin Books Australia Ltd, Ringwood,
Victoria, Australia
Penguin Books Canada Ltd, 10 Alcorn Avenue,
Toronto, Ontario, Canada M4V 3B2
Penguin Books (N.Z.) Ltd, 182–190 Wairau Road,
Auckland 10, New Zealand

Penguin Books Ltd, Registered Offices:
Harmondsworth, Middlesex, England

First published by Dutton, an imprint of New American Library,
a division of Penguin Books USA Inc.
Distributed in Canada by McClelland & Stewart Inc.

First Printing, August, 1992
10 9 8 7 6 5 4 3 2

 REGISTERED TRADEMARK—MARCA REGISTRADA

Library of Congress Cataloging-in-Publication Data

Heffernan, William, 1940-
    Corsican honor / William Heffernan.
      p. cm.
    ISBN 0-525-93465-0
    I. Title.
    PS3558.E4143C64   1992
    813'.54—dc20

PRINTED IN THE UNITED STATES OF AMERICA
Set in Plantin
Designed by Leonard Telesca

PUBLISHER'S NOTE
This is a work of fiction. Names, characters, places, and incidents either are the products
of the author's imagination or are used fictitiously, and any resemblance to actual persons,
living or dead, events, or locales is entirely coincidental.

This book is dedicated, with love, to my youngest children. To Taylor, who always reminds me what it was to be a boy. And to Max, who fills my heart each and every day. And for the little one we now await with love and expectation.

AUTHOR'S NOTE

Many events depicted in this novel are historically true, especially those immediately following World War II. In some cases, historical characters also appear under their own names. This is done purely in a fictional form. At times the sequence of events also may have been altered to achieve a more rapid flow. It is literary license, to be sure. But that is the nature of the novel, and is intended solely for the readers' enjoyment.

PROLOGUE

Wiesbaden, 1980

She felt unbelievably happy. The past three weeks—that incredibly short period of time since she had first met Dieter Rolf—had been the most amazing of her young life. She smiled at herself, at the words she had used to describe her own feelings. *Unbelievable. Incredible. Amazing.* It made her sound like a giggling teenager, not a twenty-two-year-old staff sergeant in the U.S. Army.

But it had been a long time coming. High school had not been the dream everyone had told her it would be. Not in Siesta Key, Florida, anyway. Not where a slightly plump girl didn't exactly send the boys into a frenzy when she walked along a beach, wearing a bathing suit designed to hide baby fat that never managed to get itself hid anyway. No, not for Melissa Walden. She had always been the girl nobody asked to the dances, who nobody asked anyplace. Except, maybe, for a walk on the beach at night. Asked by some boy who'd been drinking beer and who thought a lonely fat girl would do what he wanted. And who'd walk away when he got it. And then tell his friends and laugh about it.

So she had left all that and joined the army after high school. And the army had changed her. She'd lost weight, and her new friends even said she was pretty now. And Dieter thought she was beautiful, and said he was crazy about her.

She smiled to herself, recalling how she had agonized over the decision to re-up for another four years. She had finally done it because the reenlistment had carried a promotion to sergeant and had made her *somebody* at last. And they had posted her to Germany, here to Wiesbaden, and now she had met Dieter. And, oh God, everything was finally going to be all right.

Melissa stretched in her chair and tried to see beyond the sea of people who crowded the discotheque—mostly GI's from the nearby base. It was a converted German beer hall that had telephones on every table, and each table had a light above it, with a number printed on the light, so people could call each other and try to make dates, or whatever. She had liked the idea when her friends had first brought her there. But now she didn't need it. Now she had someone who was coming there just to see her, and, damn, that was so much better.

"You're drooling again, Melissa."

It was her friend, Tanya, a black girl from New York City, from that awful place called Harlem. Tanya, who liked to tease her about it all but who was really happy for her because she understood. She had run away to join the army too. Just to get away from all that shit, she had said.

"Girl, you only met this man two weeks ago, an' already you're leavin' drool marks on your shirt. Get hold a yourself."

"It's been *three* weeks," Melissa said, still not looking at her.

"Well, shit, that's all right, then. You go ahead an' drool on yourself, if you want."

Tanya started to laugh. It was a coarse, raucous laugh, and it was infectious, and Melissa started to laugh too. She couldn't help herself.

They were all laughing now, even Tyrone, the spec 4 Tanya was dating. And Tyrone almost never laughed. He said it gave away his natural camouflage in dark places; made it too easy for these Germans to see where he was. He didn't like Germans much. Didn't like most people, Melissa thought. But especially Germans. And he was always introducing himself as Jesse Owens, said he liked to shake them Germans up. Let them know he wasn't some dumb African who didn't know what their boy Hitler had done all those years ago.

But he had been nice to Dieter the one time he'd met him. Tanya had warned him he better had be or she'd have him cleaning latrines 'til he begged them to ship his ass to Alaska. Tanya was a sergeant too. And nobody messed with her.

"You all look so happy. Now I am really angry with myself for being late."

Melissa's head snapped around and she looked up into Dieter's smiling, handsome face. Her own broke into a huge grin.

Dieter slid into a chair next to her, and he took her hand and kissed it.

"I'm so sorry," he said. He lifted a briefcase with his other hand, showing it to her. "Just as I was getting ready to leave, my chairman gave me all these papers to grade. I was working on them in my office, and I lost all track of time."

Dieter was an instructor at a university in Frankfurt, and had explained to Melissa he was the lowest man on the staff of his department, and therefore got all the work no one else wanted to do.

Melissa squeezed his hand. It didn't matter. Now that he was there. And it didn't matter how low on the staff he was. She thought he was wonderful. And brilliant, and beautiful. She stared at him, pleased just to look at him. At his long blond hair and striking blue eyes. At the slender nose and finely chiseled features. She thought he looked like some kind of Teutonic god. And she wondered what he ever saw in her.

"It doesn't matter," she said. "We were just listening to the music."

Dieter glanced at the numbered light above the table. "And fighting off telephone calls from people who want to steal you away from me," he said.

He watched the woman blush. She had short dark hair and large brown eyes set in a plump, almost cherubic face. And, like her friends, she was only hours away from being a teenager, he thought. Naive and silly and slightly sophomoric. And feeling very worldly, but not even beginning to understand what worldliness involved. He smiled at her.

"I am very lucky," he said, "that you are so understanding."

Melissa beamed at the praise.

"Man, you shouldn't let them push you around like that. Make you some kinda house nigger."

It was Tyrone starting his rap, and Melissa saw Tanya shoot him a look that said: Keep your mouth shut, fool. Tyrone did as he was told. Dieter only shrugged.

"You are probably right," he said. "And, perhaps someday, I will do that." He turned his attention back to Melissa and smiled, telling her he understood, that Tyrone didn't bother him. "Let me get us all some beer," he said.

He turned and signaled to a passing waitress, who carried a large slotted metal carrier of the type milkmen had once used. It was filled with already drawn glasses of beer, and allowed her to move among the tables, dispensing drinks, picking up empty glasses, and collecting money all in one, efficient sweep. It was German ingenuity, and it also gave each waitress the biceps of budding weightlifters.

Dieter slipped his arm around Melissa as he sipped his beer, feeling her slightly plump flesh give against his fingers, thinking of the way she sweated beneath him as they made love. Trying so hard to give all she could. Trying to please him. Trying to show what a good lover she could be. He smiled at the thought of it.

"You look happy," Melissa said, laying her head against his shoulder.

"It is you. You always make me happy," he said.

She pressed her head harder against him.

"Oh, girl. You're makin' me jealous," Tanya said. She snapped around to Tyrone. "What's the matter with you? You sittin' there like some lump, while this man puts you to shame."

"I'm savin' myself," Tyrone said. "For later. Besides, Dieter's too old to do nobody no good."

"You be savin' yourself for nothin,'" Tanya warned. She turned back to Dieter. "That true? You too old, Dieter?"

Dieter smiled, flashing large white teeth. "I am afraid so. I'm thirty-three, and the end is surely near. You know what happened to Jesus at that age."

"See, woman. I told you," Tyrone said, pleased Dieter was supporting him. But still, he couldn't make himself trust the man. There was something about him. And it wasn't just that he was white, or German, or anything like that. Just something.

"Well, don't you worry, Dieter. Melissa here, she ain't gonna nail you to no cross." Tanya rolled her eyes. "She might nail you. But it ain't gonna be to no cross. That's for sure."

Melissa blushed, then began to laugh, joined by the others, and behind them, on the stage, the band struck up "Looking for Love in All the Wrong Places." Melissa began to sing along, swaying back and forth against Dieter to the music.

"Damn shitkicker music," Tyrone mumbled. "Can't play no real music here."

When the song ended, Dieter leaned into Melissa and said he had to get cigarettes, asking her to watch his briefcase until he got back. He thought she seemed pleased to be asked to do even that small thing for him.

"Got some here," Tyrone said, extending a pack of filtered menthols.

"Ah, I must have my own," Dieter said. He winked at the younger man. "We old people, we form habits that are hard to break," he said.

"Glad to see you admittin' it," Tyrone threw back.

Dieter made his way through the crush of people, almost all of them as fresh-faced and naive as the three he had just left. The United States seemed to grow that wide-eyed variety of youth, he thought. Trusting innocents, who didn't seem to receive an appropriate level of jadedness until they were well into their late twenties or early thirties. All of them so intent on having a good time, so eager to push away the need of a solitary serious thought.

A young woman seated at the bar turned slightly and offered him a coy smile as he passed. She was beautiful, as so many American women were, but with a level of subtlety that was laughable. He leaned toward her. "You look very lovely," he said. He watched her smile broaden, anticipating more. He continued past her.

He stopped at the hatcheck booth and slipped off his coat, then smiled at the dour-looking young German woman standing behind the small counter.

"Ah, it is so hot," he said in German. "May I leave this with you?"

The woman shrugged, expressionless. She was quite attractive but so sour. There was some benefit in American naivete, he told himself.

The woman fitted his coat to a hanger, then turned and looked sharply at him. "There is an envelope in the pocket," she said. "I cannot guarantee its safety." She held up the jacket so the envelope in the inside pocket was visible to him.

"Ah, it is just an old business letter," he said. "It is of no consequence."

The woman shrugged, as if to say it was of no consequence to her either, then finished hanging the coat and handed him the claim check. Again he smiled at her, pleased he was doing something to help end her sour day. He turned and walked to the cigarette machine near the door, turned again, and looked back into the crowd. There was no one watching him. He walked past the cigarette machine, and pushed through the door and went out into the fresh, still warm evening air.

He crossed the street quickly and walked to the nearby corner, then stopped and glanced at his watch. A little time, he told himself.

He took a cigarette from a nearly full pack and lighted it, then turned back and watched a handful of people enter the discotheque. The close-cut hair styles of the men told him what they were. More lambs, he told himself, failing to keep back a smile.

He glanced at his watch again, and the smile turned to a cruel smirk. He stepped quickly around the corner, out of the line of the building he had just left.

The explosion was enormous, the concussion rocking him even in his sheltered position, and bits of glass and debris flew past the corner, slamming and cutting into cars passing along the perpendicular street. He stepped back around the corner, into a sea of billowing smoke and dirt, and waited for it to settle.

When it did, he marveled—as he often had—at the effectiveness of Czechoslovakian-made plastique. It was the one thing—save tennis players—that they produced at a dependable level of competence. He smiled. The exterior of the discotheque was a twisted mass of broken rubble, and in the ruins, near what had been the front door, he saw what appeared to be the remains of a human limb.

He thought fleetingly of sweet, innocent young Melissa, who had been so close to the epicenter of the blast—without doubt unwilling to leave her duty of safeguarding his briefcase. And the two *schwarzers* she had foisted upon him for the past week. He would miss Melissa slightly. Miss her foolishness and her eager, sweating young body. Perhaps he might even miss Tanya's humor. Tyrone? The only thing he would miss about him would be the chance to have seen his face just as the bomb exploded beneath his feet. Ah, the

Americans, he thought. The way they let their *schwarzers* abuse and intimidate them. It was their ultimate weakness.

And then, of course, there was that lovely young woman at the bar, who undoubtedly would not smile with such stupid innocence again. And the dour German hatcheck girl. If you live, then you will truly have something to be sour about, he thought.

But he hoped, if she had been killed, it had been from flying debris. He would like the letter in his coat to be found. Of course, it wouldn't really matter. His group was already notifying the media that their leader, Ernst Ludwig, had again struck out at the American capitalist/military horde. But it would be so nice for them to have his handwritten message as well.

He smiled again. Time to put his latest nom de guerre, Dieter Rolf, back into the closet. He would not use it again for years, if ever. He would undoubtedly use the name Dieter again. It had been his father's name, and he took some satisfaction in that.

In the distance he could hear the wailing, staccato blasts of approaching sirens, and he turned and began to walk away. There was a woman, old and withered, standing a few feet from him, her eyes and mouth opened in shock and disbelief. He shook his head as she looked up into his face.

"It is terrible," he said. "These Americans, they make our fatherland safe for none of us."

The woman stared at him, confused, uncertain even of what he had said. He tossed his cigarette into the street and moved past her, repressing the smile that was again forming on his lips.

BOOK I

CHAPTER

1

Marseilles, 1980

Alex Moran dropped his suit coat on his office sofa, seated himself in the high-backed leather desk chair, and turned to face windows that faced out across the rue de Rome at a wall of dull, lifeless buildings. The office was located only a few blocks from the Prefecture and several more from the opera and the innumerable Corsican-run whorehouses that surrounded it. An apt decision—he had often thought—to billet the Defense Intelligence Agency staff in close proximity to the political hacks and prostitutes it so often emulated.

Until a year ago, DIA personnel had operated out of the U.S. Consulate, under a still continuing guise as a U.S. trade mission. Then the Revolutionary Guards had stormed the U.S. Embassy in Tehran and initiated a now endless hostage crisis. And suddenly the security of the consulates worldwide had become questionable, just as his staff's primary objective—monitoring East bloc shipping out of the Port of Marseilles—had fallen victim to its secondary mission, anti-terrorism. And so they had moved, and this new madness had begun.

Marseilles held an Islamic population so diverse it was rivaled only by Amman. This, together with its strategically located port, combined to make it a seat of Middle East intrigue, and Moran's staff of nine had been run ragged keeping watch on every Arab with known or suspected sympathies for their Persian brothers—which meant virtually every Arab in Marseilles.

But now even that had changed. Ernst Ludwig was in the city, and the Iranians—as Moran's Washington boss, Pat Cisco, had explained—were going to have to suck hind tit until he was caught.

Alex turned his chair back to his desk and opened Ludwig's file, which contained everything they knew about the man, sans photograph or physical description. But then, everyone who had ever seen him had been killed—by Ludwig himself—a running total that included five officers of various U.S. agencies.

There was a light rap on Alex's door before his secretary, Julie Ludlow, popped her head inside.

"You ready to start the day?" she asked as the rest of her slightly plump body eased into the room.

Julie was in her mid-thirties, favored a severe, out-of-date page boy for her dark hair, and dressed as though her job were merely a way station en route to a convent. Today she wore a flowered summer dress with a lace collar that left nothing but her arms exposed. Alex had inherited her two years before when he had been promoted to station chief, and had discovered she was deeply infatuated with him. Since that time he occasionally fantasized about how she might look with her armor stripped away. But, at best, it was a fleeting thought.

"Yeah, I suppose I am. What's first on the list?" He ran his fingers through his dark, wavy hair, then stared at the empty coffee cup on his desk.

"I'll get you some coffee," Julie said, catching his gaze. She retrieved the cup and continued to prattle. "You're supposed to see Jim Blount, the new boy in town. Give him a briefing on what you expect of him."

Alex groaned inwardly. "What's he doing now?" he asked, hoping someone had Blount well occupied.

"He's holding court on how he'd retake the embassy in Tehran. It's quite a daring plan, actually." Julie fought back a grin that almost made Alex smile.

"Good. Let's have him reassigned there and get right to it."

"Sorry, I'm afraid he's yours, for better or for worse. Shall I send him in?"

Alex nodded and turned back toward the window. *For better or for worse.* He stared at the building across the street, wondering what his wife, Stephanie, was doing at the consulate. The place where she worked, where he himself had worked until the Iranians decided to play "parade the Americans before the TV cameras." Maybe it wouldn't have happened if he'd stayed at the consulate. He snorted at the immaturity of the thought.

There was another light rap on the door, followed by the entrance of Jim Blount, a tall, angular man of twenty-four or -five—Alex couldn't remember. Somewhere on his desk was Blount's personnel folder, but he didn't much feel like looking for it.

"Grab a chair," he said, then waited for Blount to fold himself into one of two leather guest chairs across from his oversized desk.

Blount's eyes darted about the room, obviously taken with the government version of opulence bestowed on a chief of station. The room was reasonably large, furnished with leather sofa and chairs, carpeted and equipped with an executive-sized walnut desk. The walls held framed maps of France, Europe, and the countries dotting the Mediterranean, but none of the gratuitous, obligatory photographs of the boss with various political bigwigs. Even the photo of President Carter, sent routinely to every government office, was missing. It hung in Julie's outer office, only because Pat Cisco, Alex's boss, had insisted it hang someplace. But compared to the bullpen arrangement for his staff, the office was plush. The government's way of letting the staff know who was in charge, and of spending a few more pennies out of every citizen's tax bill.

"So, this is your first assignment out of training," Alex began.

"Yes, sir. I guess I'm as green as they come." Blount served up a boyish grin with the answer, one that seemed to suit him. He was tall—two or three inches taller than Alex's six feet—with the lean, rangy build of a basketball player. He had blond hair cut unfashionably short and an open, midwestern face that seemed clean-scrubbed and innocent.

"Where you from?" Alex asked.

"Tipp City, Ohio. That's about ten miles north of Dayton."

"Yeah, I know where it is," Alex said, producing an immediate grin from Blount. Apparently not many people he spoke to did.

"I've got your file here someplace, but I can't find it. Tell me about your background."

As Blount began, Julie entered carrying two mugs of coffee and placed one in front of each man. Blount was babbling on—Alex wasn't listening, had never intended to. He would read Blount's file later. This was just a necessary task he didn't much feel like doing.

Something Blount said made Julie smile, but Alex hadn't caught it. Maybe he was retaking another embassy somewhere. She was still grinning when she left the office.

"Are you married?" Alex asked when Blount had finished. The man might have already told him, but he had no way of knowing.

"No, sir. Not yet, anyway." He grinned again.

"Good. Keep it that way." The grin disappeared. "It's just easier," Alex added. "With the hours you'll have to work."

Alex leaned back in his chair. Time to get to the pertinent crap, he told himself. "What do you know about Ernst Ludwig?" he asked.

Blount's brow furrowed in concentration and he began reciting by rote. "German terrorist, age about thirty. Born in Aachen. Father a longtime communist who emigrated to East Berlin when Ernst was five. Educated in East Berlin and Moscow, trained as a terrorist in Libya. Speaks all pertinent European languages, along with Russian, English, and Arabic. Supposed to be the head of the Red Army Faction terrorist group that took responsibility for the disco bombing in Wiesbaden three weeks ago. Strong ties with the East German Stasi and its Libyan counterpart, but prefers to work independently, sort of a loose cannon."

Blount looked expectantly at Alex when he'd finished. Sorry, chum, Alex thought. No gold stars handed out here.

"You know why we don't have a picture or a physical description of this bastard?" Alex asked.

"The file said he's killed every agent who's seen him. German. French. Some of ours."

"Don't forget that part," Alex said, his left eye narrowing slightly. "You're going to be looking for him. Along with the rest of us. It's the only job we're doing right now. We've been thrown into a pressure cooker and told to find him—and to do it fast, before anybody else does. *Before* he gets out of Europe and into some Arab stronghold where we can't get to him. So we'll be pushing hard. Very hard. And I don't want to send anybody home in a box."

Blount shifted uncomfortably in his chair. "Yes, sir" was all he said.

Alex squeezed his eyes between finger and thumb, then leaned forward. "I'm assigning you to work with Stan Kolshak. He's been

around the block more times than he cares to remember. So listen
to him. Do what he says. You go out armed. We don't usually do
that, but Ludwig makes it necessary. Make sure you wear clothes
that hide the weapon. We don't want to make our French friends
nervous. Although in Marseilles a gun's about as shocking as a
necktie. But any complaints raise hackles in Washington, and back
there we've got a lot of people who'd be happy to climb over your
bruised and battered body on their way to the top floor. And not
only back there," Alex added as an afterthought.

When Blount had left, Alex gave the man a few more minutes'
thought. Kolshak would be good for him. Keep him out of trouble.
A picture of the forty-year old agent came to mind. Big and brutish,
but bright. Balding badly, with only a thick band of graying hair
over his ears. Large nose, thick, stubby hands, all of it giving him
the look of a middle-aged butcher, and making him almost indis-
tinguishable in a crowd. The perfect field agent. And thank Christ
he has no intention of retiring when he's eligible next year, Alex
thought.

Yeah, he'll keep the kid out of trouble. Kid. Alex shook his head.
At twenty-five he's only eight years younger than you are. Except,
right now, you're thirty-three going on sixty.

Funny, he had liked Blount right away, something that didn't
happen often. He was eager, genuinely so, and Alex suspected
there'd be a natural antipathy in the man toward everything they
were fighting against. Perhaps it was just that it reminded him of
how he himself had been when he had started out eleven years ago.

Alex rummaged about his desk, finally locating Blount's file. He
ran quickly through it. No, not much similarity at all. He thought
back to his own beginnings with the agency. A doctorate in com-
parative literature at twenty-two. A prodigy—based solely on a
memory that could not forget anything he had read—and headed
for a life in academia that would have bored him to death. At least
that's what his father had told him. But what else would Richard
Pierpont Moran—Piers to his friends—have said, after spending
his entire adult life in the OSS and CIA? It was not the life he had
wanted for Richard, the favored, elder son. For Richard it was
international banking. For Alexander, a chance to serve the nation,
"not squander your intelligence on endless groups of insipid middle-
class brats," as Piers had put it.

So he had been routed to the DIA, rather than his father's own agency, where he'd have had to live under Piers's overwhelming shadow. Now his father was retired and a director of the Florida bank Richard headed. And the number two son was in Marseilles, trying to catch a terrorist and keep his wife at the same time. Alex closed his eyes. Bit of self-pity there, he told himself. Bit of an Oedipus complex? No, just disgruntled at being the least-favored son.

He looked back at Blount's file. No, you're right. Not really much similarity at all.

He put the file aside and scanned his desk, thinking about all the bureaucratic bullshit he still had to wade through. He had never thought about becoming chief of station before he married, about rising in the bureaucratic hierarchy. He had liked field work, the challenge. Yes, even the danger it occasionally involved. He sure as hell didn't like the back stabbing and political games that were integral to those who directed it all. But he had done it, because it seemed like the right thing at the time. To impress Stephanie? Or was it to show his father that he too could rise in the ranks? Who the hell knew. Or cared.

He pushed it all away and turned back to Ludwig's file. The problem—the only problem—was to figure out where the bastard was holed up. The KGB would be covering him. And that meant Bugayev. He had gone up against the KGB *rezident* repeatedly over the years, and as often as not, Bugayev had won. At best the game between them had been a stalemate.

He reached into a desk drawer and pulled out a street map of Marseilles. He really didn't need it. The map, like everything he read, was imprinted on his mind. But it gave him something to do. Kept him away from the bureaucratic nonsense. Kept Stephanie out of his thoughts.

His eyes moved to the silver-framed photograph at the corner of his desk, and he reached out, took it, and slid it into the center drawer. He was good at hiding things. That was part of what being a spy was all about. Now he had to do the other part: find what the opposition didn't want him to find.

He looked back at the map. Something seedy in the Arab quarter of the old city? Could Ludwig pass as an Arab? He doubted it. Maybe something upscale. Christ, it wouldn't surprise him if Bugayev had him planted in an apartment in his own building. A few floors down.

What you need is more men on the street than you have available. Men who know every gutter and everybody who's walked through it. Leave your people to watch Bugayev's, see who they visit.

Alex sat back in his chair, accepting the inevitable. "Time to get some help from Uncle Antoine," he said aloud.

CHAPTER

2

Ernst Ludwig sat on an overstuffed sofa, head back, eyes closed, as he listened to the Chopin prelude coming from the portable stereo recorder, and ignored the words of Sergei Bugayev that floated in from across the room.

"Listen to the music, Sergei," he said. "It will calm you."

"I am calm," Bugayev said.

"If you were, I wouldn't hear the clacking of those fucking beads."

Bugayev glanced down at the Arab worry beads he held in one hand. It was an affectation, at worst a habit. Something he had picked up during a posting in Syria years before. The same place he had first met this arrogant German, he told himself.

The Russian stared across the room. Ludwig's eyes were still closed and there was a slight smirk on his lips. But then Bugayev imagined it was there when the man slept as well, something permanently affixed to his handsome Aryan face. And there especially when he killed.

He despised the man and it made his job all the harder. Ludwig was well loved at Moscow Center. The jackal who did the bidding of their jackal, the Stasi, and did it without ever leaving a trail back to the lair, back to his true masters.

The latest "victory" had been the bombing of a discotheque in Wiesbaden. Fifteen U.S. servicemen killed, along with ten West German nationals. Dozens of both types mutilated. Another victory for socialism.

Bugayev snorted to himself. And now it is your job to get this scum safely to Libya, where, no doubt, those madmen will place a medal on his tunic. And all for the *Rodina*. Mother Russia. He shook his head. Ah, Bugayev, he told himself. You are thinking treason again. Someday you will say it out loud. Then you will find yourself behind the wire instead of outside it.

"I would appreciate it, comrade, if you would give me just a few minutes of your time." Bugayev used the term comrade formally, and with obvious distaste. He crossed the room and stood before Ludwig. The man's eyes were still closed, the smirk still fixed to his lips.

Ludwig jerked forward with such suddenness, it gave Bugayev a start. The eyes snapped open and the German stood, walked slowly to a mirror, and began running long fingers through his blond hair. "Of course, comrade," he said, imitating Bugayev's distaste, still looking at himself, turning his head from side to side. "Whatever pleases you."

He glanced at Bugayev in the mirror, amused at their images juxtaposed that way. Bugayev, short, fat, and balding, with a flat, Slavic face that was one step short of being truly ugly. And still dressing in those shapeless Russian suits despite so many years in the West. He allowed his eyes to return to his own features. The fine, slender Aryan nose, the strong jaw and wide mouth, the prominent cheekbones that set off the dark blue eyes that drew so many women to him. He smiled at himself, then held the smile, enjoying his perfect teeth. If I looked like this Russian, he thought, I'd plant a bomb in my own room.

Ludwig was laughing softly to himself as he turned to face the KGB *rezident*. He even smirks when he laughs, Bugayev thought.

"Is there something funny, comrade?"

"Not really. I was just noticing how ugly you are."

Bugayev pressed his lips together in a grimace of a smile, shook his head slowly, then looked up into Ludwig's eyes. He hated looking up at the man. But at five feet ten, Ludwig was a full three inches taller than he, so he had no choice. There were, in fact, few adults he had not had to look up at in his life. But that did not make it any easier. Certainly no easier than being ugly.

"We cannot all be possessed of your Aryan good looks," he said. "But still we are needed, if for no other purpose than contrast."

The nearly hidden bitterness in the man's words made Ludwig

laugh again. "I read somewhere that all short, fat, ugly men"—he gestured toward Bugayev as though there might be some doubt about the identity of his subject—"and women too, I suppose, think of themselves as tall and slender and handsome. Is that true, comrade?"

"As long as there are no full-length mirrors present," Bugayev said.

Ludwig gave him a sidelong look and smirked again. "Or people cruel enough to remind one, eh, Bugayev?"

"There are always people cruel enough, comrade."

Ludwig's smirk turned into a genuine smile. It was as though Bugayev were saying there would always be vermin—vermin in such numbers they would consistently return no matter how many one killed. Ludwig decided he liked the thought, whether Bugayev had intended it or not. He was certain he had. He rubbed his hands together and turned back to the mirror and rotated his head from profile to profile. "So tell me about my escape to Libya," he said.

Bugayev turned and started back across the room, speaking as he did. "The ship will be here in three days, spend two days loading cargo, then off again. You will board her the day she arrives. The area will not be closely watched then because the ship will be unloading nothing. You will go on board as an officer who is replacing a man injured at sea and removed from the ship in Crete. Such an officer will arrive by plane that day and will go through all necessary customs matters. So, even if suspicions are raised, the French will have enough documentation in hand to resist any actions that might create an incident." Bugayev shrugged. "And you know how the French hate incidents. So uncivilized."

"I would prefer to board the ship just before it sails," Ludwig said. "Two extra days aboard one of your stinking cargo ships doesn't exactly appeal to me."

"It can't be helped," Bugayev said, taking private pleasure in dispensing some discomfort. "Just as it can't be helped that you must remain in this apartment until the ship arrives."

Ludwig turned his head to the right and studied the apparent start of a blemish on his left cheek. "That's nonsense," he said. "I have no intention of staying in this shithole any more than necessary."

"But it *is* necessary. Your recent . . . raid caused quite a stir. There were a few too many innocents in the discotheque when your bomb went off. But then, it's the kind of place populated by innocents, isn't it?"

Ludwig stared at Bugayev's reflection and allowed his lips to move slowly into a grin. "Do I sense disapproval, comrade?" He began to laugh, then stopped abruptly. "Innocents, you call them. I must confess, I prefer the American military's terminology for civilians who happen to get in the way of ordnance. They call it 'collateral damage.' Nice phrase, eh, comrade?" He turned to face the smaller man, his eyes and mouth hard now. "But I choose to put them in the way. And do you know why, comrade? I do it because there are no innocents. There are only those who support the cause and those who don't. And the ones who die serve as a good object lesson for the others." The snide smile returned. "It helps them understand which side they must choose." He shrugged, imitating Bugayev's earlier gesture. "And I have no intention of hiding. As you said, the French don't like incidents, so I doubt they want me caught on their territory."

"It's not the French who will try to catch you, comrade."

"Who then? The CIA?" Ludwig laughed. "They've tried before."

"The American Defense Intelligence Agency has a team in the streets now," Bugayev said. "They're good, and the man who leads them is good. I've dealt with him before."

"And they have no idea what the great monster, Ernst Ludwig, even looks like," Ludwig said. He started to laugh, then gave Bugayev a hard look. "I've killed everyone who's ever seen me, comrade. Everyone except those I know would never betray me." He continued to stare into Bugayev's eyes, making sure the full intent of his message was received. He turned back to the mirror. "And who is this American you fear so much?" he asked.

"His name is Alex Moran. And I don't fear him, comrade. I simply choose not to underestimate him." Bugayev offered another philosophical shrug. "But then, my perspective is different from yours. I don't look upon you as invincible, so I can't allow myself to underestimate him."

Ludwig's jaw tightened and his eyes flashed momentary anger. Then he began to laugh. "Well, that solves our problem, comrade. Because I do choose to underestimate him." His eyes began to glitter with pleasure. "Are you one of the many communists who still prays, Bugayev?" he asked.

Bugayev shook his head. "No," he said.

"Too bad. I was going to suggest you pray that I am right. Your masters in Moscow would be very unhappy if you failed to protect me. My death would be too great a propaganda victory for the West. And my capture . . ." He shook his head as though words could not describe the disaster that event would produce. He turned back to the mirror. "But that's your problem, not mine. Isn't that right, Bugayev?"

Bugayev offered Ludwig's reflection a cold smile. "Yes, that is right, comrade. But even more important is the great personal sadness your death or capture would cause me."

Ludwig's eyes snapped to Bugayev's reflection in the mirror. Then he threw back his head and laughed.

CHAPTER

3

The Corniche President Kennedy wound along the edge of the sea, skirting the steep limestone cliffs and sandy coves almost as if intent on showing off the stark beauty of Marseilles's coastline. Across the road, the rich villas of the bourgeoisie formed an opulent rampart, the large houses standing guard over sprawling lawns and gardens, the upper stories staring out toward the sea, blind to all else but the wealth and privilege of their owners. And amid that wealth, nearly dominating it in size and grandeur, was the villa of Antoine and Meme Pisani, the Corsican brothers who had ruled the Marseilles underworld for the past thirty years.

Alex Moran watched the Pisani villa come into view as he drove along the coastal highway. He knew the house well; he had been present, as a boy, at the party that had launched it into this community of riches—a party roundly avoided by the other denizens, who, to a person, had found themselves conveniently elsewhere rather than be forced to offer offense to two men the newspapers regularly labeled as murderous.

Alex smiled at the memory—he had not understood it then, although his father had tried to explain—but even more at the ongoing contradiction between the house and the men who owned it, and what it had been turned into by the very nature of those men.

The house, though only twenty-five years old, had been built to conform with—but in most ways to outshine—its neighbors, many of which already had been in existence for over a century, having been built by the shipping giants who dominated Marseilles during its halcyon days as a port. It was a solid, gracious house, three stories of stucco, covered by a red tile roof, with long French windows, each opening on to a series of balconies. At each corner of the house large palm trees marked the beginnings of gently sloping gardens, bisected by a long driveway that began at the encircling spiked iron fence and ended in a loop around a simple fountain that stood before the front entrance.

What viewers of this magnificent house could not see were the steel-reinforced shooting positions built into balconies at each corner and designed to handle incoming and outgoing automatic-weapons fire, and the metal plates embedded in the driveway, which at the toss of a switch would raise foot-long steel spikes capable of disabling any approaching vehicle.

What viewers could see were the two solid-looking men who stood guard at the gate, each offering the promise of weapons not far from hand and making it clear that those who lived within were men to whom violence was neither uncommon nor unexpected.

But that was only apparent to those who looked closely, those who truly understood what they were looking at. And the men who lived here were so much a part of Alex—had been so much a part of his life since childhood—that he often thought even he couldn't see them clearly. See them as they really were. They were his uncles, and as a child they had often told him he had Corsican blood, that they had given it to him when he was just a baby. And sometimes he thought it must be true.

Alex pulled up to the gate and allowed his eyes to follow the long drive up to the house itself. It was truly magnificent, he thought, again marveling, as he often had, at the difference between American and European gangsters. In the States a modern mafioso would never dare live in such obvious splendor for fear the IRS would swoop down on him like a starving vulture. Here, in Europe, and especially among members of the Corsican *milieu*, it was almost demanded, lest one's competition view a lack of display as a lack of strength.

Alex's thoughts were interrupted by a light tap on the driver's window, and he automatically pulled the latch that opened the trunk. Once the guard, whom Alex knew only as Angelo, had inspected both the trunk and the front and rear seats, he asked

Alex to step from the car to be gently frisked. He then nodded to his companion, who manually opened the gate. No matter how many times Alex had visited the Pisanis—and always telephoning ahead, as he had this time—the routine had never changed. One simply did not survive in the *milieu* by assuming your friends—or your family—would never kill you.

As he pulled the car around the fountain and stopped, the front door of the house burst open and Antoine Pisani exploded down the stairs. There was no other way to describe Antoine's movements, unless it were to compare them to the release of a bull at a *corrida*. Even at sixty he moved like a man half his age, and his blustery warmth and energy always brought an amused grin to Alex's face.

"Alex, you donkey," he roared in French, the only language the Pisanis and Alex used with one another. "You haven't visited your uncle in years."

It had actually been six weeks since Alex had come to the house to have lunch with his two "uncles," but he had no time to say it before Antoine gripped him in two bear-like arms and lifted him off the ground with bone-crushing affection.

"Why don't you ever visit me?" Antoine demanded, punctuating his question by kissing Alex on each cheek.

"I do," Alex insisted, returning Antoine's kisses as the only way he knew of being returned to the ground. "It's just that you're getting old and you forget."

Antoine released him, stepped back, and conspiratorially tapped his nose with one finger. "I forget nothing," he said. "I still remember you peeing your pants when we were boar hunting in Corsica."

"I never did," Alex snapped, playing the game they had played out many times before. "And even if I had, I was only ten when it happened."

"A pants pisser at ten will be a pants pisser at ninety," Antoine intoned. His piercing blue eyes bore into Alex, his long white mane of hair making his words seem like those of a prophet. But then his unusually ruddy complexion became even redder, and his face burst into a smile. One log-like arm encircled Alex's neck and pulled him against the older man's chest. "Damn, it's good to see you," he roared. "When I told Meme you were coming, he wouldn't believe me, it's been so long."

"How is Uncle Meme?"

"Ahh," Antoine snorted, waving one hand in disgust. "He's a pain in the ass, like he always is. How do you expect him to be?"

Alex thought of his other Corsican "uncle." Antoine's brother, Meme, was a man as different from Antoine as nature could make him. Meme was a year younger, but frail and aesthetic, a quiet, balding man with a simmering violence beneath his calm exterior, shown only in dark brown eyes that became nearly black when angry. Said to be a wizard in financial matters, he was no less violent than his elder brother. But where Antoine would kill with a club, it was said Meme would use a stiletto, and he would make sure that death was a long and painful process.

But those were in the old days, Alex reminded himself. Long ago when they had worked for his father. Now there were minions who did the killing. Hundreds of them. He wondered if that meant Antoine and Meme had mellowed.

He smiled to himself as Antoine bundled him through the front door. He had stopped trying to analyze his feelings for these two men. He understood the personal affection he felt for them, feelings ingrained in him since boyhood. And he knew how much he despised what they did "to earn their bread," as they put it: the drugs, the prostitution, illegal enterprise atop illegal enterprise, and the ever present violence that seemed a common thread through it all. So, on a business side, he dealt with them only as intelligence assets—who, as a rule, were seldom ideal. And on a personal level he ignored who and what they were. It wasn't the easiest of tightrope acts, but so far it had worked. He had become adept at disregarding the truth.

Antoine ushered him into the study, where Meme was seated on one side of a massive partner's desk the two brothers shared. The room, unlike the rest of the house, was what a film director would have—and had—offered as a gangster's study: Spacious and dark, heavy with wood paneling and leather furniture, a place of sinister brooding and filled with the residue of planned mayhem.

Meme jumped to his feet as Alex entered, a broad smile on his narrow, gaunt face, and all images of the gangster's lair disappeared from Alex's mind. He rushed across the room and embraced his "nephew," kissing his cheeks and being kissed in return. He stepped back, held Alex's shoulders at arm's length, and nodded his head. "You look tired," he said in French. "And it's too early in the day to look as tired as you do." Meme turned and guided Alex across the room toward a seating area before an unlighted fireplace. "Come. Sit. Have an aperitif. We will talk, then we will have lunch." He smiled with uneven teeth, the gift of an impoverished youth that he had never tried to alter. "But, first, tell us what news you have of your father. He is even a greater stranger here than you are."

They sat and talked for nearly a half hour before adjourning to the dining room for lunch. Alex told them of his last letter from his father, and of the quiet life he professed to be living in Palm Beach, spending most of his days at the exclusive Everglades Club, a ritual interrupted only by the occasional meetings demanded by his position as a director of the bank his elder son, Richard, headed.

Both brothers nodded sagely at the news, not believing a word of it but accepting Alex's need for discretion. CIA executives—like men in their own profession—simply did not retire, their manner said, and Alex wanted to laugh and assure them it was true, as far as he knew. But that was it. *As far as he knew.* It was a phrase he would have to add in all honesty, and one he knew they would interpret in the only way they could.

After a lunch of poached salmon they returned to the study and resumed their places before the nonexistent fire. It was time for business, the unexplained help Alex had said he would need when he had telephoned that morning.

"So tell us, nephew, what small service we can do for you," Meme began. By the simple use of the fictitious familial term it was clear whatever Alex asked would be done. No true Corsican, they believed, could refuse a family member any service, up to and including the slitting of an offending throat.

"There is a man in Marseilles that I must find," Alex began. "It's business, and my people are working on it. But the time I have is short and I need more assets on the street."

Alex went on to explain who Ludwig was, the help he was receiving from the Soviets, and the belief he was en route to Libya or another radical middle eastern nation. He could see from the look on both men's faces that the words *terrorist* and *communist* had made all additional discussion unnecessary. Alex fought back a smile. Like most of the gangsters he had ever met or heard of, they were ultra conservative and highly patriotic. It was a complete contradiction, especially when one considered they had spent most of their lives trying to subvert the very principles they espoused.

When he had finished, Meme leaned forward in his chair, looking like an aging bookkeeper about to make some point about the company accounts. "You want this man alive? Or is this unimportant?"

"Alive would be better. We could learn a great deal if he were able to talk," Alex said. "But I don't want any of your people hurt unnecessarily. The man's killed every agent who's gotten close enough to dust him or collar him. And every one of those agencies is looking for him right now. So I'd rather have him dead than add to his body count."

Meme and Antoine nodded. They understood the American terminology and appreciated the sentiment. Meme stood and adjusted the dapper suit he wore, light-years away from Antoine's rumpled sack. "I'll make arrangements now," he said. "If the man stays in Marseilles even a few days, or is foolish enough to leave his hole, we will find him." He shrugged. "If we knew what he looked like, we would not even need a few days. We'd simply put his description out on the street and watch every possible exit route. This fish would never swim out of our net. Now we will just need time to filter through the strangers in the city." He shrugged again and left the room. The accountant off to do his sums, Alex thought.

"Now, put your mind to rest on this," Antoine said, leaning back in his chair and folding his hands over his sizable but rock-hard paunch. "Tell me of your beautiful Stephanie, and when there will be a child for me to play with."

Alex quickly masked the pain that flashed across his eyes, but not before Antoine had noticed. "We both work such long hours, I don't know how we'd manage a child right now."

Antoine leaned forward, prepared to pursue the matter, then thought better of it. Alex would talk to him when he was ready. And then he would tell him everything, not just what was forced from him.

"You must tell Stephanie that we miss her. And that I refuse to let you make her a stranger to our home," he said.

Alex smiled and nodded, but the smile was a weak one.

"I'll tell her," Alex said.

Antoine and Meme stood side by side on the front steps as they watched Alex's car retreat down the driveway.

"Something is wrong with him," Meme said. "Inside, something is very wrong."

"Yes, I think you are right," Antoine answered.

CHAPTER 4

Alex poured himself a drink, his second since he had got home—two in less than an hour, a lot for him. He looked at the clock. In ten minutes Stephanie would be an hour late, although he wasn't sure what time she normally arrived, since he always got there later than she. He knew what time she finished work, and how long it should take her to reach their apartment from the consulate. He was basing it on that. If she came straight home. If that were her usual thing to do. If she wasn't tied up with something else. . . . Someone else. He pushed the thought away. Hating it. Hating himself for thinking it. Knowing he had every right to, every reason. Hating that as well.

The sound of the key turning in the lock stiffened his back, and he turned to watch Stephanie enter. Beautiful. Always so beautiful.

She seemed startled to see him. Surprised? No, startled. Of course, he was never home early. To check up on her? On when *she* got home? Was this the way it was going to be now? Fuck her. Let her think and worry about whatever she wanted.

"Hello, darling," she said. "This is a nice surprise. What finally got you home early?"

"Just couldn't stand the office anymore," Alex said.

"Good. I hope the feeling continues. I'm glad this Ludwig thing isn't driving you crazy." There was an all's right with the world smile on her face.

Alex returned it. "Want a drink?" he asked.

"Love one."

She sat on the sofa and watched him pour a glass of white wine he had already set out on ice.

"Usually something like this Ludwig matter leaves you so tense and single-minded. Is it over already?"

He came toward her, handed her the glass of chilled wine. "No, it's not over. Something else has taken precedence."

"Oh. What's that?"

"My wife sleeping with another man."

The color drained from her face; the wine glass trembled slightly.

"How did you find out?"

"Someone saw you going into a hotel with someone, saw him register, and saw you both go up to a room." He stared at her. "Then come down a few hours later." He studied his own drink. "All the intelligence services—the French, the British, everyone—have watchers in every hotel. But you knew that, didn't you?"

"I guess I forgot." Her hand was still trembling, the wine shaking in her glass. But she kept her eyes on his, almost as though she were unable to look away.

"How long has it been going on?" He watched her eyes blink, then look away. She seemed suddenly different to him, more like a young girl forced to explain something she had hoped no one would ever know.

Stephanie looked back at him, her eyes and voice soft. "Does it matter?"

"It does to me." His voice cracked slightly and he hated that it had.

"Oh, Alex. That's just torturing yourself. Next you'll want to know how many times, and where. Don't do that to yourself."

She tossed her long blond hair back with a twist of her head. It was a practiced gesture, something that drew attention to her, something he had always thought she had rehearsed, standing in front of a mirror as a young girl. He had always liked it. It was part of her. And was this part of her too? He didn't know. But he knew she was right. Knowing the details would only make it worse. But maybe he needed to know. Know how deeply he'd been cut. Maybe it would make him understand the pain he felt, eating away at his guts like a hungry animal.

He stared at her, unable to speak for a moment. She looked tall and willowy, even now seated across from him on their living room sofa. The dark blue eyes, the high cheekbones. Sculpted features that still made his breath catch at times, just looking at her. And she was dressed so perfectly, always was. Ever since he had first seen her. The fine silk blouse she wore now, the striking blue setting off her coloring so well. The tailored slacks and stylish shoes. Even here at home, alone with him, she always dressed extravagantly. But never jewelry. The only jewelry she wore were the engagement and wedding rings he had given her. She never took them off. *Never.*

They had married five years before, only months after they had met. She had been twenty-five then, a newly arrived translator at the consulate. Fresh out of Vassar and Columbia. He had teased her about that. And she had laughed, enjoyed it. But she had known she was everything he had ever been taught to look for in a woman. And she had told him so.

Alex stood and walked to the wide windows that looked out onto the Mediterranean, the azure waters glistening under a bright sun. It should be dark and overcast, he thought. Like it is when the mistral blows in winter. But it was summer now, and the days were warm and bright and beautiful, one after another.

Behind him another bank of windows looked out over the city and the rising bell tower of the nineteenth-century Basilica of Notre-Dame-de-la-Garde. It was the perfect place to live. A towering apartment on the Corniche President Kennedy. The perfect place for the perfect couple, living out the fantasy of a government posting in the south of France.

"Can you at least tell me why?" he finally asked.

Stephanie stared at his back. He was standing there in his shirt-sleeves, his body silhouetted against the bright sun as it reflected off the water. He wore a fitted shirt that hugged the slim, hard body she had always loved. So different from the man she had chosen to be with. Why? He wants to know why?

She looked down at the floor, her hair falling forward, surrounding her face like a veil. She snapped her head up, exhaled, then tossed her hair back over her shoulders.

"I'm not sure I can tell you why," she said at length. "I'm not sure I can explain it to myself, without making it sound like some cheap bloody excuse." She straightened her back, then drew another deep breath. "Sometimes," she began, then stopped. "Sometimes I feel smothered by how much you love me." She shook her head, sending her hair forward again, then tossed it back. "And sometimes I feel you don't even know I exist. You become so involved in your work, in all the things going on in your head. You don't even seem to know I'm here. Oh, I know you love me. And I know you try so hard to make me happy. But you seem to have this pre-set image of me, this pat idea of what I am, of what I need." She drew a long breath that seemed to catch in her throat. "I'm not the person you think I am. The person you want to think I am." She stared at his back again, watching the shoulders stiffen. "Oh, it's not just you. It's everyone I've ever known. Everyone who's ever been in my life."

"And your 'friend' at the consulate, he doesn't make you feel that way?" Alex had used the word *friend* like the cutting edge of a knife, slashing out at her. He regretted it at once, but knew he'd do it again.

"I don't want to talk about him. There's no point." He still hadn't turned to face her, offering only his back. Now he did, his lean, six-foot frame swiveling against the bright backdrop of the Mediterranean. Stephanie stared up at his face. It wasn't a classically handsome face. She had never thought it was. His features were strong, rugged, and in that sense it was handsome. But now it seemed soft, almost puffy.

"Have there been others?" His left eye had narrowed slightly, something that signaled a building anger, almost a warning to others, especially other men.

"Oh God, Alex. These questions don't do any good. It happened. I can't really explain it. It's nothing that anyone did or didn't do. The opportunity presented itself, and I guess I needed it, or at least wanted it." She ran the fingers of both hands through her hair, almost as though she were going to grab it, pull it. "I know this couldn't be happening at a worse time for you. I know you're under a great deal of pressure, that what you're doing now is dangerous, and you don't need all of this crowding your mind. I wish it hadn't happened now." She paused, as if correcting herself. "Especially now. Please believe that."

Alex stared at her, wondering if she regretted "it" at all, afraid to ask if she did.

"What will you do?" Her eyes entreated him.

"I don't know." The honesty of his answer surprised him.

Stephanie stood and came to him, slipping her arms under his and pressing her head against his chest. "I love you. Please believe that too."

He could feel her pressing against him, the moment slowly becoming sexual. It sent a shiver of both desire and revulsion through him.

"Come to bed with me. Please. I need you. I need to know you still love me."

Over her shoulder he could see the tower of the Basilica. It had been one of their favorite places when they were courting, walking up the steep hill from the center of the city, hand in hand, joking, teasing each other about how romantically hackneyed it all was. It seemed different now, juxtaposed against the soft, beseeching sensuality of her voice. Now he hated the sight of it.

"Please," she whispered. He could feel her tears dampening his shirt, and he wanted to push her away, strike out at her, something he had never done to any woman. And then he could feel himself hardening against her, knew she could feel it too.

"I don't know if I can," he said, hating his own weakness, knowing he wanted her to ask him to try.

"Just come into the bedroom," she said. "Let me love you." She turned and slipped her hand in his and led him across the room. He felt like a small child being taken to school on his first day.

Her mouth slid across his chest and down his body, licking him, kissing him, and his fingers gripped the sheet as if that was all that held him to the bed. Her hand cupped his testicles, the fingers moving gently, almost imperceptibly, and she took him in her mouth, her own passion seemingly ignited now, her head and mouth and tongue moving wildly, forcing him to arch his neck in the near painful pleasure of it. But he knew it was all a ruse, a way for her to make him believe she still wanted him, still loved him. And to show him how much he still wanted her. And she succeeded and yet failed at the same time, as his mind attacked him, wondering if this was what she had done for *him*. And how many times, and where. And why. Yes, most of all. Why?

And, worst of all, he could see her hand. See the rings he had given her.

CHAPTER 5

The music filled the large garret apartment, the sound captured under the eaves of the roof and held there with no escape possible.

Ernst Ludwig winced at the volume, at the mixture of cigarette and marijuana smoke that assaulted his nostrils, at the tightening grip of the young woman who held onto his arm as though afraid he might escape. It seemed as if all his senses were being attacked at once. And he loved it.

He had discovered the party that afternoon at a small café on La Canebière, when he had stopped for a coffee. Or, rather, it had discovered him. The young woman who now clung to him had been there with a small group of friends, all fellow students, and she had flirted so openly, so flagrantly, that he had been amused and simply walked to their table and joined her. Blatancy to blatancy, much to the shock and surprise of her friends, much to her delight, and from there to here—this after-classes party—in the twinkling of an insistent invitation.

The music changed, a faster, earthier, more urgent beat, and Justine—her name was Justine—began to gyrate next to him. Ludwig looked at her and smiled. She was quite lovely. Short dark hair and green eyes. A large, wide mouth that excited him, and a nose that was long and straight and very French. And her body was exquisite, even offering full breasts, so unusual for a young Frenchwoman.

"Dance with me," Justine said, smiling, tugging him toward the center of the crowded room. She used her native tongue with all the sensuality it was purported to possess.

He went and began to dance smoothly but unexcitedly, choosing instead to watch her, to enjoy the obstreperousness of her movements. She was truly fucking him without penetration, and sweating and smiling and enjoying it.

When the music ended, replaced by something mournfully romantic and French, they drifted toward a long table that was serving as a bar. There was a group of students, the males bearded to a man, the women all dressed in the obligatory black, each and every one discussing the need for revolution, the change in social structure so essential for mankind.

He wanted to laugh in their faces. Yes, the change would come. But not from these fools, who would puke their guts out if forced to stand ankle deep in the blood required of revolution, who would be horrified to discover that revolution only meant the changing of those in power, those who would hand out the "better life" to the masses, but who themselves would prove just as elite, just as corrupt as those who dispensed it now, however badly.

Justine went up on her toes to place her lips close to his ear. "You should tell them what you think. What it is really like," she whispered.

He looked at her quickly. It was almost as if she had read his mind. His eyes hardened on hers. And if not that, certainly she knew more about him than was possible. Unless . . . unless . . . "Why do you say that?" He had told her his name was Peter Luntz, that he was Swiss, and an instructor in economics at the university in Zurich.

"Because I know who you are," she whispered.

He smiled at her, trying to appear amused by her romanticism, then took her arm and led her to a quieter corner. His stomach was churning, and he could feel fresh sweat beginning to form under his shirt—sweat that was not from the dancing or the close quarters of the room. "And what have you decided I am?" he asked when they were alone.

"You're a terrorist," she said, grinning wildly. "You are certainly not Swiss but German. I can tell. I'm very good with accents. I studied acting for a time, and my teacher said I had the most natural ear he'd ever heard."

Ernst nodded. Probably while he was fucking you, he thought.

He was beginning to relax. He forced a smile and a small laugh. "I will be whatever you want me to be," he said. He slid his hand into his jacket pocket, feeling the handle of the switchblade stiletto. He could move her back into the crowd of dancers and slide the blade into her so expertly she would never make a sound. She would merely gasp and fall to the floor; he would already be moving away, and her friends and everyone else would simply think she was drunk, or stoned, and had suddenly passed out.

He looked at her again and laughed, more convincingly this time. No, the little fool offered no threat. He would let her play her game and he would enjoy her. He would kill her only if she annoyed him. Or if it amused him to do so.

"God, I'm so hungry. I could eat everything. Even you. Especially you." Justine looked at Ludwig and giggled. She was drunk and stoned and she was drawing attention to herself.

They were in a small restaurant, where she had insisted on going after leaving the party. She had just finished her second order of *sabayon*, and he was convinced she would want even more of the sickly sweet dessert. But then her mood suddenly shifted, and she began running her shoeless toe against his ankle beneath the table; there was a glint of mischief in her eyes.

"Why do you lie to me?" she asked, her voice coy rather than offended. "You tell me you're Swiss, but I can tell you're German. You tell me you're a teacher, but I know what you really are." She gave him an impish grin, then leaned forward and whispered: "You tell me your secrets, and I'll tell you mine."

"But I already know your secrets," Ludwig said.

Justine sat back and assumed a haughty look. "Oh, and what are they?"

Ludwig leaned forward, imitating Justine's feint at intimacy. "You love *sabayon*," he whispered, "and you are absolutely wicked in bed." She began to giggle. "What I don't know," he continued, "is whether it is your natural inclination, or if it is the *sabayon* that makes you depraved."

"Then you must bring some *sabayon* to my bed and conduct an experiment," she said.

Justine lived in a small apartment not far from the New Labor Exchange. It was decorated in student motif, as Ludwig suspected it would be, complete with a heroic poster of Che Guevara, to which

Justine took pains to draw his attention. It was as though she were proclaiming that she too was a revolutionary in whose company he could feel safe and at ease. The thought made him smile, and he wished he had the inclination to explain to the little fool that only those who played at revolution hung posters on their walls. Those who worked at it made themselves appear anything but what they were. But he had neither the inclination nor the interest. He had only one use for this woman, and her political education played no part in it.

Justine took his hands in hers and began slowly moving back toward the large bed that dominated one corner of the room. She was smiling lasciviously, and as he looked past her shoulder he realized the bed—actually a mattress laid atop an elevated platform—had the quality of an altar about it that was definitely intended. When they reached the foot of the platform Justine slipped her arms about him and pressed her body against his.

"Tell me how you do it," she whispered, undulating her pelvis against him with a faint, almost unnoticeable pressure that was more erotic than if it had been done with abandon. "Tell me how you kill for the revolution."

Ernst ran his hand down her back, caressing the sharp curve of her buttock, arousing himself with the firmness, the severity of it. "Why do you want to know about it?" he whispered, allowing his tongue to lightly roam the inner contour of her ear. "What will it do for you to know?"

Justine arched her back and rotated her hips. She wanted the talk to arouse him, drive him into a frenzy. She could feel what it was doing for her. She was already so wet, so ready to have him. But she wanted more. She wanted him beyond the point of control. She wanted him unable to dictate the flow of their lovemaking. She wanted to dominate him, and she wanted him to feel that domination, to know there was nothing he could do about it, and to realize that he didn't care. That his pleasure was so intense he just wanted it to continue, so intense he would beg her not to stop if he had to. It was her fantasy, and she knew if she could make it work, her own pleasure would be overwhelming.

"It will make me so hot to hear it, to hear you talk about it. I want to know how you do it. If you use a bomb or a gun. I want to know how it makes you feel: if it excites you, or makes you sad. I don't think it makes you sad. I think maybe it makes you hot."

She was rambling and she knew it, knew it was part of what she wanted to do. But still, there was some loss of control for her in doing it. And she could feel it arousing him, feel his body stiffen, and just feeling it, and hearing herself do it, was driving her into her own frenzy.

"*You* make me hot," Ernst whispered as he began to run his mouth along her neck. He was fighting back fear now, the same fear that had come to him earlier when she had begun insisting she knew he was a terrorist. But he was certain she was just playing with him, simply cajoling him into acting out her own sexual game. She knew nothing, could know nothing. But still it gnawed at him, and he could feel himself going limp with the fear it might be more.

He pulled at her clothes, ripping free buttons in his haste, struggling to rekindle his passion. And she responded, pulling his shirt open as well, then attacking his belt and drawing down his pants. She was naked now; he only partially so, standing there ridiculously dressed, naked from the waist down, his jacket and shirt still on but spread apart to reveal his chest and stomach, which Justine now wildly kissed, licked, and sucked on.

"Tell me," she begged, her tongue flicking across his belly, inching fractionally, infinitesimally lower with each movement.

"Sometimes a bomb, sometimes a gun, and sometimes this." His words were breathless and he reached into his jacket pocket and withdrew the stiletto, pressed the button, and sent the blade shooting out. "It's best with this," he said, his voice little more than a pant. "Because you're close and you can feel it. You can feel their death in your hand."

Justine dropped down, took his semi-erect penis in one hand, and looked up at him. "Tell me," she said, her voice hoarse. "Tell me how it feels."

She took him in her mouth and sucked long and hard, and, hearing his first moan of pleasure, settled to a steady, rhythmic flicking of her tongue that immediately made him begin to grow inside her.

Ernst dropped his head back, low, guttural grunts and moans coming from him, unheard, unnoticed in the pleasure that controlled him. "It's good," he said. "It feels good. It always feels good." He held her head with one hand, his other, still holding the knife he had shown her, hanging loosely at his side. She kept at him, giving him wild, unbelievable pleasure, and suddenly he could stand it no longer and he exploded into her mouth, the release continuing until he was certain she would gag on the sheer volume of his flow. But she continued, her mouth, her tongue working unabated, draining him, soothing him until he was again limp inside her. Then she withdrew and looked up at him smiling.

He stared down at her, a faint, weak smile playing across his own lips, and he took her hair in his hand and pulled back her head. Then he drew the blade of the knife across her neck, opening her throat from ear to ear.

Justine's body began to buck violently, the spasms shaking her arms and legs, and he reached down and lifted her, drawing her against him, as the blood pumping from her throat washed over him. Her head had dropped back, a head almost severed from her torso, as her body writhed in his arms, the throes of death vibrating, pulsing erratically, the only sound the steady gurgling of her throat.

And he looked down and saw that he was hard again. So hard now that it almost caused him pain.

CHAPTER 6

It was 10:00 A.M. when Alex's car pulled to a stop in front of the Basilica Notre Dame-de-la-Garde. The telephone call a half hour earlier had been nothing more than a terse message by an unrecognizable voice. "Your uncle needs to see you about the matter you discussed. Come to the Basilica." Then a dial tone.

It was very Corsican, Alex thought, as he climbed from his car. It was obscure, sinister, byzantine, all the things Corsicans cherished. But they also cherished success, and so he had come, knowing that whatever they had for him, it would be more than he would get from any other source.

Alex pushed through the heavy front door and was immediately confronted by one of Antoine's bodyguards, a short, black-eyed box of a man who had the look of someone to be challenged only at peril. He nodded perfunctorily, then gestured toward the front of the church. Alex walked down the center aisle, the heavy stone walls rising about him, the only light filtered through the long stained-glass windows and fed from the candles that filled the ornate altar. As he approached, Antoine rose from the pew in which he was seated.

"I like churches," he said. "You should go to them more often." Then he shook his head, part in disbelief, part in disgust. "This man you are after," he said. "He is a beast. Worse than a beast."

"What has he done?" Alex asked.

"He has killed a woman," Antoine said. "But it is how he has killed her." He shook his head again; he looked as though he wanted to spit, but realized it couldn't be done here.

Alex said nothing. They sat and he waited for Antoine to continue.

"It seems your man met this woman at a party, or he met her somewhere else and went to the party with her." Antoine shrugged, indicating the sequence was not important. "My men get varying stories about that, depending on who they talk to." He shrugged again. "Anyway, this party, it was all students who were there, and all of a group who consider themselves poets and philosophers and communists and radicals and revolutionaries. All of that." Again he shrugged. "The truth is, the only revolt they have in them is in their manners. And if the money ever stopped coming from home, they would all rush out and begin taking advantage of the working classes, just as they have been raised to do all their lives."

Alex nodded, trying to hide his impatience. He appreciated the background Antoine was giving him, knew it was necessary. But he wished he'd get to the meat of the story and back to the lesser details later.

Antoine slipped an arm around Alex's shoulder, then looked up at the altar, as if hoping to find solace there. "These students," he continued, making a circular gesture with his hands indicating that no one, even he, could really understand them, "they say this man the woman was with was a terrorist." He snorted. "Although some are now saying it was really a SDECE* officer posing as a terrorist."

"What made them think he was a terrorist?" Alex asked.

"The woman," Antoine said. "She kept talking about it, asking him about it." He shook his head. "If it was true, it's a wonder her mouth didn't make him leave a bomb at the party."

"If he'd had one, he probably would have," Alex said. "What description were your men able to get?"

"The usual. A different one from everyone who saw him. But there is one I trust more than the others. It was from another woman who was somewhat taken by him, although my men say they never spoke."

"Just worshiping a killer from afar, I'd guess," Alex said.

Antoine nodded. "According to her, he's slightly above average

* Service de Documentation Exterieure et du Contre-Espionage, the French intelligence service.

height—about five-ten, I'd guess—slim, with long blond hair and blue eyes. Handsome, she said. Sounds like he looks very German to me," Antoine added. There was a derogatory tone in his voice, a carryover from a war he had fought thirty-five years earlier.

"How was he dressed?"

"The woman said he could have passed for one of their younger teachers. Very casual. Sports jacket, jeans. About the right age too—thirty to thirty-five." Antoine shook his head. "My man said she talked about him as though she regretted not having had the chance to fuck him." He glanced quickly to either side, as though afraid someone might have heard the profanity. "If I had been there, I would have grabbed her by the hair and dragged her down to the morgue to see just what she missed."

Alex sighed inwardly. He knew Antoine was going to tell it all in his own way, and only then get to the pertinent information. "What did he do to the woman?" Alex asked, knowing now it had to be discussed first.

Antoine leaned forward, heavy forearms resting on even heavier thighs, and bowed his head as if he were about to pray. "He cut her throat from ear to ear," he began. "And right after she had given him pleasure." He hesitated, as though struggling to find phrasing suitable for church. It amused Alex that his uncle would even try. Antoine shook his head. "Her mouth and throat, they were filled with him." He stared at the younger man. "You understand what I mean?"

"I understand," Alex said.

"And then he fucked her," Antoine said, either forgetting to be delicate or abandoning the attempt. "And he did it either as she was dying, or after she was dead."

Alex grimaced. "How do they know that?"

Antoine shook his head, uncertain. "Something about his sperm droppings being on top of the blood instead of underneath it." He shrugged. "And some other things. Scientific things I don't understand. But it's what he did. They're certain of it." He shook his head again, forcefully this time. "A disgusting animal!" He looked at the altar again. "A man who doesn't deserve to live."

"We'll see what we can do about that," Alex said. "Do you have any idea where he is?"

Antoine nodded. "A general area. The woman had an unused book of matches in her purse. It was from a café on La Canebière.

Two of my men went there. She was there yesterday afternoon with some other students, and later they were joined by an older man who had been sitting alone." Antoine made a face. "She picked him up, and now her throat's cut. Anyway, the waiters say he matches the description we have of our man. And, if he's in hiding as you say, I think he's living in that area."

"I do too," Alex said.

"We will know soon," Antoine said. "My men are checking even now. Anyone new—especially someone who looks like a *boche*— will have French tongues wagging." He made an alligator-like mouth with his fingers and thumb and began snapping it open and closed. "La Marseillaise. Yap, yap, yap," he said. "A Corsican who talked like they do would be buried before the sun was down."

Antoine sat back, his broad, barrel-like body seeming to swallow the pew. "Anyway, I have all the information for you. The names of the people we talked to, their addresses, all of that. You can have your men talk to them. Perhaps they will learn even more."

Alex smiled at the note of gentle accusation in Antoine's voice. Antoine knew he would do exactly that—have his men double-check the information provided by the Corsicans. And he knew Alex's men would learn nothing new, perhaps even a great deal less. But it would be done anyway. Alex, they both knew, would not blindly accept the word of gangsters. Even those who worked for men he had known and loved since childhood. It was a fact they both accepted with varying degrees of regret.

Alex stood. "Will your men continue to look?"

"For as long as you wish." Antoine heaved himself up. "You would still prefer this man alive?"

"Yes."

"It is a shame," Antoine said. "It would be a pleasure to see him killed." He shrugged, indicating life could not always be as it should, then circled Alex's shoulders with one massive arm, and began walking him back up the aisle. "You should pray while you are here," he said. "A man should always pray." He received only a nod and a grunt in reply. "And how goes it with Stephanie?" he asked gently.

Alex glanced at him, then lowered his eyes. He offered a wan smile. "Not well," he said.

Antoine leaned forward, his large head and silver mane even more leonine than usual. "Are the problems that serious?" he asked.

"About as serious as they can get, Uncle."

Alex could feel the cavernous cathedral about him, hear his words against the massive, domed ceiling. He could almost see the quiet, the solemnity with the light filtering through the stained glass windows, the flickering of the altar candles. He wasn't certain why, probably never would be, but once the initial confession was made, the flow came, and kept coming, more easily than he had thought possible.

Antoine's eyes were a mixture of anger and pain. His stomach knotted, feeling a fraction of the betrayal he knew Alex now carried. "What would you have done with this man? The one who has been with her?" he asked when Alex had finished.

"Nothing. He only took what was offered to him. I don't know who he is, and I doubt we've ever met."

"He took what was not his to take," Antoine said.

Alex looked at the stone floor and smiled weakly. "If he were my friend—if I had given him my trust—then I would agree." He looked up, the weak smile becoming a painful grimace. "What she gave was hers to give. She had promised it only to me, and I trusted the honor of that promise, relied on the honor of the person who gave it. That's where the trust was broken."

He could tell Antoine did not agree. To him the debt was larger than merely an unfaithful wife. But Alex knew the man would never challenge an expressed belief. To do so would be unworthy of a friendship.

"So now it's simply a question of whether I can put this aside and try to go on with her." His face sagged, and he hated the weakness he felt showing in it. "I still love her very much," he added, knowing it was only intensifying the weakness; hating that too.

Antoine steepled his fingers in front of his broad, flat nose. "A man can love a dog even after it bites him," he said at length. "But he must accept the fact that this dog is capable of biting him again." He tilted his head to one side and offered a sad smile. "And probably will."

Alex could feel his stomach twisting. "So you would just walk away." He smiled, thinking of what Antoine probably *would* do. It was another weak smile. "Or something to that effect," he added.

Antoine gestured with his hands, trying to find the right words, to express them as inoffensively as possible. "Loyalty," he began, "at least in the mind of the person who believes he has it, can never be recaptured once it is lost." He stared at Alex, his eyes sad. "Leaving her will cause you pain. But that pain will go away in time. The pain of her unfaithfulness will never go away. But at least you won't have to look it in the eye and remember it each day." He shrugged. "We Corsicans say that vengeance soothes pain. I believe this is true. But I don't know for sure, because I've never tried without it."

"Vengeance is not something I want," Alex said.

Antoine nodded. "That is your choice. I'm an old man, and you are my adopted nephew, and I love you and will always love you. But you are still very young. And one of the few things I have learned in life is that almost anything can be replaced. Anything except honor and self-respect." He encircled Alex's shoulders again and continued back toward the door of the cathedral.

"Now we will help you find this Ludwig, this other pig of a man. And then, when you are finished with him, I hope you let me cut his throat."

They stopped at the door, the quiet solemnity of the cathedral behind them, and Alex turned to the older man. "Thank you, uncle," he said.

Antoine watched Alex step through the door, and thought how he must now go and tell his brother what he had learned. The thought of even speaking the words offended him.

The cunt, he thought. He wished Alex would go home and cut her heart out.

The morgue attendant pulled back the sheet that covered the woman's body and exposed the pale gray flesh. The Sûreté inspector who had accompanied Alex turned his head away, his long, broad nose wrinkling with distaste. He was a liaison officer, not an investigator, and human butchery was not part of his daily diet. Alex, like the morgue attendant, seemed oblivious to what lay before them. Unlike the French policeman, he had been told what to expect. The woman Ludwig had known only as Justine was no longer beautiful. Aside from the cranial and abdominal wounds of the autopsy, the cut in her throat, encrusted now with dried blood and puckered tissue, yawned up at them like a second, larger mouth. He looked past the wound, concentrating on her face. Her eyes were wide and staring, and had the irises not already faded and filmed over, he was certain he would see a look of horrified surprise imprinted there. Her mouth was slightly parted, the tips of her teeth showing through, and he knew it had been thoroughly swabbed, forced to surrender its sexual secrets. He looked away. But, of course, there were no secrets when one's death became the interest of strangers. Not even those that deserved to remain private. He looked back at the slack gray face. The nose, obviously once straight and slender, now seemed to have a faint curve to it. He reached out, allowing one finger to lightly trace it.

"You have a good eye," a voice behind him said in French. "The nose was broken. We believe when she fell. It often happens that way. The victim hits a table or chair on the way down. But it doesn't appear to be from a blow administered by someone else. But, of course, we could be wrong."

Alex turned to meet the round, smiling countenance of Gaston LeBrec, the city's chief medical examiner, a man he had dealt with numerous times in the past. LeBrec had the reputation of being something of a fool, and definitely a political hack. He was a distant relative of some sort to the city's mayor, a man who had been in office for twenty-seven years and had earned an unequaled reputation for political patronage. But Alex had found him to be highly competent, with a well-concealed but sharp, analytical mind. Now, oblivious to the corpse spread out before him, he was happily chewing on a sausage sandwich, giving full credence to his detractors.

"Good morning, Gaston," Alex said.

LeBrec inclined his head toward the body. "This is something involving one of your spies or terrorists?" he asked.

"A terrorist, we think," Alex said.

"She didn't know what she was dealing with?" LeBrec asked.

"We think she did. Or at least suspected."

LeBrec shook his head. "The snake charmer who believes he cannot be bitten," he said.

LeBrec turned and began to waddle away. "Come to my office," he said. "We will go over my findings in comfort."

Alex followed him down a long tiled hall, the Sûreté inspector trailing behind. LeBrec was short and fat, more round than pear-shaped, and his body seemed to roll rather than walk. He had short, nearly white hair with a round bald spot at the back of his head, almost identical to those of certain monks, and a cherubic face dominated by thick, wide lips.

When they reached his large office, he seated himself behind an oversized desk littered with individual papers and bound reports. A wide bookcase behind the desk was interspersed with medical volumes and bottles containing various human viscera floating in alcohol, and a human skull served as a paperweight for another sheaf of papers crammed into one corner.

"A vile business," he began, placing his sandwich on one corner of the desk. "The killer had expended himself in her mouth, and then killed her almost immediately afterward."

"How do you know that?" Alex asked.

"Because the semen was still there in quantity. There had been no time for swallowing or spitting out. And the cutting was so deep, there could be none afterward." He shook his head. "This must have aroused him, because he entered her again, undoubtedly as she was dying." He tightened his shoulders, fighting off a shiver. "None of that flow traveled into the ovarian canal. She was already dead before it could happen, and the traces of semen that fell onto her body as he exited lay atop the blood that had run down her body." He shook his head again. "He must have been covered in her blood."

Alex nodded. "The police forensic report indicated he took a shower."

LeBrec picked up his sandwich, took a large bite, and talked around it while he continued. "We know his blood type. B negative. Unusual, rare even. And he has blond pubic hair. A bite mark on her shoulder shows he has wide, even teeth. The bite was post-mortem, by the way. Probably administered while he was taking her that last time. The man belongs in a cage."

The Sûreté inspector, whose name was Auguste Miro, gave an involuntary grunt which seemed to embarrass him. He was young, no more than mid-twenties, Alex guessed, and in some ways he reminded him of his own new man, Blount.

LeBrec smiled at the inspector. "The act of love, my friend. It is not always beautiful, eh?"

The younger man ignored him, turning instead to Alex. "Why would he do this?" he asked.

"We can only guess," Alex said. "No one knows much about him, other than what he leaves behind. And that almost always involves killing. The best guess is that she said something, or he did, that made him think he'd been compromised. Based on his history, that's usually enough to make him kill."

"But to have her this way first and then to kill her." Miro shook his head. "The man must think he's untouchable. He must believe he can do anything and escape capture."

Alex glanced at LeBrec and raised an eyebrow. Whether Miro had intended it or not, he had placed his finger on the one common denominator of everyone who wantonly killed. Perhaps the Sûreté should get him out of public relations and into the field.

LeBrec smiled. "Our killer," he said, "has the tragic flaw of all psychopaths, and their cousin sociopaths. He takes himself too seriously." He stretched his round body, dismissing his own observation, then turned back to Alex. "Would you like my views as an amateur psychiatrist?"

Alex smiled. "You took courses in it in medical school, didn't you?"

"But, of course."

"Then go ahead. You're the closest thing to an expert I have."

LeBrec leaned forward and raised a lecturing finger. "I believe what he did excited him to such an extent that he will seek to be with another woman soon." He wagged the finger. "Not necessarily to kill her." He glanced at Miro and gave him an approving nod. "But to show he can do this."

"Show whom?" Alex asked.

"Oh, that doesn't matter," LeBrec said. "Show no one. The fact that he does this shows everyone, don't you see?"

Alex handed the list across his desk. Stan Kolshak took it and grunted.

"Our Corsican friends have done a lot of spade work on this, and they're usually pretty good," Alex said.

"They're usually *very* good," Kolshak corrected. He held the list in one meaty hand. "How do you want the men divided up?" he asked.

"However you think best. You keep Blount with you. Don't let him get too enthusiastic. Maybe he should concentrate on the cafés around La Canebière. He'll pass more easily as a student."

Kolshak ran a hand over his balding head, then pulled on his oversized nose. "He is enthusiastic," he said, restraining a smile. "You want everybody armed?"

"To the teeth," Alex said. "Just be quiet about it. We don't want to give our French friends any palpitations."

Kolshak flexed his heavy shoulders. "I hope we ge⁺ this bastard. I saw the photos of his handiwork."

Alex knew Kolshak had two daughters in college back in the States, both about the same age as the woman Ludwig had butchered. "I do too," he said. "I just don't want to lose anyone in the process. Let's just do this quickly and quietly, and let's use the Corsicans wherever we can. They're better at this than we are."

Kolshak grunted. "They're even better at what Ludwig does," he said.

Alex watched Kolshak's hulking back retreat from his office, taking comfort that work he should be doing himself was at least in competent hands. He stared at the telephone. He had tried to reach Stephanie at the consulate when he had returned to his office, but had been told she was out. He had not left a message and wanted to try again now, but knew he could not. It would eat at him if she still wasn't there, allow his mind to play out endless scenarios, all of which would end up in a room somewhere, as Stephanie's all too familiar ways of making love were showered on someone else.

"The area is beginning to look like a convention for the DIA and their Corsican goons," Bugayev said. "It is a time for the rabbit to stay in its hole."

Ludwig's eyes snapped up at the Russian. "Is that how you see me, comrade? As a rabbit in a hole?"

Bugayev's jaw tightened, but he hid it with a quick smile that failed to carry to his eyes. He was tired of playing to this man's excessive sensibilities, of watching his words to avoid offending him. "Just a figure of speech, my friend. You know how we Russians like our sayings and parables." Bugayev stared down at the younger man, spread out comfortably on an aging sofa. Suddenly he sprang up and stood directly in front of the KGB *rezident*.

"I know how you Russians look down on everyone who is not Russian." Ludwig's eyes were intense, almost feral, and Bugayev wondered if that was how he looked when he killed. No, he thought. Then the man smiles.

"I thought all Russians suffered from inferiority complexes,"

Bugayev said, his tone light, almost humorous. "It's what the western analysts claim."

Ludwig's features changed to a sneer, then a slow, gradual smile. "Russians suffer from an excess of caution," he said, turning and walking to a window that overlooked a small side street a block off La Canebière. "The city is overrun with tourists. The only suspicious man will be the one who stays hidden in his room."

Bugayev's back stiffened and he fought an impulse to snarl. He was not a diplomat despite his official ranking as a consular trade officer, and men he was responsible for treated his directives like prelates following canon law—if for no other reason than fear of the consequences.

"I *cannot* protect you on the streets," he emphasized. "Even if you are not readily recognizable, the faces of my men are. If I send them out with you, I might as well drop bread crumbs leading to your door."

Ludwig turned back and offered a mocking half smile. "Now we resort to children's fairy tales," he said. "Oh, Bugayev. What am I to do with you?"

"Obedience would be a novel concept," the Russian snapped.

"Subservience, you mean," Ludwig countered. "I am sorry, comrade. The revolution has arrived." He touched his chest with the fingers of both hands. "And the masses are no longer submissive to the ruling class." He watched the red come and deepen in Bugayev's face, then tilted his head back and laughed. His eyes suddenly hardened again. It was like watching a rapid change in personalities, Bugayev thought—a madman snapping from one to another.

"You said the Corsicans were asking questions about some foolish woman who managed to get herself killed. That has nothing to do with me."

"The Americans seem to think otherwise."

"Then the Americans are playing their usual role of court jester." Ludwig walked to a nearby table, picked up a small, .32-caliber Berreta automatic, and slid it into his belt at the small of his back, then slipped on a lightweight windbreaker. "Keep your minders at home, Bugayev. I don't need to be walked on a leash. Just make sure they get me aboard the ship when it arrives."

The KGB *rezident* watched in silence as Ludwig walked to the door, turned to offer one final, mocking smile, then left. Get yourself killed, he thought. Do all of us the favor. He bit off the words as soon as he had thought them. And get me sent to some posting in the Urals for failing to save you from yourself. He shook his head. Cretin, the thought. Whoreson of a fucking cretin.

CHAPTER

7

ingers gently trace her body, lingering only momentarily at her breasts, then moving again, lightly brushing the skin, continuing to stomach, to hip, then pausing just above the pubic mound, hesitating, drawing out the moment, a faint toying with the triangle of blond hair, exploring its shape, following the contours of her body to the baby soft flesh of the inner thigh. Her back arches; legs part anticipating pleasure, and her breathing changes to a soft, steady, drum-like beat.

Alex's hand tightened around the glass holding the fresh drink, causing a small amount of liquid to splash onto the back of his wrist. He glanced at his watch—eight-thirty—two hours past her normal time. The image of her making love, the ways she accepted pleasure and gave it, fought its way back to his mind, was pushed away again with another gulp of liquor. He stood and circled the living room. The number of times he had done it escaped him now. Only a month ago they had seemed happy. The short vacation they had taken to Sardinia, the quaint fishing village that offered little more than long walks amid the craggy cliffs and cove beaches. They had made love on one of those beaches, the sun beating down on them, lost in mutual abandon. And now, only a few short weeks later. Had the man been part of her life even then, or had it been only since they returned? How long? A week? A month? Three? Jesus Christ.

None of it made any difference. It existed now. That was all that mattered. But perhaps it did make a difference. What did it say about them—about her—if they could make love that way with the memory of another hanging like a specter amid every touch, every gasp of pleasure?

He drained the glass, went to the liquor cabinet, and poured another. He looked at his watch again. Five of nine. He wouldn't ask her where she had been. No, he had to. Had to know. Had to refuse the role of complacent cuckold. His "uncle" was right about that. Almost anything could be replaced. Anything except . . . He shook his head. Wisdom and morality from a man who sells heroin. No, not that. From a man you've known since childhood. A man you and your government use freely, no matter who he is or what he does.

The sound of the key in the door; the hand tightened on the glass again. Another gulp of liquor, flooding the brain with resolve.

He turned to face her. She was looking down at first, then her back straightened slightly as she saw him. She walked into the room, the failed trace of a smile quickly fleeing her face.

"Hi. Sorry, I got tied up." She eyed his drink. "I could use one of those." When he didn't move, she walked to the drinks table and began mixing one. Her back was to him. She was dressed so flawlessly again, her pale silk suit not even creased, not a solitary wrinkle.

She wants to keep it civilized, Alex thought. Maintain the charade. "Were you with him?" His voice was cold and flat, unemotional. He could see her back stiffen slightly again.

"I thought he should know." Stephanie sipped her drink, her back still to him.

"Know what?" An edge had crept into his voice, and it annoyed him that it had.

She turned slowly, eyes down. "Know that you knew." The words sounded like a schoolgirl's in her own ears. She raised her eyes. "It seemed best to me."

"You never heard of telephones?"

She looked away, her lips tightening. "I thought it was something that should be done face to face."

"Felt you owed him that much." His words were cold and cutting. He wanted to scream at her, ask her what she thought she owed *him*. Ask her if she'd fucked him one last time. Just for old time's sake. Ask her all kinds of things, except it would let her know how much she'd hurt him. And he couldn't do that. Wouldn't.

"I just wanted to do it that way." Her voice was soft, not challenging.

"Are you going to marry him?"

The question seemed to surprise her. "He's already married. And I have no interest in marrying him." She looked at him. Soft eyes. Chin trembling slightly. "I'm married to you."

"Will you see him again?"

She turned away and sipped her drink. "I don't intend to," she said. "But won't promise that. I seem to have broken enough promises already." She turned back to face him. "I want it to work between us," she said softly.

"Will there be others, Steph? Is that how it's going to work between us?"

She turned away, refusing to respond. "That's cruel, Alex."

"Yes, it is. But cruel seems to be the way things are between us right now." He put his drink down hard on the table, and the sound of it made her turn back to face him.

"What will you do?"

"I don't know. I just know I'm leaving here."

"Now?"

There was a wistful look in her eyes, as though something she had planned had been thwarted. He knew what that was and he wanted no part of it. "Yes, now," he said.

She looked down at her drink and let out a long breath. "Perhaps that's best. Maybe we can work things out more easily away from each other." She raised her eyes to him. "I hope so, Alex. I love you."

Alex didn't respond, he simply walked toward the bedroom to pack some clothing.

Antoine replaced the telephone receiver and looked across the room at his bother. "That was Alex," he said. "He seems to have found his balls again."

"He's left that cheating cow?" Meme asked.

Antoine nodded. "He asked to use one of our apartments until he can find a suitable place."

Meme nodded. "Good," he said. "But I think your first idea was right."

Antoine raised his eyebrows, questioning the statement.

Meme shrugged. "He should have cut out her heart."

CHAPTER

8

Jim Blount sat in the second row of tables in the crowded sidewalk cafe, pretending to nurse an aperitif and read an evening newspaper. Actually his attention was fixed on the blond man seated with a young woman at the café next door. He had spotted the man an hour earlier and had heard him speaking French with the faintest of German accents. It had been there, no doubt about it. If there was one thing he knew, it was European languages and the nuances of how they were spoken by various nationals. He had majored in languages at Princeton, had excelled wildly in them, and the refinements he had gained by a year's study abroad and, later, in the specialized course at "The Farm"—the DIA's training center in Virginia—had intensified that expertise. The only doubt he had now was the man's total lack of furtiveness. He acted as though he hadn't a care or concern—exactly the way an illegal operating in a foreign country was supposed to act. But he had watched dozens of illegals on training exercises in Washington and New York, and had never seen anyone this good. And this man— this target—was being hunted, and knew—had to know—just how intense that hunt was. If this was Ludwig, he told himself, he was better than good. He was damned near perfect.

Blount sipped his drink—actually just raised it to his lips and stuck his tongue in it, feigning a sip. So it probably wasn't Ludwig, but he couldn't afford to take that chance. It was ten o'clock. Kolshak had broken off their search two hours before and told him to go home and get some sleep. But he had gone back out on his

own, something that would send Kolshak up the wall if he knew
—and probably Alex Moran as well. But what could they really
say? He was on his own time, just out enjoying himself. He certainly
couldn't be dressed down for spotting Ludwig while doing so. A
slow smile formed on his lips. And what a coup it would be if this
was Ludwig. They had been treating him like a rank amateur, using
Kolshak to baby-sit him, keep him out of harm's way. It reminded
him of that television show he had watched as a kid. The one about
the sheriff in a small southern town, burdened with an incompetent
deputy, who was allowed to have only one bullet for his gun, and
who had to keep that bullet in his shirt pocket. Well, he was no
Barney Fife and this wasn't Mayberry. He was well trained and he
could do the job. And fuck them all if they couldn't understand
that.

The target was laughing now. Wide, even teeth, just like the
M.E.'s report had said. Blount could feel his pulse quicken, and
he ran one hand through his severely cut blond hair. Too damned
short, he told himself. You could pass for a goddamned GI on leave.
Got to remember to let it grow.

Blount feigned another sip of his aperitif. As he returned the still
undiminished glass to the table, he caught the eye of a young
Frenchwoman seated several tables away. She maintained eye contact for a few seconds, then looked away, her manner appearing
uninterested, almost haughty. It was as near an invitation as one
would receive in France. Blount's open midwestern face became
even more open with the pleasure he took from it. The woman was
dressed almost entirely in black—the favored color of feminine
France—save a garish flowered scarf about her neck, and her short
black hair and high cheekbones accented a wide mouth that was as
sensual as Blount had ever seen.

"Damn," he muttered, momentarily wondering if the woman
wouldn't make a wonderful cover for his surveillance. He grinned
stupidly at the foolishness of the idea, then glanced back toward
her table, hoping to at least once again catch her eye. But it was
not to be.

God, how he loved France, and especially Marseilles. It was such
an overpowering place, this, the most polyglot of French cities. All
about one, on the streets, in the cafés, came the sounds of myriad
languages—Arabic, Turkish, Italian, Vietnamese, Corsican, Farsi,
almost any tongue of Europe, Southeast Asia, the Middle East, or

north Africa. And with it the faces of the flotsam of those countries, struggling for something that could never be found at home. It virtually teemed with life and struggle and villainy, a place where the criminal element—in its quarters of the city—ruled without challenge and where life could prove as cheap as a few francs.

His first week in the city had been spent in a small old hotel on the Vieux Port, in a room with a balcony overlooking the ragtag fishing fleet that struggled in shortly before dawn each morning, the captains unloading their catches to waiting wives and children, who manned makeshift stalls from which the fish would be sold, while the men retired to the cafés along the quay to exchange the gossip of fishing and other matters of interest.

It was a place that literally burst with activity throughout the night, never finding the few quiet hours that even cities like New York and Paris and Amsterdam offered to those who lived there. Marseilles, he thought, was like life itself, a dirty, brawling, unruly creature with a heart that never stopped beating.

Blount started, nearly jumping in his chair, then caught himself. The target was up and moving, the woman he was with laughing at his side. Blount fumbled with his drink. Forgetting himself, he raised it to his lips and gulped it half down.

Damn. Stay calm . . . quiet . . . natural. Treat it like a training exercise. He rose slowly, tucked his newspaper under his arm, and wandered out onto the sidewalk, where a steady flow of people still offered the comfort of concealment. He began to relax as the training took over, the nervousness fading back below the surface. Ludwig was about thirty yards ahead, walking casually, seeming to concentrate on the woman who clung to his arm. But Blount knew he would soon stop, at a shop window, or corner, or any object that seemed natural, to pause and admire. Then he would look back and lightly scan the faces behind him, searching for any eye contact, taking in the color of clothing that he might see again and again on future checks. Blount readied himself, dropping farther back, doubling the distance between them. He knew it was impossible for one man to run a close tail, had been taught it took a minimum of three, even four to do it properly—each man dropping out at regular intervals, at least one following the target from the front—rotating regularly, never presenting the same face, the same clothing that always marked a tail. Better to stay back and risk losing the target. Always better to lose him than be spotted. Always.

The target walked on, seemingly casual and unconcerned, with Blount following—sixty to seventy yards behind—barely keeping him in sight, his mind repeatedly replaying the lectures on street craft that had been drummed into him at The Farm. But most important, he knew that when the target stopped to scan the street behind him, he had to force himself to continue walking, not stop, or turn away, or step into a doorway to avoid being seen—the natural reactions of someone wanting to avoid detection and the very things that would draw an experienced eye.

Alex placed the last of his shirts in the dresser and slowly slid the drawer shut, then turned, gathered his suitcase from the bed, and stowed it in the bedroom closet.

He glanced around the sizable bedroom, surprised at how little it took to make a person self-sufficient. No more, really, than what would be needed for an extended trip. The rest, he told himself, were creature comforts that could come—or not—in time. He caught his reflection in the dresser mirror. Perhaps. And perhaps not. Old Antoine had told him everything could be replaced except his honor, his self-respect. All the creature comforts, the money, the possessions. Yes, even the people. He offered his reflection a grim smile. The reflection offered it back. If that was all true, then why did he feel so miserable? Time, he told himself. Time solves that part.

Promise?

Yeah, I promise.

Alex walked into the oversized living room, stopping before the large picture window that looked out across the Vieux Port to the old city, where so much of Marseilles's history, and its poor, resided. He turned back, allowing his eyes to roam the well-appointed room. He knew what the apartment was—one of several the Pisanis kept to accommodate visiting gang lords of the drug trade—a place for those who had come to Marseilles surreptitiously, and who wished to avoid the public exposure of a hotel. He snorted at the idea that his marital problems might inconvenience some visiting American mafioso. He dropped into an overstuffed chair near the window. But it won't be for long, he told himself. Just until you can find something suitable for yourself. Or, until . . . He pushed the thought away.

Odd, though, he told himself. In any other branch of government service, accepting favors from known gangsters would be cause for scandal. In intelligence, not only would no one look askance, but in reality, no one, not anyone who truly mattered—anyone who could offer any type of threat—would ever even know. He was simply borrowing an apartment from people with whom he normally did business—people he had known since childhood, and considered a part of his extended family, because his father had also been part of the intelligence community. Alex smiled for the first time that day. It was absurd. So delightfully absurd.

He stared out the window at nothing in particular. But none of it—none of the madness, none of the absurdity, none of anything—changes the reality of your life, does it? And right now you don't know what that reality is. Is it Stephanie or no Stephanie? You don't even know that. Oh yeah, you left. You did that. But whether that invisible rope that ties you to her will draw you back or not, now that's the real question. And do you want to go back, or is it just ego? Just not wanting to have something taken from you? Stephanie. The only real family you have. The one you made for yourself. Alex shook his head. Something you never had in the first place. Shit.

There was a telephone on the table next to Alex's chair, and he stared at it at length before finally picking it up. His office answered on the second ring, and he quickly identified himself and gave his new telephone number. There were no questions. Not of the boss. But there would be buzzing about the office tomorrow. Fuck 'em. Let them talk.

Alex rose from the chair, walked to a built-in bar, and mixed himself a drink. He'd throw himself into his work and keep Stephanie out of mind as much as possible, he told himself. He raised the glass to his lips and found himself wondering what she was doing at that very moment. Was she alone, or had she called *someone* as soon as he had left? He squeezed his eyes shut, opened them, took a long sip of his drink, and walked to the window. Below, a line of cars, their headlights a blur of speed, raced along the Quai de Rive. It was past midnight, and Marseilles looked as though it were just awakening for the day.

Blount stood deep in the shadow of the alley, staring up at the lighted third-floor window across the street. *The target* and the woman had entered the building slightly more than two hours ago—the target standing back while the woman opened the downstairs door. It was her apartment, and Blount had waited, knowing he had to follow the target back to his hole before calling in any help. That was the coup, finding the man *and* his hole, where he could be grabbed without any witnesses, without anyone left behind yelling about American agents kidnapping people on foreign soil.

Blount glanced at his watch, the radium dial glowing in the dark of the alley. Two A.M. Christ, he hoped he wasn't sleeping over. Shit, just hope the guy isn't the woman's husband, or boyfriend, and you're not left standing in a Marseilles alley with your dick in your hand.

Blount stiffened. He wanted to move farther back in the alley— it was instinctive—but he resisted it. The street door of the building had opened and the target had stepped out onto the sidewalk. He was lighting a cigarette. Calm and cool and unconcerned. Probably just had his oil changed and all's right with the world, Blount told himself.

He remained quiet, watching the target, his breathing shallow when he breathed at all. He could feel his own heart. He couldn't hear it, but he could feel it. Damn, this was the real thing. This was no fucking exercise. This bastard, if it was him—oh, yeah, it's him, dammit, it's him—he'll blow you away as soon as sneeze. He pressed his arm against the Walther hanging in a shoulder holster under his left arm, then tried to remember if he had jacked a round into the chamber or left it empty as an added safety. It's empty, dammit. You left it empty.

The thought of doing it now flashed through his mind, but he dismissed it. The sound of the slide moving back, then forward again—even if he did it slowly, quietly—would be heard in the dead quiet of the street. He would wait until the target stopped again. Went inside again.

The man began to move, back the same way he had come with the woman. Blount inched up the alley, peered around the corner, then waited. He'd let the man get to the corner, wait for him to check behind him, then he'd move. Move quickly, catch him in the busier main street, then work the same distant tail again. Damn, don't lose him now. Not now.

Back on La Canebière, Blount cut the distance between them to fifty yards, this time running the tail from the opposite side of the wide avenue. It was a risk if the target turned into a side street and his hole was in a building close to the corner. He might be inside and gone before he could be picked up again. But at least he'd know the street and the general location of the hole. It was better than nothing, and he could pick it up tomorrow and still have his coup. Or he could call it in with what he had. No, he'd wait if that happened. He wanted this coup, every bit of it. He'd worked too hard to get it.

Up ahead, the target stopped in front of a café located at the intersection of a narrow side street, and gave a quick scan of the street behind. Blount kept walking, his eyes averted. The target moved inside the outdoor area of the café and took a table two rows in. Blount continued down the street, crossed the intersection, and settled himself in another café diagonally across from the target. He allowed his eyes to move quickly past the target. He was speaking to a waiter. Damn, his luck was holding. Just keep it coming. Keep it coming just the way it is.

Blount waited for what seemed like an hour but was only half, and the target was up again and turning into the side street. Blount didn't move. He watched in near disbelief as the target turned into the narrow side street, moved along it, then entered a building three doors down. That was it, had to be. Christ, he thought. All he had to do was wait now and make sure he didn't leave again. And he didn't even have to move.

Stephanie awoke, slipped on a freshly pressed silk robe, and walked out into the living room. It was the third time she had awakened, and it seemed useless to fight it any longer. She drew a breath and hugged herself, standing in the center of the room, trying to decide where to sit, or if she wanted to sit at all. Her body felt as though it were trembling internally, and her mouth was dry and pasty. She walked to the drinks table and poured herself a glass of red wine from a bottle she had opened earlier, then walked to a chair in front of the wide bank of windows and sat wearily, her body numb, removed from everything.

The wineglass trembled slightly as she raised it to her lips and sipped the blood red claret. He had left, cleanly and simply, unable to accept this one last bit of madness she had forced on him. Why had she done it? Had she just forced him to take the step she hadn't the courage to take herself? No, dammit. No. She wasn't even sure now why she had started the affair in the first place. Oh, what she had told Alex was true enough. There was the neglect, the fact he was never there. And when he was, she felt smothered by his love, by everything he believed her to be. And there was the thrill of it. The excitement of being wanted by someone else, someone she too found appealing. But she was a beautiful woman, and she knew, intellectually, that there were few men she couldn't have if she made herself available. God, what attractive woman couldn't? Men were so easy.

She sipped the wine again, barely tasting it, her hand still trembling. Had he been that irresistible? Had the sex been that different, that overwhelming? She shook her head. No. Be honest. It had just been the thrill of doing something forbidden. Pleasing her ego with the thought that someone was willing to take the same risk just to have her. It swelled her ego, drove away the small fears that she was no longer a young thing who was wanted just by being what she was.

Don't even ask yourself if it was worth it. The answer is too brutal, too stark. God, the look on his face when you told him Alex knew. You had wanted him to look strong, relieved even, that it was out in the open. Not that you wanted him to offer to leave his wife, or even to say it didn't matter, that you could go on just as before. But he didn't say any of that. All he wanted to know was if Alex would be difficult about it, if there was going to be trouble. Read: trouble for *him*. She let out a short, derisive breath. He didn't even ask if you were all right, or what would happen to you, or had already happened because of it.

She held the glass in both hands and sipped from it again. The look on Alex's face, the pain in his eyes, came floating back. Just like *you* never considered what it would all do to Alex. Oh, yes, you did. You knew what it would do. You just thought you'd get away with it, that he'd never know. Or you were just too damned selfish to really care.

But you don't want it to be over. You don't want Alex to stay away. Then why didn't you tell him it would never happen again? Why didn't you tell him it was a stupid mistake, that you were frightened no one else would ever want you? That you had to know that someone else still wanted to take you to their bed, found you desirable, just couldn't keep from having you.

Because you didn't want to sound like a fool. Didn't want to sound like you were begging to be forgiven. Didn't want to do all the things you'd want him to do if the situation were reversed. And what do you do now? If you tell him all those things right after he's left, will he believe you? Would you believe him?

So you wait and hope it will work out, and then you tell him later. But do you mean it? Deep down, are you sure it won't happen again? Oh, Christ. Stop it.

And what if someone comes along while you're apart, someone who wants him? You've certainly made him available, and mentally and physically ready. What would you do if you knew a man like Alex was there for the taking?

Oh, God. Stop thinking like this. Stop it. Stop it. Stop it. Stop it.

The café had closed more than an hour earlier, but Blount had returned after the waiters and countermen had made their hasty departure. The chairs had been stacked on top of the tables in the outdoor section, and Blount had simply moved back into the deepest recess of the awning-covered area, removed a chair, and continued his watch.

An hour later, Alex pulled another chair from the table, placed it next to Blount's, and allowed his gaze to lay long and heavy on the younger man.

"Tell me why you think it's Ludwig," he began without preamble. "And don't leave out how you happened to be out here when you stumbled across him."

Blount told his tale, and Alex had to admire the blatant lie of how Blount happened across this would-be Ludwig. He was pleased to see they were still recruiting people who knew how to cover their asses.

"Which building?" Alex asked.

"The side street. Third entry down. Fourth-floor front apartment."

Alex just stared at him, allowing that to be his question.

"The light went on right after he went inside," Blount explained.

Alex nodded. Apparently The Farm was still doing its job as well.

"What do you think?" Blount asked, no longer able to contain his enthusiasm.

"I think you did a damn fine job," Alex said, his eyes on the apartment window. "I'm not sure I approve of your methodology, but I can't complain about the results." He looked back at the younger man. "It may not be him, but that won't be your fault." Alex allowed himself a small smile. "If it is, you may become one of those agents the instructors tell stories about during their ridiculous motivational sessions at The Farm."

"They ought to send you back to the fucking farm." It was Kolshak, pulling another chair from the table and glaring at Blount. "You trying to get yourself killed, junior?"

"Okay," Alex said. "Let's let it go for now. We'll yell at him *after* we figure out whether or not we've got Ludwig treed."

"Just so long as I can beat him then," Kolshak said.

"Hell, if it's Ludwig, we'll give him a medal, then we'll both beat him."

Alex glanced at Kolshak, saw the beginnings of a grin flicker, then disappear from his lips, and knew he had the man mollified. Kolshak was a mother hen, pissed that one of her chicks had crossed the road without her. And that was the very reason he had paired him with Blount. But now Ludwig was the focus, the only one that mattered.

"Tell Kolshak what you told me," he ordered.

Blount repeated his tale, including the ass-covering part. Kolshak only rolled his eyes at the effort. "Sounds good," he said when Blount had finished, but more to Alex than the still woodshed-bound younger agent. "How do you want to do it?"

Alex turned to Blount. "You sure he didn't spot you? It's important."

"I'm sure," Blount said.

Alex watched his eyes, looking for some hint of doubt, saw none, and turned back to Kolshak, who was studying the building the target had entered.

"Looks like there's an alley leading to the back," Kolshak said, his eyes still on the building.

"Yeah. We'll have to have someone cover the back. Then two men in front. One near the entrance and one farther down the block. You know what Marseilles buildings can be like." Alex was referring to the many buildings in Marseilles connected to one another through their basements, often along the entire length of a block. It was something picked up from the Corsican ghetto, where holes were knocked in basement walls, creating tunnels from one building to the next in a nearly endless network. The Corsicans had used them to escape raids by the police, and others had employed the tactic during the Nazi occupation to provide escape and underground travel routes for the Resistance.

Kolshak, still thinking like a mother hen who didn't want her chick off alone, volunteered for the alley.

"Okay," Alex said, turning to Blount. "You know what he looks like, so you take the front of the building. I'll go down the block. You see someone come out at my end who looks like him, you signal me." He stared hard at the younger man. "But we're going to call in more people, including some Corsicans who can talk to the concierge. We don't want to go kicking in any doors and then find out the guy's lived here the past five years. So, if he comes out, we follow him. Nothing more. We have radios, so we can get our people to wherever he goes. Understood?" Alex didn't even look at Kolshak. He just waited for Blount's nod of assent.

Ludwig stood to the side of the sitting room window and watched the three men deploy separately. The fool who had followed him was on station in a doorway across the street, up slightly from the front of the building toward La Canebière. Another had gone to the back, and the third was somewhere farther down the block. Given the time, and the look about them, it was obvious they were a team.

And a team with more on the way, Ludwig told himself.

He moved back away from the window and paced the floor. He was annoyed with himself. He had not spotted the tail until he had stopped at the café for a final drink before returning to his hole. But the man had moved too quickly into the café across the avenue and had looked once too often in his direction. He hadn't been certain then, but now he was. He stopped pacing and debated a call to Bugayev. These were Americans. He was sure of it if for no other reason than the hair style of the one across the street. But they might be calling in French police to help them. If so, Bugayev's people would be useless. No, he must move now, before any others arrived. He must go out the front door and move quickly back to La Canebière, away from the other two. Then he would only have to deal with the one across the street. If they only followed, he would lose them. If not . . .

Blount stiffened as the target suddenly appeared on the sidewalk and began walking quickly toward La Canebière. He had been looking the other way, thinking that he would really have to start getting out socially in the evenings, not just use it as an excuse to cover his ass for unauthorized work; try to meet someone who could soothe his long-suffering libido. Someone like the woman the target had met only a few short hours before. But the target's sudden appearance exploded that daydream with grenade-like force. He glanced toward Alex's position. He too had seen him and was moving back up the street, his radio to his lips, alerting Kolshak. But he was too far back. To follow him, Blount would have to let him move ahead before stepping into the open, and by that time the bastard would be on La Canebière within easy reach of a taxi, a waiting car, whatever.

The sonofabitch knew, Blount told himself. Somehow he had been spotted—somehow he had fucked it all up—and now they were losing him, and the goddamned coup he wanted so much was flying right out the window. Shit. There would be no stories at The Farm about super agent Jim Blount.

Bullshit, Blount told himself as he stepped from the doorway, his right hand going for the Walther under his left arm. He called Ludwig's name, and at the same moment realized he still hadn't jacked a round into the chamber of the automatic. His left hand came up to the slide with practiced instinct, as everything seemed to speed up. The target had dropped into a combat shooting crouch, his weapon already out, rising, leveling toward Blount. In his peripheral vision Blount could see Alex running toward them. He would be angry, pissed off at what he had done. Angry. Angry. Angry.

Blount never heard the slide on his pistol snap forward, chambering a round. Ludwig's first shot caught him at the base of his throat, blowing out the back of his neck and severing his spinal column. He was already dying when the second shot struck his chest as he fell back into the doorway. Nor did he have time to realize there would be stories told at The Farm about Agent Jim Blount. But they would not be of a kind he would have liked.

Alex's gun was out when Ludwig spun and dropped into a shooting stance, but he was running too fast to aim and fire with any hope of hitting anything but an innocent civilian driving through the intersection on La Canebière. He skidded to a halt, still thirty yards away, but before he could level his own pistol the target had already fired twice, and he could see Blount's body flying back into the darkened doorway.

"Fucker," he screamed, firing four rapid rounds as the target turned, his own weapon rotating toward Alex.

Ludwig's free hand flew to his face, one of the four bullets having cut deeply into the flesh of his right cheek. Then he caught himself and fired two rounds at his attacker.

Alex acted instinctively as the two shots went wide. The target held his weapon in his right hand, which meant that in rapid fire, under pressure, he would jerk his hand slightly to the left—to Alex's right. He threw his body to his own left and rolled, coming up on one knee, his weapon up and level. But the target had darted into the street and, crouched low, was running toward La Canebière, an impossible shot with too much risk.

Alex could hear the pounding of feet behind him: Kolshak out of the alley and moving up fast. The sight of him had changed the odds and forced the target to run.

"I got him, Alex," Kolshak shouted as he rumbled past.

Kolshak was by him before Alex regained his feet, and ahead he could already see the target rounding the corner. He started to join the pursuit, then broke stride and ran toward Blount's fallen body. There might be a chance, and if there was, he owed it to Blount to go to him first. But even before he reached him, he knew. Something about the way his legs were draped over the low doorstep. Or perhaps it had been the way his body had flown back. But even before he looked into Blount's dead, staring face, Alex knew there would be nothing left to save.

He looked up as Kolshak's pounding feet headed back toward him.

"I lost him," Kolshak said, fighting for breath. He looked down at Blount's body. "Fuck!" he snapped. "Fuck, fuck, fuck, fuck, fuck."

Alex reached down and picked up Blount's Walther, handed it to Kolshak, then quickly removed the shoulder holster the dead agent was wearing. "Let's get out of here," he said, his voice dead and flat. "This place is going to be crawling with French cops any minute."

Kolshak stared down at Blount's body, his face a mixture of anger and pain. Leaving your dead behind sucked. But he knew the procedure. Blount would simply be an American businessman killed on a Marseilles street. Worth only a few lines in *The New York Times* on a slow news day. Deniability wasn't just the rule, it was the way of life in his business.

CHAPTER 9

Ernst Ludwig bared his teeth and his eyelids fluttered as the doctor tightened the last suture in his cheek and began tying it off.

Across the room an almost indiscernible smile played momentarily on Sergei Bugayev's lips as he watched the Soviet-paid physician minister to him. Ludwig had telephoned the Soviet consulate shortly before dawn, demanding help, and had been picked up by a team and brought to the new safe house in the old quarter of the city. Since Bugayev had arrived with the doctor, a half hour later, he had not moved from the sofa on which he still lay.

"Will there be a scar?" Ludwig asked, staring up at the doctor with eyes so filled with hatred that the man took a step back, almost as though he feared he would be held personally responsible for the injury.

"I don't believe there is any nerve damage, but it is impossible to be sure. As for scarring: Yes, I'm afraid there will be a scar. But plastic surgery—"

Ludwig cut him off with a wave of his hand. The doctor had spoken in French, and Ludwig turned to Bugayev and continued in Russian.

"Can we trust this fool?" he asked.

And what should we do, kill him if you're uncertain? Bugayev thought. "He's a member of the French Communist Party, and we have used him many times in the past," he said in Russian. "His loyalty has been proven."

Ludwig turned his head away, indicating neither pleasure nor dissatisfaction with the answer. "Get him out of here," he said in a softer voice.

The doctor looked at Bugayev, uncertainty and a hint of fear in his eyes. The Russian smiled, crossed the room to him, then took his arm and guided him to the door. "Again you have served us well, my friend," he said. "Again, my thanks." He paused. "Is there anything special we should do for him?" He indicated Ludwig with a toss of his head.

The doctor pulled a small pad from his suit coat pocket, scribbled quickly, and handed over a slip of paper, bearing a prescription.

"For pain," he said. "Otherwise there is nothing."

Bugayev saw the doctor out, thanking him again, then stared at the prescription in his hand, momentarily thought of stuffing it in his pocket and allowing Ludwig all the pain possible, then handed it to one of his men and ordered him to get it filled. He turned and crossed the room to the sofa, pulled up a wooden chair, and sat facing his "wounded hero of the Revolution," as he now referred to Ludwig in his mind.

"So, tell me, my friend," he began. "Tell me how all this happened. The cafés are already buzzing with stories of wild shooting outside your former apartment early this morning."

Ludwig glared at him, aware now that Bugayev had already had men scouring the neighborhood for information. "The Americans found your not-so-safe safe house," he snapped. "I found three of them watching it."

"Could it be they followed you there?" Bugayev's voice was light, almost syrupy. He was thoroughly enjoying himself.

"It could be they simply placed all the safe houses you ineptly run under surveillance," Ludwig snapped back. "I couldn't take the risk."

"So you killed one of them. And one of them wounded you," Bugayev said.

Ludwig's eyes narrowed. "A man called Alex," he said, almost hissing the name. "One of them called him that. Who is he? He saw my face."

Ah, Bugayev thought. The great fear that the myth of invisibility has been breached. "I can only guess," he said. "But it undoubtedly was Alex Moran. The man I told you about, the head of the American Defense Intelligence Agency station here in Marseilles." He shook his head. "A difficult man. And obviously a decent shot."

Ludwig glared at him, looking for a moment as if he might leap off the sofa and go for the Russian's throat. Bugayev almost wished he would try.

"I want to know where he lives," Ludwig said.

"We don't kill each other's agents, and certainly not each other's station chiefs. Not unless it's unavoidable," Bugayev said.

"I know about your stupid unwritten rules," Ludwig said. "But they don't apply to me. I don't require approval from Moscow Center to kill capitalist agents. So you can give me his address, or I'll find someone at the Center to order you to. I know you have it. Not to would be an unbelievable incompetence."

Ludwig tried to smile, but the effort caused him to wince with pain. Bugayev offered up the smile for him, but not at Ludwig's words as it might seem. Perhaps Alex would be more successful this time, he thought. If he were less committed to his own beliefs he might even telephone him.

"You'll have your address. Now tell me what happened. And leave out nothing. It may just help us keep you alive." Bugayev smiled again. "Oh, and there will be men here with you this time. Whether you want them here or not." The Russian's eyes hardened. "And if you go out hunting American agents, you go alone. And *I* shall advise Moscow Center of your plans, *and* my decision. Is that understood, comrade?"

The consulate had arranged for the pickup of Blount's body, following an autopsy by French authorities, and had put out a story about the murder of an American businessman during an attempted robbery on a Marseilles street. It wouldn't do much either way to the reputation of France's second largest city, since the French themselves already referred to it as France's Chicago.

But those facts didn't concern Alex Moran as he sat at his desk in the late afternoon. What did bother him was his inability to offer some kind of official recognition to a man assigned to his office, however briefly. That, and the fact he wasn't even close to finding the sonofabitch who killed him.

He had seen Ludwig's face—the man no one could supposedly identify. He had seen him in profile as he murdered Blount, and then again as he had faced him to try his luck a second time. And now he was wounded. Not badly, but somewhere on the right side of his head. Alex allowed the man's image to float across his mind. It was a face he wouldn't forget.

And when I find you, I'll treat you with all the pity you showed that poor, hapless bastard you blew apart on a filthy French street, he told himself.

Except maybe that poor hapless bastard would still be alive if you'd been out doing your job instead of pacing floors wondering who your wife was fucking.

Alex spun in his chair and stared out at the dull, monotonous view offered by his lone window. It was the question that had been gnawing at him, the reality that he had sent his men out to do a dangerous job while he concentrated on the shit that was piling up on his own doorstep. And if he hadn't been, would the outcome have been different? He squeezed his eyes shut. It damned well should have been.

There was no question in his mind that had he been out there, he would have kept Blount with him, if for no other reason than to evaluate what capabilities, if any, he had. And if he had ordered Blount to break off and go home, he would have. No matter how eager, the man had not been a fool. He had been ambitious, and would never have played his Lone Ranger game on the one man who could have shipped his ass back to the States on a whim.

But you weren't there. You were at home, waiting for Stephanie. Waiting to see if she was still playing her game. Waiting to challenge her after-work jaunt, to find out if she was still dropping her drawers for someone else. Then you were packing your things, moving out. Playing the wounded cuckold for all it was worth. Playing for an audience of two in your own fucking soap opera.

So you pawned him off on Kolshak—let Kolshak do your job for you—and now one overeager kid, fresh out of training, was being shipped home in a box without even the dignity of anyone acknowledging why or what he died trying to do. Shit. It was all shit. And your part in it was the shittiest part of all.

Alex spun around, facing his desk and the still unwritten report explaining how and why Blount had died. His eyes drifted to the telephone. Even now all you want to do is call Stephanie and find out where she is and what she's doing. Try to find out if her final words—that she still loved you, still hoped things could work out between you—were just another lie, just another part of her game.

Alex ground his teeth, the muscles along his jaw dancing wildly.

He reached out and punched the speak button on his intercom. "Please ask Kolshak to come in here," he said when his secretary answered.

A minute later, Kolshak entered, looking gaunt and grim and exhausted.

"I'm going to the airport to see them put Blount on the plane," Alex said without preamble. "I know we can't do anything officially, but I think I owe him that much. You wanna come?"

"Yeah, I'd like that," Kolshak said. "Then I want to find that fuck Ludwig, and blow his ass to kingdom come."

Ludwig turned the note over in his hand. It was a single sheet of plain, unidentifiable paper that had been hand-delivered by one of Bugayev's lackeys. On it an address and apartment number had been typed. No doubt using a typewriter that had since been destroyed, Ludwig thought, mentally snorting at the cowardice of the KGB.

But Alex Moran wouldn't be the first station chief to die at the hands of a revolutionary. He would simply be more deserving than the others.

Ludwig ran his fingers gingerly over the heavy bandage that covered most of his right cheek. The man had not only seen him, he had marked him for others. Now it would take plastic surgery to remove the scar that would certainly be there. He walked to the large mirror that hung on one wall and stared at his bandaged face, his eyes alight with the hatred he felt boiling inside. The wound throbbed with the blood coursing through his face, telling him it was time for another dose of pills the doctor had prescribed. But they made him drowsy and dulled his reflexes, and there would be no more of them until he had killed the man who had made them necessary.

And kill anyone who was with him. Making Alex Moran get on his knees and watch their deaths, knowing his own was only moments away. Then a stomach wound, administered with a silenced pistol, so he could sit and watch him die, lying in his own vomit, his own piss and shit. That was the price he'd pay for marking him.

Ludwig's fingers reached for the bandage again, and he noticed they were trembling. But not from fear. No, not from fear at all.

CHAPTER

10

Stephanie stared at the telephone, willing it to ring, willing Alex to call, just to speak to her, to say anything at all. When she arrived home there had not been a message from him on the answering machine as she had hoped. She had not called him at his office, hoping he would call first. But he hadn't, and now it was ten o'clock and she didn't even know how to reach him.

She could call his office and ask them to locate him, but she was afraid that might embarrass him, might even widen the chasm that already existed. She ran her hands through her hair, almost pulling it, thinking about pulling it. She could call Antoine. He would know where Alex was. Yes, she could call Antoine. Old Uncle Antoine, a man she had always secretly despised.

She fumbled in her purse, finding her address book, and quickly located the Pisanis' number. She dialed it, listened to it ring endlessly, then finally heard an answering click, followed by a brutish voice. She asked for Antoine, said who she was, then waited again. Several minutes passed, then the brutish voice returned telling her Antoine Pisani wasn't at home. She replaced the receiver.

"Bastard," she said.

Stephanie walked to the drinks table and poured herself several fingers of brandy, a drink she seldom touched. But she needed it, needed something strong to push down the fear. She walked to the window and stared out at the night. She was dressed in black pleated slacks and a white blouse—as always presentable if she suddenly had to go out. It was something that had been drilled into her since childhood. Something, she felt, she never quite achieved.

The drink fell from her hand at the sound of the doorbell, splashing the amber liquid over the pale oriental carpet. She turned, ignoring the spilled drink, and hurried to the door. It was Alex, she told herself. It had to be Alex. No one else ever came this late at night.

The opened hand pushed into her face as soon as the door swung back, the fingers squeezing her cheeks, keeping her from pulling away. The barrel of the gun pointed straight at the bridge of her nose, held high and awkwardly so she could see it, the aperture at its end seeming enormous, almost like a small tunnel.

She staggered back, seeing the man behind the gun clearly for the first time. He was blond, with blazing blue eyes, and his right cheek was covered with a large bandage.

"Where is your husband?" he whispered. "Where is Alex?"

Stephanie tried to speak, but the fingers squeezing her cheeks made it almost impossible, and her words came out mumbled and distorted, sounding like some character in a cartoon.

"You call out and I'll kill you instantly," the man said.

Stephanie stared into his eyes and believed him. She tried to nod her head against his hand. Her legs had begun to tremble so violently she thought they might collapse beneath her.

The man dropped his hand from her mouth, seized her wrist, and spun her around, then forced it up behind her back. He laid the barrel of the gun against her cheek and marched her from room to room, checking each one. Stephanie could feel the sweat on the hand that held her wrist, and the man's breathing seemed too fast, almost as if coming in short, panting gasps.

The search ended in the bedroom—the man was not here—and Ludwig could feel his adrenaline begin to ease. He shoved the woman forward brutally, sending her sprawling on the bed. She turned to face him, sitting on the edge of the bed. There was fear in her eyes, but not enough, he thought. He leveled the gun between her ample breasts, then turned it from side to side.

"This device on the end of the gun is a silencer," he said, his voice almost crooning. "If I shoot you, no one will hear."

He snapped the pistol to the left and fired into the mattress only a foot from the woman's right hip. She stared at the smoldering hole in the bedding, then jumped to her left, as if belatedly dodging the bullet. The sight of it brought a smile to Ludwig's face.

"When will Alex be home?" he asked.

The woman's chin trembled uncontrollably, as she fought the words out.

"I . . . I . . . don't know."

Stephanie's mind was racing. If she told him Alex wasn't coming home, that he didn't live here anymore, what would he do to her? If he thought he'd be home any minute, would he leave? No. He wasn't here for her. He was here for Alex. To hurt him. Her eyes widened. Even to kill him.

"Tell me!" Ludwig's voice was a feral growl.

Stephanie stammered, getting nothing intelligible out, then stopped, drawing a breath. "He left me," she said, her voice barely audible. "He moved out," louder this time. "Yesterday."

Ludwig's eyes narrowed, and his face glowed with rage. "Where is he now?"

Stephanie's entire body shook, and she clutched her opposite arms with her hands, hugging herself. "I . . . I . . . don't know."

Ludwig took a quick step forward and raised a hand as if to strike her. She shrunk back, her chin pressing down against her chest, her shoulders rising to fend off the blow. It didn't come, and she risked a look up at him. The hand was still raised, waiting, threatening.

"Tell me!" he growled again.

"He hasn't called. I don't know where he is. No one will tell me where he is." The last came out in a sudden sob.

Ludwig stared at her, thinking. His eyes narrowed to a shrewd line. "Caught you fucking someone, did he?"

"Y-y-es," Stephanie stammered, sobbing again.

Ludwig threw back his head and laughed, then caught himself, as if suddenly acknowledging the unexpected complication. He began to slowly pace the room. He stopped and stared at her, a smile coming gradually to his lips.

"But he'll come for you, won't he?" He looked at her, his eyes drinking in the litheness of her body. She cringed, reading his thoughts.

Ludwig studied her fear, her sudden realization that he could do whatever he wished with her. The sight of it sent a sensation of warmth through his groin.

"Oh, yes, he'll come. He'll come wherever I tell him to." His smile widened. "And his pain, when I speak to him, will be wondrous." His face hardened, his features changing with the speed of a switch being thrown. "Get up! And get your coat!" he snapped.

Alex got to the office late—ten o'clock—a full hour and a half past his normal time. He had stayed up drinking the night before —in part because of Blount, but mostly due to images of Stephanie, images he had never wanted to see.

His secretary looked at him reproachfully. Not because he was late, he thought. But because he looked like what he had done.

"Stop being a surrogate mother," he threw at her, marching past her desk and into his office.

She followed him in moments later, as he was just settling behind his desk, his coat already off and thrown carelessly onto the sofa. She placed a cup of coffee on the desk in front of him, looked down at him for a moment, then turned to leave.

"If you have something to say, Julie, just say it and go away," he said.

"Why would I have anything to say?" she said, starting for the door. "I'm not that kind of employee." She moved to the door. "The general wants you to call him," she said as she reached for the doorknob, then casually glanced over her shoulder. "Oh, by the way. You look like shit," she said.

"Thank you," Alex said as the door closed behind her.

He eased back in his chair and drew a breath. The general was Pat Cisco, director of the DIA, a man who had been his friend and "rabbi" in the agency, but still very definitely a man whose call he could neither ignore nor postpone. He pushed the intercom button. "Please get the general for me," he said when Julie responded.

"His phone's ringing now," she said.

"Damned woman's too efficient," he muttered, picking up the receiver. "I've got it," he said to Julie just as Cisco's secretary answered.

When Pat Cisco got on the line, he began talking as though their conversation had been going on for several minutes. "This kid Blount," he said. "It was Ludwig who got him?"

"Yeah, it was Ludwig," Alex said.

"Fucker," Cisco said. "I want this bastard's ass. He's on a short list, of maybe five, that have been running circles around us. Around everybody. Carlos, Abu Nidal, hell, you know who they all are. Motherfucking bastards."

Cisco was a retired army general who had never lost his military "in-the-field" idiom. Alex had always wondered if he used it with the president. He doubted it. The man was slick when he wanted to be. He was the type who could walk across a chocolate cake and never leave footprints. But he stuck by his people. Over and above anything else, he stuck by them like glue.

"If he's getable, we'll get him," Alex said. "He was hit in the shootout," he added.

"Bad?" Cisco asked, a note of hope and some unmistakable pleasure in his voice.

"Not bad enough," Alex said. "Flesh wound somewhere on the right side of his head. Bled pretty heavy, but then all head wounds do. He still had enough in him to run like an elk," he added.

Cisco grunted. "You get him?" he asked.

"Yeah. One lucky round out of four."

"So tell me about Blount." The real reason for the call.

"I fucked up," Alex said.

"How so?"

"Wasn't doing my job earlier in the day. Wasn't out there supervising him like I should have been. He went off on his own that night, after the guy who was told him to go home. He got lucky and spotted Ludwig." Alex paused, drawing a breath. "Ludwig must have picked up on the tail. As soon as we were deployed, and waiting for backup, he was out the door and walking away. Blount made a move he shouldn't have made, and Ludwig blew him away. It was a general fuck-up, but it started at my door."

"Happens," Cisco said. "Don't put any of that in the official report. Just leave it clean and simple. Never know who's gonna read that shit."

Alex felt gratitude but no lessening of guilt.

"I hear you and Stephanie split up," Cisco said.

Shit, Alex thought. The man's pipeline was unreal. "Yeah, for now anyway."

"Sorry to hear it. I always liked the lady."

Yeah, me too, Alex thought, grateful that Cisco hadn't expressed any hackneyed hope things would work out. Probably even knows who she was sleeping with, he decided.

"I'll get my mind back on my job," he said.

"That would be good," Cisco said. "All the way around. You go get that fuck, Alex. The KGB's got to be hiding him out. Go sit on every asset and safe house you know about. You using Pisani's people?"

"Full time," Alex said.

"Good. Those fucking Corsicans are better'n bloodhounds. Don't put any restrictions on them. Let them cut the bastard's balls off when they find him. The promise of a little blood sport seems to make them work harder, I've noticed."

"You got it, General," Alex said.

"Good," Cisco said. "And, Alex. Take an old man's advice. Take your time with Stephanie. And go easy on yourself."

"Thanks, General. I'll try."

Alex replaced the receiver and stared at it. Pat Cisco had been the man who had guided his career—safeguarded it from agency politics—a job he had mistakenly thought his father would assume.

He was just beginning to think about that when the intercom buzzed. He pushed the button. "Yes, Julie," he said.

"Consulate on line two," she said. "A Gerard Morganthau. Sounds very Boston brahmin."

Alex punched the appropriate button. Gerard Morganthau began nervously, explained there was something he felt they should discuss, and suggested they meet for lunch. Alex immediately knew who the man was. He felt his stomach tighten.

"We're kind of up to our ears here right now," Alex said. "Let's do this on the phone, then maybe meet later when things quiet down around here."

Morganthau paused, as if gathering his thoughts. "Yes," he said, then paused again.

Tough thing to say, Alex thought. Excuse me, but I've been fucking your wife. No offense intended, really.

"I understand Stephanie has told you about us," Morganthau began.

"She told me there was someone. I didn't know who," Alex said. Take that little surprise, he added to himself.

"Oh," Morganthau said, then stopped, gathering himself from his unexpected faux pas. "I was sure she had." He paused again. "And I thought I should call and explain." Another pause. "As well as assure you that everything is over between us." The final words were rushed, coming from someone eager to please.

Fuck you, Alex thought. He said nothing.

Morganthau waited, then realized he would get only silence for now. "It was just something that happened. Not something either of us planned. God, I know that sounds like the worst of clichés, but it *is* true." He paused again.

"Go on," Alex said. He wished he could grab the silly, babbling bastard by the throat and shake him.

"Well, I-I just wanted you to know that. Especially that it's over." He hesitated again. "I hope there won't be any difficulty between us."

Alex closed his eyes, the muscles along his jaw doing a rapid dance. It was the diplomat's view of spooks, as they called them. People whose linchpin of life, they believed, was gratuitous, never ending violence.

"I have no intention of doing anything to you or about you, Morganthau," Alex said. "Whether you keep seeing Stephanie or not. That's a decision she'll make, and something we'll each deal with individually."

"Oh, I . . ." He hesitated again, and Alex could almost hear him wondering if he were simply being put off guard, if Alex thought the conversation might be recorded, if, if, if, if, if.

"Well, I just want to assure you it *is* over," he added.

"Good-bye, Morganthau," Alex said and hung up. Sonofabitch, he thought. Goddamned weasel of a sonofabitch.

"You! You! You! *Out!*" Bugayev jabbed a finger at each of his men, punctuating his words, then turned on Ludwig, face flushed, eyes gleaming. "You have lost your mind!" he snapped. "And the KGB will have no part in your insanity."

"I'm amazed, comrade," Ludwig said, his own eyes filled with open delight at Bugayev's rage. "I thought you would leap at the chance to help me."

Bugayev fought for control, normally an easy matter for him. But not with this man. "There will be no men here with you," he said. "Not now. Not when you finish whatever it is you plan. When the ship is ready for you, we will tell you. If you get there, you will be allowed to board." He paused, staring at the man. "For one, I hope you never get there."

"I am touched by your solicitousness, comrade," Ludwig taunted.

Bugayev turned, walked to the door, then turned back. "You are a disgrace to socialism," he said. "You disgrace my country for having dealt with you. You disgrace the agency of that government I serve. I only wish you worked for the other side, where you belong." He stared at the younger man. "Because then I could personally arrange your extermination."

Bugayev left to the sound of Ludwig's laughter.

But the laughter faded and stopped within moments, replaced by a look of seething hatred. They were all alike, Ludwig told himself. The lackeys of both sides, both applying rules of morality that didn't exist, were never practiced in any way, but were always mouthed whenever reality made them squeamish.

He turned on his heel, marched to the closed bedroom door, and threw it open, forcing it to crash loudly against the wall. The sound, and the sight of him standing there, made the woman jump in place. He stared down at her. She was seated on the end of the bed, her mouth gagged, hands tied behind her back.

"Get up!" he ordered. "We are going to telephone your husband. You will tell him only that you are well, that you are with *Ernst Ludwig*, and that I shall kill you if he doesn't do exactly as I say." He paused, glaring at her for effect. "Then you will come back in here and you will shut the door with your foot. If you don't do *exactly* as I have said, your husband will hear you die over the telephone. Do . . . you . . . understand?"

He watched Stephanie nod her head like a foolish puppet, then crossed the room to her and ripped the tape from her mouth.

"Now we go to the telephone," he said, pushing her ahead of him.

Alex's hand gripped the receiver as though he were trying to crush it as he listened to Stephanie's words.

"Are you all right?" he asked.

He heard her say yes, then a cry of surprise as the telephone was yanked away from her. "Go," he heard a voice say.

A few seconds later the same voice purred into the phone. "Good morning, Alex," the voice said. "I hope I'm not interrupting any vital government business."

"Just tell me what you want, Ludwig," Alex said, his own voice barely under control.

"Ah, the ever practical American," Ludwig said. He paused and let out a soft laugh. "What I want is to be able to avoid killing your wife. Will you help me do that?"

Before Alex could answer, Ludwig continued, "Of course you will. She is such a marvel in bed, isn't she?" He paused again, enjoying what he perceived to be Alex's shocked silence. "I especially like the way she plays with my balls when she has me in her mouth. But I'm sure you know that little trick of hers as well as I. It was what so attracted me to her—let's see, three, or is it four, months ago now."

"Get to the point, Ludwig." Alex's hands were trembling, and he was fighting to keep it from his voice.

"The point, my friend, is that I have no need to kill a woman with such splendid talents. But you seem to offer me little choice, except to threaten to do exactly that. And I always make good on my threats. But of course you know that, don't you?"

"Tell me what you want," Alex said. His teeth were clenched to keep any tremor from his voice.

"Oh, it is so simple," Ludwig said, his voice light, goading. "I will need a passport. I would prefer West German, but American will do. It must be blank and unnumbered, but, of course, the appropriate seals must be in place. I have the ability to number it and affix the necessary photograph and name." He continued, his voice almost purring again. "And, please, no infrared markings or other ways of identifying it. It will be thoroughly checked, and any foolishness of that sort will be treated very badly."

"Is that all?" Again the clenched teeth.

"Oh, no. You must also call off your dogs. I will not telephone again unless I see that you have. I will simply send you a note about where to have dear Stephanie's body collected."

"You've got it. I'd like to speak to her again."

"I'll let you know where, and when, the passport is to be delivered." He paused, drawing out the moment for effect. "And I'm afraid you won't be able to speak to your wife again right now. I'm going to entertain her. She does so love to be entertained."

Ludwig replaced the receiver, then turned and walked slowly back to the bedroom. He opened the door and walked casually to the bed, removing his shirt as he did. He let it drop to the floor, then unbuckled his trousers and removed them as well.

He stared down at Stephanie, who was again seated on the edge of the bed. Her eyes were wide, terrified.

"I have something delightful for you," he said, his voice soft, almost gentle. "It must never be said that Ernst Ludwig was caught out in a lie."

CHAPTER

11

Antoine Pisani's face was a rigid mask as he listened to Alex relate the telephone conversation with Ludwig. Alex spared no detail, hid nothing in the telling of it. He wanted his "uncle" to know everything, wanted it clear he must do exactly what he was asked. As he listened, Antoine's fingers gripped the arms of his chair as though he might rip them free at any moment. To Antoine, any attack against a member of his family was an attack against every member, an attack against his own being. To the aging Corsican, right or wrong, justice or injustice, played no part in the equation. Any attack required only one response, and it must be swift, and it must be overwhelming. And to Antoine's mind—though it was nothing more than a fabrication created over the years—Alex was very much a part of his family.

"So what would you have me do to help you?" Antoine asked when Alex had finished. There was a hint of concern in his voice, a note of suspicion that Alex was prepared to do something unwise, something foolhardy.

"I need your people off the street," Alex said. His hands were twisting on the arms of his own chair, the fingers opening and closing as though he were exercising his grip with rubber balls.

Antoine picked up on the nervous gesture, the look in Alex's eyes, the panic that seemed to pour off him. The man was not operating in anger, he was operating in fear. It was not fear for himself, but it was fear nonetheless. And that, Antoine knew, was a harbinger of disaster.

"I've already pulled *my* people off," Alex continued. "There's no choice. I know this man, I know his history. He'll kill her, Uncle. Just as sure as we sit here."

Antoine gathered himself, forcing the anger away. No one, he knew, truly listened to an angry man.

"You know this man—this pig—intends to kill you." It was a statement, not a question. He watched Alex nod his head. "When he tells you where to come, will you take men with you? Preferably my men?"

"I don't know. I haven't thought that far ahead," Alex conceded.

"Have you talked to General Cisco?"

Alex shook his head.

Antoine reached across the small distance between their two chairs and laid a beefy hand on Alex's arm. "I don't say this to hurt you," he said softly. "I only say it for the sake of reality. But have you considered the fact that this man—this animal of the worst kind—will kill Stephanie no matter what you do? That she will be dead even before you go to him?"

Alex's face drained of the little color left in it. "I have to gamble that she won't be," he said. "I don't have any other choice."

There was a look of abject resignation in Alex's eyes, in the tone of his voice, and Antoine wondered if it was due to Alex's comprehension that he was starting out on his own funeral march, or because of what Ludwig had told him—that he had been with Stephanie for months now—which, if true, had already drained the will to live from him.

"He has lied to you about her, you know," Antoine said. "This shit he speaks about being with her before. It is his way of torturing you."

Alex stared at him, his eyes, his face void of expression. "Are you sure?" he said, his voice as flat as his features.

"I am sure," Antoine said. He sat back, releasing Alex's arm. "When you go to him, how will you kill him?" he asked at length.

Alex shook his head slowly. "I don't know. First I'll make sure she's safe."

"You must have people with you, then." There was no question, no room for argument in Antoine's words.

Alex nodded. He was staring at the floor. "Yes, you're right about that." He looked up suddenly, his eyes sharp. "But far back. Just to make sure he doesn't get away if he kills me, if he kills . . ." He allowed the sentence to die unfinished.

Antoine nodded, his face set and grim. The man was not thinking, he told himself, but there was nothing he could do to change the fact.

"I will be there for whatever you need," he said.

When Alex had left, Antoine summoned his driver and headed for the opera district, where his original business venture, the nightclub, Club Paradise, was located. Little had changed over the years, save the names and ownership of various businesses in the neighborhood. The area was still rife with houses of prostitution, mostly located on the upper floors of four- and five-story tenements, masking themselves as hotels, each requiring clients to ascend long, narrow stairways that were easily guarded against police or other troublemakers, and allowing the whores to lean out the windows and cast inviting smiles on would-be customers.

On the corners, Corsicans working for the Pisanis sat at outdoor cafés, guarding the street against attack or other trouble that might develop. It was an armed camp—had always been so—but to the uninitiated eye, appeared no different than any other struggling business area, a bit more seedy perhaps, but merely a place where the disadvantaged were attempting to eke out a living, which, in fact, was true. In most cases it simply was not an honest living.

Inside the club, the bright light of daytime revealed the dinginess that was hidden by low-wattage neon and the fabricated glamour employed at night.

Antoine moved quickly past the massive circular bar, through a door guarded by two of his men, and into a long hallway that led to an office at the rear. It was an office he and his brother had used from the beginning and still did—although much of their work was now done in the house they shared—keeping the old office more out of sentiment than practicality.

When Antoine entered, Meme was seated at a large desk, bent over an accounts ledger. Antoine fell into an old, comfortable stuffed chair opposite—another remnant of the past with which both brothers refused to part—and quickly recounted Alex's visit.

Meme's dark eyes glowed with suppressed rage, and his smaller body became unnaturally still.

"You promised him we would do as he asked?" Meme's voice was soft, like a faint wind blowing across frozen water. When he spoke that way, it sent a chill through Antoine.

"Yes," Antoine said.

Meme just stared at him, waiting for more. His eyes were like his voice.

"We will do what has to be done," Antoine said. "We will put everyone on the street, even ask other factions of the *milieu* for help if necessary. We will find this bastard before Alex can go to him. And we will kill him."

"And the woman?"

"The woman is no longer of consequence. She saw to that herself."

Meme nodded. "You said Alex has called off his own men, and has not contacted General Cisco. Will you call him?"

Antoine shook his head slowly, then shrugged, making a face of uncertain displeasure at the idea. "He is a man of scruples, and you can never trust a man of scruples," he said.

Three days had passed since Bugayev left the safe house after issuing his ultimatum to Ludwig. The safe house was located in the Arab quarter of the old city, a downtrodden, battered-looking area whose predominant population was Palestinian, a people whose loyalties—what there were of them—were more inclined toward the Soviets than any other nation, and whose inherent lack of trust made them difficult for even the Corsicans to penetrate.

As Bugayev entered the apartment, he found Ludwig seated on the sofa, the woman, hands still bound, in a chair across the room. She was wearing only undergarments and her eyes were like those of a frightened animal.

Bugayev removed his hat and held it before his face, hiding it from her. "Get her out of here," he demanded.

When Ludwig had locked the woman away in the bedroom and resumed his casual place on the sofa, Bugayev started in on him. "You seem very casual and relaxed for a hunted man," he said.

"I saw you coming," Ludwig replied. He seemed smug, almost bored.

"Then why didn't you lock the woman away?"

"I didn't want to," Ludwig said.

Bugayev clenched his teeth, but chose to ignore the arrogance. "You must let the woman go and leave," he said.

"Why?" Ludwig picked up a magazine lying next to him on the sofa, exposing a pistol hidden there. The threat was so blatant and ridiculous it almost made Bugayev laugh in his face.

"Because the Corsicans have covered this city with a net of humanity even a fly could not escape," Bugayev said.

"I expected as much," Ludwig said, his voice still bored. "What about Moran's people?" he asked.

"They are nowhere to be seen," Bugayev said. "I doubt he knows what the Corsicans are doing. His relationship with the Pisanis is almost familial. They would protect him whether he wanted them to or not."

"His own men have been called off?" Ludwig said. Bugayev nodded, and Ludwig grunted in response. "I must confess, that surprises me."

"So you expected him to continue hunting you despite your threat?"

"Of course."

"And why?"

"Because his wife is a slut and he knows it. What man would risk his life for a slut?" Ludwig smiled up at the Russian. "Oh, I knew he'd come for her, and that he'd make it appear he was alone. That is simply a question of machismo. But I thought he'd try to get to me first. And I was certain when he came, there would be men with him, and that they would attack regardless of what it meant for the woman." He smiled with pleasure. "You see, I never intended to kill him face to face. But I never realized the man was a fool either."

"He is not a fool," Bugayev snapped. "Do not underestimate the man." He watched Ludwig's face fill with a smirk. "And don't underestimate the Pisanis and their people. They control the docks and everything else that moves in this city. You will never escape if you carry out your plan."

"And don't you underestimate me!" Ludwig snapped.

Bugayev drew a long breath. "It is my job to get you out of this city alive. I can only do that if you listen to what I know to be true. If you kill Alex Moran, or if you simply attempt to and fail, all the forces of U.S. intelligence will be hunting you, whether Moran wants it or not." He paused for effect. "Along with the French police, French customs, the entire French government. All that, combined with the Pisanis, is simply too formidable."

The formality of the Russian's language, combined with the rigidity of his posture, made Ludwig smirk again. "You take life too seriously," Ludwig chided him.

"And you value life not one bit," Bugayev snapped back.

"That is possibly true," Ludwig said and began to laugh.

"Will you call off your plan, then?" The Russian's voice held a note of insistence.

"Perhaps I'll simply modify it," Ludwig said.

"And precisely what does that mean?" Bugayev's eyes narrowed. His lack of trust of the man virtually poured from him.

"It means I will do nothing that does not include the certainty of my leaving France," he said. "When will the ship be ready?"

"It is ready now. You can board anytime after eight o'clock this evening. It leaves on the morning tide. Within days you will be in Libya," with others of your ilk, Bugayev added to himself.

Ludwig offered up a long, lazy stretch. "Good. I shall be aboard before midnight. A sea voyage and the warmth of the Libyan sun will do wonders for me."

Bugayev held his eyes, probing for some hint of what the man planned. "I don't feel you answered my question," he said at length.

"I gave you all the answer I intended, comrade."

The smirk was back on Ludwig's face. Bugayev had seen enough of it. He turned and without another word he left the apartment.

Alex had returned to his own apartment, hoping without any real hope that Ludwig might anticipate the move and come for him there. He had left instructions that any calls for him—no matter from whom—be patched through to him there. Now, seated in a chair facing the front door, his pistol on a table close to his right hand, the telephone next to it, he waited.

He had arrived straight from work, and except for a quick search of the rooms to ensure he was alone, he had remained in the living room. The other rooms, each in their own way, held too much of Stephanie, too much to distract him, to plague an imagination already on overload.

He had been living on Antoine Pisani's words—that Ludwig's

claim of a lengthy relationship with Stephanie was nothing more than an attempt to torture him. But the scenario kept replaying itself. If a Morganthau had existed, why not a Ludwig? Why not a man whose real identity she hadn't known, a man who had stumbled across the wife of the DIA station chief—or even intentionally sought her out—and found, to his delight, that she was looking for an extracurricular roll in the hay?

The scenario played again, and he forced it down, away. As far below the surface as it would go. But other thoughts wouldn't leave. He had not been here when Ludwig had come for him. Had he, there was little doubt Ludwig would have killed him. He did not walk around his own home armed, did not answer the door weapon in hand. Despite Hollywood's portrayals, the real world of espionage simply didn't work that way. The private lives of spies were more like insurance salesmen's than film heroes.

But he might have killed Stephanie too. Especially if she had seen his face. And that was the other gnawing question. Ludwig would not leave her alive now. Not after she had seen him, had learned who he was. But he just might hold onto her until he was certain Alex had stepped completely into his trap; he might just choose to kill her in front of him—or to kill *him* in front of her, depending on his particular bent of mind. It was his one hope, and knowing that in itself terrified him.

Alex glanced at his watch. Late, very late. And that was the other possibility. That Ludwig had simply used Stephanie to abort the search for him, and now, having killed her, had left the city, leaving everyone standing in place, impotent, until her body was eventually discovered.

The sound of the telephone made him jump in his chair, and he reached quickly for it before catching himself, forcing himself to let it ring a second time, just to give himself time for some degree of calm.

Ludwig's voice purred at him as soon as he answered, the tone mocking, filled with the delight of a school yard bully. "You must have wondered why it has taken me so long to call you," he began, the jeering sound in his voice flowing across the line so thickly Alex thought he could feel it, like a finger jabbing him in the chest.

"I assumed you were being cautious," Alex said, his own voice flat, as unemotional as he could manage.

"Oh, of course. I am always that," Ludwig purred. "But, I must confess, I've also been a bit distracted."

Alex's hand tightened on the receiver, knowing what was coming, what he would be forced to hear.

"Have you ever noticed . . ." Ludwig paused, playing out the moment. "How can I describe it? Yes. Have you ever noticed that little gasp—that tiny little gasp—that Stephanie gives when you first enter her? Or the way the tip of her tongue protrudes ever so slightly as she closes her eyes to concentrate on the pleasure? It is such a—"

"Cut the crap, Ludwig. I've done what you wanted. Now tell me when and where to deliver the passport." Alex's hands were trembling—something he fought to keep from his voice—and he brought his second hand up to steady the receiver, afraid he might drop it.

"Ah, and I thought we might share something together. But I see that is not to be." He paused again, letting the seconds draw out, waiting until he knew Alex would have begun to wonder if he was still on the line. "Do you know the Street of Pistols, in the old quarter?" he finally said. "It is quite a small street, only a few buildings."

"I know where it is," Alex said.

"You will come there in one hour, no sooner. If anyone even slightly suspicious comes there before . . . well, I needn't go on, need I?"

"I understand," Alex said. "Which building?"

Ludwig let his silence play out again. He had no fear of a telephone tap. That would take time, and the phone he was using was an innocuous one, and he would be away from it—far away—in a matter of moments. "There will be a small piece of paper pinned to the outer door—something you will have to look closely to find. There will be a simple X on the paper. X marks the spot, as you Americans say." He laughed, short and harsh. "You will find me in the basement of that building." He hesitated again. "But only if you are alone and have come when you were told."

"I'll be there," Alex said.

"Yes, I think you will be," Ludwig said.

Ludwig stared into the Street of Pistols, then began to walk, too quickly at first, then slower. He was dressed in a dark sailor's peacoat, the large collar pulled up to hide the sutures in his cheek—the bandage having been removed to make him less noticeable to anyone who knew he had been wounded. A seaman's watch cap covered his blond hair, and he walked with a slight hunch to make himself appear older. He hadn't shaved since being wounded, and the growth of beard gave him a grizzled look, he thought.

His hands were thrust into his pockets, but even there they were trembling. He felt exposed and vulnerable, and it frightened him. And he felt beaten. Alex Moran's chances were too good—the only man who had ever seen his face and lived. But at this point the fact was moot. All the others had died quickly, before they could pass on his description. By now Moran had had a composite drawing made, had made sure it was as close to a perfect rendering as possible. The face of Ernst Ludwig was no longer a mystery to those who hunted him. And the death of Alex Moran would not change that fact. Now, harming him would only provide an unmeasurable amount of pleasure.

But there were too many people hunting him. Too many who held the advantage of hunting on their own terrain. Bugayev was right. He should flee, get aboard the ship while Moran and his Corsican goons were concentrating on the Street of Pistols. He didn't need the passport he had asked for. It was only a ploy to lure Moran in—a part of the game to make him think he had a chance. That was the problem, playing the game out, doing what he must do and getting to the ship before they found him and killed him. But it was important that Moran be made to pay. It was important to destroy his life, and to do it so he knew it came at the hands of Ernst Ludwig.

Ludwig tightened his fists into balls and forced them deeper into the pockets of his coat. It helped hide the trembling—from himself.

CHAPTER

12

lex stood back in the shadows at one entrance to the short, wide alley known as the Street of Pistols. He was dressed in a black trenchcoat, the collar pulled high to keep any light from his face, and his right hand was deep in the pocket, gripping a Walther PPK/S automatic, the pistol cocked and ready, the safety already disengaged.

He scanned one side of the street, illuminated only by a single street lamp located at the opposite corner. Ludwig had chosen well. To find the proper entry among the ten or so on the street, he would have to go from door to darkened door, looking for the small slip of paper marked with an X, and making himself an easy target for anyone shooting from a building or rooftop opposite. It was a suicidal walk if that was the way Ludwig had decided he would die. But it was only one of several ways. A booby trap in the basement he would enter couldn't be overlooked. The man's penchant for explosives was too well documented. And his selection of the Arab quarter of the old city made that possibility all too real. More than a few PLO bomb factories were known to have existed there over the years.

But there was nothing he could do about any of it; any precautions would risk Stephanie's life. He had to hope that Ludwig wanted a face-to-face confrontation, wanted the satisfaction of seeing the fear and hatred in his eyes when he killed him. Wanted, once more, to tell him how much he had enjoyed his wife and to see the effect it had, perhaps even force her to tell him how much she had enjoyed Ludwig.

He pushed it all down. He was only replaying scenarios with which he had tortured himself for hours. He stared into the street. Almost every apartment was dark, lifeless. It was a poor, working-class neighborhood, and the people who lived there played no part in the city's endless nightlife, unless it was to scratch out a living serving those who did. He glanced at his watch. It was half past midnight, the exact time Ludwig had appointed.

He had met Antoine's men a half hour earlier, a few blocks away on the Street of Refuge. He had ordered them to keep well away from the target area, and they had given him the look Corsicans use when they know they are dealing with a fool but cannot say so—a blank stare and a simple shrug. But they would stay back, cutting off any escape in that direction, while others—Antoine among them, he suspected—would seal off the lower end of the street. But it was useless, he knew. The basements of the old buildings were a labyrinth of tunnels that could take a man who knew them, or someone with local help, almost anywhere. The bastard had chosen well on that count too. He had everything the way he wanted it. He was winning his dirty little game, and Alex could see nothing that would change it. Unless you get lucky and can kill him before he kills you.

He stepped out into the street and began walking, his rubber-soled shoes moving soundlessly on the well-worn cobblestones. A light rain had begun to fall, slicking his face so it matched the sweat in his palms.

He stepped to the first entry, cooking smells drifting out through the closed door, the door itself empty of any marking. He moved to the second, a sensation heavy in the center of his back, awaiting the blow that would come when a bullet smashed into him. His body was lathered in sweat now, despite the chill dampness of the rain, which had begun to fall more heavily. A third door, a fourth, nothing. Across the narrow street, exposed to the rooftops and upper floors of the buildings he had just left, the sensation in his back stronger, more certain.

It was at the third entry, only two from the end, that he found the slip of paper—only a two-inch square affixed low on the glass door panel near the doorknob—a heavy black X filling its surface. He pushed through the door quickly, closing it behind him and flattening himself against one wall, his breathing loud and rapid, his mind shouting at his carelessness for not checking the door for traps before entering, then arguing back that he'd had to get off the street and escape the bullet screaming toward his back. But no bullet had come, and he stood there, pistol up beside his cheek, his left hand cupping the heel of his right, which held the weapon, fighting to control the trembling which would nullify the steadiness sought by a two-handed shooting stance.

God. He willed the trembling to ease, willed his brain to begin to function, start spewing out the training that had been drummed into him years before. Too many years, he told himself.

The basement. A doorway leading to it somewhere back under the stairway that lay ahead of him. The entry hall was dark, whatever light there had once been now extinguished, the darkness registering for the first time. He slid down the wall, crouching low, lessening the target he offered backlighted against the faint glow coming through the glass door panel, then began to move slowly forward, his heart pounding in his ears.

There was a door ahead of him, but not enough light to check its edges for wires or any other telltales that would indicate an explosive device. He reached into his pocket and removed a penlight that felt slippery against his sweating hand. He held it out to the side, as far away from his body as possible, flicked it on, and played it over the edges of the door.

A thud on the floor above him. A man coughing. The penlight winked off and he froze, waiting, listening.

Another cough—a cigarette smoker's hack—then quiet again. Alex's breathing slowed, the tension ebbing slightly, the butt of the pistol slick with sweat from his palm. He turned the penlight back on and finished his search along the edges of the door. Nothing. At least nothing he could find.

He eased himself up, took two quick steps across the hall, and flattened himself against the wall next to the door. Alex could feel the sweat gathering again, running in cold rivulets against his skin, as he reached for the doorknob. Stephanie's down there, he kept telling himself. Your family. The one you created for yourself. You have to get to her. Have to. Now. He turned the knob, waiting for the explosion from wires he could not see. He eased the door open a crack, then gently played his fingers inside the opening, feeling for the telltales. Again nothing.

Faint light filtered out from the opening, rising from the basement, and he stared into it, trying to force his eyes to adjust to the change. He drew a breath, then swung the door back and spun into the opening, the pistol out in front of him in two hands, the left shoulder slightly forward, the tip of the right index finger applying two pounds of pressure to the trigger's seven-pound pull, both eyes open, squared over the rear sight, the front sight and the target area a faint blur. Textbook. They teach you everything except how badly your hands will tremble.

Slowly, the weapon still out in front, like a weight drawing him forward, Alex started down the stairs.

Two blocks to the south, Antoine Pisani sat in the rear of a large black bullet-proof car, the tinted rear window lowered six inches so he could see clearly into the street. A World War II vintage Colt .45 automatic lay on the seat beside him—the only personal weapon he had carried over the past thirty-five years, on the rare times he carried one at all. It had been a gift from Piers Moran, Alex's father, a weapon, he had thought then—with pleasure—that had been pilfered from the occupying U.S. Army.

One of Pisani's men sat in the front seat, an Uzi across his lap, his left hand holding up a portable field radio so Antoine could hear conversations among his men.

"Tell them to start into the tunnels at both ends," he snapped.

His man looked at him, then did as he was told. Alex's instructions had been clear. No one was to go anywhere near the target area until it was over, or until shots were heard and the net for Ludwig needed to be drawn shut. But Antoine didn't give a shit what Alex had said. If the man wanted to try to get himself killed over a whore of a wife, that was something he couldn't control. But Pisani men would be there to try to stop it, and the bastard, Ludwig, would not escape. No matter what, that would not happen.

Antoine swung the rear door open and climbed out, dragging the old automatic with him. "Let's get closer," he snapped. "We need to be close."

Alex reached the bottom of the stairs and found himself in a narrow hall that led to a large, open room he could see ahead. Light flooded from that area, bright and glaring, picking up the heavy layer of dirt and scattered debris that littered the stone floor. He moved forward in a crouch, then stopped before a final turn that would take him into the room that spread out, largely unseen, to his right. He straightened, slipping the pistol back in his pocket, his hand still on it.

"Ludwig," he called. "I'm coming in."

There was no answer.

He stepped forward, body tense, ready to fall back to the safety of the hall, and turned into the room.

He froze, staring, then sank to his knees.

Stephanie's naked body hung from a rafter, tied at the wrists, her toes touching the floor. Her head was tilted back and to one side; a second, yawning mouth, where her throat had been, gaped at him; her blood washed over her shoulders, her eyes lifeless slits, as though squinting at something she couldn't quite see. A single word had been cut across her breasts—*Slut*—and the incisions had dribbled blood across her belly.

Alex's mouth hung open, and his body shook in violent spasms. He crawled forward, oblivious to any need for self-preservation. Then struggling up, using her legs to support himself, he clung to her swaying body. A low moan, growing slowly to a howl, flowed from him.

When Antoine and his men came through the tunnels, they found Alex kneeling on the dirt-covered floor, cradling Stephanie in his arms. He was staring straight ahead, seeing nothing other than whatever grotesque scenario played across his mind.

Antoine motioned his men forward, signaling with his head that they should check the area. But he knew it was useless. Ludwig was not there, had not been for hours from the look of the pale, lifeless husk Alex hugged tenderly to his chest. Antoine moved next to him and knelt, gently stroking his head, his voice soft as though comforting a small child.

"We must go, Alex. We must go and call the police. Let them do what must be done for her." He nodded to one of his men, who knelt and began to lift Stephanie from Alex's arms. His grip tightened, but his mind didn't seem to register the fact. Gently the man pried his hands loose and lifted the body up, and Antoine engulfed Alex's shoulders in one bear-like arm and raised him to his feet.

"We will go now, Alex."

Alex's head snapped around, glaring into his "uncle's" face.

"And then we will find this pig, and we will slaughter him," Antoine said, his voice still soft, almost as if reciting the words of a lullaby.

Alex's eyes glowed like coals, and his lips began to move, but no words could be heard.

Ludwig stood at the rail of the ship and watched the pilot boat pull away, headed back to shore. In a few days he would be in Libya and he would force himself to forget his failure. Then he would concentrate on the execution of the American general he had marked for death back in Germany. He raised one hand, gently touching the bandages that again covered the wound on his cheek. But first he would heal. First the wounds he had suffered would be allowed to fade from him. All of them.

The boy ran across the street, straight for the man dressed in the uniform of a Stasi colonel. The man stood tall and rigid, and as the boy drew closer, his body slowed instinctively upon seeing the hard, rigid eyes that dominated the man's face.

"I have spoken to your teacher," the man said, his voice low and cold. "I have told you what I expect," he said. "What I do not expect is for my son to be a disgrace to me. The teacher tells me that others in your class are doing work beyond what you are capable of doing. How do you explain this?"

The boy was seven and his lips began to tremble as he tried to speak. The man glared down at him, and the boy lowered his eyes, staring at the glistening riding boots that stood, feet splayed apart, before him.

"I will do better," the boy said, his voice barely above a whisper.

"Look at me!"

The man's voice stung him like a whip, and the boy's head snapped up.

A gloved hand lashed out, stinging his cheek.

"You will do better," the man snapped back.

Ludwig's eyes glared at the sea. How he hated his father, he thought. How he still hated him, even all these years after his death.

He turned away from the rail and walked along the deck, headed aft, where the passageway that led to his cabin was located.

Libya would be warm, he told himself. If nothing else, Libya would be warm.

CHAPTER

13

Alex awoke in a large bedroom on the second floor of the Pisani house. He had been brought there the previous night, although the trip itself existed in a haze: the climbing of the stairs, undressing, falling into bed, all the stuff of somnambulists. Now he was awake, naked beneath the covers, lying on his back, his mind replaying every moment, every vision. And he was still trembling, with fear, or rage, or madness, he was not certain.

There was a small crack in the ceiling that ran wildly for a few feet, then disappeared. It became the yawning wound in Stephanie's throat and remained. He turned on his side, staring blindly at the furniture on that side of the room. Old and highly polished furniture, older than himself—antiques, he supposed—furniture that would exist long after he was dead. Unless someone destroyed it first.

A tree, to a piece of wood, to a fashioned item of furniture. Something inanimate, something dead, that would outlive the living.

The door to the bedroom opened and Antoine entered, carrying a tray of croissants and butter and coffee. He crossed the room, placed the tray on a bedside table, then pulled up a chair and sat next to Alex's head.

"It's good you're awake," he said. "It is time we began."

Alex sat up, swung his legs out of the bed, and reached out for the coffee Antoine had already poured.

He looked thinner, less powerful naked, Antoine thought. But he supposed most men did.

"My men are already working," he said. "Yours as well. I took the liberty of calling your man Kolshak. He too is hunting."

"Kolshak won't be able to do what's needed." Alex's voice was cold and flat, lacking any emotion. It momentarily surprised Antoine, then pleased him. The man had recovered from the previous night, when he had found him sitting like a vegetable, holding the woman's body. Antoine had been unable to understand it as anything more than a terrible weakness. Now it was gone.

"Why do you say this?" Antoine asked.

Alex gulped the coffee down, then poured another cup. "The only way we'll find him quickly is to pull in every sympathizer we know about, everyone who's ever aided a terrorist, been part of a terrorist organization—even on the fringe—everyone who's ever worked with the Russians, or any other East bloc intelligence agency, and get it out of them by whatever means we have to use." Alex put the cup down. "And we're not allowed to do that. We have to work through SDECE, or the police, or both, and by the time that can be arranged, Ludwig will be sitting in Moscow, or any other fucking place he wants to be." He looked up. "Kolshak won't break that agreement. He knows one complaint by a foreign national, and the agency's in the shit."

Antoine looked straight into Alex's eyes for the first time, and found them like his voice, flat and without emotion. He thought he could detect pain beneath the surface—was certain it had to be there—but if it was, it was hidden deep, deeper than anyone but the man himself would ever go.

"We have . . . collected some people," Antoine said, offering a shrug that seemed to say: What else would we do? "But they will never complain to the police. They understand us—we have made sure of that."

"Have you gotten anything?" Alex's body tightened in anticipation, like a spring suddenly coiled.

"Little other than rumors that someone important was in the old city—in the Arab quarter." Antoine smiled. "But we have someone now, a doctor who is known to do work for the communists. If Ludwig was wounded, as you say, he is the one they would go to."

"What has he told you?" Alex's voice showed no trace of excitement. It was like someone discussing the price of beef, Antoine thought. In many ways he was like his father, Antoine told himself. The forced patrician reserve that must never show a crack. But Alex was more human than Piers had ever hoped to be, even if he hid it well. And that was his flaw—a dangerous one for a man disposed to kill.

"I told my men to leave him for us," Antoine explained. "He is in a room in one of the whorehouses not far from my nightclub. We can be there in only a few minutes."

Alex stood without speaking and began pulling on his clothes. Cold and calm, like a man readying himself for a day at the office. Yes, very much like his father, Antoine thought. But not enough. Not nearly enough. It was something, he knew, that Alex would not be pleased to hear.

The room was on the third floor of a onetime tenement in the city's Opera district, reached by a narrow staircase that opened into a small central room that had a simple hotel counter with a bank of numbered keys hanging behind it. The counter—unmanned now—allowed customers to "rent" rooms in which they would just happen to find a beautiful young woman whose official job was that of a chambermaid. It was a simple guise against any police crackdown, something that happened rarely now. But it was a custom from days past, and the "clerks" who ran the desks were faintly disguised bouncers who kept order by whatever means necessary.

A series of numbered doors led off the central room, and as Antoine and Alex approached, a man standing before one opened it for them.

The room was no bigger than a good-sized bedroom, with a bed, two wooden chairs, a low table, a small dresser, and a bidet. A middle-aged man sat in one of the chairs, his arms and legs bound to it with rope. There was a look of abject fear in his eyes, and his jaw trembled. The low table had been drawn up in front of him; his pants were opened, and his penis lay atop the table, held there by a taut piece of string tied to its end. Next to his penis a meat cleaver was embedded in the tabletop. Several scars in the wood indicated the cleaver's cutting edge had been adequately demonstrated.

Antoine pulled up the second wooden chair and sat before the man. "You know who I am?" he asked without preamble.

The man nodded. "I know," he said, barely able to get the words out.

"How do you know?" Antoine asked.

"The newspapers," the man said.

Antoine nodded. "They say terrible things about me, do they not?"

"Yes."

Antoine shrugged. "Well, they are true." He tilted his head to the side, studying the man, almost as though he were deciding whether or not to eat him. He suddenly clapped his hands and began rubbing the palms as if to warm them. The sound made the man jump in place.

"Let me tell you what we know," Antoine continued, seeming not to notice the man's fear. "We know you are a doctor and a communist." Antoine stared into his eyes. "I do not like communists. I have never liked communists. Mostly I have killed them when they interfered with my business. But if they haven't, I have simply ignored them as the unimportant insects they are. Do you understand?"

The man nodded, his jaw trembling too hard to reply with words.

"Another thing we know is that you treated a man recently for a gunshot wound. He also was a communist. Of the German variety."

Antoine sat back in his chair, folded his hands across his belly, and motioned toward Alex with his head. "Now, this man you see behind me, he is my nephew, a member of my *family*." He emphasized the final word. "Last night, this man you treated—this man you offered your help—he murdered my nephew's wife."

The man's eyes darted to Alex, then back to Antoine. "I-I didn't know," he stammered. "I had no way t-t-to know."

Antoine waved an impatient hand before the man's face. "None of that matters," he snapped. "This man has offended me. He has attacked my family, attacked its honor. Normally, anyone who helped him would share in that offense, and would pay a price for doing so. And that price would be a heavy one." Antoine stared down at the man's penis. "If it were only up to me," he said, "this pathetic little weapon of yours would already be in a box on its way to your mistress." He shrugged. "But my nephew will decide that."

"Where is the man you treated, Doctor?" Alex's voice came from behind Antoine, and even though he had been standing there throughout, it seemed to surprise the man, causing him to again jump in place.

"I-I don't know. They never told me."

"Cut it off! Now!" Alex snapped.

"No. No . . . please. Monsieur, you must believe me. I was told nothing. Nothing at all. I was only brought there to treat him, and I was told only they needed treatment quickly because they were taking him out of the country." The man's eyes had followed Antoine's hand to the cleaver, and the terror had forced him to speak so rapidly Alex had difficulty following his French. The man began to sob as Antoine—his hand still on the cleaver—turned and repeated what he had said in English.

"Who brought you to the man?" Alex's voice was low and cold, and it seemed to intensify the man's terror.

"Comrade Bugayev," he said, his voice almost a whine. "I believe he is KGB, even though he has never told me so in the years I've known him. But he never tells me anything. Nothing of importance. I simply do what I am asked."

"Where did you treat him?" Alex stared down at the doctor, his eyes boring into him with open hatred.

"An apartment in the old quarter. I will take you there. I will show you." He looked back at Antoine's hand still on the handle of the cleaver, then back to Alex. "I will do anything you ask, monsieur. Anything. Anything. Only please—"

"Shut your mouth," Antoine snapped. "You will show us now. And if we believe you, maybe you will save that useless prick of yours."

The apartment was empty, as Alex knew it would be. He stood in the doorway of the bedroom, staring down at the bed on which Stephanie must have been held. The apartment was only a block from the Street of Pistols, from the basement where he had found her, and there was no blood here. Ludwig had led her away, walked her through the street, or through one of the tunnels, and had butchered her there.

Butchered. It was the only word to describe what had been done to her. Hung up and slaughtered like a farm animal. Then left hanging to bleed out like a piece of meat being readied for market.

He turned back to the main room. The doctor, seated in a chair with men on either side of him, stared back with imploring eyes.

"Where did they take him?"

The doctor began to tremble, realizing quickly that the threat to him had not ended. "They did not tell me." The words were spoken rapidly in a shaky contralto.

Antoine, who had been standing behind the doctor, moved forward to glare down at him. The image of the hulking Corsican had its effect.

"I understand just a little Russian," the doctor began, his voice still high and uncertain. "The men who drove me here, they seemed to dislike the man, and they said something about him going to that madman Kadafy. That's what they said: 'that madman Kadafy.' They said that was where he belonged."

"When?" It was Antoine this time, his tone unmistakable.

"They didn't say. But Bugayev said they were in a hurry. Bugayev knows. You must ask him. He knows. I am sure he knows."

Alex turned his back on the man. "Let him go," he said, then listened as the man's hands were untied and he went rushing and stumbling for the door.

Antoine came up behind Alex and placed a hand on his shoulder. "I'm a curious man," he said. "If this fool had not told us what he did, would you have had me cut off his prick?"

"No," Alex said. He glanced into Antoine's face, then turned and started for the door. "I would have done it myself."

"I will help you, of course," Antoine said. "But this is a mistake. And you will pay a great price if you do it."

Alex gave him a flat, cold stare, his features showing no hint of condemnation or disappointment. "If you think the repercussions for you and your men will be too great, I'll understand." His voice matched the look on his face.

They were in the back of Antoine's car, moving slowly through the city's clogged streets. Antoine shook his head. "There will be no price for me. My faction serves your government for certain considerations. It has been so for thirty-five years now. And you, Alex. You are the representative of that government. Even if you tell them later, that you were acting without authority"—Antoine made a weighing gesture with each hand—"that this was a matter of personal honor, we will simply say we were ignorant of this. We thought we were serving our American friends. The men in Washington will believe that."

"Are you sure?" Alex asked.

Antoine offered a rare smile. Alex decided it was very much like one a bear might give—if bears smiled—upon finding something special to eat.

"Yes, I am sure. Americans are a very strange people. Especially in matters dealing with others who are foreign to them." He served up his unnerving smile once again. "They always believe things are as they would have them be. They never let reality get in the way of their thinking. They simply choose to ignore it as an irrelevance." Antoine shrugged, his eyes offering an apology. "I hope I do not offend your sense of pride in your country," he said.

Alex felt a tinge of amusement, something Antoine's Corsican philosophy always managed to produce. It was a clever insult. And he was sure it was intended as such. If he accepted it, he accepted that his government operated under a principle of naive arrogance. If he took offense, he too was choosing to ignore reality.

"You have an interesting view of my government, Uncle," he said. "I hope, for your sake, they see things as you expect them to."

"I am certain of it," Antoine said. "Just as I am certain of the consequences for you." He reached out and laid a hand on Alex's arm. "I can protect you from many things," he said. "But I am not certain I can protect you from all the men the Russians will send if you do this thing. I think even your own country will turn its back on you."

"No. They won't," Alex said.

Antoine raised a doubtful eyebrow.

"They'll join them and help hunt me down," Alex said.

Alex waited, listening to Kolshak's words of sympathy and outrage come across the telephone. He was in a phone booth on the street, the unparalleled bustle of Marseilles at midday surging about him. He felt like a cork in an angry sea as people pushed past him, jockeying for advantage on the crowded street, nudging him back until he was pressed against the phone, smiling or shrugging apologies as they stepped on his shoes or ignored him completely, considering any intrusion on his person the price to be expected for impeding the flow of humanity.

Alex turned his back on the crowd, choosing to take the blows from behind, cupping his free hand over the mouthpiece so he could be heard.

"I appreciate it, Stan. I mean that. But there's something you have to do now. And it's an order. I want you to pull everybody off the streets. Nobody works on this thing. Nobody."

Kolshak started to object, but Alex cut him off. "I'm going to take an action, Stan. And it's something the agency can't be involved in." Kolshak began to object, rushing to tell him that Pat Cisco had called, urging him to reach out for him before he did anything.

"I don't have time," Alex said. "You'll just have to trust my judgment on that. But you get back to the general and tell him what I said. And tell him I said this was personal, and he should get the word out on that."

Kolshak began to object again, but Alex cut him off. "Just do it, Stan. This is real cover-your-ass time. People will get hurt if you don't."

He heard Kolshak's muttered epithet, and knew it meant he would do as he was told. He was pissed, but he'd do it.

"Thanks," he said, and hung up the phone.

Sergei Bugayev came out of the restaurant and stood on the sidewalk, picking his teeth as he stared at the fishing boats tied up to the quay of the Vieux Port. The bouillabaisse had been extraordinary, as it always was in this restaurant. And even the price, which was great, had not stopped him from coming there every Friday, a day that many French Catholics still devoted to fish, and which Bugayev believed, inspired the chefs to even greater heights.

He drew in a satisfied breath of sea air, then turned and started up the crowded street for the walk back to his consulate office.

The body pressed against his side, and he could feel the pressure of the pistol's barrel in his ribs.

"Good afternoon, Sergei. I see you're still stuffing yourself with bouillabaisse every Friday. Bad habit, that. Don't your trainers teach the perils of falling into a pattern?"

Bugayev glanced up into Alex's face and found none of the chiding amusement that was carried in his voice.

"You can't be serious, Alex. This breaks all the rules. You know that."

"This is personal, Sergei. There are no rules." He jabbed the gun barrel firmly into Bugayev's ribs. "That car up ahead. In the backseat. I don't mind blowing out your kneecap and dragging you if I have to."

Bugayev shrugged and shook his head. "I regret what this will cost you, Alex."

"Just make sure you're around to see it, my friend. It will be a wonderful story to tell your grandchildren, if you live to have any."

Bugayev entered the rear seat of Antoine's car and found himself pressed between the hulking Corsican and Alex. The pistol was still firmly planted in his ribs.

He looked at Antoine, trying to measure him with his eyes, immediately realizing it wouldn't work. "So the Corsicans are in this too," he said.

"We serve our American friends. It is no secret, Russian."

Bugayev glanced at Alex. He had said it was personal, and now Pisani had indicated it was business. Either Alex had lied to the Corsican, or they were simply covering him from future difficulty. It didn't matter, really. There was no way the KGB would agree to move against the Corsican *milieu*. That would only produce a suicidal body count that would benefit no one.

"Where are you taking me?" Bugayev asked.

"To a basement in the Arab quarter," Alex said. "It's a place your friend Ludwig found to his liking. I thought I might give it a try myself."

Bugayev's wrists were tied to the same rafter where Stephanie's body had hung only twelve hours earlier. His feet stood squarely on the floor stained with her blood.

The police had finished their forensic investigation, and the two officers left to guard the crime scene had been convinced by the Corsicans to make a long, profitable visit to a nearby café.

Alex stood in front of the Russian, far enough back so he was out of the bloodstained circle. It had taken all his strength to return to the basement, and even now he could feel his body trembling with rage as the lingering smells of blood and death assaulted his nostrils.

"You know what happened here," he said softly. There was no question, just a simple declarative sentence.

"I had nothing to do with it, Alex," Bugayev said. "If I had been here, I would have stopped it."

"But you just took a walk," Alex said. "You washed your hands of your paid killer and let him play out his game."

"What choice did I have?" Bugayev's voice was angry. More with himself than with Alex. "My job was to transport him. Nothing else. These animals we both use, you know how unpredictable they are. It's why we use them. They will do what no sane man would even consider."

"Spare me your philosophy on the evils of contemporary intelligence," Alex snapped. "I want to know where that sonofabitch is, and I want to know it now."

Bugayev let out a long breath. "You know I can tell you nothing. Admit nothing. If I could kill him myself, I would gladly do it. But we all play by the same insane rules, Alex. If I tell you nothing, I can forget what happened here. If you force me to talk, I must make a report. It will be my duty."

And your head if they find out you didn't, Alex told himself.

Bugayev looked at him, chilled by the mask that had taken over Alex's face. "And if you kill me, my friend, it will not be difficult for Moscow Center to deduce the purpose and cause of my death."

Antoine came out of the shadows, where he had been standing, and walked up to the Russian, bringing their faces only a foot apart. He had stepped into the bloodstained circle on the floor as casually as if it had not existed. The sight of him doing so had made Alex wince.

"I want to tell you a story, Russian," Antoine began. "It has become something of a Corsican legend, even though it happened fairly recently. Around the time of the first World War.

"It is about a countryman of mine. A man called Buonaparte Sartene. He is dead now. But before his death he became the head of a great faction in the *milieu*. One that virtually controlled Southeast Asia."

Antoine waved his hand, dismissing what he had said as irrelevant. "But then, at the time of this story, he was just a young man living in Calvi, content with the simple life." Antoine paused. His eyes hardened.

"There were French soldiers in the area, and one of them decided he wanted Buonaparte's young sister. The child was only fifteen or sixteen, but this didn't matter to the French pig and two of his friends. They simply took her away and raped and killed her. Buonaparte found her body, and in her hand was the military insignia of her killer. She had ripped it from his collar in an attempt to save her honor."

Antoine paused again, his face drawing even closer to Bugayev's.

"Buonaparte was only a young man then, really little more than a child himself. But he tracked the men down and found them sleeping in their tent one night. And he saw the missing insignia on the man's tunic. He killed the first two men—the friends—simply and quickly. But the man who had killed his sister—the one with the missing insignia—he killed slowly, and with pleasure. They found him staked out to the ground, his arms and legs spread—much the way your arms are spread now. And his eyes were missing. Taken out and replaced with his testicles. While he was still alive, it is said. And his prick was cut off and stuffed into his mouth. The newspapers said the man died from a loss of blood."

Antoine stepped back and turned to one of his men. "Get some rope," he said. "And tie the Russian's legs so they are spread apart."

Bugayev drew a long, trembling breath and stared past Antoine to Alex. "Ludwig is on a ship bound for Libya," he said. "It is a Russian vessel called the *Midnight Sun*. It will dock in Tripoli in two days."

"Thank you, Sergei," Alex said.

CHAPTER

14

The men in the gray suits gathered.

Unlike a meeting of diplomats there were no reporters, no photographers. There was no ballyhoo that members of opposing sides were gathering together. The men who ran the various intelligence agencies operated as they lived: in secret. This was a meeting where rules, and the violation of rules, had to be discussed. And there had to be rules in the community of spies. Otherwise they could not perform their function and would surely cease to exist. And governments could not successfully operate without them. It was simply not possible to have workable agreements among politicians unless each side knew what the other was likely to do. Wars resulted from miscalculations on that basic point.

Rear Admiral Walter Hennesey entered the large stone house, set far back from the banks of Lake Geneva. The house was owned by the Swiss government, and had been made available—as it often was—for delicate meetings between nations when privacy and secrecy were considered vital.

Hennesey was a portrait of physical extremes. Tall, overweight, and just turned sixty. Like most career military men, he wore civilian clothes poorly, always appearing slightly rumpled, slightly ill at ease to be out of uniform, very much uncertain about how the various parts should be put together. There were simply too many choices about matching one piece, one color to another. But that uncertainty did not make him unsure of himself. He was the newly appointed assistant deputy director, operations, of the CIA.

And only two men in the agency had more power than he, and one of them—the director—was a politician whose true function was to listen to the advice of the professionals beneath him, pass those positions on to the president, when necessary, then close his eyes and hope for the best. That, in truth, left Hennesey's boss, the deputy director, operations, as the most powerful. And he was a man who believed in delegating authority. That, Hennesey knew, gave him more power than any member of the cabinet and, in some cases, the president himself. For there was no accountability in his job, except on those rare occasions—and they were truly rare, despite what newspapers would have one believe—that the agency screwed up and got caught in the act. Oh, they screwed up often —Hennesey would be quick to admit that. But they only occasionally got caught.

The man waiting for Hennesey in the building's foyer was Richard Giordano, Pat Cisco's right-hand man in the DIA—and fellow wop, Hennesey told himself. But his presence also meant that Cisco was prepared to play hardball to save his agent, and that was not Hennesey's brief. He would like it to be. He was a longtime friend of Alex's father, Piers Moran. And he was a firm believer that stepping on Russian toes—stepping very hard indeed—was not something to be discouraged. But that wasn't a practical position. And that was what the CIA wanted. A practical position. And, after all, Alex Moran was not one of their own.

"You ready to get this thing over with?" Giordano chirped as Hennesey reached his side. He was a short, swarthy man with a stocky build and an unusually high voice. He was balding badly, but it gave him a somewhat distinguished look, as did the clothing he wore. He was a career intelligence officer, non-military, and the tailoring was impeccable. It annoyed Hennesey to an irrational degree.

Hennesey took out a pipe and reamed the bowl before filling it, stuck it in his mouth, and allowed it to remain unlit. The pipe was a tool more than a pleasure. It gave him time to think, and he was constantly playing with it.

"Seems like we're rather between the proverbial rock and hard place," Hennesey said. "What do you propose?"

"What *we* don't propose is selling our man down the river," Giordano snapped.

"No one wants that," Hennesey said. "But, as you know, this

has gone all the way to the president. And, while he sympathizes with Moran—finds what happened to his wife inexcusable—he's not willing to risk open warfare among the agencies. Yours, ours, the KGB, whomever."

"I know that. Cisco spoke with him," Giordano said. "But we want time to bring him in. If possible."

"We can agree to that," Hennesey said. "But we can't reject a sanction, or any willingness to cooperate. That's our position. Our *government's* position. If we can get him to give it up and accept suitable reprimand, all to the good. But if the Ruskies get to him first, we can't stop them." Hennesey paused to light his pipe. "Do you know where he is?" he asked, almost as an afterthought.

Giordano shook his head.

"Do the Corsicans have him?"

"Who the hell knows what the Corsicans have or don't have? If they do, they're not saying. Moran's like family to the Pisani brothers. If he wasn't, and they had him, they'd give him to us. For a price." Giordano spoke the final words with contempt.

Just like any dago bastard would, Hennesey thought. He drew long and heavily on his pipe. "Well, let's see what our Russian brothers are willing to do," he said.

"The KGB can only accept the strictest application of the agreement."

Boris Rostoff was a man of equal rank to Hennesey in the KGB, a fact intended as a clear message that Moscow Center placed extreme importance on the matter under discussion. It was the same reason Hennesey and Giordano had been sent. All messages delivered and received, Hennesey thought.

Rostoff was a large man with thick white hair and bushy eyebrows, and a flat, Slavic face with a large, vein-lined nose that spoke of a love affair with vodka. He held the rank of full general, and his badly fitted Russian suit gave him a further affinity for Hennesey.

Rostoff was flanked by his counterpart in the GRU, the Russian equivalent of the DIA, another general—a tall, still trim septuagenarian named Nicolae Poltikov—whose narrow, aesthetic face and thinning hair made him appear paper-like, despite his physique, someone who might be blown away by a strong wind.

But it was clear Poltikov was there for window dressing, solely because the DIA was involved. The KGB was in charge—would make the necessary decisions—just as Hennesey believed he, and the CIA, would do on their side.

"You must admit this is an unusual situation," Giordano said. "Your man Ludwig butchered Moran's wife."

"The Soviet Union does not employ terrorists," Rostoff said.

"Oh, let's stop the bullshit, General. Ludwig, right now, is aboard a Russian vessel headed for Libya. His background is no secret. Whom he works for is no secret. And what he did to Moran's wife is no secret."

Hennesey jumped in, cutting off Giordano and the reply Rostoff was readying. "We accept the fact that Moran broke the rules. And we accept what the penalty for doing so is. We are only saying that—in this rare case—there are unusual circumstances."

A flicker of a smile momentarily played across Poltikov's thin lips. He likes the terminology used to describe the butchering of an American agent's wife, Hennesey thought. To him it's a show of weakness. Hennesey decided to scotch that snake.

"We don't want open warfare with your agencies. But if you force it, we'll accept it." He raised a hand as Rostoff's face reddened in preparation for an angry response. "We will not interfere with your hunt of Moran. We will even assist it, as per the agreement. What we want—what we insist upon—is the opportunity to give him a final offer before he's taken." Hennesey raised his hand again. "And only if we find him first. And only if the final offer is acceptable to you."

Rostoff sat back, satisfied like a well-fed cat. "It is fair," he said. "But if we find him first, as we expect to, we will have no obligation to notify you before he is sanctioned. He is a dangerous man, and we will not risk the lives of our men."

Hennesey turned to Giordano, his eyes saying it was as far as the CIA was willing to go. Giordano's face reddened, then he gave a curt nod of his head.

"Done," Hennesey said.

CHAPTER

15

Corsica

A lex sat on a low wall at the edge of the village and stared down at the distant sea. The village of Cervione was perched on the side of the mountain, near the summit, and below it lay the tangled mass of the *maquis*, and below that the cultivated vineyards in which many of the villagers worked, and which, like so much of the impoverished and insular countryside, were among the numerous holdings of the Pisani brothers, on this, their native Corsican soil.

A narrow, winding road led up from the sea, twisting and turning as it followed the contours of the rising terrain, the sole direct route to the village. The only other road was one which ran parallel to the mountain, moving from village to village just below the summit. It was a fortress, pure and simple, one that no man could approach without being seen. And to which few, save the occasional tourist, ever ventured. Even the French police station serving the village was located halfway down the mountain, a place where the gendarmerie remained behind locked doors, admitting only those who had been scrutinized through a narrow peephole. And only then if absolutely necessary. Seldom would the police venture to the village itself, and then, if forced to, only in overwhelming numbers, and never with even a small hope of success. They were an occupation force imprisoned by their own hand, fully at the mercy of their captives.

The village had been selected as Alex's rabbit hole while he plotted his incursion into Libya. It was a foolhardy plan, but one he considered his only chance to reach Ludwig before he disappeared into the ever ethereal terrorist network, to be seen again only when he chose.

And that would not do. Alex had to reach him where he felt safe. Where his guard would be as low as it ever got. Reach him while he was resting up for his next outrage. Planning his own strategy of the lives he planned to take. Kill the sonofabitch before he had time to react. Kill him like he had killed Stephanie. Butcher him like an animal being readied for market.

Alex's hands began to tremble beyond control, and he clenched his fists and turned back toward the village, walking quickly to a small café with a tiny, covered outdoor patio. He took a seat at one of three tables, and when the owner's son appeared, he ordered a Corsican brandy known as marc. The other tables were occupied by village men, all of whom nodded somberly in acknowledgment of his presence. The word had no doubt been passed that Alex was there under the protection of the Pisani brothers. It was as strong an imprimatur as one could receive.

In the narrow street outside the patio, an ancient woman moved steadily up the rising cobblestones on legs accustomed to climbing. She was dressed entirely in black, a coarse black shawl covering her head so only her long nose and pointed chin protruded. She carried a market basket that looked as old as she, and which, when she passed by again on her way home, would undoubtedly hold the bread and cheese and meats she would later serve her family.

Farther up from the patio, the street opened into a small square, where young children played on the sharply rising steps of the village "cathedral," a small, modest church which had been given that lofty designation centuries earlier, an honor that was still a matter of pride to the village's few hundred souls whose ancestors had tilled the ground on which it had been built. The other sides of the square were occupied by connected four- and five-story buildings, each so old that pipes for latter-day plumbing ran down exterior walls, which were cracked and scarred and leaning with age.

The floor of each building had a single apartment, rambling collections of rooms which could be easily divided to serve the extended families—often as not three generations—that lived within. It was in one of these apartments that Alex had been housed, as the visiting cousin of a man who worked as foreman for the Pisani vineyard. The household, named Sabatini, included the family patriarch, a wizened, weatherworn grandfather with a flowing white mustache, addressed solely as Grand-père, his equally ancient wife, whom villagers and family alike referred to as Madame, their son, the vineyard foreman, Rene, his wife Juliet, and an eighteen-year-old daughter, Michelle, who had been designated as Alex's guide and protector during the weeks he would be with them.

The mere presence of a young Corsican woman with a lone man outside the safety of her family's home was normally enough to produce a flash of weapons. But in Alex's case the couple were never alone. Trailing at a distance behind him, at all times, were the ever present figures of two Pisani bodyguards, men whose coats concealed automatic weapons that could deter any but the heaviest assault. And in the insular mountain village that was the Pisanis' domain, any assault at all would require miraculous intervention to succeed.

Alex sipped his marc, allowing the warm, rich liquid to sear his throat and spread a comforting warmth through his stomach. He felt safe and secure, almost as though he had returned to the womb. Across the narrow street he could see the two young men who would make that safety inviolate, even at the cost of their lives.

He watched the young woman cross the street and smile innocently at the two men. She had collectively dubbed them the *duegne*, insisting with only a hint of a smile that the Pisani brothers had provided these chaperones not to protect Alex, but to ensure her honor remained intact.

Young Michelle, as Alex thought of her, was truly beautiful. He had noticed the beauty of her face when he first arrived at the family apartment two days before. It had soft, delicate lines made even softer, more delicate by long, flowing brown hair that held faint hints of red and blond. And there was a lovely sense of childish innocence about her. Her brown eyes flashed with life, and her wide mouth seemed to burst into a smile at any provocation.

He hadn't noticed her figure then, other than that she was only moderately tall and slender. But as she crossed the street, headed toward him, he couldn't help but notice her lithe, supple movements, the delicate curves and shapes of a recent child who had blossomed in ways any woman would covet, and he wondered why two days had passed without him noticing she was much more woman than child. But, of course, she wasn't. She was lovely and gentle and naive. And he envied her her innocence.

Michelle smiled at him as she approached, the warmth of it flooding Alex's face like sunlight. It was a smile that in another place might be mistaken as something else. But not on Corsica, where such a misinterpretation could mean a man's life. Here, as Alex knew, a woman could offer warmth and friendship, if she chose, without fear it might be misunderstood as something more.

Before she reached Alex's table she stopped at another, where one of the village men who had nodded so somberly to Alex was seated. His young son had joined him there, a boy of perhaps five or six, and Michelle commented on how much he had grown and what a truly beautiful child he was. The boy blushed and lowered his eyes, and the father beamed with pride, his hands running over the boy's head and shoulders—stroking, almost petting him—in a display of affection common for Corsican men, something seen so seldom in other places.

Watching the man made Alex think of his own father and the absence of overt affection in his own childhood. It was not an absence of love, Alex told himself. He loved his father, needed to believe even now that his love was returned, had always been. But for his father, as for so many men of his time and place, such displays were avoided lest the child's sense of masculinity be somehow subverted. It was permitted with daughters—although even then it was sometimes withheld—and he wondered now if it was due to some fear of misinterpretation. That a child might lose some sense of parental authority or, even worse, that a father's public image might somehow deteriorate.

It was not so with Corsican men, something, Alex realized now, he had noticed even as a child, the many times he had visited the island. Displays of affection were given freely, openly. It was part of the fierce loyalty Corsicans felt toward any member of their family, he decided. Part of their idea of honor that they would defend at any time, at any cost. But it was not a personalized sense of honor, he told himself. It was more the belief that those they loved were worthy of honor and should be treated honorably. And no exception to that idea could be tolerated. And that they themselves must offer the same to others. To do otherwise would be akin to an act against nature.

Michelle turned from the boy and his father, and came and sat next to him. She smiled again, and again he felt the warmth of it. "Why are you sitting here in the shade on such a beautiful day?" she asked.

Alex nodded toward the other men on the patio. "They seem to find the shade comforting and pleasant," he said.

"Ah, but they have been working in the sun all day," she said, her smile returning, a bit more mischievously now. "You have been locked away in your room, studying your strange maps and papers."

Alex looked at her. "How do you know about my strange maps and papers?" he asked. There was no hint of anger or irritation in his voice, none felt.

"I saw them, of course, when I went to make your bed. Are they secret?"

"No."

"Good. Because if they were, you should certainly hide them away. I am a very curious woman."

Alex smiled at her use of the word. She was certainly a woman, albeit a very young one. But he had difficulty thinking of her that way, was surprised to hear it was how she thought of herself. He was fifteen years older than she, but it seemed a much greater expanse of age. He wondered if she were twenty-six or twenty-seven, and he forty-one or forty-two if he would feel the same. He pushed the thought away. It was foolish, pointless.

"From now on I shall hide my papers," he said.

"Oh, no, don't hide them. Simply put them away. If you hid them, it would be like a game, a challenge to find them."

A faint smile flickered across Alex's lips, then disappeared. Michelle watched him, taking in the depth of his sorrow.

When Antoine had brought him to her home, she had asked about him. Antoine had been reluctant to tell her, but then he had. He always gave her what she wanted, had done so since she was a small child. He often snarled at her, accusing her of being a nosy little girl, as he had this time. But he always acquiesced. He had never, in all the years she could remember, found the courage to deny her anything. She thought it was because he knew she loved him.

Meme Pisani was different. She loved him as well, but the depth of feeling between them had never been as strong. And yet Meme seemed to regard her more seriously. He seemed more aware of her intelligence and abilities. Seemed to view her more as a whole person rather than merely a child who charmed him and brought him pleasure.

Michelle continued to look at Alex, taking in the pain that seemed ingrained in his eyes, the weariness that drew the life from his face. He must have loved his wife deeply, she thought, and it helped her understand the anger and hatred she had seen flash across his face, although she wished it were not there, not such an integral part of him.

"Dinner will soon be ready," she said. "Madame is making a special soup that is so rich with garlic, I will not need the *duegne* to protect me from you."

"Your honor is safe," Alex said. "Garlic or no garlic."

"Ah, you say so. But we are not so primitive in this tiny village that we have not heard about Americans."

"Let us eat the garlic soup, then," Alex said. "It will guarantee safety for both of us."

Alex watched Grand-père eating his soup, his flowing white mustache twitching with each mouthful, his eyes twinkling with the pleasure of the meal. His wife, Madame, watched as well, and it seemed to Alex that she still took pleasure in the way he looked, the dignified, almost regal bearing he exuded in the way he held his head, the way he smiled and spoke in his soft, gentle voice. Madame was a woman who had grown thick with age, with sturdy features that spoke of strength and eyes that seemed to look at all around her with satisfaction. She was proud of her family, proud to be with them. He decided he would not want to encounter her if he ever abused any of them.

Rene and Juliet, Michelle's father and mother, were in their forties, and seemed more than content with their lives. Rene spoke of the vineyard he supervised with great pride, complaining only of the French government's practice of denying Corsicans the right to export their fine wines to France, but turning their heads when French winemakers illegally used smuggled Corsican vintages to doctor their own wines when a poor year made that necessary.

Juliet nodded with her husband's complaint, supporting his views, then distracting him from anger by urging more food upon him. She seemed intent on forcing food and comfort on Alex as well, and he was certain it was not merely out of respect for a Pisani guest in her home, but rather a genuine wish to make her home a place that gave pleasure to all who entered it.

She was a beautiful woman, Alex thought, and it was easy to see that Michelle would look almost exactly the same twenty or twenty-five years from now. He found himself wondering how Stephanie would have looked in middle age, and he felt a rush of hatred that he would never now know.

And the man who had denied him that was less than nine hundred miles across the Mediterranean, sitting in safety and comfort, satisfied with what he had done.

Michelle watched the fury come into Alex's eyes, and she knew he was thinking of his dead wife again, and of the man who had killed her, and of the vendetta that would soon take him across the sea and perhaps to his own death. She understood vendettas. The word had originated in the Corsican language and was soaked into its soil like the blood that had flowed so freely for so many generations. And she knew she could do nothing to stop it now for this strange, handsome American for whom she felt such attraction.

"You are making a face. Is it Madame's soup that displeases you?" she asked, startling him.

"Oh, no. Not at all," Alex insisted. He smiled at the old woman and nodded his head stupidly. "The soup is wonderful."

Juliet immediately picked up the terrine that held still more, and began ladling another portion into Alex's bowl. She sprinkled a spoonful of grated cheese atop the soup. "We have a wonderful roast pork that Michelle cooked especially for you," she said. "The soup is so light you will still have room for it."

Alex glanced at Michelle. She had not said anything about cooking any part of the meal.

"I'll be sure to save room," he said. He was surprised to see that Michelle was blushing.

They walked along the dusty dirt road that ran parallel to the summit, the two Pisani bodyguards—Michelle's *duegne*, as Alex now thought of them—trailing behind. It was morning, but the sun was already warm, and from below, rising on winds from the *maquis*, the air was scented with the smells of buckthorn and juniper and bayberry and wild thyme.

Napoleon, Alex recalled, had once said that he would know his native Corsica solely by its smell, and he knew now that the French emperor had been speaking about the wild beauty of the *maquis*, that impenetrable, tangled mass of foliage that burst forth every spring in a blinding sea of flowers, and which throughout the year filled the air with its spicy scents, just as the wild boar to which it was home filled the larders of the Corsicans who hunted them.

"You came here to Corsica as a child, did you not?" Michelle asked. She was walking beside him, dressed in loose-fitting slacks and sturdy shoes, and a billowing blouse that hid all her youthful womanliness.

"A number of times. My father worked for the American government in Paris, and he and the Pisani brothers had become friends after the war, and they often invited him to Marseilles and here to Cervione during his holidays. They used to hunt boar here, and once, when I was ten, I was allowed to go with them. It was very frightening and very thrilling for me."

Michelle smiled up at him. She wondered what he had been like as a child. Whether he had been the pampered son of a government official, or a little boy she would have liked as a child herself. The latter, she told herself. Spoiled little boys did not grow up to be men like this.

"My father and uncles always hunt the pigs," she said. "But they would never take me with them. Even though I am a better shot than they are. I should have asked Antoine. He always did what I asked of him. But I never knew he hunted. He had a big house just outside the village, and it was always crowded with men from the *milieu*, and I seldom went there. So I only saw him when he came into town each day, or down at the vineyard."

"You're a better shot than your uncles?" Alex asked.

"Of course. Don't be a chauvinist."

"Ah, you've been reading American magazines."

"It would surprise you what I know. What I believe in."

Alex held up his hands in surrender. "I don't think anything about you would surprise me," he said.

"Yes. Many things would," Michelle answered.

"So you grew up with Antoine and Meme," he said. "I did too. They are like uncles to me. In fact, I call them uncle."

"I know," she said.

"I only wish they were in a different line of work."

Michelle's head snapped around. "There is nothing wrong with their work." Her voice was sharp, defensive.

So she doesn't know what they do. At least not the drugs, Alex thought.

"I meant no offense to them," Alex said. "Or to you."

They continued walking, Michelle silent, brooding, Alex thought.

"You just don't understand," she said at length, her voice softer, with only a hint of an edge to it.

"What is it I don't understand?"

"What it is like to be a Corsican. What drives men like Antoine and Meme into the *milieu*." She paused, gathering herself. "If you are smart and capable, it makes no difference here. If you want to stay here, or in France, you are always just a Corsican. You can be a servant, work for a Frenchman, or a French business. But you will never be given the opportunity to run that business. And if you have your own business, you are subject to French regulations that keep you under their heel. We are treated like you Americans treat your Hispanics and your blacks. I have read about your people in Puerto Rico. And it is the same here for us."

Her voice had risen again, and her vehemence cut the air. Alex said nothing, preferring to listen.

"So, if a Corsican wants to succeed, wants to have more than is allowed by the French, there is the *milieu*. And many choose it. My father works for the Pisanis, and therefore for the *milieu*. If he worked for a French-owned vineyard, he would pick the grapes, not manage the people who do. A Frenchman would be brought in to do that."

She was quiet for a time, and Alex waited for her to continue.

"I know there is violence in the *milieu*, that there are things I cannot condone. But many of those who are part of it have been forced into that life. To have a life other than the *milieu*, other than what the French will allow them, they would be forced to leave their homeland, forced to leave all they know." She hesitated again. "Do you know the term: *un vrai monsieur?*" she asked.

"I've heard it," Alex said.

"It is a title given to those who head a faction within the *milieu*," she said, ignoring his response. "It means a man of honor." Her eyes flashed at him. "Antoine and Meme have that title, and I believe in my heart that for them it is a true one."

Alex stopped and turned to her, taking her arms in his hands. "I believe that too," he said. "And even though I don't approve of all they do, I trust them. And I love them." He offered her a faint smile. "I have trusted my life to them."

Michelle lowered her eyes. She seemed embarrassed that he was holding her, even at arm's length. He let her go.

"I am sorry I became angry," she said.

"No, don't be sorry. I enjoy hearing what you think. And I enjoy walking with you. Promise me we will do it again."

Michelle started walking again, Alex beside her. Her eyes were still lowered.

"We will walk again tomorrow morning," she said. "There is something I want to show you."

"What?"

"I will show you tomorrow."

CHAPTER 16

They walked along the same road, but this time in the opposite direction from the village. Again the two *duegne* followed at a respectful distance. They were truly like chaperones, Alex thought. Except for the Mach 10 submachine guns under their coats.

"You said yesterday you had something you wanted to show me," Alex said as they were leaving the village. He spoke to her in French, the only language they had used together. And although his French was good, he spoke it formally, and the sentences always sounded stiff and unnatural to him.

"It is not far," Michelle said.

She was dressed in a skirt today, full and unrevealing, and a dark blouse with long sleeves and a collar that she had turned up in a nod to fashion.

Ahead a solitary donkey ambled toward them down the road, almost as though it were off to market to pick out a few choice carrots. As they passed, the donkey stopped and watched them with open curiosity, then, with a slight shake of its head, continued.

When they rounded a bend in the road, they saw four stray pigs snuffling in the dirt. They were huge and fat, the kind of pigs, it was said, that wild boars would lure into the *maquis*, mate with, and produce a variety that was even wilder and more ferocious than the boar itself. A young boy came around another bend, carrying a long pole.

"*Ça va*, Michelle," he called, waving his free hand.

"*Ça va*, Pierre," Michelle called back.

The boy, who was no more than eight, circled the pigs, then began prodding and hitting them with the pole, calling out oaths in Corsican that Alex didn't understand. Slowly, unwillingly, the pigs began to move back along the road, until they finally broke into a trot, the boy still behind them, still jabbing them and shouting in his native tongue.

"What is he saying to them?" Alex asked.

The trace of a smile played across Michelle's lips then was replaced by a sterner expression that did not carry to her eyes. "If his mother heard him, he would be in great difficulty," she said. She turned her head away from him, and he knew she was smiling again.

They stopped, no more than two hundred yards from the village, and Michelle pointed to a gently sloping area below the road. One section, some fifty yards square, held a small, walled cemetery, and from above Alex could see that almost all the graves held freshly cut flowers.

"This is what I wanted to show you," Michelle said, leading him down a narrow path and through an iron gate.

The cemetery was made up mostly of stone slabs, some of which were elevated and enclosed on three sides, others flush with the ground. Most of the more recent ones held glass-enclosed photographs of the dead, placed just above the names and dates cut into the stone. Dotted throughout the cemetery were some small family vaults, almost all done in the Genoese style, with black and white stone roofs laid in an alternating checked pattern.

Alex stopped just inside the gate. "When I was a boy, I remember wanting to come and look at a Corsican cemetery. But Meme told me I couldn't. He said Corsicans became offended if they found strangers prowling about among their dead. He told me about a French tourist who had been driven off with sticks by women of the village because he had been found photographing the graves."

"It is true," Michelle said. "But it seldom becomes violent now. We have become more used to tourists, so there is more tolerance."

She began walking down one row of graves. "Do you know the other customs we have about our dead?" she asked.

"No," Alex said.

She stopped and turned to him. "Every day the eldest woman in a family—mother, daughter, grandmother—must come and tend to the family's dead. She often brings flowers, makes sure there has been no damage, clears away any weeds that have grown up about the grave." She smiled faintly at what she was about to say. "It is believed the dead will place a curse on the family if they are forgotten and their graves are left uncared for."

"What if a family has no women left? If the mother has died and the daughters have moved away, or the sons have not married?"

"Then the eldest male must do it," Michelle said. "They say women were chosen to do this centuries ago, because the men were often away at sea or hiding in the *maquis*, fighting whatever nation was occupying the country at that time—Roman, Genoese, French, whoever." She allowed her eyes to roam the graves. "I like to think it was because women were more dependable, more conscientious about such things. Today, because so many children have left the island, you see many old men coming to care for the dead." She looked up at him, her eyes sad. "The dead have a very large place in Corsica."

Michelle turned and led him on down the path, finally stopping before a family plot that held numerous graves. It was marked by a large headstone that held various photographs. Three of them, old photographs all in a row together, were of young men.

"This is the Santisini family," she said. "The father owned a small store in the village. He sold meats and cheese and canned goods, and made a small but decent living for his family. Another family, the Barellis, had been friends of the Santisinis' for generations. Some of their children and cousins had even married in the old days." She shrugged. "But then, it is almost impossible to find two families here who have not had some marriages between them.

"Anyway, the head of the Barelli family, the father, had long envied the Santisini store, wishing he too could provide for his family in such a steady way. So he saved his money and one day opened a store of his own. The Santisini family was offended. They saw it as an attempt to take bread from the mouths of their children. One day Santisini and Barelli argued in the street, and Santisini killed Barelli, stabbed him to death. A month later Santisini was killed by one of Barelli's sons. And then that Barelli son was killed. It went on that way for several years, until finally the Barellis moved to another village. But even today the two families hate each other. They are taught about the vendetta from the time they are children." She looked down at the grave. "This all happened thirty years ago, but one day a Santisini or a Barelli will be killed, and the vendetta will continue for another generation."

Michelle drew a deep breath. "I could show you many graves here that hold similar stories. Most involve families from different villages, and in most cases the offense that started the vendetta was more serious. But the result has been the same. The deaths continue because no one will stop them. No one will let the authorities intervene. Corsica is an island bathed in its own blood because of this. And because of it, it never stops bleeding."

Alex looked at her and remained silent. He understood what Michelle was telling him; was not offended by it.

"I have to do this thing," he said at length.

"I know," she said. "But it will not ease your pain. It will not make your wife rest more easily."

"He butchered her. She *was* my family. And he took it from me." Alex's voice caught as he spoke, and he took time to steady himself. Then he told her about it, as gently as he could. He told her about Ludwig, how he had wounded him. About the kidnapping and the telephone calls, and how Ludwig had brought him to the filthy basement to find her body. "It is all I have left," he said. "Killing him."

Tears had come to Michelle's eyes, and she reached out and gently stroked his cheek. "I know there is much violence in you. I can see it there. But I can also see gentleness. This man should die for what he has done. And he should die badly. I believe that. But I don't want you to die, Alex. I don't want the women of your family tending your grave."

"I have too much hatred, Michelle. It won't go away until I've killed him."

"Yes, I can see it in you," she said. She lowered her eyes. "There is a saying that if you seek revenge, you must first dig two graves. I hope one of them is not yours, Alex."

Michelle walked down the path, turned, and crossed the cemetery, then turned again. She had picked some flowers along the roadside as they walked, and she stopped before a grave and laid the flowers atop it. The marker, Alex saw, bore her familial name.

"Was there a vendetta in your family?" he asked as he stood beside her.

"Oh, yes," she said. "There is always a vendetta. Some say without the blood, nothing would grow here." She turned to him. "Do you think that is true?"

"No," he said. "No, I don't."

His name was Alberto Montani, and he was twenty-two, and already he had been fighting for Corsican independence for five years. It had begun when he was a boy in nearby San Nicolao, when he had shot the French policeman who had been extorting money from his widowed mother. She had been running a small bakery his father had begun years before and which she had continued as her only means to support her family after his death. But then the French *flic* had wanted his share of the weekly profits, and soon—in his greed—he wanted more, until there were hardly any profits at all.

His mother's friends told her to go to the *milieu* and have them deal with the French pig. But his mother said they were pigs themselves—and even worse than pigs, they were killers and gangsters. And so she paid, until there was little food for the three children she was struggling to raise.

It was then that Alberto had taken his father's old shotgun, and had blown the kneecap off the *flic* as he climbed from his car one night. And then he had run and hidden in the *maquis* until the police had lost interest in their investigation, and had sent their crippled pig home to France on a fat pension.

A year later, at the university in Corte, Alberto learned that the abuse visited on his mother had not been isolated. He discovered how the French exploited the people throughout his island, and he joined the Corsican Liberation Front and vowed to spend his life —all of it, if necessary—fighting to free Corsica of French domination. It was then too that he became a communist, although few in the movement were, convinced it was the only way to free Corsica of all exploiters, including its own, the *milieu*.

And the communists saw to his needs, sending funds from France to support the cause. And he, in turn, served them. It was how he came to inform the Soviet consulate in Marseilles that the Pisani brothers were hiding an American in Cervione. And it was how he decided to kill the American pig himself, if only to repay the long-standing debt he owed to those who supported him and his cause.

His Soviet handler did not ask him to take that action. In fact, he was told only to watch and await further instructions, and to tell them if the American was moved. But Alberto decided to kill the American himself. He knew that no foreigner would ever breach Cervione and live, and that only a Corsican could get close enough to the American for a sure kill. It would be a blow against an imperialist supporter of the French, and an even greater blow against that other abuser of his people, the *milieu*.

Alberto was a handsome young man, and like most of the independence fighters in the region, he was known to the people of the village. He was short and slender, with a shock of black curly hair, and his mouth never seemed to carry a smile. He was a didactic young man whose words were largely ignored, but his attack against the French police officer was known to all, and so he was considered a young man of honor and courage, and therefore his fanaticism was tolerated.

Alberto had been coming to the village for three days, under the guise of recruiting young men for the cause, and he had discovered that the American would sometimes slip out of the apartment where he was hidden and walk alone at night. Thus, he had taken a position at the top of the small village square, seemingly to talk to some of the teenagers who gathered there in the early evening, but actually to watch the entry of the building where the American was being guarded.

It was eight o'clock when the American emerged that night, and Alberto watched as he passed the café and turned into the road that led along the *maquis*. Then he left the teenagers as quickly as he could, and walked slowly across the small square, to avoid raising any suspicion, and quietly slipped into the brush that grew below the road the American had taken. He had no gun with him—that would have been too obvious to the people in the village. They would have remembered that he had been armed. And after the American's body was found, the *milieu* would know, and they would hunt him for the rest of his life. But he had a knife, and he knew how to use it. He had no need of a gun. It would only have made it easier.

Alex walked along the road, knowing it would be foolish to go far. Even the walk itself, without the ever present bodyguards, was foolish. But he needed time to himself. Time to think. Time to be alone with his pain. And in a few days he would be in Libya, and then he would be very much alone anyway. And in far greater danger.

He walked as far as the cemetery, then turned and headed back, his mind filled with the words beautiful young Michelle had spoken that morning. But she couldn't understand the pain that gnawed at his gut like some hungry animal. She saw only the senselessness of killing—and there was no argument against that. She couldn't understand the pain and anguish and hatred that could fill someone's mind and heart. And there was no way for her to know the type of animal who lived in the world, whom only killing could stop.

And he was glad she did not. Let her have her innocence for as long as life would allow it. For her entire life if possible. There were people who went through the world untouched by anything more than their newspapers or television sets. He hoped it would be that way for her. He could wish her nothing better in life than untainted innocence.

He was almost back to the village when he stopped along the edge of the road and looked down into the *maquis*, taking in the earthy smells of buckthorn and juniper and all the other herbs and flowering plants that permeated the tangled mass of vegetation. So beautiful, and yet so impenetrable that the resistance fighters in World War II had adopted the name as their own. And so much like life. A dense covering that left all but the surface unseen.

He had never brought Stephanie to Corsica, had never shown her the beauty he had found here as a boy. His uncles had offended her sensibilities, and she had bristled the one time Antoine had spoken of his nephew's Corsican blood and how much he was a part of their lives. She hadn't understood—had no way of knowing how much that praise, that affection, had meant to him. And he hadn't tried to explain, certain she could never comprehend how two aging gangsters had been more a father to him than his own had ever attempted to be. And now she never would understand, and, oddly, all that was left of him was the Corsican blood that would exact the price of her life.

He turned and started back the final fifty yards to the village. As he rounded the last bend he stiffened at the sight of a man walking slowly toward him. Then he relaxed, telling himself it was only someone headed home from the café. Killers, unless they were fools, didn't come alone. Even Ludwig worked with the support of a group and his Russian protectors. And no stranger, he knew, could make his way into Cervione, even at night, without being noticed.

There was a half moon, but still not enough light to make out the man's features, but when he was twenty yards away he called out to Alex.

"*Ça va, monsieur. Comment allez-vous?*" It was a young voice, but one Alex did not recognize.

"*Ça va,*" he replied, the man only five yards from him now.

He stiffened again. This man too, he realized, could not make out *his* features. The blade of the knife flashed in the faint moonlight, but Alex was ready for it and slipped away from the thrust, then grabbed the man's wrist, twisting the arm to one side. His knee drove into the man's groin—a glancing blow, but enough to cause pain and force him to drop the knife.

Alberto was young and agile and strong, but the stiffened fingers Alex next sent to the base of his throat took the breath from him, and the chopping strike that followed to the side of his neck dropped him to the ground, temporarily paralyzed along one side of his body. Still holding his wrist, Alex pulled his arm straight, then drove his knee into the back of his elbow, snapping the joint and bringing forth a scream of pain.

When he dragged the man back to the village, he found one of the bodyguards standing in the square, having a cigarette. The guard quickly got the other, and within minutes additional men had been summoned by telephone.

"Who is he?" the one who seemed in charge asked.

"I have no idea," Alex said. "He was good, and he got close enough. But he made a mistake."

The young man glared at him through his pain.

"I made no mistake, American," he spat. "You were just lucky this time."

Alex stared at him, wondering at his rage, knowing it really did not matter.

"You spoke French to me. Not Corsican, or a mixture of French and Corsican, as you would have with another villager," he explained. "But you couldn't see me. You couldn't have known I wasn't just another Corsican making his way home. Not unless you'd been following me." He paused, still staring at the man. "You fucked up, kid. And I don't think you're going to get another chance."

The leader of the group of bodyguards grabbed Alberto by the hair and yanked his head back. "Who are you? And who sent you?" he demanded.

"Fuck you, and your whore of a mother," Alberto spat back.

The head bodyguard drove his knee into Alberto's groin, producing a cry of strangled pain.

"Not here," Alex snapped. "I don't want the young girl or her family to know of this."

The head guard grunted. "You are right," he said. He looked down into Alberto's stricken face. "We will go someplace where it is quiet. And then we will have a long talk."

Alex watched them drag the young man away. He regretted what would happen to him, but there was little he could do about it. It was as Antoine and Meme often said. When you go into the whorehouse, you must pay the price for the whore.

The two Russians got off the ferry in Bastia, walked through the large parking lot and across the street to the car rental agency. The consulate in Marseilles had reserved a car for them, and it was waiting, cleaned and fully gassed.

While one of the Russians filled out the papers, the second consulted a map, reassuring himself of the best route to take them to Cervione. It seemed simple enough, he thought. Only twenty or so kilometers to the south. With luck they should be able to get there, kill the American, and be at the airport for the afternoon flight to Marseilles.

They had taken the overnight ferry to Corsica so they could bring weapons with them. There were no security checks or metal detectors for the ferry, and when they took the flight back they would no longer have the weapons in their possession. They would leave them behind for the group of separatists, whose leader had told the consulate of the American who was being hidden in the mountain village. This particular man was a communist, a rarity among those fighting the cause of Corsican nationalism. They had been lucky. It had been nothing more than that.

The car was a Citroen, long and sleek and low to the ground, and it maneuvered easily through the heavy morning traffic of the northern capital city. Unlike most countries, Corsica had two capitals, Bastia on the northeastern coast and Ajaccio on its central western shores. As in most things Corsican, even the location of a capital could not be agreed upon. Corsica was little more than a chain of mountains surrounded by four hundred miles of coastline, and the rugged, isolating terrain that divided the island so severely had also created a parochialism that could not be breached.

But the Russians had no knowledge of this, and would have cared little if they had. They were from the Action Directorate of the KGB, and had been brought in from East Berlin at Moscow's direction to perform a specific task. The Russians called it "wet work," and despite the wishes of contemporary fiction, any assassinations, kidnappings, and other acts of violence in foreign countries required approval at Politburo level. The fact that they were there only emphasized how seriously Moscow regarded Alex Moran's actions.

The Russian who drove remained silent, his bulk and massive hands dwarfing the steering wheel, his flat, slavic face pointed intently at the road. The man beside him was equally large and even harder looking. He had a narrow, rat-like face and small dark eyes that looked as though they would see in the blackest night. He concentrated on checking their weapons, making sure they would function properly, then stowed them under his seat. Both men were dressed as tourists, in loud, short-sleeve shirts. The man in the passenger seat even had a camera around his neck.

About five kilometers from the turnoff to Cervione, the driver slowed the car. Ahead, a French gendarme stood before a barricade, waving all southerly traffic to a halt. At the roadside next to him, a work crew swung picks and shovels at the berm. The gendarme spoke briefly to each of the three drivers ahead of the Russians, then when northern traffic cleared, directed them around the barrier. The Russian who was driving checked his rearview mirror, and was surprised to see there were no cars behind.

When the Russian pulled up to the barrier, the uniformed gendarme walked to the lowered window, bent down, smiled, and placed the barrel of a revolver against the driver's temple. Across the car a sawed-off shotgun had been leveled at the face of the passenger.

Without a word the Russian driver was pushed away from the steering wheel, replaced there by the gendarme, as three of the laborers piled into the rear seat and placed weapons against the heads of the Russians. The gendarme drove away, while another laborer threw the barrier into the rear of a van and followed.

They drove another four kilometers, then turned east along a short road that led to the coast. At the end of the road was a large garage, and there another man waited, opening the door as the car approached so it could drive inside.

As the door closed behind them, the Russians were forced from the car, and found themselves standing before the body of a man tied into an old, battered swivel chair. They could clearly see the man had a single bullet hole in his forehead, and as the gendarme kicked the chair and the body slowly turned, they were offered a view of the gaping hole the exit wound had made.

"Take off all your clothes. Shoes and socks, everything but your underwear," the gendarme said in surprisingly good German.

The Russians remained silent and did as they were told.

"You now have three choices," the gendarme said. "You can remain here and explain this body to the police. You can leave— and I suggest you walk along the beach in your state of dress—and arrange for new clothing and weapons, then come to Cervione and die as this man has died. Or you can re-clothe yourselves and return home to your masters, and explain that no Russian, or friend of Russians, will live more than an hour after he steps on Corsican soil. You may also tell them that Alex Moran has no interest in killing Russians unless they come to kill him first."

The Russian who had been the passenger looked again at the dead man before him, then back at the gendarme.

"Who was he?" he asked.

"The man who telephoned your consulate," the gendarme said. "The *milieu* also has its informants. And no one of significance comes to Corsica without its knowing."

The two Russians looked at each other, then at the car, where their concealed weapons were now being removed. The one who had been the driver nodded at no one in particular. "We go now?" he asked.

"Whenever you wish," the gendarme said.

"You are an interesting policeman," the other Russian said.

"I am not a policeman," the gendarme answered. "But please try not to come back," he added. "It causes unnecessary traffic delays."

Alex had no knowledge of the confrontation taking place a few kilometers below Cervione. The message that had been delivered in his name had come from Meme Pisani, along with instructions that the Russian hit team be harmed only if they refused to listen to reason. It was a political message to the Russians, one Meme hoped they would heed.

Walking with Michelle now, back along the road to the village, Alex contented himself with the beauty of the *maquis* stretched out below him. At first, when they had started out, he had struggled to understand why he had unburdened himself to the young woman the day before. But he had given up any hope of an answer, finally attributing it to the low ebb of emotion that had dominated his waking hours since. . . . He had pushed the thought away then. Now it returned again. Since. . . . He found he couldn't even finish it in his mind.

"Have you spent all your life here on Corsica?" he asked Michelle, again driving away the thought.

"I have visited France with my mother," she said. "We have relatives in Brittany. The coast is very beautiful there, only colder and without the mountains. And, of course, I've been to Marseilles. This fall I'm supposed to go to Paris to study at the Sorbonne."

"That should be very exciting for you."

"Yes. But I shall miss Corsica." She looked at him and smiled, but there was still some sadness in her eyes. He wished he could remove it.

"My father has never been off our island, and has seldom gone far from our village." She smiled again. "He likes to say he lives on the most beautiful island in the world, and in the most beautiful village of that island. So there is no need to go somewhere else." She looked away, down at the *maquis*. "It is very provincial of him, but in many ways I agree."

"There are much worse places to spend one's life," Alex said.

"And worse ways?" Michelle added.

"And worse ways," Alex said.

They entered the village and went to the café, deciding to have the breakfast they had forsaken for their walk. They took a table on the small patio, the *duegne* taking up their positions across the road. The coffee and croissants had just arrived when a man approached the two bodyguards, spoke to them briefly, then walked to the café and seated himself at their table.

The man, who an hour earlier had been dressed as a French

gendarme, and who the night before had dragged Alberto away, nodded respectfully to Michelle, then to Alex.

"Two Russians were stopped on the road from Bastia," he began without preamble. "They have been sent away unharmed, but I was told to advise you that these men now know where you are."

Alex responded only by narrowing his eyes, and the man continued. "If they come back—even if they come back with many men—they will never enter this village. But it would be wise for you to remain close to the village." He hesitated, then added, "And to remain alone." He spoke the final words softly, not wishing to give offense.

"Thank you," Alex said. "And please thank the other men who helped protect me."

The man nodded, smiled again at Michelle, then stood and left. Alex remained silent.

"Why do the Russians come for you?" Michelle finally asked.

"This man—the one who murdered my wife—he works for them." Alex drew a long breath, wishing he didn't have to explain but knowing not to do so would hurt her, perhaps even intensify her fears. "When I needed to find out where he had gone, I forced the information from a man in their government, their intelligence service. It is something that is not permitted, and it carries a heavy penalty."

Michelle looked down into her coffee, her hands gripping the edge of the table to stop her trembling.

"I'm afraid it means we will not be able to take our walks," Alex said.

Michelle looked up at him, and her eyes filled with pain. She rose quickly from the table and rushed out into the street. She ran toward her apartment, had difficulty seeing the way. There were tears staining her cheeks.

CHAPTER

17

The limousine pulled up in front of the Pisani brothers home. The passenger in the rear waited for the driver to open the door, then gradually stretched up to his full height and stood staring up at the impressive, familiar facade.

Piers Moran was in his early sixties, but had the look and bearing of a much younger man. He was tall and slender, with longish white hair that turned silver in the sun and seemed due more to premature whitening than to age. Moran had a long, bony face that looked more British than American, as did the off-white linen suit he wore, complete with Scots Guards regimental tie. All together it made him appear somewhat arrogant rather than commanding.

Yet he would have been pleased by the description, although unlike many American anglophiles who worked for their government, he had never served in Britain. He was pure American WASP, and as such simply admired the certain flair the British demonstrated.

If Piers Moran was anything, he had often thought, he was a man with flair. If others thought him arrogant, so be it.

The door to the Pisani house opened, and Antoine rumbled down the stairs and rushed toward him. Behind the bull-like Corsican, Meme followed at a more sedate pace.

Antoine threw his arms around Moran, pinning his own to his sides and hugged him ferociously. "God dammit," he bellowed. "You don't ever age. You must have one of those paintings in your attic that does it for you."

Antoine released him, and Moran stepped back, gasping slightly. "I didn't know you'd read that story," he said. "I didn't," Antoine said. "I saw the movie."

Moran threw back his head and laughed, then turned to Meme and clasped his hand warmly.

"It is good to see you, my friend," Meme said, using the French they always spoke. "We have missed you."

"And I, you," Moran said. "I'm only sorry I come to you with difficulties."

Antoine waved his hands. "There are no difficulties among friends." He wagged a finger at his old comrade. "In the old days, then there were difficulties. I thought you would kill me that day I threw that labor leader—that communist pig of a Frenchman— into the harbor."

"He almost drowned," Moran said. "And we needed him. You could have asked him if he knew how to swim."

Antoine shrugged. "One assumes some things of a man who has grown up around water."

"Besides," Moran added. "I would never have killed you—at least not myself. I was terrified of you in those days."

Antoine wagged his finger again. "You have never been terrified of anyone," he said.

They entered the house and went immediately to the large study the brothers shared, and a third chair was drawn up before the unlighted fireplace.

The place of conferences, Moran thought, wondering how many times he had sat in this very place and discussed things that had eventually cost other men everything they had.

"The Russians know where Alex is," Meme began. "They will never reach him there, not even with an army of men. But they know."

"Yes. Walter Hennesey told me. He was not pleased with your intervention, but he understands there is little he can do about it." Moran leaned forward, his features slightly pained. "The Russians won't come for Alex. They know it would be a public bloodbath, and they don't want that. They will sit and wait for Alex to move. And even if you take him over the mountains where they can't follow, they know where he will go. And by now Ludwig knows too. Alex doesn't have a prayer of succeeding."

"I have told him that," Meme said. "It does not seem to matter to him."

"Yes," Moran said, drawing out the word. "That's the part that may get him killed. He seems to believe that what happened to Stephanie is worth dying for." He shook his head. "Romantic nonsense."

"You know what happened between them before she was killed?" Antoine asked.

Moran nodded, his lips pinched together with distaste. "It all came out in the investigation the DIA did after her death. This man at the consulate—Morganthau—didn't know what a pile of shit he was falling in by not keeping his trousers zipped. He'll find himself posted to Cameroon or some other godforsaken hellhole."

Antoine noted the man's name for the future. "It should be worse for him," he said.

"Yes, it should," Moran said. The anger in his eyes was a clear message.

Antoine wondered if the woman's affair with this Morganthau angered Piers because of the pain it had brought his son, or because it had produced a scandal and gossip he found distasteful. With Piers it was difficult to tell.

"What does the CIA want from us?" Meme asked. He too had been watching Moran, and now wanted to cut to the quick of the matter.

Moran drew a breath and sat back in his chair. He folded his hands on one crossed knee. "They want you to withdraw your protection and allow them to take Alex. They assure me they will take him alive, and that he will be forced out of the service, forced to retire."

"He will never agree," Meme said, his voice soft. His eyes suddenly hardened, taking on the glare that had so frightened so many people over the years. "And I will not agree to remove our protection." He turned his eyes on Moran. "I am surprised you would suggest it."

"There is not a great deal of choice," Moran said. "This could cost you a great deal, and no one wants that. There is great interest in your continued success. You know that."

"Our success will continue no matter what the Americans think," Meme said. He had looked away and was staring into the unlighted fireplace. "Even if it was not Alex we were talking about," he continued, "we could never allow *anyone* to come into our village, our *home*"—he almost shouted the final word—"and take someone we had pledged our honor to protect."

"But it would be with your permission."

"Such permission would never be given, except out of great weakness. And the Pisani faction must never be seen to act out of weakness." He looked back at Moran, his eyes still black and cold.

Moran turned to Antoine, hoping he might find an ally there. "Alex would fight no matter who came for him," Antoine said. He shrugged. "No matter what they tell you, they will have to kill him." Antoine shook his head. "And no one takes a life that we protect. And never in Cervione."

Moran pursed his lips and raised one hand to his tie, straightening it. "There seems no alternative," he said.

"There is," Meme said.

"And what is that?" A hint of annoyance had crept into Moran's voice.

Meme pressed his palms together and gestured with them. "You must promise Alex an alternative, and you must get the CIA to agree." Moran began to speak, but Meme's hands cut him off. "Even if the alternative is never acted upon." He waited, allowing comprehension to register in Moran's eyes. "And you must convince the Russians to help you. That will be the difficult part." He shook his head. "I am afraid they will never agree to let him stay in Europe. And we shall miss him."

Moran was annoyed by the wistful digression. "And how am I to convince the Russians to help? What can I offer them that they might accept?"

Meme's eyes narrowed, but with cunning this time. "You will only need the help of a few Russians. And you know what you can offer them. These Russians are greedy like all men." His face broke into a rare, if fleeting, smile. "Whatever is decided upon in Moscow, the recommendations will come from the Russians who are here. They only need a reason to make those recommendations favorable."

Moran stared down at the shoe of his crossed leg. It was rocking nervously. "I will suggest it," he said.

"Do more than suggest it," Meme said.

The meeting was set in Geneva, in the same room that had been used a week earlier. The Americans arrived first—Walter Hennesey and Piers Moran. This time the DIA had been excluded. They were not even aware the meeting was taking place.

The Russians had also changed players. The GRU had been left behind. Instead, Rostoff was accompanied by Sergei Bugayev. No less than the injured party himself, Moran thought, as the two men entered and seated themselves across the long, polished table.

Moran knew Rostoff, had dealt directly with him in the past. And he knew enough about Bugayev to feel comfortable dealing with him. He had read the man's file, observed the results of his work, ferreted out his secrets. Until his retirement five years before, Moran had held the post now occupied by Hennesey. It had simply been his job to know those things.

"It is good to see you again, Boris," Moran began. "Although I wish it were under more pleasant circumstances."

The Russian nodded, then cocked his head to one side. "I was surprised to hear you would be here. Have you ended your retirement?"

Moran forced a smile, tried to move it to his eyes and failed. The man places a sanction on your son and then expresses surprise you're here. "I have a vested interest," Moran said.

The Russian nodded again. "But we are not here to discuss vested interests," he said. He gestured toward Bugayev. "Bugayev here also has a vested interest. But we are not discussing that either. We are discussing an agreement that has been broken. And we wish to know what you intend to do."

"What is it you wish?" Moran asked.

"We want the Corsicans to remove their protection of your son so appropriate action can be taken."

Moran felt every muscle in his body tighten, and he fought to keep it from his face. He despised these Russian bastards. They spoke about killing a man's son, straight to his face, just as if they were haggling over some trade agreement.

"The Corsicans won't do that," Moran said.

"Then you must make them."

"We are both aware that is not practical." It was Hennesey this time, and his words were firm, as though he were still commanding a ship at sea.

"Practical?" Rostoff raised his eyebrows. "I was not aware practicality came into this agreement. I thought the purpose of the agreement was that *it* was practical."

Hennesey ignored him. "Will you trade Ludwig for Alex Moran?"

"Ludwig is not part of the equation," Rostoff snapped. "He is not a member of the KGB, or any other intelligence agency serving the Soviet people or its allies."

"He works for you, was trained by you, acts under your orders, and with your knowledge and support," Hennesey said.

It was Rostoff's turn to ignore facts. "He is not a member of any intelligence agency and is not subject to our agreement."

"Neither are the Corsicans," Hennesey responded. "Does that mean they can sanction the wife of a Soviet official?"

Rostoff looked away, then up at the ceiling. "We do not say you cannot hunt Ludwig for what he has done."

"But you do not offer your assistance. Nor do you tell us that you will ask the Libyans to withdraw their protection from the man." Hennesey was leaning forward, forearms on the table: a fighting stance for this type of negotiation.

"We do not control the Libyans," Rostoff said. He snorted. "Even the Libyans do not control the Libyans."

"And we do not control the Corsicans," Hennesey countered. "And we are not prepared to enter into a bloodbath that you yourself would not undertake. Because it is simply *not practical*."

Rostoff's face reddened, and he seemed about to stand and leave.

"But we can suggest an alternative." It was Moran again.

"We have already reached an understanding," Rostoff said. "If your son will agree to accept dismissal, if he will end this insane hunt, we will remove our sanction. What more do you expect of us?"

"Only one thing," Moran said. He paused, gathering himself for his final offer. "Ludwig must disappear and he must not be active again in Europe." Moran raised a hand, begging patience. "You can change his name. You can send him elsewhere. South America might be a choice. You can continue to *use* him."

"To what purpose?" Rostoff asked.

"I believe we can get Alex to accept disgrace. If for no other reason than the good of the service. But I will never get him to agree to end his hunt for Ludwig." Moran paused again. "He won't lie to me. He won't say he'll agree and then go out on his own again. But if I promise him it is only a question of time, that he will be given a chance at Ludwig when he reappears at a later date, then he *will* agree. Ludwig must simply not reappear."

"And how am I to get Moscow Center to agree to this?"

"You simply do it," Hennesey said. "We both know you, and you alone, direct your assets and approve their use by other agencies."

"And what if one day someone in Moscow Center says he wants Ludwig for a particular task?"

"He will simply be too hot to use in Europe. Whatever. You will find an excuse."

Rostoff snorted again. "And what will we get if we agree to this madness?"

"The Soviet Union? Nothing," Moran said. "You gentlemen individually? Something very interesting indeed."

Moran could see both men stiffen. They knew they were about to be bribed, and it was about to take place in front of each other. That was dangerous ground. Especially if the offer was too good to refuse. Moran knew that it was. But he wanted them to be frightened of each other. He wanted them both to know that if they agreed, then one of them backed away from the plan later, there was someone else who could bring them down. It was the only way the plan could work.

Rostoff turned and stared Bugayev down. It was a battle of wills, and there was no question who would win. Moran knew that Bugayev had turned a few tricks in the past, and he was certain Rostoff knew it as well. It was something that was expected, and was overlooked. Unless, and until, the man became an enemy. Then it was used to destroy him.

Rostoff turned back to Hennesey and Moran. "And why would we want to agree to something that will give you power over our heads?" he asked.

"Because you will have the same power over our heads," Moran said. He smiled, wondering what Rostoff would think if he knew how he had been forced to threaten Hennesey to get *him* to agree.

Rostoff's eyebrows rose again. "Tell us about this offer," he said.

Moran smiled. "We have something of value we want to share with you," he began.

CHAPTER 18

Michelle knelt on the stone floor, her hands clasped at her waist, her head bowed and covered by a scarf. She was kneeling in the tiny Romanesque Chapel of St. Christine in the Valle di Campoloro, which was located a few hundred meters below Cervione and reached by a narrow footpath cut like stairs into the mountainside. It took twenty minutes to navigate the narrow, steep steps, and thirty-five more to make the ascent back to her village, but Michelle came there often, at times when she was sad, or lonely, or frightened by what the future might hold, or when she simply needed to be alone with her God in a place that offered comfort and safety and solitude.

The chapel was a modest whitewashed building almost lost in a wilderness of flowers, and adjoining the ruins of an old Roman water mill. It was a place easily overlooked as quaint and curious, but not worthy of the rugged, tiring climb required to reach it. But inside it was something rich and unique, with twin, semi-domed, vaulted apses, each covered with delicate, pale frescoes dating back to the fifteenth century.

Michelle allowed her eyes to roam the cracked, faded paintings —scenes of Christ majestically enthroned, and of the Annunciation and Crucifixion—and she prayed for Alex's deliverance from the men who would kill him, and for the soul of his wife, whose name she didn't even know. She had thought to pray for his success in finding and killing the monster he would soon hunt. But it had seemed wrong to do so, an offense against God in His own house.

When she had finished praying, she rose and turned in a slow circle, as if looking at this special place a final time. There were no benches, no pews, just the floor of cut, square stones, and as she started for the small arched door, her footsteps echoed through the chapel as though bidding it farewell.

Outside, the warm late morning sun caressed her face, her body. She was dressed modestly in a skirt and blouse, and as she removed her scarf, she revealed hair that had been tied back in a single long, flowing braid. It seemed to emphasize the delicate, soft lines of her face, the fine, almost fragile curve of her jaw. She stepped forward into a sea of flowers, bent, and began gathering a bouquet to take back for her mother's table. She saw Alex only at meals now, and they were precious times for her, times she knew would soon be over and would never come to her again.

A small tear formed at the edge of her eye, and moved slowly down her cheek. Just keep him alive, she thought. Sweet God, don't let them kill him.

Alex sat in his room, the small table he hunched over covered with maps and reports he had removed from his office before fleeing Marseilles. It had been a comic adventure, stealing into his own office, talking his way past the young trainee on lone duty for the night, waiting for the young man to find his balls and challenge a superior who might end his career with a single telephone call, or at least call someone to find out what in hell he should do. But none of it had happened, all the wasted sweat notwithstanding, and he had waltzed out of the office with a bag full of documents that would help him reach Ludwig, possibly with breath still in his lungs.

His eyes burned into a map of North Africa. The men who awaited him, he thought, would expect him to arrive in Libya itself, perhaps directly in Tripoli by plane or boat, or somewhere to the west near Benghazi. But he would land instead south of Tunis, a favorite of Corsican smugglers who plied their trade throughout the Tunisian coast and knew every harbor and crevice that could be safely breached. They would drop him there, as close to the Libyan border as seemed safe, and he would then make his way along the several hundred miles of coastline by the least conspicuous means he could find.

He replaced the map with another of Tripoli and its environs.

The Libyans were known to have a resort to the west of the city, where visiting terrorists were believed to be entertained. There was also a training camp to the south, where these "dignitaries" were allowed to hone their skills, or offer counsel to those being readied to join the myriad terrorist factions—the IRA, Bieder-Meinhoff, the Red Brigade, or any number of names and collective letters that all spelled mindless and indiscriminate destruction and death.

He had often postulated, in his mind, a day when victim nations of the world would sicken of the killing and band together and raid these camps and destroy the destroyers. But, of course, it would never happen. Politicians lacked the will, and some savored the occasional indirect advantage the terrorists provided, while others feared their own safety might be jeopardized. And the world was ruled by politicians.

He pushed the maps away, submitting to his fears that Ludwig might already have been warned and spirited away to safer terrain. But he would find out where and follow. Sooner or later he would catch up with him and kill him or . . .

Sounds from the kitchen drove the thought away, and he pushed himself from the table and made his way into the hall. Juliet stood chattering excitedly at the door, and he could see Michelle busying herself at the sink, eyes lowered, waiting to be addressed before she turned.

Standing in the doorway was Antoine Pisani, his massive bulk obscuring all but the surrounding frame, his eyes warm on the woman, his face creased with a smile.

He looked up and saw Alex, the smile broadening, then he stepped into the apartment and to one side, revealing Alex's father standing to his rear, dressed in a suit and tie, and carrying a briefcase like a man on his way to the office, not one visiting his outlaw son.

Alex came forward and embraced Piers, receiving strong pats on the back in lieu of the kiss Antoine would have provided.

Piers took his arm in one hand and stepped back, holding him a short distance away. "You look well," he said. "Far better than I expected." His eyes drifted to Juliet, then to Michelle, who had turned now to watch the reunion. He smiled, keeping his eyes on them as he spoke. "These lovely women have done well by you. Very well indeed."

Alex made the introductions, then turned and embraced Antoine, receiving the kiss he wished his father had offered.

Antoine gestured them all to the kitchen table, then smiled imploringly at the women, who immediately and discreetly left the room. Piers followed them with his eyes, then looked at Antoine for reassurance.

"Anything they hear will go to their graves with them," he said. "We are safe here."

Piers leaned forward and grasped Alex's forearm. "I'm sorry about Stephanie," he said. "Your mother and I felt very strongly about her, and I shall help you see that the bastard pays for what he has done."

Alex's eyes brightened and his pulse began to race. He had not expected this. Help from his father, help from the CIA legend who still regularly lunched at Langley, who was still consulted on decisions that touched his area of expertise, even now, five years after he had left them. Then the euphoria crashed with his father's next words.

"But not now, Alex. Not now."

"Why?" Alex's voice was almost a croak. His throat was dry, and he felt—absurdly—as though he might cry.

"They're there waiting for you. Antoine and his people can get you away from here. They can probably get you past the CIA and DIA people who have been forced to join the Russians in the hunt." He shook his head. "But you knew that would happen. You knew the agreement they would be forced to live up to." He tightened his grip on Alex's arm. "But in Libya the net will be too tight. No matter how good you are—and I don't doubt your abilities—you'll never get within shooting distance of the bastard. And I know you want to be even closer than that." Piers released his arm and began slapping his palm lightly on the table. "I'm not even certain the Ruskies haven't already moved him. I'd be flabbergasted if they hadn't. If he were my asset I'd have him stashed away in an apartment in Minsk, surrounded by a company of KGB guards. It would be too great an embarrassment if a single rogue agent were able to track him down and kill him."

The words *rogue agent* hit Alex squarely, caused him to blink. Not that he hadn't thought of himself in those terms, didn't recognize the truth of it. It was hearing it from his father's lips. His anger flared.

"I should have known," he said. "I thought you'd come to help me. Finally to do something for me when I needed you. I should

have known better. You're still their boy, still the agency's puppet."
He stopped to stare at his father. "Well, fuck you, Dad. I'll get
him with you or without you. And I'm sorry I've embarrassed you
by becoming a rogue."

Piers recognized the reaction, had counted on it. "You are a
rogue," he said. "But it doesn't embarrass me. Actually, I'm quite
proud of you." He grabbed Alex's arm again. "And we'll let them
treat you like a rogue. There will be a punishment for you," he
said, changing directions, creating a new concern. "Forced retirement." He let the words sink in, waving the stick before he dropped
the carrot into view. "But Ludwig won't hide forever. He'll crawl
out of his hole one day. And we'll be waiting for him. And it won't
be long. I promise you. And then I'll personally help you get the
bastard. And the agency will help you as well."

Piers looked toward the room where Michelle and her mother
had gone. "And there will be no danger brought to those who have
sheltered you," he added.

Alex closed his eyes and recalled the recent attack. He hadn't
thought of the danger to others, even then. He'd been too consumed
by his own need.

"I can go somewhere else. Somewhere no one else can be
harmed," he said weakly.

Piers raised his eyebrows, as if questioning where. "There is
another alternative," he said.

Piers pulled his briefcase onto the table and patted it with one
hand. "I have something in here for you," he said. "It's a letter
from Walter Hennesey on CIA stationary. When Ludwig
emerges—and he will—they'll help you get to him. We will *all*
help you get to him. You won't be acting officially. You won't ever
be brought back in. You'll be forever deniable. But we'll get you
to him and give you whatever you need to do it. And a copy of this
letter will stay in Hennesey's safe, so if he's replaced, the promise
won't be forgotten. And I shall never let them forget. You have
my word on that."

Alex's face became a mask, and his fists tightened. He turned to
Antoine. "Does this mean I no longer have your help?" he asked.

Antoine's eyes hardened and he looked away from Alex and stared
at Piers as he spoke. "You will have whatever help I can give you.
The Pisani faction will take you wherever you want to go. If you
choose to stay here, it is here you will stay with our full protection.

You will be buried here if you die of old age. And no one will reach you before then." He looked back at Alex, his eyes softer now. "But your father is right. If you wait, you will still have our help. And you will have the help of others. You will be able to get to this pig and kill him the way he deserves to die. And you will live to savor it."

Hearing the words from his uncle—from a man he trusted more than any other—made the breath rush out of Alex as though he had been holding it for a long time, and he seemed to sag visibly in his chair.

"What do I have to do?" he asked. There was no bitterness, no fight in his voice, and he felt like a weight had been lifted from him. But his gut felt hollow. Everything, even the air about him, seemed empty.

"You'll fly back with me," Piers said, gripping his forearm again. "Hennesey will meet us at the airport in Marseilles, and we'll fly directly back to the States. The Russians have agreed to back off if you leave with us. And they'll scratch your name from their list. Permanently."

Alex's face darkened, and his left eye narrowed almost imperceptibly. "And when I kill Ludwig?" he asked.

"Enough time will have passed," Piers said. "It will just be the fortunes of war. And you won't be part of any agency when you do it. They don't expect their bastards to live forever. None of us do."

Michelle had listened. She understood English and had heard the agreement the men had reached at the table where she took her meals every day. She had felt a surge of relief, then of renewed fear, knowing it was only a postponement in what Alex must do to unburden his soul.

And as he packed his bag now, she also realized she would never see him again, would never walk with him, speak with him. But he would be safe for now. And perhaps Ludwig would die at someone else's hand, or a plane he was on would fall from the sky. She would go to the chapel and pray that it would happen, and if it offended God in His own house, so be it.

She was sitting in a chair in the family living room, and her mother came to her and sat on a stool beside her.

"You love him, don't you?" she asked. She watched her daughter's eyes fill with tears, and she leaned forward and kissed her forehead and gently stroked her cheek.

Michelle knew what her mother said was true. Alex was the gentlest, most honorable man she had ever known. And despite the suffering that had darkened his soul—the hatred it had produced, the need to kill—he was everything she believed a man should be.

"I want him to be safe," Michelle said. "All I want is for him to be safe."

"He will be," her mother said. "He is going home to the people he belongs to. They will keep him safe. They will give his hatred time to die, and they will help him find a new life."

"How do you know?" Michelle's eyes implored her mother for some proof, something she could hold on to.

"I saw it in Antoine's eyes," she said. "They have lied to him, and it displeases him that they have. But he has allowed it because he loves him, just as you do."

Michelle stared down into her lap, where her hands were clenched together. Juliet knew what her child, who was no longer a child, was thinking, how she had lost this man forever.

"It is good that you loved him," she said. "He is a good man, and it is good to have loved one like him. But, one day soon, there will be another good man. And you will love him too. And that will be even better, because then it will be time."

Tears began to move down Michelle's cheeks, and she quickly wiped them away as she heard the men moving down the hall. Alex stepped into the doorway to the living room. Antoine and his father remained in the kitchen.

Alex smiled down at them. "Thank you, Juliet," he said. "I shall never forget your home or your kindness." He put his bag on the floor and walked over to Michelle and knelt in front of her. He reached out and took her hand. "I wish you great success at the Sorbonne," he said. "I shall think of you there. And I shall think of you here. And of our walks and the things we talked about."

He wanted to tell her to write to him, that he would write to her. But he knew it was foolish, and something he should not do. He leaned across and kissed her gently on the cheek.

"Good-bye," he said. And then he was gone.

Michelle sat quietly, her fingers touching the place where he had kissed her, brushing back her tears so they would not wash it away.

CHAPTER

19

One Month Later

Gerard Morganthau left the consulate shortly after five o'clock, momentarily stood on the sidewalk, and tried to decide whether to take a taxi or to walk. Finally, he turned left and headed down the street, and let his mind fill with the young woman who had joined his staff that morning.

He would have liked to have lingered at the office, taken the time to talk to her, perhaps even take her out for a drink. She was truly exquisite. But he was due to meet his wife. They were to go to a reception that Gaston Defferre, Marseilles's mayor, was hosting. It was obligatory and unavoidable. Defferre had ruled Marseilles since shortly after World War II, and *ruled* was not too strong a word. Morganthau, despite his affected Boston accent, had been raised in Chicago and had grown up under the reign of Richard Daley, and Gaston was the closest thing to Daley in the Western world. Some even said Daley was an amateur by comparison. And old Gaston had once headed an Allied intelligence network in the south of France, so the obligation carried even more weight.

But there would be time for the consulate's latest acquisition, Morganthau told himself. There was always time, and given the nature of diplomatic work, the supply was constantly replenished.

He glanced at his watch and began walking more quickly, taking a side street that would bring him to the café where he had agreed to meet his wife. He did not notice the car moving up slowly behind him, did not see it stop, did not see two of its occupants get out. The first he knew of what was happening was the feel of the gun jammed into his ribs, the soft voice and hard eyes that told him he was to get in the back of the car, and of the two hands that gripped his arms on either side and hurried him to the open rear door.

He was being kidnapped. The horror of it flooded his mind as he was jammed between the two men, the gun still against his ribs, the two men no longer looking at him or speaking a word.

He tried to remember what they had told him during his training. Instructions of what to do if kidnapped. But most of what he could remember dealt with how to avoid being taken. And that was long past any use. For the life of him he could not remember what he was supposed to do now. *For the life of him.* The phrase sent a shudder through his body.

The car picked up speed, raced past the Vieux Port, past the City Hall, where Gaston Defferre was no doubt preparing to leave for his reception, and into the old quarter. There the car slowed and made several turns, seeming at times to turn back on itself in the labyrinth of streets that were a maze to those unfamiliar with them, until it finally pulled into a large warehouse that Morganthau thought must be somewhere near the Bassin de la Grande Joliette, the city's new port. At least he could hear the sounds of ships in the distance.

Another car waited inside, but he could see no one behind its darkened windows, which became even darker as the doors of the warehouse closed behind him.

One of the men pulled him from the rear of the car, and pushed him roughly into the center of the large, empty room. The second of the men who had taken him from the street approached slowly, a tire iron dangling loosely from one hand.

"Look, gentlemen," Morganthau began, fighting to keep his voice even and controlled, "I'm sure the United States government will give you what you want if you'll just telephone and explain."

The man with the tire iron smiled and shrugged, and Morganthau could read in his eyes that the United States could not offer anything that might interest him.

The tire iron came faster than he expected, making a wide, looping arc and carrying all the power of the man's shoulder and arm. It crashed into his left knee, shattering the bone in a blinding flash of pain that sent Morganthau's body crumpling to the floor.

The second blow came immediately, smashing his right knee before the first howl of pain had completely escaped Morganthau's lips. Then a third blow crushed his right elbow, and as he sobbed hysterically, he could feel the man using his foot to turn his body on his other side. Then the fourth blow came, destroying his left elbow, and finally, with merciful speed, a fifth strike, smashing his nose and forcing his upper teeth into his mouth.

He was on his back now, unable to hold any of his wounds, staring up at the man through the blood that covered his face. The man readied the tire iron a final time, and brought it down between his legs, crushing his testicles.

Morganthau let out a final cry, coughing on his own blood, then fainted. When he awoke, several minutes later, he looked up into the face of Antoine Pisani. He recognized the face, had seen it often in the newspapers, and he was certain now that he would die.

Antoine bent over and spat into Morganthau's face.

"In six months, when you get out of the hospital, we will come and visit you again," he said. "Then, when you leave the hospital again, we will come to you. And we will keep coming until you run to a part of the world where we cannot find you. And if you tell anyone who has done this to you, we will kill you. And we will do it in a way that will make this seem a pleasant dream." Antoine was quiet for almost a minute. "When you fuck a man's wife," he said at length, "well, then, you must expect to pay a price for the whore."

Antoine turned and walked back to his car, and the last thing Morganthau heard before he fainted again was the sound of it leaving the warehouse.

BOOK II

CHAPTER

20

Marseilles, 1947

The line of people waiting to buy food stretched down the street, wound around one corner, then still another, and continued on almost out of sight. It numbered in the thousands, and to a casual observer it might seem these people were waiting for medical attention, so many were using canes or crutches or were missing limbs, and few, if any, looked as though they had eaten well in a long time. But it was not medical attention they sought. It was only food. And there was little of that to be had.

The mood of the crowd was not subdued; it was not the mood of beggars awaiting some token gift, or of those so desperate they would endure anything. There was a steady murmur of angry voices, intermixed with occasional oaths, and the soft October rain that had begun to fall seemed to further darken the gaunt, unhappy faces. And, as people shifted impatiently from side to side, the line took on the look of an anxious snake, writhing with displeasure.

The reason for the sullen, angry mood was not the long wait to buy the little food there was. The people had become used to that. The war, and now its aftermath, had conditioned them, and one had only to look at the surrounding buildings, torn and shattered by the Allied bombings, to know that things were not as they once were—would not be for a long time, perhaps would never be again. No, the anger was not about food, or the lack of it. It was about the decision of the newly elected mayor, Michel Carlini, to raise the tram fares, the only means the people had to move about their battered city: to get to the little food there was, to reach their jobs, if they had any, or to travel about to seek one if they had none.

Now, years after the war had ended, years after the last Nazi had been driven from France, the average worker was earning sixty-five percent of what he had during the Great Depression, and eating eighteen percent less than he had eaten then. Even the government had acknowledged it and had promised the people it would soon get better. But its solution had not been more food, more work. It had been to raise the price of a tram ride, which already took food from the mouths of the hungry.

"What do they want from us?" a man shouted from somewhere in the middle of the mass of people. "Why don't they let us die in the street, then sweep us up like so much garbage?"

"No," shouted back another. "They can run us over with their empty trams. Then Carlini can sell what's left in the food shops, fucking pig that he is."

There was no laughter among the crowd, no display of black humor, or appreciation of it, and the police who moved along the street, watching the line, waiting to quell any small disturbance, looked at each other with nervous eyes.

Strikes had already broken out throughout the city—threatened to spread to all of France—and any driver who dared take his tram into the streets was met with barricades and a hail of rocks. And the police, who controlled the people to what measure they could, knew that they—men who took ample wages home to their families—were no longer regarded as protectors. They were now hated almost as much as the Gestapo had been hated before them, almost as much as the gangsters who controlled the black market and preyed off the misery of the first vanquished, now "liberated" populace, and who were so comfortably in bed with the politicians the people despised more than anyone. And it was getting worse.

Less than a mile from the long, angry line of people, in a nightclub in the Opera district known as Club Paradise, Antoine and Meme Pisani sat at a table talking with an American and the man from the mayor's office who had brought them all together. They were twenty-seven and twenty-six respectively, and they were dressed in wide-shouldered suits and garish neckties. In the shadows of the large, empty room, other young men, who worked for the two brothers, waited expectantly to see how deep Antoine and Meme would be allowed to dip their beaks—as the Corsican saying went—into the profit political turmoil always offered.

The American was tall and rangy, with carefully manicured hands, and he was dressed in a double-breasted pin-striped suit that made him look more like a banker than an official of the United States government. He had been introduced only as Jorgenson, no first name, no official title, but the brothers were sure he represented what had been known as the OSS—the Office of Strategic Services—and which, they had been told, had just the previous month been reorganized into something called the Central Intelligence Agency. They had both dealt with the OSS during the war as part of the Resistance, and this man Jorgenson—if that was truly his name—had the look of those they had known then.

The other man, Pierre Ferri, was a fellow Corsican who worked in some indefinable way for the new mayor. He was a small, plump man of about forty, dressed in a tattered but well-pressed brown suit that made his sallow complexion seem washed out and faded in the dimly lighted room. He smiled often, almost endlessly, with poor teeth as he spoke, and the brothers knew his type well—a man not of the *milieu*, but one who had emigrated from their native land and chosen politics as his way to wealth.

There was a plate of cheese and bread and fruit on the table before them, and Ferri picked at it as he spoke, more out of habit than hunger.

"Monsieur Jorgenson has a proposition for your faction," Ferri said around a bit of bread. He saw the pleasure come to Antoine's eyes—not Meme's, who hid his feelings better—and he knew his acknowledgment that they now headed their own group within the *milieu* was still a matter of pride between them. For years the brothers had worked for the faction headed by Paul Carbone, who together with François Sirito had dominated the criminal organization for more than a decade, and they had labored as little more than triggermen and leg breakers. But Carbone had been killed in 1943, when the Resistance had bombed a train on which he was riding, and Spirito, who had collaborated with the Nazis, had fled the country in 1944 with the Fascist ex-deputy mayor Simon Sabiani. Now, with Carbone and Spirito gone, they were among a handful of new leaders within the *milieu* who were struggling for dominance.

"As you know," Ferri continued, cutting himself a small slice of cheese, "the communist labor unions, and those among the city council who share their ideology, are attempting to manipulate this increase in the tram fares to bring violence to the streets, and use it to pave their way to power."

Antoine and Meme remained silent. They knew that nothing of the sort was true. The men who led the Communist–Socialist labor coalition were being blackjacked into support of the unauthorized strikes that were spreading throughout the city. These labor leaders, many of whom had fought with the communist-led Resistance, were far from wild-eyed revolutionaries, but conservative middle-aged men who now wanted some part in the governance of their country. But they were also realists, who understood that the mayor's hike of tram fares was needed to curb a growing fiscal deficit. And while communist politicians had jumped to the side of the strikers, Ferri's assertion that this was a combined plot between communist-led unions and politicians was nothing more than a means to beat back dangerous political opposition.

But none of that mattered to the Pisani brothers. What did matter was that they were being offered the chance to gain strong political alliances. And they had learned, from both Carbone and Spirito, that this, even more than the knife and the gun, was the strongest path to dominance in the *milieu*.

"Our American friends are concerned that this is only the beginning, that it will lead to a communist wave throughout Europe." Ferri moved his hand in a flowing gesture to emphasize his point. "And Europe is at its most vulnerable. The people are hungry and ready to follow anyone who will offer them power."

Meme nodded agreement, although he knew this too was false. The people only wanted adequate food and shelter and work. What they didn't want was the heel of any politician's boot, no matter what his stripe. They were not ready for revolution. People who were preoccupied with getting enough food into their mouths would accept anyone they thought could help them, and throw them out as quickly as they failed. France, he believed, would be going through constant political changes for many years. And in those changes there would be great profit. And it was the Americans who would direct the flow of currency. And if the Americans wanted to believe in a communist menace in France, who was he to argue? The Americans, he knew, would change political allegiances as one anti-communist faction ebbed and another surged ahead. And throughout it all those who remained with them would become rich.

"My brother and I are honored that you would share your concerns with us," Meme said. He was a small, slightly built young man—a sharp contrast to his bull-like brother, who looked as though he would burst from his suit at any moment—but his hawk-like face and dark, penetrating eyes spoke of someone who could be taken lightly only at peril.

Jorgenson leaned forward and offered a false smile. He knows we speak only shit here, Meme thought. And he knows that we know it too.

"My government is well aware of both of your heroics during the Occupation," Jorgenson continued. He gestured to Meme. "We know how you were so deservedly awarded the Légion d'Honneur. And we believe you are men who can be trusted. Men of honor, who will do what is necessary."

Antoine raised his heavy hands, as if lifting something from the table, then let them fall back. "We always do what is necessary," he said. "Corsicans learn that simple truth in the cradle."

Jorgenson's smile became more genuine. He liked venality in those with whom he dealt. Venality was something you could hold on to, something you could manipulate to your own ends.

"My government, through its newly formed Central Intelligence Agency, wants to cut off any possibility of a general strike," he said. "But if that's not possible, we want the strike crushed, and we want it crushed quickly." He tilted his head to one side. "We would like it done with as little bloodshed as possible, but we're realists enough to understand that circumstances may lead us down a different road. And we know we will need forceful people to handle that. People who are not outsiders."

Meme folded his hands in front of him, offering the sincerity and innocence of a schoolboy. "We, my brother and I, are of course anxious to help the American friends we learned to trust during the war." He spoke the lie smoothly, easily. "But there are others in our group whose welfare we must consider, and we must be able to explain what benefits our faction will receive for our help."

"There will be adequate benefits," Jorgenson said. "There will be monetary benefits now, but even more important"—he glanced at Ferri—"and I believe I speak for those who run the government"—Ferri quickly nodded agreement—"there will be a certain amount of leeway and protection offered your many enterprises in the future. This as a way of additional compensation. Let us just say you will be making friends who will not forget you."

Meme gestured expansively. He knew that Ferri and those he worked for might lose power, but that those who replaced them would be obligated by the Americans, to that same promise. "One could ask for no more," he said. "Tell us what you would have us do."

Jorgenson nodded, reached below the table, and lifted a briefcase to his lap. From inside, he withdrew an envelope and laid it on the table between them.

"This is for your use," he said. "It will cover any initial expenses you might have. It's fifteen thousand dollars U.S., and there will be more when it is needed."

Antoine picked up the envelope, opened it, and slid out the money. He did not count it, not wishing to insult the American. The amount, a virtual fortune in France at this time, made Ferri's eyes bulge. Antoine discreetly slid the money into his suit coat pocket.

"At some time within the next month," Jorgenson continued, "the CIA will be sending in a psychological warfare team to make a general strike unpalatable to the population." He nodded at each of the brothers in turn. "You will follow the direction of the man who heads that team. He will be here for several years, we expect—even after the strike threat has passed—just to insure we maintain a level of political stability."

Ferri smiled broadly at the use of the terminology, but the Pisani brothers knew it did not necessarily mean political stability for him and his masters. It meant the Americans would only allow those they could work with to remain in power, and that they would interfere with the choice of the electorate only to that degree.

"In the meantime," Jorgenson added, "we want your faction to do whatever is needed to disrupt any street demonstrations. We are well aware that historically in France the street demonstration has always been as important as the ballot box in influencing politics. And we just can't allow that to be the case."

"I believe we can serve you very well," Meme said.

Jorgenson smiled his false smile. "I believe you can," he said.

When Jorgenson and Ferri had left, Antoine and Meme went to their office at the rear of the club and counted the money.

A broad smile creased Antoine's face. "There are people who would gladly kill us for this much," he said.

Meme returned the smile. "There are people who would kill us for free."

"You are thinking of Marcel Francisci," Antoine said.

"He is one," Meme said. "But I am very happy the Americans came to us instead of him. With this much"—he patted the stack of bills that lay on a desk between them—"and the support of the Americans, Francisci's faction would be stronger than us. And he is like a wolf. When he sees something weak, he must kill it."

Antoine nodded. "Maybe we should show the wolf what it is like for the lamb."

Meme shook his head. "I would rather see Francisci come to us to beg our benevolence. It would hurt him more than death."

Antoine drummed his fingers on the desk. "The only thing that offends me is that the Americans think they have bought us with this money." He too patted the stack of bills. "But then . . ." He finished the sentence with another smile.

"Sometimes those who receive the money are the ones who have done the buying," Meme said.

Antoine inclined his head to one side, weighing the idea. "Let it be that way with us," he said.

"We shall see to it," Meme answered.

CHAPTER

21

The man from the CIA was no older than they themselves, and the fact of it surprised the Pisani brothers, although they said nothing. It was November 12, almost a month to the day of their meeting with Jorgenson and Ferri, and during the intervening time Pisani men had moved against barricades the strikers had set up to stop the trams, smashing them and the heads behind them with whatever force was needed. Yet no one had died, as the CIA had instructed, and many of the barricades had not been discovered in time. They were like the fleas on a dog, first here, then somewhere else, and it was impossible to anticipate where they would next appear.

But those who manned the barricades had learned to go to them in fear. But they also went with resolve, and that was something more difficult to crush.

Richard Pierpont Moran—Piers, as he said he preferred to be called—was a tall, angular young man with the bearing of an aristocrat. He spoke French formally and well, having difficulty only with the odd idiom or the colloquial terms used among members of the *milieu*. But soon he was referring to the police as *flics*, money as the *blé*, a strong-arm soldier of a faction as a *casseur*, and myriad other terms that had grown out of custom from years past.

Moran had arrived five days earlier with his psychological warfare team, a full week ahead of the time indicated by Jorgenson. The Pisanis could only assume it was an indication of American resolve.

Based on past experience with the OSS, they could not conceive it was the result of efficiency. Piers had kept his men apart from the Pisanis, preferring to deal with them only himself. It was a management technique that Meme—who instinctively understood these things—recognized for what it was, a desire to keep instructions simple and clear—at both ends—and to avoid any misdirection or misunderstanding.

At first Antoine had been offended, believing that Piers felt his men too good to deal directly with Corsican inferiors. But Meme had explained, and Antoine—far quicker to grasp things than his bulk and manner led many to believe—recognized the wisdom of the decision. And he stored it away, to use later himself.

They were gathered in the office at the rear of Club Paradise in the old Opera district, and one of the *poules*, who had been given the day off at the whorehouse where she worked, brought them coffee and croissants and a plate of butter and jams from the black market stores in the basement.

Meme noticed that Piers's eyes lingered on the woman, who was no more than nineteen, and whose name was Colette Minot. She was a beautiful young woman, among the most enticing who worked for the Pisanis, and Antoine and Meme had both enjoyed her skills, which were proficient to a rare degree. And, most important, she was not Corsican, as far too many in other stables were. The Pisanis' respect for Corsican womanhood was too deeply ingrained to permit that to happen. Meme would have liked to keep the woman with them, and take advantage of Piers's obvious attraction for her. But Colette was from Lyon, a good enough place but one not imbued with an understanding of Corsican silence, and so she could not be trusted to hear the conversations of men.

Piers bit into a croissant and immediately dusted his thin lips with a napkin. He had pale blue eyes that were striking and attractive to women, but which betrayed the falseness of his exterior patrician warmth. He was coldly pragmatic, something the Pisanis found unusual in so young an American, but it was also something they could trust and admire. It would not be hard to take orders from this man, they had quickly decided. As long as the money continued as promised, and as long as Piers could accept their own, more subtle direction.

"So the communists among the city council appear to be a major problem," Piers said, dusting another crumb from his mouth. "How would you deal with them if they were causing you business difficulties?"

Meme tapped his nose with one finger. "I would ignore them, ride out their efforts. Politicians quickly lose interest in things that do not directly affect the maintenance of their power. The tram fares will not do this. Whether they remain in effect or not, the mere fact they have opposed them will serve their purpose."

"And if it were something that would not go away, that would cause you permanent harm?"

"It would depend on what it was," Meme answered honestly. "If it meant a loss of too much *blé*, or if it threatened to cripple our faction, we would kill one and hope the others took the lesson to heart."

"Short of killing someone," Piers urged.

"A good beating is sometimes enough," Antoine said. "But it must be understood that more will follow. Some will accept the price of one beating. But few who know they don't have the power to stop it from happening again and again will fail to do what is needed to end it."

"What if a beating were to take place in the council chambers itself? What if all the communist councilors were beaten at once?"

"The people would be angry," Meme said. "They would react."

"At first, yes," Piers said. "But would it show them their protectors could not even protect themselves? And when they themselves were hurt later, would it not say to them"—he gestured with one hand—"why continue this strike, there is no one who can help us?"

The brothers were silent for several moments, then Meme's face broke into an uncharacteristic smile. "Yes," he said. "I think that would happen. There would be a reaction at first, and I think it would be angry and would come quickly. But it would be small in numbers, and if met with violence I think it would have the effect you seek."

Piers nodded. "I believe the council is meeting this afternoon. And I think it may be a good time to test our theory," he said.

When the Pisanis and their men had left, Piers lingered behind. Meme had suggested it would be better if he was not seen near the council chambers, and had offered Colette as a means of relaxation and diversion.

Moran was not accustomed to prostitutes. He had been with one once, while a student at Yale, but he had been drunk and in a group of his peers, and it had been a loud, rakish, stupid event filled with absurd taunting. He found Colette in the small kitchen that served the nightclub, washing up the cups and dishes they had used, and he leaned against the counter, trying to seem casual and at ease.

Colette understood. Neither Meme nor Antoine had given her any specific instructions, but she had been in this position before and knew what would be expected of her. At least this one was young and handsome, and he seemed polite, and possibly gentle, although she could not be sure. Even the most innocuous of men, she had found, could turn brutal when they knew she was available for money. It had something to do with power, she thought. And a woman who sold her body had no power over it.

But she would have to be careful with this one. He seemed important to the brothers, more important than most. She would not steal from him. The Pisanis forbade stealing from customers; they said it was bad for business. But when the opportunity presented itself, she stole anyway. It was a way of getting back at them, she told herself. And she also liked the money.

"Tell me about Lyon," Piers said. "I've never been there." Colette's back was to him, and he was studying the view of her bottom. It was full and wonderfully shaped—not large, perfect really. He recalled a line from Hemingway about a woman similarly endowed. He had said it was one that "definitely would not require a pillow." The author was speaking about the ability to achieve the deepest of penetrations with such a woman, and undoubtedly trying to imply that his character was so sizably proportioned it was a serious consideration. Piers had no such concerns. He was a normal man. But he liked the thought of it.

Colette turned, but only partway, knowing it would give this man a view of her tight blouse and the shape of what lay beneath. She was a beautiful woman; she understood that. She also believed it was the only thing of value she possessed, the only means she had to the life she wanted.

"It is a city like any other," she said. She offered a small shrug, a small smile. "If you grow up among the *filou* it is wonderful. If you are poor, it is *merde*."

She spoke English mixed with her own idiom, and it surprised Piers that she knew the language. But then, the occupation forces had been there for several years, and he supposed a clever whore would have to. Competition on the streets had been severe. The poverty and the hunger had seen to it.

"You speak my language well," he said, switching back himself.

"I like to practice," Colette said. "I want to go there someday."

"Why? France is so beautiful."

The small shrug returned. "It is where the money is," she said.

Piers laughed, pleased by her blatant honesty. "There are those who believe the money will be here. Much of Europe will have to be rebuilt. That will mean money."

Another shrug. "Then maybe I will stay. For the money. But later I will go there."

"Why, then?"

"Because I want to live someplace where people will not know I worked as a *poule*." She offered him a broad, self-mocking smile and shook her long dark hair. "I want to be respectable," she said.

Piers laughed again. The woman was enchanting; she seemed to lack the coarseness and humorlessness of so many of the prostitutes he had seen on the streets. And she was able to joke about her own greed. In a strange way that had a certain charm.

"How long have you been here in Marseilles?" Piers asked.

Much nicer than asking, How long have you been fucking for a living? Colette told herself. She smiled inwardly. He was nice, had good manners. He had a certain class to him. Unlike some of the barbaric American soldiers she had been with.

"Two years," she said. "I came here when I was seventeen." She wanted him to know she was only nineteen. She thought it would please him, would be an advantage.

"You must know the city well," he said. "I only arrived a few days ago, and I haven't seen much of it yet."

She wanted to tell him she had seen little of it too, outside of the Opera district and the shops along La Canebière. But she didn't want him to think she had spent all of her time on her back. It might frighten him away.

"Is your wife here with you?" she asked. She had noticed the gold band on his finger, and she was curious.

"No," Piers said. "She's at home. She just had a child. A son. Our second."

"Then you have been married a long time."

"We were married right after I graduated from college. The war had just begun—for us, anyway—and everyone was trying to pack as much into life as possible before they were sent off." He imitated her shrug. "But then I was stationed in Washington. Never heard a shot fired in anger, as they say."

"And now you are here, and you are lonely," she said.

"And now I am here," Piers said.

Colette smiled at him. She had a beautiful mouth, wide and sensuous, and her features were delicate, her eyes a dark brown that seemed to drink him in.

"Would you like to walk me home?" she asked. "It is not far, a small apartment a few blocks from here."

"Yes," Piers said. "I'd like that very much."

He lay in bed, staring at the ceiling while she ministered to him. There was no other way to describe it. She played with him, brought him to points of arousal that seemed impossible to maintain, then allowed him to escape, and brought him back, even higher than before. He could feel her fingers, her mouth, her tongue manipulating various parts of him, and he luxuriated in it, wanted it never to end. He had never been made love to like this, and somewhere in the back of his mind—what little of it was functioning—he told himself he would have to find a way to teach his wife these exotic offerings. If only there was a school she could go to, he thought. He almost laughed, but could not. Colette had intensified her ministrations again.

When they had finished and lay beside each other, he thought of what she had done, the immense pleasure she had given him, the pleasure she seemed to take from it herself. A man could love a woman like this endlessly, he told himself. If only she wasn't what she was.

He wondered if he should offer her money. Wondered if she would accept it. Certainly she would not be offended. Perhaps Meme had told her to accept nothing. Perhaps she feared he might ask if she had. Perhaps she had simply wanted him. He knew he would like to think that she had.

He decided to test it. He rose to one elbow and looked down at her. She was truly lovely, and he found himself wanting her again. "What can I do for you?" he asked.

She smiled, coyly, he thought. "You have done everything I could want," she said. The smile broadened, making him think of the width of her mouth and the way she had used it. He wanted her to use it again.

"But you could take me to lunch, if you like," she said.

"I would love that," he said. He felt himself growing hard again at the thought she did not want his money. "But first . . ." He bent to her and brushed his lips lightly against her mouth. And they began again.

CHAPTER

22

The council chambers were chaotic, the members fighting to shout each other down, anger so intense it seemed to go beyond the mere vitriolic bile of politicians. The terms communist and fascist filled the air. There were no friendships here, no words that would be forgotten once the session had ended. They would not adjourn together for a drink, for conversation about other things. These were men who hated each other's beliefs. Men who had fought a war against a common enemy but from different quarters, and who had hated each other almost as much as they hated the enemy they fought.

Michel Dubois rose from his seat and shouted into the tide of voices. He was an enormous man, and his girth seemed to attack the space around him, demanding room for his person and his words. He waved a meaty fist, almost as if swinging something about his head, and his deep baritone thundered over the other voices, threatening to beat them down into the floor.

"How dare you speak to us of justice?" he roared. "There is no such commodity in Marseilles today. Or in all of France." He drew in a deep breath, preparing to blow out more abuse. "Not since the Nazi filth was driven from our city have its workers been treated as mere slaves to those who rule over them. But what could be expected from those who for years before the Nazis came waved the fascist banner so proudly?"

The final sentence brought shouts of anger and derision. There was only one greater insult than to suggest someone had worked for the fascists who had riddled France before the war—and that was to suggest collaboration with the Nazis. And, as everyone knew but would refuse to admit, France was also rife with collaborators as well.

Dubois stretched out his arms in a theatrical gesture of disbelief. "How else," he roared, "how else can we view this incredible increase in the cost of a simple tram ride? How else can we view this picking of the pockets of workers who lack even adequate bread for the mouths of their children? And now we would imprison those who take to the streets to cry out against this injustice."

The roar heightened again, mixed with cries of "Anarchy!" Dubois paused, raising his chin and looking down the length of his ample nose at those who surrounded him. "Anarchy, you say?" His voice rose several octaves to indicate his disbelief. "If it is anarchy to go into the streets to demand justice, to demand mercy for one's hungry children, then I must say"—his voice rose to a crescendo —"let us have anarchy throughout France."

The large rock that came down from the balcony struck Dubois in the back of the head and hurled his body forward. Only the seats in front of him, and his great size, kept him from crashing to the floor. Few around him seemed to notice the attack, their shouts and opposing shouts taking up the whole of their attention. It was not until a group of tough young men forced their way onto the floor and began beating the members on the communist side of the aisle that what was happening dawned upon others in the assembly. They were horrified, thinking at first that they too would also be attacked. But when it was clear the communists were the only target, they fell back in silence, only a few coming to the aid of those being beaten.

Dubois was among the few who struck back at his attackers, but it was useless. The Pisani men were armed with pipes and clubs and brass knuckles, and they were younger and proficient in their task. The councilors, mostly middle-aged men, fell like sacks of wet laundry, and from the rear of the balcony Antoine and Meme looked down, satisfied with the work. Only Antoine was slightly disappointed. He would have liked to have been in the middle of it all, dealing out blows himself. But those days were past, he knew. *Le patriarche* of a faction within the *milieu* did not soil his hands with the work of a *casseur*. To do so would diminish his status. And especially if he hoped to become a *paceri*, a leader among leaders. But still, he knew, he would miss it.

He watched Dubois fight back against two of his men. He was a *dur*, a tough one. Like Antoine himself, under the layer of fat, the man was a bull. And Antoine thought he would like to give him a few minutes of his time. But then Dubois fell. A set of brass knuckles had crashed into his jaw, surely breaking it, and opening a deep gash in his chin. Antoine shrugged and turned to his brother. It was time to *cavaler*, to scram before the police woke up and made things difficult.

Meme winked at his massive brother, instinctively knowing what he felt. "A good day's work," he said. "Not as interesting as the old days, but I think our American friend will be pleased."

"As long as he continues to pay for his pleasure," Antoine said.

The beatings of the communist council members occurred at three o'clock, and word of it spread rapidly through the city, and by four, police estimated that forty thousand people had gathered in front of City Hall. Matters were getting out of hand, and even the battered and bloodied councilman, Michel Dubois, could not appease the crowd.

The handful of police present, who had no hope to bring the situation under control, called upon the Communist ex-mayor, Jean Cristofol, to beseech those present to return to their homes. Cristofol, a powerful speaker but an unsuccessful mayor—and a man many of these same people had voted out of office—suddenly became the one person the shocked and frightened crowd was willing to believe.

He assured them none of the councilors had been seriously hurt, and that the police would soon arrest the thugs and gangsters who had perpetrated the outrage. Within thirty minutes the crowd had dispersed, and by six-thirty all appeared quiet again.

But it was not over. A handful of young workers gathered nearby at the Vieux Port, and decided that the terms "thugs and gangsters" could only mean one collective villain: the Pisani brothers.

At seven o'clock Antoine and Meme sat near the front window of their nightclub, awaiting a response to their attack in the council chambers. Twenty of their men waited with them, each of them armed, as were the two brothers.

176 / WILLIAM HEFFERNAN

Word had come several hours earlier, by way of a telephone call from a terrified Pierre Ferri, that a sea of humanity had gathered before City Hall and was crying out for blood. Meme had listened to the frightened clichés, certain Ferri was exaggerating the danger. But it made little difference. He and his brother could not run and hide, for the loss of face within the *milieu* would be too devastating. So he had called in men and prepared for a fight, even if it proved to be his last.

Shortly after seven o'clock they heard a mob of nearly forty men moving down the street, smashing windows as they came. To the average citizen the Opera district was the headquarters of the underworld, replete with its nightclubs and brothels, and the control point for the black market which dominated their purses. And as such, it was a legitimate target for working-class anger.

When the mob came into view, Meme snorted derision. He turned to Antoine, noting the small smile on his brother's lips. "It would seem our 'sea of humanity' is nothing more than a filthy mud puddle," he said.

Meme told his men to remain inside, but to make their presence—and those of their weapons—visible through the window. Then he and Antoine stepped outside, guns in hand.

The crowd stopped on seeing them and began shouting taunts and threats.

Neither Meme nor Antoine said a word. They simply raised their guns and fired into the crowd. Five men fell, badly wounded, and the remainder of the mob broke and ran.

The following day one of the wounded men died.

CHAPTER

The next day Antoine and Meme were arrested. That morning the city's Communist newspaper, *La Marseillaise*, reported that it had been Pisani men who attacked the municipal councilors, and that later, the Pisani brothers themselves had fired into a crowd of workers marching to protest the attack. The charges were not seriously rebutted in the Socialist paper, *Le Provençal*, or the Gaullist *Méridional*. It appeared, on the surface, the Pisanis were about to be thrown to the dogs.

Yet Meme and Antoine did not appear concerned as they sat with Piers Moran and Pierre Ferri in the rear office of Club Paradise.

"Why did you shoot them yourselves?" Piers asked. "I thought leaders in the *milieu* remained above the dirty work."

"There are times when you must show you have not forgotten how to deal out violence with your own hands," Meme said. "These men, they were attacking our club. *Our* club." He gestured to his brother and himself to emphasize the point. "So they found themselves facing *us*."

Piers was sure the lesson was meant more for their opposition within the *milieu* than a handful of ragtag workers. But he saw no point in pursuing the matter.

"You do not think the object lesson you sought was made more forceful by what happened?" It was Antoine this time, and the question carried a hint of anger in it.

"I do indeed," Piers said. "But we now have the problem of

keeping you out of jail. We have no interest in losing you at this point."

The Pisanis had been bailed out of jail that morning by one of their men, with money provided by Piers Moran. It was not that they lacked the funds. It was intended as a show of support that would not be missed by the politicians who learned of it. And it had brought Ferri to this meeting. Otherwise, after reading the morning's newspapers, he would have remained far away.

"There are witnesses," Ferri said. "Two police officers claim to have seen the shooting."

"Witnesses can be dealt with," Antoine said. "We only need to know who they are."

"That I can discover," Ferri said. "The question of what happened in the council chambers I think will go away by itself. We are claiming it was a spontaneous reaction to the slanderous statements of Michel Dubois. It will be difficult to prove otherwise."

"Tell me more about these police officers," Piers said.

Ferri scratched his head, sending a cascade of dandruff onto his blue suit. "They are honest men, always the most difficult kind to deal with."

Piers smiled at the politician. "Certainly there are ranking officers in your police department who could convince these men they made a mistake—that they really didn't see our friends here firing into the mob." He smiled at Ferri. "Perhaps they were just too far away. After all, if they were really that close they should have stopped it."

Meme was studying Piers closely, and a very faint, almost unrecognizable smile was forming on his lips.

Ferri twisted nervously in his chair. "But the people would be outraged if they thought we were corrupting our own police," he said.

Piers leaned back in his chair and stared up at the ceiling. "The people are hungry," he said. "Many do not have jobs. They believe this is unfair. And, of course, it is. But it has been my experience that when people lack food, and the work to get it, they're resentful of those who have both readily available to them, and are prepared to believe the worst about them." He sat up and let his gaze fall heavily on the mayor's man. "I don't think their outrage would be too lasting," he said.

"I do not think I could get the mayor to agree," Ferri said.

Piers drummed the fingers of both hands now. "Then perhaps we need a new mayor," he said. He studied the shock on Ferri's face, then smiled. "This does not mean that you, my friend, could not be part of a new administration. Loyalty is something we never forget."

Meme saw Ferri crumbling inwardly. "Gaston Defferre would be the man," he said. "He is the leader of the Socialist party, and a man we have dealt with before. He is a realist." Meme offered his faint smile again. "And he has worked with your people before. He headed an intelligence network in the south of France during the war. I think, perhaps, he would be willing to continue in that role. He hates the communists, and only agrees to work with them for political reasons."

Piers nodded, then glanced back at Ferri. "What do you think of Defferre?" he asked.

"He is a good man and a powerful one. I think he is honest. But he also understands the way politics work."

Antoine snorted. "He understands how his relatives work. Every time a government worker leaves his house, he is afraid he will find one of Gaston's relatives sitting at his desk when he arrives at his office."

Piers smiled broadly at the evaluation of Defferre. "It's something that has been known to happen in many countries," he said. "But it sounds as though Gaston may be our man. If not for this strike, then certainly for the next."

"You expect more of the same?" Ferri asked.

"I was told to expect to be here for several years," Piers said. "And it was not because my government expected *this* difficulty to last that long."

Ferri let out a long breath. "I will talk to the mayor," he said. "But I do not know if he will agree. But I will try."

"Only tell him what we want," Piers said. "If he chooses not to listen . . ." He raised his hands in a shrugging gesture. He knew Ferri would tell the mayor much more.

This American was becoming very Corsican, Meme thought. Even his gestures were becoming so.

"I will speak to him," Ferri said. "And, I assure you, I would have no difficulty working with Gaston."

"I'm sure you wouldn't," Piers said. He paused, folding his hands before him. "For now we must deal with the charges against our friends here," he said. "We must arrange to have them dropped. Then we can get back to the business of ending this strike."

Four days later the two officers appeared in court and recanted their earlier statements that they had seen the Pisani brothers fire into the crowd. The court did not act immediately on the new information. To do so would incite the public. The court, in fact, would not drop the charges against the Pisanis until December 10, almost a month later. But, in effect, the case against the Pisanis was over.

Now Piers could concentrate on the strike—and the other interests he had found in Marseilles. He looked forward to the pleasures of both.

Colette allowed her fingers to roam softly, gently, the fingers barely touching him, just a faint flicker of movement across his skin. Her head rested on his stomach and she watched him become more aroused with each caress. She liked to watch him, to hear his breathing catch with pleasure, to feel his stomach muscles tighten against her face as his passion grew and surged. It was as though he had not been loved in a long time and the pleasure of it was alien to him. Perhaps he had never been loved. Oh, she knew he had been with women, many of them. He had been skilled enough, even from the beginning. But she did not think he had been *given* true pleasure. She thought he had been with women who simply took it for themselves, or those who gave only what they had to give and got it over with quickly. She knew there were such women. She had heard them talk about men, about the demands they made and how those demands never seemed to end. It had puzzled her that a woman would not wish to be wanted with such intensity, that it would not please her that a man she had chosen to be with would find her so desirable, he could not stay away. She could not understand how a woman would not want that power over a man.

She felt Piers's stomach muscles tighten, and she felt his fingers come into her hair, run through it, entwine with it.

It was different for a *poule*, who had to be with almost any man who had the price of it. Those women, the ones who complained so much, they should have a little *foutre* with some of the *mecs* she had been with. It would teach them how different it was to give to a man who loved you. And she believed that Piers did love her, in his way.

She felt his fingers tighten slightly in her hair, and a small smile formed on her lips. She wondered if she loved him. She had told herself she did, then had forced the idea away, had told herself not to be a fool. But the feeling had returned again and again.

He was a man of power, she could tell it was so. And so young. She had been with others like that. Meme and Antoine were such men. But they just took what she had as their due, and she never felt the need in them. Piers—what a strange name, she thought again. With him there was so much need, so much surprise, that she *wanted* to make him happy. At first she had thought he would be just another *mec* the Pisanis had forced on her. And she had wanted to steal from him, even though she knew it would be dangerous to do so. She liked to steal from her *mecs*. But with him it had been different almost from the start.

The way he had stood in the kitchen, talking to her. He had been like a young boy waiting for the right moment to ask for a date for the first time. And even after they had been together, he had taken her to lunch and talked to her about her life in Lyon, and about his own life, and about the things he had done as a boy and as a young man. He had not talked about what he did to earn his bread—still did not talk about it—but she understood that. Some men could not talk about such things. And he was gentle with her. And tender. And she wondered if it meant he was a tender man. She did not know. But she knew he did not treat her like a *poule*, and that, more than anything else, made her want him.

His breath was coming faster now, and she reached for him, took him in her hand, and began to stroke him. It was so pleasurable to touch him there. He was so hard and yet so soft and smooth at the same time, and she could feel his long, slender *piqûre* jump in her hand with a will of its own.

She was so wet now, so very wet, and she wanted him inside her. But she would wait. First she would take him in her mouth, and then she would let him do the same to her, if he wanted. The faint trace of a smile returned. But he always wanted that. He knew it drove her to a frenzy. But she wanted it too. And then she would have what she wanted most of all.

"Do you love me?" she whispered.

"I love everything about France," Piers said. "Especially you."

CHAPTER

24

Two hundred men and women and children gathered in front of the labor exchange, carrying banners and placards demanding higher wages and more jobs and lower prices for food. They were only a fraction of the eighty thousand on strike throughout the city, but their numbers were duplicated many times in many places. But it was this time and this place the Pisani brothers had chosen to let some blood.

The strikers had chosen this new tactic—the presence of women and children—to stop the attacks that had come randomly every day, reasoning that the thugs would not risk the public outcry of having French women and children beaten in their own streets.

But the Pisanis had chosen this group for just that reason. It was an escalation of terror; it forced the strikers to recognize there would be no safety, no sanctuary; no person, or place, or situation that could shield them from inevitable violence.

The Pisani men—some forty strong—had gathered out of sight a block north of the demonstrators, armed with clubs and lead pipes and blackjacks and brass knuckles, weapons designed to maim but not to kill if wielded by experts. And if the Pisani men were nothing else, they were experts at dispensing mayhem and pain.

A large contingent of police were to move in first, ostensibly to set up barricades, but also to strip the strikers of any obvious weapons. The police would then withdraw several blocks to the south and await the Pisani attack. When the demonstrators were driven toward them, they would use it as an excuse to strike out at a mob rampaging through the streets, using their own clubs to beat them down. It left the demonstrators trapped between assailants and would-be protectors with no hope of escape.

Piers Moran watched from a rooftop several blocks to the north. He felt like a general in Napoleonic times, viewing his troops from a nearby hilltop, waiting to see how the battle would go, and to make adjustments to any unanticipated moves by the enemy. But there would be no unanticipated moves. This was a battle between lambs and wolves, and the outcome was predestined. Piers thought he should be sitting atop a horse—a large white one—just to make the illusion complete.

The Pisani men moved in mass, slowly, casually, almost like a group of young men on their way to a sporting event. When the strikers saw them they were momentarily defiant, taking heart in their greater numbers. They moved the women and children to the rear and prepared to fight. But when the first blows were struck and the first line of strikers crumbled to the ground, it was obvious their numbers meant nothing. Within minutes of the attack the strikers were beaten, and they broke and ran, fighting only to shield the women and children from the pursuing thugs.

The children were spared—the Pisanis, ever conscious of their image, had so instructed their men—but not so the women. It was regarded as a further defeat, a further humiliation, that the workers were not even able to protect their wives and girlfriends from harm.

From the rooftop, through a pair of field glasses, Piers watched a young woman stumble and fall. She looked about the same age as Colette, he thought, and he could tell that she was quite beautiful. She started to rise, but a club came out of nowhere and smashed into her face. She fell back unconscious, her features covered with blood.

Piers winced at the sight, then raised the glasses to follow the crowd. He watched the Pisani men stop about a block before the police line, then slowly begin to disperse. But the strikers continued rushing toward the safety of the police cordon. Then the police charged, wielding their clubs with equal viciousness, and the crowd's retreat turned into a rout with people scattering in every direction, knowing now that safety would be found only in continued flight.

Piers lowered the glasses, his face expressionless. These were beaten people, he told himself. They had been beaten down by the

Nazis, and then the Nazis had been driven away and they had rediscovered their balls. But they had had a savior then. Now they were being beaten by their own people. And there was no savior in sight. It would only be a matter of time, and a matter of escalation. There was no question of the outcome.

Days after the beatings in front of the labor exchange, the strikers changed their tactics. They abandoned their use of smaller groups of demonstrators spread throughout the city, opting instead for larger shows of force. Demonstrations that numbered in the thousands were called for, but the violence had already taken its toll on the minds and hearts of the strikers, and fifteen hundred was the largest crowd the organizers were able to muster at one time. And women and children were told to remain at home.

But the Pisanis changed their tactics as well. Their men attacked not with clubs and pipes and blackjacks, but with pistols and sawed-off shotguns, firing at the legs of the demonstrators, still trying to maim rather than kill. But some were killed, the few hapless souls who fell to the ground and into the murderous line of fire.

Again Piers watched from a nearby rooftop, and again he saw these larger crowds routed. He was convinced more than ever the strike was drawing to a close.

But the murders produced an unexpected backlash, and the number of demonstrators suddenly grew. Piers was stymied. He could not order wholesale slaughter, and even the Pisanis and the police combined didn't have the strength needed to overcome demonstrations that had suddenly grown to three and four thousand people.

He decided on another approach. And that would require seeking the help of the French government in Paris, something he had hoped to avoid.

Upon his return from Paris, Piers strolled through Marseilles's old quarter, listening with interest as Meme recited some of its more recent history. All about them the buildings were scarred and battered, with huge chunks torn away, and workmen busied themselves on scaffolds, making long-awaited repairs.

"The people of the quarter rose up against the Nazis in 1943," Meme explained. "The Germans found the entire area uncontrollable, so they simply turned out the forty thousand who lived here, then trained their heavy guns on the area and blasted it to ruin." He nudged Piers lightly in the ribs. "Not much different from what you have arranged," he said.

Piers had heard from Paris that morning that the minister had agreed to his plan. "Except my plan is only bluff and bluster," he said.

"That is why it was accepted so quickly in Paris," Meme said. "They understand bluff and bluster there. They thrive on it. It is like their mother's tit to them."

Piers smiled inwardly. "And to think I almost didn't go to Paris," he said.

"Why?" Meme asked.

"No one in Washington cares to do business with the DeGaulle government, or have anything to do with *Le Grand Charles*. Oddly enough, it turns out he and his minions are just as terrified of the communists as our people in Washington are."

Meme gave him a sidelong glance. "And you," he asked, "are you terrified of this communist menace? Now that you have seen it?"

"The communists don't have the chance of a snowball in hell of taking over this country," Piers said. "But those who hold the power in Washington believe they have. And to tell them otherwise would be very foolish for a man of ambition."

"You certainly will never be accused of lacking ambition," Meme said, slapping his friend on the shoulder.

Piers laughed. The powers in Washington would soon see how great that ambition was. The thought kept a smile on his lips. He was feeling almost lightheaded with his impending success. Tomorrow's newspapers would announce the decision of the French government to mobilize two hundred thousand troops and eighty thousand reservists to force an end to the strike, and the following day Gaston Defferre's newspaper would break the news of Piers's own part of the plan. It was December 7, the anniversary of "the day that would live in infamy," and Piers was about to launch his own sneak attack against the workers of Marseilles.

"Why is it that Parisians and the people of Marseilles hold each other in such disregard?" Piers asked, still smiling to himself.

"It is a conflict of the spirit," Meme said. "Paris is a city of monuments, and those who live there view themselves as monumental." He waved his arm in a grand gesture. "Marseilles is a city of people."

Piers laughed again. He was truly beginning to enjoy Meme and Antoine, and he had begun to value their friendship, and to recognize what it could mean to him in the years to come.

"I think your plan will work," Meme said at length as they continued along the narrow street.

"I'm certain it will," Piers said.

"But you must be careful about how you make it work," Meme warned.

"How so?"

"Well, it is all right to turn a man into a beggar," Meme said. "But when you do it, you must be able to point the finger at another villain."

"I intend to," Piers said. "Or, rather, Gaston Defferre will do it for me."

"Are you sure you can trust him?" Meme asked. "He's a politician, and they tend to look to their own interests first."

Piers grinned almost boyishly. "It *is* in his interests. I'm sure my masters wouldn't want me to tell you this, but I would have anyway. Just in case Gaston plans to shake you down for political contributions." His smile widened. "Washington has decided that Gaston should be mayor, and that his Socialist party should be dominant here in Marseilles. So they've given him a million dollars, with the promise of more to come each year. Providing he plays by the agenda we set."

"*Mon dieu,*" Meme said. The sum was staggering. He nodded. "It will be nice leverage for us to have when he does come begging. Or if he decides to do other things that might offend us."

"Leverage is always nice to have," Piers said.

On December 9, with the city already fearful of the impending assault by French troops, Gaston Defferre's Socialist newspaper, *Le Provençal,* announced that the American government was preparing to ship sixty-five thousand sacks of flour, intended to ease the city's hunger, back to the United States, unless dockworkers began to unload them immediately. In a front-page editorial, the paper also accused the Communists of leading the workers into a bloodbath, followed by starvation.

The specter of violence and hunger was too great, and that same day the Communist-led labor coalition called for an end to the strike, and workers immediately returned to work. Piers Moran had his victory, and it proved as sweet as he had hoped.

Christmas Eve, 1947

The party was held in the afternoon, hosted by the Pisanis in Club Paradise, and was attended not only by members of the *milieu* but by politicians of every stripe, save the Communists. It was a men-only affair, and the Pisanis had emptied their brothels of prostitutes to serve as companions for the evening.

Piers Moran was a special guest of honor, and he found that fact, and the overall environment, more than a little amusing. He had never spent Christmas Eve in the company of hookers and gangsters, and it made him feel like a time traveler who had been transported back to a Roaring Twenties party hosted by Al Capone. He wondered if he would ever be able to tell his wife about it.

Colette clung to Piers's arm, watching the other *poules* work the crowd, offering their favors, as instructed, to any *mec* who sought them. But she was special. She would be only with Piers, and she knew the others were deeply envious of her unique treatment.

And she knew Piers was special too. She had finally learned what all the meetings were about, all the violence that had engulfed the city for almost a month. Piers had crushed the insane strike, and he had used the Pisanis to do it. He had done it for his government, had been sent here to do that specific job. And now he was feeding the entire city. He was, without question, she told herself, the most powerful man in Marseilles.

And that power had also fallen to the Pisanis as well. There was no question they were now the most powerful faction in the *milieu*. They had the support of the Americans. And the Americans were the only power that mattered now.

She had seen it earlier, when Marcel Francisci, the Pisanis' most powerful rival in the *milieu*, had come, hat in hand, to the party, a gesture of respect that also acknowledged he was now subservient to them. Colette realized how ideal her position was. She worked for the Pisanis, and she was Piers's mistress. Even more important, she had accepted the fact that she loved him. And, even if he chose to remain married to his wife, it did not matter. She would be his mistress as long as he wanted her.

Piers had also noticed the arrival of Marcel Francisci. He knew who the man was, had even made plans to turn to him if the Pisanis had failed. But that was now moot. Meme and Antoine had done everything asked of them, and would continue to do so. There would be more work ahead, and more problems. Marseilles—France itself—was politically volatile and would remain so until economic reconstruction was complete.

Piers had been placed in charge of the south of France, and it was only a question of time before he would run all CIA operations throughout the country. Then it would take only a few more successes, perhaps over as short a time as the next decade, and he would find himself back in Washington, well on his way up the administrative ladder.

Marcel Francisci came to Piers before leaving. He was of the same generation as Meme and Antoine, and somewhere in between the physical differences that separated the two brothers. He was of average size but trim and well built, and he dressed impeccably but casually, favoring an open-necked shirt under a tailored suit. Like all Corsican gangsters, Francisci wore expensive, highly polished shoes—something Antoine had explained as the product of youthful impoverishment, when lack of shoes was often the rule—and he looked very much like what he was. From his receding hairline to his crooked boxer's nose and square, solid chin, Marcel Francisci was a hoodlum. And he obviously resented being out of the running for toughest kid on the block.

"Monsieur Moran," he began, taking Piers's hand. "My congratulations. Your success has been an inspiration."

"Thank you, Monsieur Francisci."

"My only regret is that I did not have the opportunity to dip my beak into that success," Francisci added. He shrugged. "But such is life."

"Perhaps there will be time another day," Piers said.

"I certainly hope so," Francisci said. "It would be an honor to be of service to you *and* your country."

Piers only smiled in response.

When Francisci had left, Meme made his way across the room. "What did that scum Francisci want?" he asked.

"He wanted your job, of course," Piers said.

Meme grunted. "He would like my job, and my balls hanging from a hook in his office."

"Well, I'll guarantee your job. You'll have to take care of your balls yourself," Piers said.

"I have done so all my life," Meme said. He looked around the room with satisfaction. "How do you like our little celebration?" he asked.

Piers smiled. "As Monsieur Francisci would say, its success is an inspiration."

They laughed, and Piers circled Meme's shoulders with his arm. He glanced at his watch. "Now I'd like to show you and Antoine another inspiration," he said. "It will only take us away from the party for a short time."

Piers, accompanied by Meme, Antoine, and Colette, drove the short distance to the maritime railroad station, which was adjacent to the Joliette Ship Basin. The afternoon sun was bright and warm, cutting the effect of the winter mistral that blew steadily in from the sea.

When they left the car, Piers directed them away from the station and out along the outer seawall, which overlooked both the port and the railyard. A train was just pulling into the station. It held eighty-seven boxcars, carrying flour, milk, sugar, and fruit. A banner running the length of five cars simply stated: "GIFTS FROM THE AMERICAN PEOPLE." Along the station platform hundreds of schoolchildren stood cheering and waving tiny American flags.

Up on the seawall, the four watchers began to laugh.

"*Magnifique*," Antoine said.

"Yes," Piers said. "It is, isn't it?"

CHAPTER

25

Marseilles, 1950

T he causes of the new strike brewed slowly, and the outcome should not have come as a surprise.

It surprised Piers Moran. And it surprised the Pisani brothers and members of Gaston Defferre's Socialist party, who had made dramatic political advances in the intervening three years, but who had not kept touch with the people.

The strike was centered on the docks, and it began in January with what seemed no more than a political protest. The French were embroiled in a war in Indochina against the forces of Ho Chi Minh. The Vietnamese revolutionary was a popular figure in France, and especially among leftist workers in Marseilles, and during his years in France he had helped found the French Communist party. Now, in January, Marseilles dockworkers came to his aid with selective boycotts of freighters carrying supplies to the war zone.

But on February 3, the labor coalition surprised its opponents when it demanded the return of the French Expeditionary Corps from Indochina, and urged workers to take the most effective actions possible against the war in Vietnam. That produced an immediate shutdown of Marseilles's port, along with stoppages in smaller, less important ports along the Atlantic, and by mid-February the strike had spread to the metal industries, mines, and the railways.

But the strike was only indirectly about the war—it was little more than an excuse, a flashpoint. Since 1947 the lot of French workers had not significantly improved. Wages were still low, jobs were still scarce, and the influx of American food had solved only one part of the myriad problems facing the average family.

Yet throughout most of France, the strike was halfhearted, at best, and the Paris newspaper *Combat* reported that Marseilles was once again the hard core, with seventy percent of its dockworkers on strike, compared to only two percent in Bordeaux, twenty percent in Toulouse, and twenty percent in Nice. But the port of Marseilles was the key, and without it France was effectively cut off from the sea.

This inadvertently laid the blame at Piers Moran's doorstep, and threatened to stall, or even kill, his rising star within the CIA.

"We have fucked up royally," Piers insisted when Antoine and Meme arrived at his office in the U.S. consulate. He was seeking to lay blame, and the Pisanis were the easiest target. Over the intervening three years their strength within the *milieu* had grown dramatically, and they had greatly expanded their activities in art thefts, international smuggling, and counterfeiting. At present their illegal bank accounts were bulging with money earned from smuggling "tax-free" American cigarettes from North Africa into France. They had not taken care of business—his business—Piers believed. But then, neither had he, and he knew Meme and Antoine were little more than convenient scapegoats.

Meme and Antoine knew it as well, and they waited in silence to see how far their friend would push his accusations.

Piers paced his office. The two sets of hard eyes that bored into him were quickly bringing him back to reality. Blame, passed on to his masters in Washington, would not solve the problem. It would only allow his star to sputter on until he brought the dockworkers of Marseilles to heel. And he couldn't do that without the Pisani brothers.

"Shit," he said as he fell back into his chair. Coarse language was uncommon for Piers, and two epithets in two sentences only emphasized the stress he was under.

"We should have listened to what the people were grumbling about. Washington should have listened, or Defferre. *Somebody* should have listened to them." Piers knew that somebody was he. Now his newly found power was slipping away because he had chosen to ignore the obvious. The only saving factor was that his

CIA superiors and the State Department had ignored the warnings as well. So they would cover their asses, and also his, at least temporarily.

"If we don't control the docks, we don't control Marseilles," he said. "And the coalition can shut us down whenever they want." He sat forward, squeezing his eyes with thumb and index finger. "How many people, loyal to your faction, do you have working on the docks?" he asked.

"A few hundred," Antoine said. "But they are *durs*, tough ones, and there are other Corsicans there who will do as they are told."

Piers knew that more than ten percent of Marseilles's population was Corsican, but it still wasn't enough. They would have to go to war with the strikers again. It would be the only way to end the strike quickly. And that was what Washington would expect. The same results Piers had achieved three years ago.

"Perhaps the government can threaten to send in troops again," Meme suggested.

"We can ask," Piers said. "But the political climate is different. The best we can hope for is to use troops to help the non-striking workers load ships. And we'll still have to get them across the picket lines."

"We'll get them across," Antoine said. "You tell me when and how many. I'll shove their strike so far up their asses, they'll choke on it."

Piers smiled for the first time. Meme and Antoine were better dressed and more affluent, but they were still the same men he had discovered three years before. And they had considerably more men and power now.

"We'll need more of your men working on the docks," Piers said. "You're going to have to shove them down the labor coalition's throat, but we have to have them there." Piers thought a moment. "And be careful," he said. "We don't want any union martyrs. I want them seen as failures, not as heroes."

"We will see to it," Meme said.

When the Pisanis left, Piers remained behind his desk reflecting on the causes of this near debacle. Even the fact that the brothers had been here, in his office, demonstrated how careless and cavalier they'd all become. He looked around at the trappings of his office.

It showed it as well. Great effort had gone into it—largely with his wife, Cyn's, help. He was a firm believer in the effect of display, and had used his own money—and his wife's—to achieve the desired result.

He had brought his family to France in 1948, and housed them in an aging villa outside Aix-en-Provence, some thirty kilometers north of Marseilles. And he had found Colette a new, and more fashionable, apartment off the Boulevard de la Corderie. He had literally been living the life of a French aristocrat, and like many of those self-indulgent libertines, he had forgotten to take care of business along the way. It was a mistake he vowed not to make again.

But that had been largely Cyn's fault, he told himself. If only she were a bit more like Colette. If only there were a bit more sin in Cyn. Then the indulgence would not have been necessary.

The thick carpeting and rich leather furniture stared back at him now, almost as a reproach. In 1947 he had virtually worked out of a closet, had roamed the streets and alleyways with Meme and Antoine, and had not been afraid to get his hands dirty. He would get back to that, he told himself, and he would use this setback as an object lesson not to be forgotten.

Antoine pushed his way into the Communist union's strike headquarters that had been set up in a warehouse office on one of the docks. Antoine was backed up by five of his men, but had he come alone he would have met with little resistance. Such was the new power of the Pisani faction.

The union leaders—five of them—were in the midst of a meeting when Antoine kicked open the door. Not only had these men resisted adding new members of the *milieu* to their work force, they had threatened to fire those already on the payroll for refusing to honor the strike.

The men jumped to their feet as Antoine burst through the door, but it was more out of shock, and fear of survival, than any move to fight. Only the union head, a grizzled old Resistance fighter named Jules Millau, stood his ground.

"It is easier, Monsieur Pisani, to use the doorknob rather than your foot," he said.

Antoine glared at him. "The doorknob is going up your ass,

followed by my foot," he snapped. "And you will be buried with it sticking out of your mouth unless I get the action I want without delay."

Millau paled. Not because he was a man easily frightened, but rather because he was one who understood reality.

"This is a union matter," Millau said. "It is not a personal assault against your group."

"I have made it personal," Antoine said. "And I intend to make each of you pay personally if you continue this strike."

"But that is madness," Millau shouted, losing control of his tongue. "You cannot tell us how and when to strike. We are a free labor union."

"You are a bunch of communist pigs," Antoine shouted back. "And I will herd you all to the slaughterhouse myself."

The others shrunk back, but Millau's anger grew.

Antoine motioned with his head to the men behind him. "I want these men put to work at once," he snapped. "And I will send more tomorrow, and more the next day."

Millau leaned forward, his fists supporting his weight on the table that separated them.

"Not only will these men not be hired, monsieur, but I will go out to the docks and fire the other scum you have working here."

Antoine's hand shot out before Millau could react, and grabbed him by the throat and dragged him across the table. His other hand grabbed the seat of Millau's pants, and he propelled him out the door, through the warehouse, and out onto the dock. There he shifted his hand so he had a firm grip on Millau's testicles and his throat, and lifted him off the ground and threw him into the harbor.

Antoine stared down at the union boss as he came to the surface sputtering and splashing in the oily water.

"I do not think he can swim," one of Antoine's men said.

Antoine continued to stare at Millau. "Then he will drown," he said as he turned and walked away.

Other dockworkers pulled Millau from the water, and within the hour the five Pisani men were at work on the docks. The next day, twenty more joined them, and the day after that, fifty more were added to the work force.

Piers stared at him in disbelief. "Jesus Christ, Antoine. I specifically told you we didn't want any martyrs."

Three days had passed before Piers heard of the incident, and Antoine had just confirmed it. But by now the fruits of the act were already obvious. Pisani men were everywhere on the docks.

They were sitting at the bar of the Pisanis' new nightclub, The Parakeet, which was still being readied for its grand opening. Piers shook his head, part in wonder, part in frustration. "The fool could have drowned," he complained.

"A man who cannot swim should stay away from the water," Antoine said. "Perhaps he has learned a valuable lesson."

Piers shook his head again and fought back laughter. That morning he had heard from Paris that French troops would be arriving in two weeks to begin working the docks. There was nothing that could dampen his elation, and his only concern now was to get them across the picket lines.

"Your men will have to be ready when the troops arrive," Piers said. "I want them moved across without one soldier being hurt."

"They will go across smoothly and quickly," Antoine promised. "They will go across like shit coming out of a frightened man."

Piers's wife, Cynthia, was working in her flower garden when he arrived home that night, checking rose bushes that had been banked and covered for the winter. She was a beautiful woman with light blond hair, blue eyes, and a slightly vapid smile. She seemed aloof, not because she lacked warmth, but rather because she was a bit unaware of all that surrounded her and preferred it that way. She liked order—in her life and her garden—and became ruffled when she discovered it wasn't there.

The two boys were playing at the rear of the long, sloping yard behind the house. Richard, who was six, was attempting to climb a tree that was too much for him, and little Alex, just three, was watching with enthusiasm, jumping up and down and clapping his small hands.

Piers watched the scene and was grateful for it. It seemed perfect, an ideal that any man should envy. But he should have a drink in hand as he viewed it, he thought. Then the picture would be complete.

His wife looked up as his shadow fell across her, and she smiled, rose to her feet, removed her gardening gloves, and extended her cheek for a kiss. Another perfect picture, he thought. It was all so genteel.

"Are you home for the night?" Cynthia asked.

Piers made a face. "Afraid not. I'll have to go back in, but I wanted to steal some time with you all."

Cynthia looked slightly mournful, then brightened. "I swear, the garden is going to bloom by March if this weather keeps up. Don't you agree?"

"It could indeed," he said.

The boys had seen him now and were running toward him across the wide lawn. Richard was out in front, legs pumping in that slightly awkward way of young boys who have not yet achieved full coordination; Alex behind, tottering from side to side, a great grin on his face.

Richard stopped at his side, breathing hard, and began jabbering about needing a ladder for his tree. Piers ruffled his hair, then scooped up Alex as he fell into his legs and raised him up to sit on his forearm. The child hugged his neck and kissed him. Then he too began talking about the tree, asking if he could climb it, even though Richard said he couldn't.

"When you're a bit older," Piers said. He looked down at Richard. "We'll try to build a ladder this weekend," he added.

All that settled, the boys ran off again, and Cynthia led Piers up to the terrace that ran along the rear of the old stone house. It was a wonderful house, Piers thought. An old *manoir*, parts of which dated back to the fourteenth century, it had been the ancestral home of an aging count who had not been able to hide his money from the Nazis and was now forced to rent it out to avoid losing it.

They sat on the terrace, and a maid brought them two dry martinis, which she had been taught to make. It was unseasonably warm for February, more like April.

"How were the boys today?" Piers asked.

"Wonderful," Cynthia said. "But Alex is beginning to ask the strangest things. He asked me today if flowers went to heaven when they died, or if they were just born again the next year. It was almost as though he'd been thinking about reincarnation."

Piers laughed. "I doubt that. It seems like a natural progression of thought."

"Do you think so? Goodness, I didn't."

They sipped their drinks in quiet, enjoying the mild weather,

Cynthia watching the boys, who were back at the tree again, Piers thinking how much he enjoyed the few moments of peace he was able to snatch from the madness that surrounded him. But he loved the madness too, he knew. There was an adventure about it he had always wanted in his life.

"When will you have to go back in?" Cynthia asked.

"An hour. Two at the most."

She offered a mock pout. "Will you be very late?"

"Mmm. Might even have to stay in the night."

"I suppose you'll be with those dreadful Pisani brothers."

She knew about the strike, had read about the violence that surrounded it. But she preferred not to talk about it. She had met the Pisani brothers once, when she and Piers had given a house-warming party, and she had avoided all contact thereafter. It was easier, more comfortable, to blame them for her husband's work.

"They're not so dreadful, Cyn." He laughed. "Well, they are dreadful, but they're very useful to me, and I rather enjoy them. It's like going to a zoo and seeing the dangerous animals, minus the bars."

"They *should* be caged," she said. "When I read about them in the papers, I shudder that you have to deal with them."

He was surprised that Cyn read that type of news at all. "The newspapers exaggerate," he lied. "They're crooks, but they're not killers. They're just different from the type of thief you're used to. They don't steal on the stock market. They do it the old-fashioned way. With guns. Or, rather, they have people who do it for them."

"I think they're despicable. And, worse, they're crude."

Piers laughed again. "You think with better manners, you'd find them more agreeable?"

Cynthia ignored him. "I understand they run brothels as well," she said, as though it were a final debasement.

"Well, that's somewhat of a French tradition," he said. "Some Frenchmen are too old, or lazy, to procure for themselves."

"Well, don't you partake," she said. "Not even if they offer."

Piers smiled at her. "I'm neither too old nor too lazy," he said.

Cynthia slapped at him playfully with her hand.

After dinner Piers sat with Alex on his knee, listening to the eclectic series of events that had fascinated the child during the day. Richard was working on a puzzle spread out on the stone floor, agonizing over one small piece, determined to find where it fit among the hundreds scattered before him.

Cynthia sat on a nearby sofa, flipping through a Paris magazine, her brow wrinkling in disbelief from time to time. "Who wears these clothes?" she said to no one in particular. "They're so outlandish."

"No one wears them," Piers said. "They're intended as a statement of the lines fashion should follow. Besides, no one has the money to buy clothing now. Not in Europe anyway."

"It seems a shame," Cynthia said. "About the money, I mean."

"They'll get it back. There are fortunes to be made in the reconstruction that's already begun."

"Yes, but the wrong people always seem to make *that* money."

"It's because they know how to work," Piers said. "The aristocrats, and pseudo aristocrats, never had to learn that undervalued art."

Cynthia raised an eyebrow. "You're feeling rather egalitarian, aren't you?"

"It comes from hanging about with the Pisani brothers," he said.

She gave a mock shudder. "I'm glad no one will ever have to know about that," she said. "There is some merit, after all, in being a spy."

"I'm not a spy," Piers teased. "I'm a cultural attaché, or military attaché, or whatever type attaché the agency prescribes."

"What's a spy, Daddy?" Alex asked.

"Someone who sneaks up and watches people when they're not looking," he explained.

"I sneak up on Richbird," the child said, using his name for his brother.

"Rich-ard," Richard said, not taking his eyes off the puzzle.

"My God, Cyn, the boy's a spy," Piers said in mock horror, eliciting giggles from the child. "We'll have to send you to your room without any supper."

"I ate supper," Alex said.

"Then we shall have to. . . ." he paused, drawing the word out. "We shall have to *tickle* you until you promise not to spy anymore."

He ran his fingers over the boy's ribs, bringing on squirms and giggles and false protestations. He put the child back on the floor, then glanced at his watch.

"Have to go," he said.

"No, Daddy, no," Alex said, reaching up to hug him, hold him there.

"Afraid so," Piers said.

He ruffled the boy's hair. He did not believe in kissing little boys.

Colette was waiting for him when he arrived. She was dressed in sheer lounging pajamas he had bought for her, and the flowing, clinging material accented every line of her body with just enough mystery to provoke erotic fantasies about what lay beneath. They had maintained their relationship for the past three years, the arrival of his family causing only a slight alteration in his routine. But excuses were easy, on all sides. And the nature of his work removed any difficulty.

He had found her the large, airy apartment in which they now stood, and had decorated it himself, or rather, led her to choose things that would please him. It was somewhat like *Pygmalion*, he thought, but there were still touches of the gauche—things she had brought with her—that, no matter how much he hinted, she would not part with.

Colette slipped her arms about his neck and kissed him with heat, and led him immediately to the bedroom. He had made her leave her job at the brothel, claiming he feared disease, and telling himself he simply did not wish to make love to her with the remnants of others still clinging inside her. But he simply did not want to share her, although he often asked her to describe in lurid detail what she had once done to the *mecs* she had serviced. It greatly aroused him, he found. He particularly liked one story—and often fantasized about it—about a man with an enormous cock, and the difficulty she had had taking it in her mouth, and how much she had hated it. The story seemed to provide him a special comfort.

She began to undress him now. She liked to undress him, liked him to undress her. It was something Cyn had never done, never thought of doing, he believed. And he knew it was something Colette had never done in the brothel. She had told him so. There, the routine was predetermined. She would be dressed only in a robe when the *mec* arrived, and as he undressed, she would remove the robe and go to the bidet and wash herself to assure him she was clean from the one before him. Then she would go to him, collect her money, and ask what he wanted. If he wanted her to suck him, she would put the condom she always carried in one hand discreetly in her mouth. She had been taught how to put it on a man with her mouth, without his knowing, and she said she always enjoyed the surprise on the *mec*'s face when she had finished and he saw the full condom on his cock. She had done it for Piers, at his request, and he had been amazed to find he had never felt a thing.

He lay on his back and she ran her lips over his body, his chest, his stomach. She was bending over him, kneeling to his side, her legs spread so he could reach out and play with her. She wanted him to touch her, to feel how wet she was for him, and as his fingers excited her clitoris, she lowered herself closer and closer to the bed, until she was almost pressed against it, squirming with pleasure.

She came against his touch, and took him in her mouth as she did, playing her tongue wildly against the shaft of his penis, then taking it in her hand and, holding it away from her mouth, licking it. She liked the way it became even harder when she did this. "Blue steel," he had called it, and while she didn't understand what that meant, she liked the sound of it.

She loved to give him pleasure, loved the sense of power it gave her to have him so under her control. It was not that she wanted to dominate him, just that she knew when she had him that way he could never bring himself to leave her, could think only of her and what she was doing to him, for him.

She knew he liked to come in her mouth on occasion—thought it was partly because she had never let the *mecs* do that, having always used a condom—and though she didn't particularly like doing it—didn't particularly like the taste of it—she liked doing it for him.

But this time she wanted him inside her, wanted to come again with him thrusting and groaning beneath her, and she climbed onto him and carefully guided him inside.

It was pure pleasure, and she came again almost immediately, as did he, and she leaned down, letting her hair fall to each side of his face, and began kissing and licking his lips. They would make love again, she knew. But this first time was always the best, the most rewarding. She missed him when he was not with her, and when he returned, it was as though he had never been away. And that was the way she wanted it.

"When will you have to leave?" she whispered, barely able to get the words out.

"I'll be staying the night," he said.

She smiled against his shoulder. And already she began to want him again.

CHAPTER

26

The picket line stretched along the entire front of the Joliette Ship Basin, the striking dockworkers moving slowly, almost lethargically, only a few of the men even bothering to speak or joke among themselves. Word had come down from the union that the worst was to be expected, that the government planned to have troops brought across the line and that they would be brought across with violence if necessary.

Already, Pisani "workers," numbering over three hundred, were loading ships in defiance of the strike, filling their holes with war supplies that had been allowed to pile up on the docks. If the picket lines were breached and more "workers" and troops, and more supplies, were allowed to cross, the strike would effectively come to an end. But the strikers would fight that, and their reticence and the absence of humor reflected their determination and also the fear that they would fail. They were tough men, *durs* to the last man. But they were no match for the Corsican gangsters and their weapons.

The Corsicans arrived on the backs of seven flatbed trucks, armed with an assortment of weapons ranging from clubs to shotguns and pistols. There were two hundred of them, and the trucks that carried them stretched across the full length of the line.

When the trucks stopped, a volley of shots was fired at the legs of the strikers, and the Corsicans followed, jumping from the truck beds, already swinging their clubs, offering no chance of retreat or surrender. The strikers fought bravely with hands and feet and clubs of their own, and for several minutes they seemed to be holding off the better-armed Pisani thugs.

Then the attack came from the rear, unexpected by the strikers. The three hundred Pisani "workers" rushed in from the docks, each man as well armed as those from the trucks, and they caught the strikers between them and mercilessly beat them into the ground.

When the French troops arrived a half hour later, their trucks moved past the bleeding and battered remnants of the picket line, whose remaining members were being loaded into ambulances called in by police. The line had been located only two blocks from police headquarters, but not surprisingly, not a single police officer had been present to witness the violence. Miraculously, not one of the strikers had been killed. But several had been maimed for life.

Meme and Antoine were supervising the final details of their new club, The Parakeet, with the help of Colette, who had been called in to advise them. The brothers had sought the former *poule*'s help because they greatly admired the decoration of her new apartment, which they believed she had undertaken completely by herself. It would never have occurred to them that Piers—or any man, for that matter—would have wasted his time seeing to such domestic concerns. And Colette had not said anything to change that belief. She liked the attention and respect she was finally—she thought—receiving.

The Pisanis had men stationed outside along the street, as was their custom, and additional men inside, all of whom were armed. Whenever violence was in the wind they took added precautions. One never knew where, or how, violence would spread.

"I think you should have them paint the trim gold," Colette said. She was dressed in a suit Piers had picked out for her, and looked more like the young wife of an aristocrat than the *poule* they had known for five years, Meme thought. She was twenty-two now, and she had grown more beautiful with the years, he also decided.

"What good would the paint do?" Antoine asked. "The club is only open at night, and it is kept dark. Who will see it?"

Colette gave him a look that said he was a barbarian without saying it, and Antoine grew sullen, then shouted at the workers, ordering them to paint the trim gold.

Colette smiled, then walked over to the bar, where new glasses were being unpacked. She picked one up and held it to the light. "These are very cheap, very ordinary," she said.

"They break," Antoine growled. "They break all the fucking time. You think the donkeys who work for us should be handling crystal?"

She shrugged, put the glass down, and walked away. Each gesture spoke of the uselessness of speaking about such things with such a man.

Meme watched his brother grow more sullen by the moment. He smiled to himself. He was beginning to understand what was happening, beginning to realize that Colette was playing out a fantasy of being the great lady. He liked her for it. She had balls.

"So, what else?" Antoine demanded.

Colette placed one hand on one hip and surveyed the room. "I think you should put down carpet," she said. "Everywhere but the dance floor. It will add some class."

Meme watched Antoine redden. "It is a good idea," he said. "I think we should have carpet. What color?" he asked.

"Something neutral and patterned," Colette said. "So it won't show the dirt." She smiled at Meme. "I'll help you pick it out, if you wish."

If I wish, Meme thought. Two years ago she was still working in the whorehouse, dropping dripping condoms into a wastepaper basket that was half full by the end of the day. Now it is *If I wish*. I could love this woman, he thought. Her balls are as big as my own.

The bomb crashed through the window and exploded three seconds later. It had been thrown from a passing car, and the Pisani men outside had immediately opened fire, killing the two men inside. But they had had no chance of keeping the bomb from being thrown. Nor had the men inside, two of whom would die in the blast.

The three-second delay did give the brothers time to dive for cover. With them it was instinctive, a natural will for survival, and the bomb did little more than soil their clothing and leave them slightly bruised and shaken.

But Colette had no instincts for survival save the coyness of her smile, her beautiful body, and her abilities at using it. She just stood there, confused, uncertain, and the blast picked her up and threw her back amid a shower of deadly debris. When Meme and

Antoine reached her, she was unconscious but alive. The left side of her face was little more than pulp.

Piers found Meme and Antoine waiting at the hospital when he arrived. He had been called and told what had happened, and he had come immediately.

"How bad is it?" he asked when they had secreted themselves in a small office made available by a nurse who had grown up in the Pisanis' village in Corsica.

"She will live," Meme said. "But she will be disfigured." There was a rage growing in him, simmering like a caldron ready to spit forth pain and fury, and it unnerved Piers just seeing it brew.

"But certainly, with plastic surgery . . ." Piers began, never finishing the sentence as what Meme had said sunk in.

Meme turned away, turning his eyes and his rage toward the window.

Antoine shook his head. "He blames himself," he said of his brother. "He asked her to come there to help us with the decoration of the new club." Antoine drew a breath and took Piers's upper arm in one hand. His grip was like a vice. "The doctors," he began, stopping, then starting again. "They say they can fix some of the damage." He gestured helplessly with his free hand. It seemed odd to see Antoine appear helpless, Piers thought. "They can fix some of the bone in her cheek that was blown away, but only some. They can replace the skin, and see to it there is only a little scarring. But they say nerves were destroyed. And there is nothing they can do for that. And her left arm. The nerves were destroyed there too. It will be useless to her. They say . . ." He gestured helplessly again, then dropped his gaze. "She will never be beautiful again."

"My God," Piers said. They had been standing, and he sat in a chair, as though uncertain his legs would continue to hold him up. He seemed to stare at his own thoughts, then surrender to them. He drew a long breath, as if gathering himself again. "Well, we must do what we can for her," he said. "She was a delightful young woman. And to have this . . ." Again he let the sentence die. He ended it by shaking his head.

There was a distance in the tone of his voice, and it caused Meme to turn and stare at him. His eyes were hard, accusing.

"She was only a *poule*," he said. "That is the way the newspapers will describe her. And tomorrow, when people read of it over their croissants and coffee, they will shrug and fill their mouths, and they will forget it." Meme's eyes were black now, a glowing black, but, oddly, his voice had grown softer, terrifyingly so, Piers thought. "But she was *our poule*," he continued. "And we will take care of her."

"We have a house in Corsica," Antoine said. "And she can go there. She will have work, and she will have comfort."

Meme had continued talking as Antoine spoke, but his voice was so soft Piers had not heard the words.

"What did you say?" he asked him.

But Meme was silent now.

"He said, we will also take care of the people who hurt her," Antoine said.

"But I was told the men who did this were killed." Piers was staring at Meme as he spoke, almost as though he were afraid to take his eyes from him.

Meme stared back. "It is not enough," he said.

Piers began to object, then thought better of it.

"Do you want to see her?" Antoine asked.

"Oh, yes. Yes, of course." He stood, looking uncertain of where to go or what to do.

"I will show you," Antoine said.

Colette lay on her back, the left side of her face heavily bandaged, the right side so badly bruised and swollen Piers barely recognized her.

There were tubes coming from her nose and mouth and right arm, and a catheter bag hung from the bed. She seemed barely alive, but the monitors above her head indicated a strong heartbeat, and the doctor he had spoken with in the hall had assured him she was stable and would survive. He thought that perhaps that was the worst that had happened to her.

He seemed uncertain again. Colette's right eye, the only one he could see, was closed, and Piers didn't know if he should disturb her.

"Meme seems very upset," he whispered to Antoine, as a way of marking time. "I hope—"

"It is a business matter," Antoine said, cutting him off.

But Piers thought it was personal too.

He went to the bed and gently took Colette's right hand in his.

Her eye flickered, opened. She seemed to have trouble focusing on him. Then the eye became more steady, and her lips moved slightly, as though she were trying to speak.

He made a hushing sound and stroked the back of her hand with his thumb. "You'll be all right," he said. "You'll be fine. Everything is being done for you."

The words sounded foolish, banal to him, but he struggled on. He could barely stand to look at her, to see her this way, and to know it would never really change.

"You must rest now." Foolish again. "It's best that you rest."

A tear formed in Colette's right eye, then rolled down her cheek, and he could not tell if it came from pain or from what she saw in his face.

Two Pisani men smashed open the door of Rene Gault's house, and Meme and Antoine entered, leaving the men outside. Gault was the new leader of the Communist union. He was the youngest member of the ruling committee, and had taken over when Jules Millau had resigned after being thrown into the harbor. No one else had wanted the job.

Gault had been shaving, and he stumbled down the stairs in his underwear upon hearing the screams of his wife, his face still partially lathered, his legs looking like two frail white sticks that had not seen sunlight in years. He was only thirty years old, but he looked suddenly older upon seeing the men who confronted him.

Antoine pushed his wife into a chair, then turned and wrenched the straight razor from Gault's hand, spun him roughly around like a child, then took him from behind in a great bear hug that pinned his arms to his sides.

Meme came forward, a long, needle-like stiletto flicking open in one hand. The hand shot forward, the wrist twisting and snapping, slicing open Gault's left cheek and cutting the nose so its lower portion hung to one side on a flap of skin. Then he plunged the knife into his left shoulder, twisting it, then drawing it down the length of his upper arm.

Gault screamed in anguish and horror, and Antoine released him and allowed him to fall to the floor in his pooling blood.

Neither of the Pisanis had spoken a word, and they turned now and left the house to the echoes of Gault's sobs and his wife's screams.

The strike was over. On March 13, the government announced that despite a continuing boycott by communist strikers, nine hundred dockworkers and supplementary troops had restored normal operations on Marseilles's waterfront.

It was also the death knell for the communist-led labor coalition and the Communist party in Marseilles. In the next election Gaston Defferre would be elected mayor, and he would rule over the city for more than thirty years.

And the Pisani brothers would rule over the Marseilles docks as a reward for their role in crushing the strike. And with that new power they would control the majority of shipping entering and leaving France for the next four decades.

And most of all, it was another coup for Piers Moran. The strike had been crushed in slightly more than a month, only two weeks longer than the 1947 debacle. Washington was elated, and Piers's star was truly in the ascension. He had just turned thirty years of age.

The Pisanis held a great celebration at The Parakeet club, which had been repaired and completed with the changes Colette had suggested. Even the glassware had been replaced at Meme's order, and it was now a finer quality, and would remain so for as long as it lasted.

Colette was at the Pisani house in Corsica. The initial surgery had gone as well as could be expected, and she would have to wait before more reconstruction could be attempted. She had insisted on keeping house for them—to earn her bread, she said—and Meme had agreed to her wishes and had given her a generous salary. He had also had all the mirrors removed from the house.

Colette had not seen Piers again. He had written, had sent flowers, but he had never again visited the hospital. She understood. It simply confirmed all she had ever thought about herself.

The party was well attended. The members of the *milieu* and the city's new political powers all came to pay homage to the Pisanis, who, it was known, had been given complete control of the waterfront by their American friends.

Piers arrived with another man, a tall, swarthy American with eyes that seemed a mirror image of Meme's.

After greeting everyone present, Piers asked the brothers to join him and his friend in the small office at the rear of the club.

There, Piers explained that he was leaving Marseilles, was being placed in charge of CIA operations for all of France. It would force a move to Paris, he said. But it was something that could not be helped. He only hoped the distance would not alter their friendship. He was assured by the brothers that this could never happen.

He then introduced the man with him and explained that he had performed a great service for the OSS during the war and now sought a favor in return.

Meme nodded. He understood completely. It was the way things were done.

"Our friend has run into some difficulty in Italy," Piers said. "There were certain services being performed there that are no longer possible. The Italian government—under pressure from my government, I'm afraid—has placed some severe restrictions on its pharmaceutical industry. And it has made it impossible to have . . . certain commodities processed there. We would like you to consider performing that function here in Marseilles," Piers said.

Meme looked at the other man for further explanation. The man nodded. He did not speak French, but the Pisanis' English was good enough for him to be understood.

"I have the ability to have opium delivered from Turkey," he began. "And I understand you gentlemen have the ability to bring anything through the Port of Marseilles that you want." He gestured with both hands, indicating his admiration of the Pisanis' power.

"I need this opium processed into number four heroin, and I would like to have it done here by men of respect and trust. I am told that you are such men, and I believe that."

The man leaned forward, his hands clasped before him as a gesture of sincerity. "Associates of mine in America have spoken with friends in Sicily, and have been assured you are men of great honor. So we want to form an alliance with your faction—become partners in a way—and I can assure you there will be profits for all of us if you agree."

Meme nodded, then shrugged. He had heard of this man, knew he was a serious person. "The only problem I see is that we know nothing about operating this type of refinery," he said.

"This is not a problem," the man said. "Any chemist can do

this. And I'm told the war has made beggars out of many here. Security is the problem," he said. "And my people have no way of providing that in France."

Meme glanced at Antoine and received a supporting nod. "Then we have no problem," he said. "And our faction will be happy to serve you if we can agree on a price."

Piers leaned forward, imitating the other man's gesture. "I can assure you that's a matter you need not concern yourself about," he said. "If there are ever any problems—about anything—you can bring them directly to me. Whether my office is in Paris or Washington or wherever. You have my word on that."

Meme looked at the other man for confirmation. It was always best, he knew, to settle potential disagreements before they happened.

Lucky Luciano rose and shook both of the brothers' hands. "Price will never be a problem between us," he said.

CHAPTER

27

Piers Moran arrived in Cervione with his son, Alex, who was now ten years old. His elder son, Richard, was away at boarding school in the United States, and Piers decided to bring Alex with him for the annual boar hunt the Pisanis were to host.

Alex had won the brothers' hearts two years earlier—especially Antoine's—when he had accompanied his father to the house-warming of the Pisanis' new home in Marseilles. He had been told then to call them "uncle" and had happily obliged, since he had no uncles of his own. Both Piers and his wife, Cynthia, were only children.

The previous year, when Piers had brought Richard to the hunt, Antoine had been clearly disappointed and had asked why Alex had not come. Then, later, he had heard Richard telling his father, in a disparaging way, that he had seen Antoine pissing off the balcony of the house. It was true, and Antoine saw nothing wrong with it, but since Richard obviously did, it made him a *mouchard*, a squealer, and Antoine could not abide that in anyone, even a child. But Alex was his *pote*, his pal, and Antoine was sure the boy would have pissed off the balcony with him. And then kept his mouth shut about it.

"Ahhhh!" Antoine roared as they stepped from the car that had brought them from the airport. "Here is my little nephew." He scooped Alex up in his arms and kissed him on both cheeks. "Are you ready to shoot a great pig?" he demanded. "One even bigger than me?"

Alex's eyes widened a bit at the thought of it. "Are they really bigger than you?" he asked.

"Some of them," Antoine said. "Fatter anyway." He laughed. "Some of them weigh more than three hundred pounds. Even I am not so fat."

He returned Alex to the ground, and the boy glanced at his father. "Can I?" he asked.

"The boy will hunt with me," Antoine insisted. "He will be safer than in his mother's arms."

"It will be good for you," Piers said. "But I think you may be too young for your own gun."

Alex seemed uncertain by the mixed answer, but quickly recovered and grinned. He turned back to Antoine and received a quick, surreptitious wink. It was as though his "uncle" was saying, Wait, when we are out in the *maquis* there may be a surprise for you.

"When will we go? After the pigs?" Alex asked. There was a touch of awe in the boy's voice.

"Tomorrow morning, before it is even light," Antoine said. "Do you think you can get up that early?"

"Yes," Alex said, wondering if he would sleep at all that night. "I'll be up whenever you say, Uncle."

Antoine smiled down at the boy. He was a handsome lad, with soft brown hair and green eyes flecked with gray, and Antoine thought he looked more like his mother than Piers, though he had met the woman only once. The boy was thin and gangly, as were most boys his age, but he was tall and had wide shoulders, and Antoine knew he would grow into a strong young man one day.

He looked at Piers, still smiling. "It is about time you brought my nephew to shoot pigs with me," he said. "Now come into the house and have a *patis*, and relax. Meme waits to talk business with you, and I will take Alex into the village to see what there is to see."

The house was a large stucco building with a red-tiled roof, not dissimilar to the Pisanis' home in Marseilles, only smaller. It was close to the side of the mountain, just behind and to the south of the village, and it was surrounded by a high stone wall, and reached only by a long, winding drive. The house stood on higher ground than the wall, and from the great terrace that ran along the front and one side, there was a clear view of the distant sea.

Corsicans seemed to need a view of the sea, wherever they lived, Piers thought as he sat on the terrace sipping the licorice-flavored *patis*. He wondered if it was due to their history of constant invasions—a need to see who was coming at them next—or simply to have an escape route always in sight.

Meme was seated next to him, and he asked him, jokingly, which it was.

"Both," Meme answered. "But for escape we would always choose first the mountains and the *maquis*. There a man would never be found, unless he wanted to be. And then . . ." He used his thumb to make a cutting gesture across his throat.

In a large garden below the terrace, Piers caught sight of a woman gathering vegetables. She was dressed in oversized clothing, with a full skirt that hung down to her ankles, and her head was covered with a scarf. But he was certain it was Colette.

He drew in a breath. She had not been here on his previous visits to the house, and Meme had always explained, without being asked, that she was away, visiting relatives in Lyon or seeing her doctors in Marseilles. Piers had been grateful then that she was absent, and he had assumed Meme had planned it that way.

"Is that Colette?" he asked, his eyes still on the woman.

"Yes," Meme said. "Did you wish to speak with her?"

"No," Piers said. "I think it's best I don't."

Meme looked out toward the sea. He was disappointed in his friend, felt a lessening of respect for him. But it was not his business, and a Corsican never criticized a guest in his home.

"How are things going for you in Marseilles?" Piers asked, changing the subject.

"Ahh, Francisci nips at our heels," Meme said. "But they are small nips and not worth killing over. But someday we will have to deal with him. But it will not happen until he thinks we are weak enough." He turned to Piers and offered an uncharacteristic wink. "The trick will be to make him think we are weaker when we are not. Then the other factions will believe he got what he deserved."

Piers knew that within the *milieu*, even the most powerful faction could not attack another, weaker one, without risking broad reprisals. A weaker faction could attack a stronger if it was a question of economic survival, and equals could attack equals for the same reason. But in each case, attacking factions would have to accept the consequences of their actions. It was a question of justice, or rather the Corsican view of it, Piers told himself.

"And how does it go with our Italian friends in the United States?" Piers asked.

"We have no problems with them. The money comes as it always has. If anything, there is too much of it." He shook his head. "So much money is difficult to hide."

"I can help you with that if you need it," Piers said.

Meme nodded. "I have my books here if you wish to look at them," he said.

"No," Piers said. "I have no need to see them." He knew it would be an insult to accept Meme's offer. It would question that what he said was true.

"Tell me something," Meme said at length. "Does it not bother you? This heroin in your country? If it were here, in Corsica, I would kill the men who brought it."

"In my country, it is only used by the blacks, what the Italians call the *melanzanes*, the eggplants. And some musicians," he added as an afterthought.

Meme nodded. "We have them in Marseilles also," he said. "The one are like animals, the other are crazy."

Antoine walked along the dusty road, his arm around Alex's shoulder, stroking and patting him, and pointing out anything he thought might be of interest to the boy. Neither he nor Meme had ever married, and had no children they knew of, but that had been a conscious choice because of the life they lived and the violence that surrounded it. He liked children and often wished he had chosen a different path because of it.

As they walked, Antoine stopped to speak with everyone they passed, and those he spoke with called him *Patriarche*. Alex asked him why.

"It is an honorary title, offered out of respect," Antoine said. "It is the most important thing a man can have in his life, this respect. It is more important than money, than power, even than life itself." He squeezed the boy's shoulder. "You must always remember that, if you remember nothing else."

When they reached the village, Antoine led him up a cobblestone street that rose on a steady incline to the small village square. There was a couple walking ahead of them, dressed in garish summer clothing and trailing a small white poodle behind them on a leash. Antoine gestured toward them with his chin. "Tourists," he whispered. "A Corsican would never own such a silly dog. We want dogs that will chase the pigs. But you will see that tomorrow."

They stopped outside a church, the stucco facade painted a dark yellow, with large, slab stone steps leading up to massive wooden doors.

"Our cathedral," Antoine said. "It was built in 1580 by Alexander Sauli, the bishop of Aleria, and it is named for St. Erasmus, the patron saint of sailors. Bishop Sauli was beatified—that means someday he may be made a saint by the pope, and he must have been a very rich man, because it is said he built the cathedral with his own money." He looked down at the boy and winked. "He had the same name as you," he said. "Maybe you will be a saint one day." He laughed. "Better you should have as much money as old Sauli."

He led Alex around to the side, and they entered the cathedral. The tourist woman had entered ahead of them, the man waiting outside so the dog could lift its leg against a nearby building.

Antoine stopped inside the door, dipped his hand into the holy water font, and blessed himself. Alex did the same, although he was not Catholic and didn't know why he was doing it, other than respect for his uncle. Antoine understood and stroked the boy's head.

They walked up the center aisle, past the lady tourist, and stopped ten yards from the altar rail, where an old man knelt in prayer. The church was small inside, unlike the cathedrals Alex had seen in Paris, and it was badly in need of paint. It was a poor church, he decided, but he thought it was very beautiful.

His attention was drawn back to the altar by the old man, who had risen and turned. There was a fierce look of anger on his face, and he reached into his pocket and withdrew a knife, opened it, and made a cutting motion across his throat. The old man seemed to be staring at them, and as he started forward, Alex instinctively jumped back. Antoine simply turned his head to look behind, unconcerned.

The other tourist had followed his wife into the church, bringing the dog with him. Now he was running, his wife behind him, screaming in French for her life, the dog yelping as it was dragged along, and leaving a trail of urine in its wake.

Antoine threw back his head and roared with laughter. "The French," he said. "They have this unmistakable wish for death."

They left the cathedral, and Alex could see the couple racing down the hill, the old man tottering as fast as he could behind them. The knife was still in his hand.

"Will he kill them?" Alex asked.

"Only if he catches them," Antoine said. "And he is too old, and they are too frightened."

They entered a café filled with men of varying ages, and Antoine walked to the small bar, accepting the greetings of all. The men also called him *Patriarche*, and he introduced Alex as his nephew, explaining that he was from America and could not speak Corsican, but spoke French very well. The men immediately switched to French.

"These men will hunt with us tomorrow," he told Alex. He turned to one of the men. "Show him your scars, Michel."

The man called Michel obliged, raising his shirt to reveal long, jagged scars along his ribs, then lifted his pants leg to show a large gouge in his calf. "*Cochon*," he said. Pig. "They are mean bastards."

Alex's jaw had dropped, and Antoine rubbed his head and laughed. "Tomorrow," he said. "Tomorrow, I predict my nephew here will shoot the largest pig of all."

Several of the men grunted and nodded agreement. "I believe it," one said. "But we must make sure the pig does not eat him first."

That night at dinner, Alex told his father and Meme about the old man in the cathedral. They laughed, and his father said he wished he had been there to see it. Meme said he wished the old man had caught them and had slit their throats—and the throat of their stupid dog.

Alex smiled sheepishly, certain his uncle had not meant what he said. But not completely certain.

He thought about the men in the café, and he remembered his father telling a friend in Paris about one of his boar hunting trips in Corsica. He had described the men who had hunted with him as a group who looked as though they had just been released from prison by mistake. He had not understood what his father had meant then, but now he thought he did.

The men in the café had looked rough and strong, and he thought of Michel showing his scars, and of the look in his eye that said he was pleased to be going out again. He wondered if he would ever be that strong, that brave, and he was suddenly afraid he might show fear on the hunt tomorrow. He hoped that he would not.

Alex wanted to tell his father about Michel and the great scars he carried, and how he must be the bravest man in the village. But he was afraid he might change his mind and not let him go.

He decided that was silly. His father had been on many hunts with his uncles, and so he would have to know about it. Maybe he even knew Michel. And so he told him.

"Yes, I've met Michel," his father said. He glanced at Antoine, a slight look of reproach, mixed with knowing humor, in his eyes. "I think Antoine had him show me his scars before my first hunt." He looked back at his son. "And he is very brave. All the men you will hunt with tomorrow are very brave." Piers rested his elbows on the table and folded his hands before his face. He leaned forward and inclined his head toward his son. "They call the hunt the *battu*, and in the Corsican language that means 'to beat.' And that is what they do. The men go through the *maquis* behind the dogs, and they beat the thick brush with sticks, and they call out to the boar and sing to it, challenging it to attack them. The idea is to drive the boar toward the shooters, who have been placed on the outer edges of the hunt. But sometimes the boar listens to the singing, and it turns and attacks the beaters and the dogs."

Alex's eyes had grown wide, and his father offered him a comforting smile. "But you will be with Antoine, and he will be one of the shooters," he said. "And although the boar may still charge, you will be with him and you will be safe."

"Of course you will," Antoine roared. "There is not a pig in all of Corsica that would have the courage to charge Antoine Pisani."

Meme snorted. "Just make sure you bring some extra pants for my brother," he said. "Just in case he pisses them when he sees the first pig."

Antoine roared again, this time in mock outrage.

"And pay no attention to the scars," Meme continued. "Sometimes I think these men cut themselves with knives when no one is looking just so they will have great stories to tell in the cafés."

He made a slicing gesture with his fork for emphasis. "In Corsica," he added, "it is very important to be looked on as a man who has been brave enough to face danger."

"And has survived?" Piers asked.

Meme shrugged. "Survival is less important. It is the facing of it with courage that matters."

"My Alex will have courage tomorrow," Antoine insisted. "If a boar comes after us, he will bite it on the balls." He glanced at Piers, suddenly concerned he had been too crude in front of the boy. But Piers seemed unconcerned, and Alex was giggling. "And after we kill this pig and eat him, we will have the head stuffed to hang on Alex's bedroom wall. And maybe the balls too." He raised his thumb and index finger, holding them only an inch apart. "Just so his friends can see the little teeth marks," he said.

They were all laughing now, and Antoine began telling about the boar he had shot the previous summer, and how it had killed three dogs before he could see it well enough to shoot. He described its tusks, hooking his fingers along the sides of his mouth, and he grunted and snorted and shook his head from side to side.

"That is why the pigs do not charge him," Meme said. "He is uglier than they are, so they fear him."

The door to the kitchen swung open, and a woman entered, carrying a tray of desserts with one hand. The other hand hung helplessly at the end of a dead arm, and Alex noticed that the left side of the woman's face was also deformed. There was a small hollow place where her cheekbone should have been, and her left eye and the left corner of her mouth drooped. But the right side of her face was beautiful, Alex thought, and when she saw him, she gave him a crooked smile that was full of warmth.

The woman served each of them, placing the tray on the table, then removing a plate, then picking up the tray and moving on again, all with one hand. She did it so gracefully, Alex thought, you hardly noticed her handicap at all.

When she reached his father, Alex saw that he kept his eyes fixed on the table in front of him, and simply nodded his thanks when the woman placed the plate before him. But the woman didn't seem to notice, and she was smiling when she reached his place at the table.

"This is *flan*," she said as she placed the caramel-colored dessert in front of him. "It is a custard, and it is very good, very sweet.

But I have a piece of *gâteau au chocolat* in the kitchen if you prefer it." She glanced across the table at Antoine, her face stern. "I have only one piece," she said. "Antoine ate the rest of it at breakfast. He will eat anything," she added. "It is like living in a house with a goat."

Antoine waved a dismissive hand at her. "Go away, woman," he said. "You are interrupting the talk of men. And bring me that piece of chocolate cake."

"Never," the woman said, and she picked up her tray and returned to the kitchen.

Antoine shook his head, then winked at Alex. "Ah, she is a difficult woman. But, then, all women are difficult, eh, my nephew?"

Alex began to laugh again.

"We will remain bachelors, eh, Alex?" Antoine continued. "It is safer that way."

Out in the kitchen, Colette placed the tray on the counter, then sat heavily in a wooden chair. She used her good hand to place the other in her lap, and felt her fingers tremble against the dead flesh. The child was beautiful, she thought. And well mannered. He had seen her ugliness and he had ignored it. He had not stared at her and made a face, as some children did. She understood when that happened. It happened mostly in France. Here in Corsica, children were used to seeing people who had injuries that had never been properly treated. But in France such people were freaks.

But the boy lived in Paris, and he lived among the *filou*, the sharp operators who had the money and the power. And still he had not shrunk from her. He had smiled, and he had listened to what she said. And his smile had been sweet.

Not like his father, who had been unable to look at her, to speak her name. But she understood that too. She was a *poule*. And she was no longer desirable. And he was a *mec* who had paid for her —just in a different way. She wished now that she had robbed him when she had had the chance. Just like the other *mecs* she had robbed. She had done it to get back at them, she now knew. It had meant just as much as the money.

She squeezed her eyes shut. No, she thought. You would never have robbed him. Not even if you knew what would happen between you. You had loved him too much for that.

Colette opened her eyes and saw the piece of chocolate cake sitting on the counter. She would take it to the boy, and she would see his sweet smile again. And she would see his father.

Alex lay in the large, soft bed, unable to sleep. He was thinking about the wild boars that even now were crashing through the *maquis*, grunting and snorting and shaking their heads from side to side, as Uncle Antoine had done. He wondered if they knew the hunters were coming, if something inside told them it was going to happen. He had studied about animal instincts in school. About how some animals—birds and fish and even large animals—could travel great distances, always going to the same place every year, because something inside them told them it was where they had to be. And the teacher had said that animals knew when danger was coming. A big storm, or a flood, or an earthquake. He wondered if they knew when hunters were coming too. No, he told himself. Then they wouldn't be there when the hunters came. They would have run away and hid.

But maybe the wild boar wouldn't do that. Antoine had said they loved to fight. That they only ran away from sounds they didn't understand. But when they saw something—another animal, or a man—they wanted to fight; they wanted to kill it.

He turned on his side and drew his knees up to his stomach. It would be scary tomorrow, he decided. But it would also be exciting, and he wanted very much to do it. And he would be with Antoine and Meme and his father. And with Michel, who wasn't afraid of anything.

CHAPTER

ntoine came into Alex's bedroom at five o'clock and gently shook him. "Get up, my little donkey," he said. "There are pigs in the *maquis* who need killing."

Alex sat up and looked around, momentarily uncertain where he was. Then he saw his uncle towering over him, dressed in rough clothes and smiling at him. He looked at the window. It was still dark outside, and he wondered how they would see the boar, how they would know where it was.

Antoine seemed to read his thoughts. "It will be light soon, and the pigs will be waking up, and they will be hungry. It is the best time to hunt them. So get out of bed, you donkey, and get dressed."

He stood and watched Alex pull on his clothes, and he could see the excitement building in his face.

"And brush your teeth," he said. "If you stink too much, the pig might fall in love with you and want to marry you." He ruffled the boy's hair. "Then come down to the kitchen so you can eat. You need a full belly to kill pigs," he said.

When Alex came into the kitchen, Meme and Antoine were already there, and the woman who had served the dessert the night before was preparing a basket of food. There were long loaves of bread, and pâtés and large chunks of cheese and sausages.

Antoine saw him eyeing the food. "It is for our lunch," he said. "You will be hungry again by noon. But you can't eat all of it. Uncle Antoine will have to eat too." He patted his stomach. "I get very hungry when I hunt pigs."

"You can eat a tin can, like any goat," Colette said over her shoulder. She turned to Alex and smiled, then pointed at the kitchen table. "Come and sit," she said. "I have croissants and jam and butter. And I have made you some hot chocolate."

"Do I get chocolate?" Antoine asked. He winked at Alex.

"Drink your coffee," Colette said. "And then get out of here, so I can do my work." She glanced at Meme. "Both of you." She banged a dish on the counter. "You both tell everyone you never married because you didn't want to force the life you lead on wives and children. But I know the real reason." She glared at each of them. "It is because no woman would have either one of you."

Alex saw that Meme was smiling, then the smile faded, and Alex turned and saw that his father had come into the kitchen.

He stopped just inside the doorway, and he seemed uncertain about something, Alex thought. Then he walked to the counter and poured himself a cup of coffee.

Piers looked at Meme, wondering if they would leave the kitchen and take their coffee in the dining room. But Meme didn't move, and neither did Antoine, and Alex was already seated at the table, eating his breakfast.

Piers went to the table and sat next to his son. "Are you ready for the hunt?" he asked.

Alex nodded, unable to speak around the mouthful of croissant. Colette came to the table and put another basket of croissants next to his father's arm. Piers seemed to stiffen, then he looked up at her and nodded.

"Thank you," Piers said, then turned back to his son. "So it will be a big day for you," he said, and Alex could tell he was speaking by rote, not really paying attention to what he was saying. He did that sometimes when things were on his mind and he was distracted. He was probably thinking about the hunt, Alex told himself.

They left the house and loaded the shotguns into the trunk of a car and climbed inside, Meme taking the wheel. There was another car behind them, filled with men who worked at the house. But their shotguns were inside the car with them, and they followed closely behind as the cars headed down the long, winding drive.

On the road, other cars waited, headlights on, engines running. There were now eight cars in all, and they drove south along the narrow dirt road at speeds that defied the road itself.

"Corsicans like to drive fast," Meme told Alex over his shoulder.

"And the narrower the road, the faster they must drive. It is like hunting the pigs," he said. "They must show everyone they are brave enough to do it."

The road twisted along the side of the mountain, and in the distance, as the road curved out again, Alex could see another line of headlights, and he knew it was another group of hunters headed for a place where they believed they would find wild boar.

They drove for three or four miles, no more, then pulled off onto a wide shoulder and stopped. The sun was just rising over the distant sea, and below them the *maquis* seemed to stretch endlessly north and south, a jumble of brambles and bushes and small trees, faint in the morning light, appearing so dense as to be impenetrable.

The men climbed from the cars and took up their weapons, and joked and laughed among themselves. They spoke Corsican, which was similar to Italian, and Alex could not understand what they were saying. But he knew they were teasing one another about the hunt. It was the same thing the boys he knew did. And these men were boys again now, at least for today.

Alex liked the sound of their language. It was rough and harsh and musical at the same time. He had seen it written as they had driven from the airport, on the road signs indicating which towns they were passing. The names were in French, but they had been crossed out with paint and the Corsican spelling substituted. His father had said it was the way the Corsicans told the French not to assume too much, not to try to take their language from them.

One of the men opened the back of a truck, and more than a dozen dogs jumped out, barking and running around the legs of the men, taking time only to urinate on nearby rocks before starting again. Alex had thought the dogs would be large and fierce-looking, and a few were, but most were small and were of mixed breeds that seemed to be at least part terrier. They all had large bells hanging from their necks.

"Why are the dogs wearing bells?" he asked.

Michel was standing nearby and he grinned at him. "It is so we can hear them and know where they are. We don't want to shoot a dog by mistake. We lose enough of them to the pigs." He made a cutting gesture along his stomach, dragging his thumb up toward his chest. His grin widened as he did so.

Alex drew a deep breath, the fragrance of the *maquis* filling his nostrils. The smell distracted him from Michel's answer. It was like going into a store that sold perfumes, he thought, or that part of a grocery that had barrels of herbs and spices. He liked the way it smelled. He had never before been to a place that smelled like this.

Alex felt a hand on his shoulder and looked up to see Antoine grinning down at him.

"It is time to go," Antoine said. "It is a long climb down, and it is difficult in parts. If you find a place that is too steep for you, tell me and I will carry you."

Alex knew he didn't want to be carried, and he was glad Antoine left the decision up to him. He would do it by himself. He knew it was important that he did. He wanted his father and his uncles to be proud of him, and not think of him as a baby, as his mother sometimes did.

His father came over and squatted in front of him. "Stay close to Antoine," he said. "And do as he tells you. If you want to come up early, don't be afraid to say so. It will be all right if you do."

Alex nodded. He would never say he wanted to leave the hunt early. He would never do that. Never. Not in a million years.

His father squeezed his shoulder, then rose and joined Meme, and they started down a steep path into the *maquis*.

"Come," Antoine said. "We go on a different path. It is a secret place that only I know about, and there is certain to be a great, ferocious pig there."

Alex went with Antoine, walking beside him where the path was wide enough, falling in behind when it narrowed.

"These are old pig trails," Antoine explained. "Only the pigs and the hunters use them. In the old days the bandits of the *maquis* used them too. But there are no more bandits now." He turned and winked at the boy. "At least that is what we tell the police."

"Why would bandits come here?" Alex asked. "So they could hide and jump out on to the road and rob people?"

"No," Antoine said. "They came here to hide from the police. They were not really bandits. Just men who had some disagreement with the police. Sometimes they would kidnap people and bring them here until a ransom was paid. But they only kidnapped the foreigners who tried to take our country from us. So they were really patriots, not bandits."

They climbed steadily down, traversing large outcroppings of gray rock, and moving around thick tangles of foliage that Alex was sure no man could pass through. In the distance they could hear the beaters and the occasional bell of one of the dogs. The beaters were calling out and singing, just as Meme had said they would, and Alex wondered if another boar would charge Michel, and if he would have another scar to show off in the café.

The sound of the bells also made him wonder if a boar might be close, and he noticed that the double-barreled shotgun Antoine carried was broken open, and that there were no shells in the chambers. He hoped the gun would be loaded before they saw a boar. But he did want to see one, he told himself. He really did.

They climbed down for more than twenty minutes, and Alex's legs felt the strain, and he was breathing hard. But the climb didn't seem to affect Antoine at all, and he moved slowly and steadily, looking back occasionally to make sure Alex was still behind him. Never once, even when they climbed down steep sections of rock, did he suggest Alex might need to be carried. Alex was pleased that he did not.

The path they were on forked at a large outcropping, one path going off and down into a thick maze to the right, the other going off to the left, then rising in the direction from which they had just come.

Antoine moved out on the rock face. A small snake slithered across his path, and he kicked it with his boot and sent it tumbling and writhing into the brush as he muttered oaths in Corsican that Alex did not understand.

His father had warned him there were poisonous snakes in the *maquis*, and that was why he had to wear the high boots he had bought him. He had wanted to wear his sneakers—he always wanted to wear them—but he was glad now he had listened to his father and had worn the thick leather that went halfway up his calf.

"Was that snake poisonous?" he asked Antoine.

"I don't know. It didn't bite me," Antoine said. "The next one we see, I will let it bite, and if I drop dead you will know."

He laughed and rubbed Alex's hair, then raised a finger to his lips. "It is time to be quiet now. To wait and listen for the dogs, so we will know the way the hunt is going, and to watch for old *cochon*."

Alex looked behind him and was surprised to see they were on a precipice with a drop of more than five hundred feet. The outcropping was narrow, and the only way off was the way they had come. If a boar charged them there was no way to run, no escape.

He wondered why Antoine had chosen such a place. He considered it, then thought he had the answer. The boar would have used the paths many times, and it would know there was no reason to come this way, or even look in this direction. So, if it came along one of the paths that forked in front of them, they would see it before it saw them. He decided his uncle was a very smart hunter.

The morning wore on, the sun rising at their backs, the warmth beating down on them. It had been cold early in the morning, and they had worn jackets against it. Now they took their jackets off and dropped them at their feet, and the sun felt warm and dry and comforting.

The sound of dogs—the barking and the bells—came from their right, and Antoine pointed down into a deep ravine. There was a tiny clearing, and a flash of brown moved across it and was gone.

"Pig," Antoine whispered.

Moments later two dogs raced through the same clearing and disappeared again.

"*Cochon* is headed down to the place where Meme and your father are. He won't come up to us unless he stops to fight the dogs, then changes direction." He glanced at his watch. "It is a good time to go up and eat some food," he said. He noted the look of disappointment in Alex's eyes. "We will come back after we eat. This is the time the men usually gather for food." He raised a finger. "Just a bite. It is not time for lunch yet. But we will eat, and we will listen to what the others have seen. And perhaps we will learn some secrets about the way the pigs are running today."

They gathered up their coats and started up again, and Alex wondered how many times they would climb up and down the steep terrain before the hunt was over.

"Do you think Meme or my father will shoot that pig we saw?" he asked Antoine's back.

"It is hard to say. It is very thick down there, and sometimes a pig can be very close, but still you cannot see him." He turned around and tapped his nose. "It is why my secret place is so much better. If the pig comes, we will see him."

The men were gathered on the road when Alex and Antoine climbed out of the *maquis*, some sitting on rocks, eating bread and drinking coffee from thermos jugs, others standing in small groups, speaking of what they had seen that morning.

One, a burly man with bright red hair, was sitting on a long, flat rock with two others, quietly sharpening his knife. When he had finished, he feathered the blade with his thumb and gave it a look of concern. The man beside him had taken off his shirt, and his back was thickly matted with black hair. The redhead slid quietly next to him and, holding the knife like a straight razor, scraped it along his back. Then he looked at the blade, at the bald spot on the man's back, and smiled.

The man, who had been shaved, turned his head and muttered something in Corsican, and the redhead laughed and slid the knife into its sheath.

Alex sat on a rock, eating a chunk of bread smeared with pâté and drinking from a thermos of milk. It was nine o'clock when they had started up, and the new warmth of the sun had made him sweat heavily on the climb, and he felt tired. He watched the men and saw that few of them seemed affected by the heat, and he wondered if they were simply used to it, or were so strong it didn't bother them. He thought about what it would be like in the middle of the day, and he hoped Antoine would stay down longer next time. Then he remembered the great lunch they had brought with them, and he knew he would not.

Antoine was talking with a group of men, and he made comic gestures describing the boar and the dogs they had seen. One of the men pointed down into the *maquis* and made a sweeping gesture with one arm, and Alex thought he was probably telling Antoine how he thought the boar would have gone.

Antoine nodded, slapped the man on the shoulder, then came to Alex, taking a final bite from a huge chunk of bread he was eating. "We go back now," he said. "I have told the beaters about our pig, and they will make a great circle and drive him back to us."

Alex stood, renewed excitement draining the fatigue from his body. "Do you think it will come?" he asked.

"It is hard to tell with pigs," Antoine said. "But I think so. I have decided to tie you to a stick and dangle you over the edge of the cliff. Then the pig will come like a fish to a worm." He cuffed the boy lightly, then pulled him to his side and hugged him. "Come. This old pig is laughing at us, and we must seek revenge," he said.

As they headed toward their path, Meme and Piers came up out of the *maquis*, and Antoine gave his brother a disgusted wave. "There was a pig so close to you, I'm surprised it didn't bite you on the ass," he shouted. "Stop sleeping down there." Meme returned the wave, but Antoine ignored it. "And if you are looking for food, there is none. We ate it all," he roared.

Piers nodded to his son, and Alex noticed he was mopping his face and neck with a large handkerchief, and the sight of it made his legs feel suddenly stronger. At least he wasn't the only one the heat and the *maquis* had beaten down.

The climb down seemed shorter this time, and Alex recognized many of the twists and turns they had taken earlier. The scent of the *maquis* seemed stronger too; it was deeper and richer, as though the sun had baked the foliage and made it more aromatic.

When they reached the precipice, Alex scanned the ground for the snake that had been there earlier, but it had not returned, and they took up their position and stared down into the ravine where they had seen the boar.

They saw the beaters a half hour later, four dogs running in front, their bells clanging as they forced their way through the thick tangle of foliage. Alex could hear the men calling and singing more clearly now. The voice of one man—a heavy baritone—rose and fell several octaves, and the solemnness of the melody made the boy think of someone singing in church.

The beaters turned north, and at times Alex could barely make them out as they were swallowed by the *maquis*. Then they began to make a large circle, and though he could not see them, the sound of their voices told him they had turned and were headed back toward them.

He saw Antoine's body tense, and then he pointed into the ravine. Alex tried to follow where he was pointing, but could see nothing. Then he heard the bells and the barking of the dogs, and he saw them rush through a small clearing and disappear again.

The sound of the dogs was rising toward them, but the foliage was so thick he could not see even the movement of branches. Then he heard the boar, a deep, guttural snorting, almost like short, repetitive growls, and his eyes moved to the sound, but again there was nothing he could see.

The snorting and the barking of the dogs seemed to draw closer together—the sounds were only thirty or forty yards away now, and suddenly there was a great thrashing sound in the brush just below them. Branches snapped, and a thick tangle of brush seemed to wave back and forth, and suddenly one of the dogs yelped, and its body flew up into the air, almost ten feet above the ground. The dog's stomach appeared to be trailing a long, gray cord, and Alex was confused by it, then realized it was the dog's intestine hanging from its body. His arms and legs began to tremble.

There was another yelp, followed by a long whine of pain, and then the crashing stopped and Alex could hear the snorting draw even closer. Antoine had raised his shotgun to his shoulder and was following the sound along the length of the barrel.

The boar broke into a clearing only fifty feet in front of them, and Antoine squeezed the trigger, but the firing pin fell against a dead percussion cap. He cursed in Corsican, then squeezed the second trigger. The shotgun roared, and the boar, struck just above the shoulder, staggered and fell to its knees.

Antoine broke the shotgun and flipped out the shells, cursing and grumbling, but the only word Alex recognized was *merde*, which his uncle repeated several times. His uncle forced two new shells into the chambers, and snapped the shotgun closed. The boar was up now, and it seemed to jump in place to face them, and Alex saw the murderous glint in its small eyes. Never before had he seen a look of pure hatred, and it both fascinated and terrified him. But he realized that his legs and arms had stopped shaking, and he stared at the boar, mesmerized.

The boar came at them like a freight train, with a speed that seemed impossible for its bulk and size, and its head, held low to the ground, moved from side to side, the great tusks that curved up from its snout glinting in the sun.

Antoine leveled the shotgun and fired, and it was almost as though the boar had struck an invisible wall. Its body seemed to stop momentarily, and then it flipped over, coming forward again, its hind legs almost striking Antoine's knee as it fell at their feet.

Antoine let out a long breath, then cursed.

"*Merde*," he said. "I have ruined the head." The boar grunted, its hind legs kicking out, and Alex, his legs trembling again, jumped back.

"Ah, there is still some life in him," Antoine said, and he reached behind him and pulled Alex forward. "You must finish him off," he said, getting behind the boy and fixing the shotgun in his hands.

He adjusted the weapon against the boy's shoulder, helped him level it at the boar's heart, then stepped back.

"Now. Now," he said.

Alex squeezed the trigger, and the shotgun jumped in his hands, the butt slamming into his shoulder and driving him back into Antoine's arms. The body of the boar jumped on the ground, then was still, and as the ringing sound faded from his ears, Alex heard Antoine laughing with unmistakable joy.

"You have killed the old bastard," Antoine roared. "And it is a good pig. Well over three hundred pounds, I think."

He knelt beside the boy and took his shoulders between his large hands, and he could feel him tremble with the fear and excitement of the kill. But the boy had not run, had not cried out in his fear, and Antoine was proud of the courage he had shown. He pulled him to his chest and gave him a great hug.

He stood, still hugging the boy with one arm, and took the shotgun from him.

"Now we must see to the dogs," he said. "I think at least two of them have been killed. But we must put them out of their misery if they are still alive and badly hurt."

He led the boy down to the thick foliage where the dogs had battled the boar. Two of the dogs were dead, and two others were sniffing about their bodies. Antoine kicked at the other dogs, driving them away. He was glad the dogs were already dead. He did not want to have to kill them in front of the boy. He had debated whether he should go to the dogs himself, but had decided the boy must see all of what they had done. It was the only way for him to understand.

Alex stared at one of the dead animals. Its belly was ripped open from pelvis to sternum, and its entrails lay on the ground, still steaming in the air. He thought about the boar they had killed, and of the way it had charged them and the murderous look in its eye. It would have killed us, he thought. Just like it killed the dogs, and he felt no sorrow for the boar they had shot. He only felt sorrow for the dogs.

Antoine led him back to the dead pig, and Alex saw now that there was a large hole in the center of its forehead, and he thought his own shot had been unnecessary, was just something his uncle had done to please him.

He looked up at his uncle and smiled. "I thought you said the boar would never charge you," he said. "That it would be too afraid."

"It must have been a foreign pig," Antoine said. "One that swam to our island and did not know who he was dealing with."

He pulled the boy to him again. "I am proud of you," he said. "You showed great courage, and that is good. You have Corsican honor, just as I knew you would."

He knelt, dipped his thumb into the boar's blood, then stood again, and made a mark on Alex's forehead. "You are a hunter now, and never again will you fear anyone who attacks you." He nodded. "Because now you have Corsican blood, and you have learned the most important truth. You have learned you will not run away."

Alex felt enormous pride, greater than he had ever known.

The beaters made their way into the clearing and gathered around the boar, assessing its size and weight, and examining the shots that had taken it down.

"Three shots, *Patriarche*," one of the men said. "That is a great many for you."

"The boy killed the pig," Antoine said proudly. "And one of the shells misfired, so the first shot was hurried and missed its mark."

The men tied the boar's legs to a long pole, and took turns carrying it up the steep rise to the road. Antoine did not help them. He and Alex walked behind, like great hunters basking in the glory of their kill. The boar's body swayed heavily, its great weight bending the pole, its curved tusks flashing as its head swung back and forth, the tongue protruding from the side of its long snout. Alex felt some sorrow now that the boar was dead. It was a great, powerful creature, he thought, and it must have ruled its part of the *maquis* like a king. It had no enemies except the hunters, and it simply had defended its home against the dogs and the men. He decided the boar was not truly evil, even though it wanted to kill anything that crossed its path. It did not go into the village and attack the people who lived there. That would make it really bad. And he couldn't think of many animals who did that, except some lions and tigers he had read about, that had grown too old to catch food. And, of course, there was man.

He wanted to talk to Antoine about those things, but he thought he would sound foolish, and he didn't think his uncle would understand what he meant. He didn't think his father or his uncle Meme would either. Perhaps he could ask his mother, but only if she promised not to tell his father. He didn't want to tarnish the pride everyone would feel for him. But he wanted to understand what he and his uncle had done. And he wanted to know why he felt pleased they had killed the boar.

There were two more shots as they climbed up out of the *maquis*, and when they had gathered on the road, two other groups of hunters brought up boars that had been shot. Both of the boars were smaller than theirs, and one—which the men said was a sow and weighed less than one hundred pounds—had been shot by Meme.

Antoine teased him about his kill, claiming he and Alex had seen three pigs of that size.

"We just kicked them in the ass and sent them on their way," he boasted. "My nephew and I are hunters. We do not kill piglets," he said.

"You are lucky the boy shot the pig for you," Meme countered. "It saved you from being shamed in front of these brave men."

Piers knelt before the boar, then gave it a firm pat, and looked up at his son. "It's a fine boar," he said. "As large as any I've ever seen." He lowered his voice. "Did you really shoot it?" he asked.

Alex nodded. "But Uncle Antoine shot it first," he whispered in English, to be certain the men would not hear. "I think it was almost dead when I did."

His father smiled at him, pleased by his honesty. "I've seen more than one boar that everyone thought was dead get up and raise holy hell with the hunters," he said.

Alex's eyes brightened, and he stood a little straighter. He was happy his father had told him that.

Antoine came over and lifted Alex up on his shoulder. "Come, my little Corsican," he said. "We have a great pig to show the people of the village. And tomorrow we will cook it and have a great feast."

The men loaded the boars into the rear of a truck, and the caravan of cars drove back to the village. As they drew close, the men blasted the horns of their cars, and the villagers came out to see the day's kill.

People gathered around the rear of the truck, and there were words of praise for the large pig. And when Antoine told them that his nephew had shot the boar, there was praise for Alex too, and several people patted his back and stroked his hair as signs of affection and respect.

Antoine beamed with pride, and he told the villagers that tomorrow there would be a feast at his and his brother's home, and that the whole village was invited to come and eat the pig.

"You may tell your relatives in other villages as well," he said. "This is a great pig, and there will be food enough for everyone."

There were murmurs of pleasure and excitement among the crowd, and Alex thought they somehow felt honored to be invited to the Pisani home. He wondered why that was.

On the drive back to the house, Alex asked Antoine if he really knew how to cook a pig.

His uncle looked at him and raised his chin, assuming an offended pose. "I am one of the great cookers of pigs in the entire world," he intoned. "Books have been written about my secret recipe."

"Books could be written about his eating of pigs," Meme snapped from behind the wheel. "That is truly great," he added.

CHAPTER

29

Antoine stood next to the shallow pit that had been dug in the ground, and basted the boar with a thick sauce, as one of his men slowly turned the handle of the spit from which the pig hung.

Alex stood next to his uncle, watching the boar turn, its skin already a golden brown, the smell of the cooking flesh assaulting his nostrils and making his stomach rumble with hunger. The grounds were already filled with the people of Cervione, the young and the old and the children, and all had brought food to add to the feast. The village priest had come and blessed the food and the boar as it hung from the spit, and Alex had learned that the boar Meme had killed had been cut up and divided among families whose men had died during the year.

Alex played with some of the children, but then returned to Antoine's side and took up his role as joint provider of the feast. He felt very proud to be with his uncle, to have been part of the hunt. And the other children had treated him with a certain awe, and that had pleased him too.

At a long table some twenty yards from the spit, Colette arranged an array of food, leaving a large space for the platter of meat that would be placed there, and which would signal the start of the feast. Children wandered up to the table to stare at the abundance, and Colette sneaked them tidbits and sent them on their way, smiling and laughing.

Alex watched her. The side of her face that was undamaged was turned toward him, and he thought again that she was very beautiful.

"How was Colette hurt?" he asked Antoine.

His uncle's face became somber, and he kept his eyes on the boar and continued basting it.

"She was injured by a bomb," Antoine said. "Some men—some communists—set it off because they could not have what they wanted."

"Why did they want to hurt her?" Alex asked. He was confused, not wanting to believe anyone would want to hurt the woman.

"They didn't want to hurt *her*," Antoine said. "She was just there when it happened. But they didn't care who they hurt. People who use bombs are like that. They are cowards. They have no honor."

Alex looked at Colette again, and he felt sad she had been hurt. But he was happy she had not been killed by the bomb.

"What happened to the men who hurt her?" he asked.

"They were killed," Antoine said. "By men of honor."

Alex was glad the men had died. He wondered if it was wrong to feel that way.

Meme and Piers sat on the terrace, surveying the crowd.

"It is quite a gathering," Piers said. "The people of Cervione show you great respect."

"We are a part of them," Meme said. "And what we have achieved brings honor to them. And we also care for them and help them earn their bread."

He waved a hand down toward the sea. "The vineyard below the village is ours. We bought it several years ago from the Frenchman who owned it." He smiled. "He agreed to our price without much difficulty, and then returned to France to a safer, happier life. The orchards beyond are also ours, and between the two, it provides steady work for many in the village."

He turned his head to Piers and winked. "Some still go to sea, as their fathers and their fathers' fathers did before them. And many of them work for us too."

"It must give you great power and authority here," Piers said.

"It gives us more," Meme said. "It gives us respect, and it gives us safety. Any man who entered this village to do us harm would find an army waiting for him."

"I still notice you have not abandoned your bodyguards," Piers said.

"Only a fool lets down his guard," Meme said. "Even in a place where safety is assured."

The feast went on into the night, and when the villagers finally left, Alex stumbled to his room and fell immediately asleep. He dreamed of the hunt and of the great boar, as he had the night before, and he dreamed of Colette and of the bomb that had destroyed her face.

The next morning after breakfast, he helped Colette work in the garden, while Meme and Antoine and his father talked in the house.

"It's unfortunate you cannot stay longer," Meme said. "You do not visit us often enough, and when you do, the visit is always too short."

Piers nodded. "Not like the old days, when I was practically living in your hip pockets," he said.

"That is because you didn't trust us," Antoine said. "You thought we would kill everyone in sight, then pick the gold from their teeth."

"And you would have," Piers said. He laughed. "Christ, you were a rough lot in those days. It seems impossible it was ten years ago."

"Much has happened," Meme said. "And we owe much to you." He leaned back in his chair, enjoying the luxury of reminiscence. They were in a large sitting room with a wall of French windows that opened to the terrace and a view of the sea, and there were glasses of marc before all of them.

"We were clawing our way then—all of us were—holding onto what little we had by our fingernails." He took time to light a cigarette, a strong, foul-smelling Turkish brand. "Everyone in the *milieu* then were babies. All the old ones—Spiritu, Carbone, and the rest—had all been killed off, or had been driven away because of the stupid choices they made during the war. The old factions were all run by men in their late twenties who only understood the knife and the gun and the garotte." He blew a long stream of smoke toward the ceiling. "It could never be so again," he said. "It was an . . ." He waved one hand, searching for the word.

"An aberration," Piers said.

"Yes, that is it," Meme agreed. "Oh, we all dreamed of it, all the young Turks. Just as they do today. But then, after the war, there were no strong organizations to be challenged. If it had not been so, we would still be working for some hard old bastard, and maybe ten years from now, we would be strong enough to make our move." He shrugged. "So much of life is fate," he said. "Being born to the right generation of men."

"You still have to be smart enough to seize fate by the throat," Piers said. "Men only become powerful and rich if they have daring."

"Large balls," Antoine offered, and laughed.

"Enormous balls," Piers agreed.

"And you must keep them," Meme said. "If they shrivel up, if you become too content, too pleased with yourself, someone with big, hungry ones will come and snatch the eggs from your nest."

"That is unlikely with you," Piers said. "You have the money, and you have the political power. And somehow I can't imagine either of you becoming too content with yourselves."

"It is why my brother comes back to Cervione," Antoine said. "That, and to renew his Corsican blood. He likes to remind himself of what he was, what he came from, and what he would be if he stopped clawing his way through life."

"You sound as though you don't think well of these people," Piers said.

"No, I love them," Antoine said. "But they have been seduced by this island. They see its beauty, and the beauty of its simple ways, and they say: 'What more do I need? I have my family, I have Corsica. I am a fortunate man.' " He shook his head. "Perhaps they are right. Perhaps it is better than seeking more and risking a bullet in your head." He smiled. "Sometimes I think . . . ahh . . ." He waved his hand, dismissing his own words.

Meme laughed softly. "Can you see my brother working in the vineyard, then coming home to his fat wife and taking his son to the café so he could sit over a glass of *patis* and talk with the other men about the great harvest that is coming?" He ground out his cigarette. "If he didn't have heads to break, he would be like a whore without a cunt."

Piers laughed at the crude reference, but it made him think of Colette, of her life in Corsica, and what it must be like for her. He recalled how much she had loved Marseilles, the fine restaurants, the beautiful clothes. Now she dressed like some young peasant woman, and her face—what the bastards had left of it—even denied her the warmth and comfort and companionship of a lover.

Colette without sex, he thought. It was like denying a great virtuoso his violin. He had never known a woman with her talents. Not before, not since. He doubted he ever would again.

"Tell me about Colette," he said, surprising himself but realizing he needed to know.

Meme stared at him. He was pleased he had finally asked. He did not object to what Piers had done to the woman. She had been a *poule*, and *poules* could never be taken seriously. But it was the way he had done it. It had lacked honor, manliness, and men like that, he knew, could never be fully trusted. He smiled inwardly at the thought. But then, no man could, he told himself.

"She lives a simple life here." He raised his chin toward his brother. "She works hard at teaching good, French manners to Antoine."

Antoine raised his arms, then let them fall, and rolled his eyes at the ceiling. "If the woman acted this way when she worked in the brothel, she would have starved," he said.

"But I think she is happy here," Meme continued. He shook his head, as if trying to find the correct words, or perhaps trying to understand what he was about to say. He looked across at Piers. "Women who sell themselves are very strange. Most are beautiful. But they have no love for themselves, no respect for themselves. And it is not because of what they do. They are that way before they begin that life." He grimaced. "Maybe their fathers fucked them. Or maybe they came to believe that their cunts were all they had to offer, the only way to make their way in the world. Who knows, except the poule herself? It is men who do this to them." He gestured at all of them. "Men like us. All men. Sometimes I think if they didn't have that thing between their legs, we would hunt them every year, like deer. We don't respect them. And we don't because they cannot beat us. They cannot overpower us physically. We respect them when they are old and ugly, because then we realize they are strong and wise. And we know this because they have survived us. And we respect them when they are our mothers, because they have had power over us and they have used it fairly. Men are asses," he added, a bit ruefully, Piers thought. "We have something good, and we have a need to abuse it."

"Does she have a man now?" Piers asked.

Meme shook his head. "She has no need of a man. I think she has finally come to believe she is better off without one. I think she would like children. But . . ." He let the idea die, then picked it up again. "I see her with children sometimes." He grimaced again. "But men don't see beyond the face and the body. They refuse to recognize that everyone will be old and ugly one day." He laughed. "That is why so many end their lives married to shrews."

"I often think of her," Piers said.

"Ah, but you think of what you knew between her legs." He waved his hand. "I don't criticize you for this. It is natural. It is how we have been taught to think. It is why men are never happy, never content. When it comes to women, they think with their pricks in their hands."

"Some settle for even less," Piers said.

Meme wondered if he was thinking of his own wife now. "And some men settle for men," he said. "I have never understood that either."

Piers glanced at his watch.

"When does your plane leave?" Antoine asked.

"Two hours. We had better get down to business." He raised his glass of *marc*. "First an announcement. I am leaving Paris. I am being called back to Washington. It is a promotion, and I will be in charge of all operations in Western Europe."

"*Merde*," Antoine said. "Now we will never see you. And my nephew will become a stranger to me."

"No, I will be back regularly. And I will bring Alex with me whenever I can. It will be good for him to grow up in his own country, but I want both my sons to have the benefits of Europe as well. Europe is where the money will be. In twenty years or so, it will be rich again. Rich and growing. And those who know it will have a great advantage."

"Does this mean we will work through someone else now?" Meme asked.

"No," Piers said. "The fewer who know of our arrangement, the better." He leaned forward. "My associates who control the American end will still do that. But I will also be there to watch them more closely."

"You think they are cheating us?" Antoine asked.

"No. But I think the men they deal with would like to control what you control. It would make sense from their standpoint." He pursed his lips. "But that would not be good for anyone. Not for the business, not for my agency. These American Italians would come here, and within a year they would have lost all the political strength you now have. They don't understand Europe, and especially not France, and they never will."

"They would find it difficult to rob our nests in our own tree," Antoine said.

"But I think they already try to go around us," Meme said. "I think they ship some of their product to Amsterdam. But it is a small amount, so we ignore it."

"Amsterdam is not a safe port," Piers said. "Not like Marseilles. So they can't ship it there in quantity. And they cannot bring it here and then ship it to Amsterdam, because once it comes here, you control it."

"Perhaps we will let them tranship some there," Meme said. "For a fee. We run at full capacity now, and the business is growing, and it would be more profitable than to pay more protection for more laboratories." He laughed. "Now we must pay even the fire department because the process is so explosive."

"Someday some fool will light a match, and the opera district will disappear," Antoine said.

"You should move it all to the country before that happens," Piers said. "Buy an old farm."

"I like it under my nose," Meme said. "Here I have people who watch it for me, and it is easier to watch the watchers."

Piers pursed his lips again. He couldn't argue with the sentiment. It was the way he ran his own business. He glanced at the time. "I'm afraid we have to get to the technical side of things," he said.

Meme nodded. Piers's move to Washington would require some changes, but they would be only minor ones. And it would be good for business. It would make it safer. It was good to have people in high places. And there was no place higher than Washington.

Alex carried the basket of tomatoes to the long table that had been used for the feast the previous day. He and Colette had been working in the garden for over an hour, and the baskets of various vegetables had grown so, it appeared large enough for yet another party. But she had explained they were needed to satisfy Antoine's appetite. And she made another reference to living with a goat in the house. He laughed and she joined him in the laughter, and he knew she really liked his uncle when she did.

They had also picked lemons and oranges from the trees that dotted the property, and one had been located next to a large burial vault that was down near the front gate. It was empty, she explained, and had been built for the day Antoine and Meme died.

"The *filou*," she said, "like to be buried on their own patch. They don't like to rot with the rest of us."

But it had been fun. Except for picking lemons near the burial vault. That was spooky, and he had this vision of the roots of the tree growing up into the vault someday and into the caskets that were sitting there. All the movies he had watched—the ones his mother never wanted him to see, the ones he sneaked off to anyway—always had scenes in cemeteries, where the trees were all gnarled and scary, and made him think they were going to reach out and grab anyone who walked by.

They sat under a different tree now, eating oranges. Colette's head leaned back against the trunk, and the fine features of the right side of her face looked peaceful and relaxed.

"Where in Paris do you live?" she asked.

"Off the Boulevard des Italiens," Alex said. "Not far from the Opera and the Place Vendome. It's near where my father works, so he can just walk there."

"Do you like it?" she asked.

"Paris? Yes, very much." He hesitated. "Some of the people aren't very nice if they think you're a foreigner. But most of them are fine. And I don't tell them I'm an American."

"You speak French very well. Better than me. You talk like a French *filou*."

Alex smiled, pleased by what she had said. She had told him what a *filou* was, and he liked the idea of being thought of as a "sharp operator."

"Have you been to Paris?" he asked.

Her eyes seemed to grow distant. "Once," she said. "A friend took me there." She looked at him and smiled. "Far back, when you were only a baby. But it was very beautiful, and I loved being there."

"You should go back," Alex said. "Come and visit me."

Colette gave him a faint smile. "I would like that very much," she said. "But Paris is not for me anymore. I live here now, and here it is also very beautiful. And I go to Marseilles sometimes, and I go to Lyon to visit my parents. It is enough."

"But then I'll only see you when I come to Corsica," Alex said.

"So you must come more often. And you must stay longer." She hesitated. "Does your father never bring your mother when he comes?"

"No," Alex said. "I don't think she likes my uncles too much. I'm not sure why, but I just don't think so."

Colette thought about asking him about his mother. Piers had never told her much about the woman. But she decided it was better not to know.

"It is probably because Antoine eats like a goat," she said. She looked away, off toward the house, and was silent for a long time. Alex wondered what she was thinking about.

"Does your brother ever come?" she asked at length.

"Sometimes. But he's back home in the United States now, going to boarding school. Richbird likes it better there, I think."

Colette questioned the name Richbird, and Alex explained it was his baby name for Richard, and that his brother had always hated it.

"But he's a pain most of the time," he said. "So I still call him that because it makes him mad."

Colette laughed at the idea. "I had an older sister who was always mean to me," she said. "And I used to hide her good clothes or her special jewelry when she had a date with a man. She never knew I did it. She always blamed my other sister, who was closer to her age. But she was mean to me too, so I never cared."

"Why were they mean to you?" Alex asked. He wondered how anyone could ever be mean to Colette.

"Oh, it was just because I was younger. They are nice to me now. Someday *Richbird*,"—she struggled with the name, laughing as she did—"someday he will be nice to you too."

"I doubt it," Alex said. "He's a jerk." He said the word in English, and had to explain what it meant. Colette laughed again.

"It is fun being the youngest," she said. "Especially if there are many children. Then no one has time to watch you very closely. But it is difficult too. Sometimes you have to grow up too quickly. Don't do that, my sweet Alex. Don't grow up too quickly."

Alex wasn't sure how you did that—kept from growing up

quickly or slowly, and he decided it was just something grown-ups said. But he did want to get bigger soon. He had a fantasy about being as big as Richbird and of punching him in the nose.

"Would you like to play a game?" Colette asked.

"Yes. Sure."

"What is your favorite game?" she asked.

"Hide and go seek," he said.

"I know that game well," she said. "Who will be it first?"

"I will," Alex said, feeling very gallant. "But no hiding in the burial vault," he added.

"And, why not?"

"It's too scary down there," he said.

She laughed again. "Very well," she said. "We will only hide outside, and only in places that are not scary."

Alex turned his face to the tree and began counting.

"You must not peek," Colette called as she ran off toward the rear of the house.

"I won't," Alex called back. Then he turned his head slightly so he could see where she was going. But it was all right, he told himself. He had known by the sound of her voice anyway.

Piers and Antoine and Meme had a final glass of *marc* to celebrate Piers's promotion and his visit and the agreements they had reached, then walked out to the car that would take them to the airport.

Piers saw Alex over by the garden and was surprised to see he was with Colette. He had seen him earlier, running across the lawn, and had assumed he was alone, happily exploring the grounds.

Now, seeing him with the woman, he felt a twinge of nervousness, and wondered what Colette might have said to him, might have told him about knowing his father in the past.

Antoine followed his gaze and realized how much he would miss the boy. "Why do you not leave Alex here for a few more days?" he suggested. "It would be good for him, and I would take him in the car to see other parts of the island."

"No, I'm afraid I can't," Piers said, his voice distant. He turned back and smiled—with regret, he hoped. "His mother dotes on him. Especially now that Richard is away at school. It was difficult enough bringing him with me."

Antoine grunted. "It is why I never married," he lied. "Women never want a man to do anything except bring money home and carry out the trash. It is bad enough having Colette here. A wife would be impossible."

He glanced across at the boy again and wished he had been out playing with him for the past hour instead of sitting inside discussing business with his father. It was all *merde*, he thought. A great pile of shit that Meme could as easily have handled by himself. But now it was too late to change it.

Piers called to his son and saw Alex start toward him, then turn and run back to Colette to give her a farewell hug. She knelt for a moment and spoke to the boy, and Piers wondered what she was telling him.

When Alex came running to them, Antoine scooped him up and gave him a great hug. "So, my little Corsican donkey," he said, "now you go back to the fancy city of Paris, and you will forget all about your poor uncles, eh?"

"No, I won't," Alex said. "And I'll come back soon, and I'll stay longer next time." He looked to his father. "Won't I?" he asked.

"We both will," Piers said. "I want you to see what the Corsicans call the "white spring," when the *maquis* is in bloom. It's very beautiful."

"You should come even before that," Antoine said, reluctantly putting the boy down so he could hug Meme as well.

"We'll try," Piers said. "We'll try very hard."

As the car headed down the mountain, Alex looked back out the window at the village and the Pisani house, and he wondered when he would see it again, and if he would ever spend a long time there and what it would be like if he did. He thought about Colette too, and about what she had said to him before he left. He hadn't really understood, but there were other things she had said that he hadn't understood either. She used a lot of slang, he decided. Words he had never heard before.

The car turned onto the main road and headed north toward Bastia, where the airport was located, and he watched the farms and the vegetable stands slide quickly past as the car accelerated. It was not as pretty as it was up in the mountains and in the high, isolated villages that he could barely see from the road. But he decided he still liked it and would miss it as well.

"Did you have a good time?" his father asked.

"Yes, it was great," he said. "And I really do want to come back."

"We shall," Piers said. "And soon."

He hesitated, knowing what he wanted to ask, uncertain exactly how he should phrase it. "I saw you with Colette before we left," he said.

"Yeah," Alex said. "She's really nice."

"Yes, I'm sure she is," Piers said. He hesitated again, then pushed on. "I noticed she said something to you before you left, and I was wondering what it was."

Alex seemed slightly embarrassed, or perhaps just confused, Piers thought. He felt a tightening in his stomach.

"It was kind of funny, Dad," he said. "She told me to love you. She said you were a man who needed to be loved because you didn't understand what it was."

Alex looked up at his father, wondering if he would explain, and he noticed his face had turned suddenly red. It was the only time he had ever seen it do so.

BOOK III

CHAPTER

Middletown, Vermont, 1990

The official residence of the Middletown College president was an old pile of Georgian brick with two enclosed porches at either end, one screened, the other glassed in against the frigid Vermont winters. The front of the house was dominated by large, formal rooms divided by a long foyer which had a massive staircase with ornate newel post and banister. It spoke of the days when the state had been ravaged by the lumber barons, who had built great homes for themselves and then disappeared with the trees that had sustained them. The houses had been bought up by funeral homes and law firms and colleges, and so had survived, giving the illusion of affluence to small towns that no longer possessed it.

The house, which was located just off the grounds of the campus, was filled now with life of a sort. Every window, at least, was bright and lighted. A party, one of many hosted by the president, was in full flower, and faculty and administrators filled the rooms, glasses in hand, and spoke unkindly about their peers, the curriculum, the school itself. Only the students were spared their invective, for to speak badly of them would reflect upon themselves, and this was something distinctly avoided.

Two men stood by an ornate mantel—one tall and reedy and distinguished, with moderately long white hair and half glasses, which he was now peering over; the second short and fat, with a tightly curled, wild, abundant, frizzy dome, thick lips, and a fleshy face that made him look like a young Charles Laughton. They were associate professors of English. And they were unhappy, which was their normal state of being.

The object of their current unhappiness was Alex Moran, who was standing at the opposite end of the large room with a beautiful twenty-five-year-old graduate student named Jody Walker at his side.

"I don't know how he continues to get away with it. It's not as though complaints haven't been made." It was the fat one, whose name was Warren Fairchild and whose eyes were not truly on Moran, but on the tightly sheathed buttocks of Jody Walker.

"He's done it for years, my good man. It's been something of a movable feast for him. This one's what? Number four, or five?" The second man was Milton Whitingham, a Shakespearean scholar who favored British colloquialisms. "It's not as though he's the only one dipping his wicket into the graduate pool, after all. What offends me is the other special treatment he's received."

"But the others don't *live* with their wenches and bring them to faculty affairs. They don't flout the rules with such impunity," Fairchild insisted.

"Indeed not. But it's the *other* special treatment, don't you see? That truly boggles the mind." Whitingham sipped his sherry. He too had begun to study Jody Walker's well-shaped rump. He preferred men if given a choice, but he could appreciate beauty wherever he found it. And Jody Walker was a lovely young thing, he decided.

They were silent for almost a minute, momentarily content with their views.

"I am still waiting for someone to explain to me how he did it," Whitingham said.

"Did what?" Fairchild asked.

"Came here with tenure, of course. Without one teaching credential to his credit."

"Well, there are rumors about that, of course," Fairchild said. "Some definite pull there. Government, or money, or whatever. I, for one, suspect government." He wagged his bushy eyebrows up and down, turning back to Whitingham. "Have you ever seen him loading his car with those cased weapons he takes up to that shooting club he belongs to?" He widened his eyes as if the statement proved his point beyond question.

"It's all that contemporary literature you teach. If one can call it that," Whitingham added spitefully. "Too many spies and outlandish villains. No, I'd place my wager on old money. A purchased position, with the promise of more." He tapped his nose with one finger. "But cleverly done—the money going to another area so as not to reflect back on what was bought." He tilted his head to get a better view of Jody, who had been momentarily hidden by another group. "But still, I can see how you might be led astray. He is a terrible loner, except for his wenching frenzies."

"He does play chess with Marley," Fairchild said. "And he does grunt to one occasionally when passing in the hall. But he hasn't spoken at a faculty meeting in over a year. And he's never sober. Absolutely never. Not completely."

"Can't object to a man who likes his nip now and then," Whitingham said. "And he does publish. We have to give him that."

"Trash. He publishes trash," Fairchild said. "But he has tenure, and peer acceptance means nothing to him, so what does he care?"

Fairchild had turned back to look at Moran "and his mistress," as he thought of her. He felt what Whitingham would have called a stirring of the loins, just watching her.

"But you wait and see. It will all come out someday. And you'll see I was right," he said at length.

Jody slipped her arm into Alex's and squeezed it lightly. He had just insulted his fifth faculty wife, and although he had done it with wit and charm and the woman seemed not to have noticed, he was reaching the dangerous stage she had seen before. She leaned up to his ear and whispered.

"We should go. It's getting late, and you have an eight o'clock tomorrow."

"I have an eight o'clock every teaching day," he said. "My peers see to it."

Alex was simply grousing, Jody knew. He preferred his eight o'clock classes. He was up at six every morning anyway, doing a regimen of exercise that would put most middle-aged men in traction. She bit her lip. She didn't like to think of him as middle-aged, although she knew the idea didn't offend him. But it bothered her. It made her think others would think she had a daddy complex.

She was a beautiful woman, with long blond hair and blue eyes and fine-boned features. She was tall and lithe, and she knew men enjoyed looking at her body. She also knew she was a replica of the other women with whom Alex had lived over the years, and very much like the pictures she had seen of his dead wife. But it didn't offend her, it only made her nervous. She didn't mind being one of several who reminded him of his wife. She only wanted to be the last. She was in love with him.

"I need another drink," Alex said. "Then we'll go."

"Why don't we have it at home?" she suggested.

"I'm out," he said. "So one more here."

She knew it was a lie, but didn't argue. There were enough people who degraded him publicly without her adding herself to the list. If he wanted to get drunk, she didn't care. She just didn't want him making a fool of himself. Or her.

He left and returned from the bar with John Marley in tow, and Jody knew it would mean another half hour and at least one more drink. Marley was an expert on Yeats, a passion Alex shared, and they played chess together, and Marley had even been taken to Alex's shooting club, something not even she had managed.

Marley was a small, almost delicate man with an open smile and boyish features that belied his fifty-three years. His graying hair flopped across his forehead, adding to a carefully planned disheveled look which many adopt in graduate school and which he had never abandoned. He was a perennial schoolboy, who had never been away from a classroom since entering kindergarten, and he had the open, naive, satisfied view of the world of a man who had experienced it from textbooks and newspapers and magazines. But Alex liked him. He said he was the only honest man he had met "in the whole damned school."

Jody liked him as well. She even liked his repeated offers—always made in Alex's presence—to be her next lover, so she could learn "the ecstasy of non-macho virility." Marley was happily married with six children, who kept him penniless, and Jody always responded that she saw ample proof of his virility and it terrified her.

Marley, she noticed, was also slightly drunk, and it was confirmed with his first words.

"Are you enjoying this gathering of mental mysophiliacs?" he asked, making sure his voice carried to those around him. He was grinning, awaiting chastisement that didn't come. "I, for one, adore these little gatherings. I'm not sure if it's the cerebral stimulation or the free booze. But I'm working on that." He scratched his head. "Martha, our beloved hostess and first lady of the campus, just told me to stop acting like a twit. My God, where has the woman been? Twits are the only form of academic life more than three steps beyond the primordial ooze. The rest are just amoeba, swallowing each other whole."

"You're drunk," Jody said.

"Of course. So's Alex. It's the only way to survive all this gaiety. Why aren't you drunk?" Marley demanded.

"I'm hoping to seduce Alex later," Jody whispered. "I'm not very good at it when I'm slobbering."

Marley clutched Alex's sleeve. "My God, man, I am weak at the knees."

"She only says those things to get you twitching. She never does them," Alex said.

"She has succeeded," Marley said. "I am definitely twitching."

Jody laughed. "God help your wife. Number seven may be imminent."

"Never!" Marley insisted. "I've been vasectomized."

"You have not!" Jody said. "Your wife told me she'd begged you to do it and you wouldn't."

"That's true. But I like to tell beautiful graduate students that I have been," he said. "Somehow it seems to make me more appealing. I used to tell them I was sterile. Then the children started arriving and I had to switch tactics."

"Did either ever work?" Jody asked.

Marley stood as tall as he could, which at five-foot-seven left him an inch shorter than Jody. "Woman!" he intoned. "You are in the presence of a living legend in matters sexual."

"I know," Jody said. "Your wife told me about that as well."

"God," Marley said, "the woman knows no shame."

Alex gulped his bourbon. "None of them do," he said. "They only want us as sex objects."

He smiled, making small lines appear at the corners of his eyes. His hair was flecked with gray now, and more often than not, his mouth formed a slight frown. His current smile was uncommon. He seldom wore it. Only Jody made him smile with any regularity. He was unable to do the same for her.

"When are you going to take me shooting again?" Marley asked. "I fear my trigger finger is becoming atrophied."

"Whenever you want."

Marley turned to Jody. "I am also one of the great shots of the Western world," he said.

"I have no doubt," she said.

"I think there's some connection between shooting and sexuality, but I haven't quite worked it out yet. But blasting away *is* so much more satisfying than teaching the genius of Yeats to mean little minds."

"You should do an article on it," Jody said.

"On mean little minds?"

"No. On the connection between shooting and sexuality," she said.

Marley clutched Alex's sleeve again. "She's doing it to me again," he said. "Are you sure it's all pretense?"

"Positive," Alex said.

Fairchild was weaving his way past, headed for the bar. He stopped.

"Marley. Moran. Ms. Walker," he said, nodding to each in turn. "Do I hear that a new article is in the offing?" He was smiling, ingenuously, he hoped.

"Yes," Marley said, straightening to his full height again. "On the similarities between sexuality and shooting."

"Ah," Fairchild said, stroking his chin for effect. "Then I take it Moran and Walker here are providing you with expert research."

Alex saw Jody stiffen; her smile faded.

"Well, the viper speaks," Marley said.

"Tut, tut. We must not lose our sense of humor." Fairchild glanced at Alex and Jody. "Neither must we lose our sense of reality," he added.

Alex reached out and laid his hand on Fairchild's shoulder. The gesture was friendly, and his smile matched it. His finger and thumb moved to the pressure point in the trapezius muscle and he squeezed firmly.

Fairchild let out a yelp and sank to his knees, the left side of his body numbed with pain.

Alex bent, placing his lips close to Fairchild's ear. "And we must never lose our manners," he whispered. "If you ever do again, I'll cripple you, you simpering little bastard."

He took Fairchild's elbow and began raising him to his feet. "Are you drunk, man?" he asked. "Let me help you."

Fairchild staggered back, his face red and horrified, the feeling only now returning to his arm and shoulder and side. "You barbarian," he shouted. "You cretin!"

"And you must never forget it," Alex said softly. He shook his head, his eyes sad. "I think you definitely should stay away from the sherry," he said.

Others had turned to stare, and Winston Cambridge, the college president, was making his way toward them.

"What's wrong here?" Cambridge asked, looking from Fairchild to Alex to Marley. He seemed confused and embarrassed.

"He assaulted me," Fairchild snapped, jutting an angry chin toward Alex.

Alex shook his head. "I think my colleague has had too much to drink. He stumbled, and I caught him."

"Definitely too much," Marley confirmed.

"This is outrageous," Fairchild ranted. His jowls and lips were quivering, and had he been a different sort of man, Alex might have thought he was about to attack him.

Cambridge held up a hand to both men. "Let's just separate and put this aside," he said. He turned to Fairchild. "Why don't you go to the bar and get your drink, and we'll talk later."

Alex turned to Jody as Cambridge directed his attention to him. "I think we should go," he said. "This is embarrassing." He turned back to Cambridge. "Thank you for a lovely evening," he said.

Cambridge momentarily closed his eyes, then nodded. Alex and Jody headed for the door.

"Did you wear a coat?" Alex asked.

"No, I did not," she said. Her voice was cold. "It's summer."

"Mmm," Alex said as he opened the front door.

"A minute, Alex." It was Cambridge coming up behind. He smiled at Jody. "Could you give us just a private moment, please?" he asked.

Jody went out and closed the door, and Alex turned into Cambridge's weary smile.

"Jesus Christ, Alex," he began. "I know the man's an ass, but I simply can't have you assaulting people—especially fellow faculty—in my home, or anywhere on college property." He watched Alex shrug helplessly, indifferently, he thought. "I've made a great many allowances for you over the past years, and I've made them because I was told to." Cambridge was nearly whispering. "Somehow my predecessor allowed your presence here to be tied into some government grant money this college very much wants and very much needs. But, damn it, man, I cannot have this type of thing going on in my own home. It is embarrassing, to say the least. And if Fairchild brings you up on charges before the faculty senate, there isn't a helluva lot I can do. Do you understand that?"

"He was drunk," Alex said. "I have witnesses."

"Thank God you do," Cambridge said. "This time. But if it happens again, it won't be believed. Witnesses or not."

Cambridge slumped his shoulders and pulled on his rather long nose. He was a pleasant man, with all the physical dignity and personal ineptness of most college presidents. He simply wanted things to go smoothly.

"I'll see it doesn't happen again," Alex said. He winked at Cambridge.

Cambridge shook his head, and Alex turned and joined Jody outside.

"What did he want?" she asked. "Are you going to be brought up on charges?"

"He just wanted to compliment me on an article I'd written," Alex said. He slipped his arm around her and started down the sidewalk.

"You haven't written any articles," Jody said.

"He thought I had," Alex said. "I didn't correct him. It would have been rude."

"God forbid you should be rude," Jody said.

They walked in silence for several minutes.

"You shouldn't have done that," Jody finally said. "The man's an idiot, and he hates you. You just gave him ammunition to use against you."

"You're right. I should have shot him instead."

"Now *you're* being an ass."

"Thank you. And all this time I thought I was defending your honor."

"I can defend my own honor, if and when I think it needs it."

"I'll remember that."

"Please do."

They continued in silence again.

"I suppose this means I don't get laid tonight," Alex said at length.

Jody laughed, and placed her head against his shoulder. They began to walk more crookedly.

"Oh, Alex, I don't understand this need you have for self-destruction. You have so much. There isn't a graduate student here who wouldn't trade places with you in a minute."

"It's because they all want your body," Alex said.

"Stop ignoring what I'm saying!"

Alex let out a long breath. "Let's just go home," he said. "I'm tired, and I have an eight o'clock tomorrow."

Jody knew the subject was closed. For now. She'd try again tomorrow.

Jody was just getting out of bed when Alex returned from his eight o'clock class. She looked especially beautiful, he thought, when she was rumpled and tousled with sleep. He smiled at her and went to the kitchen for coffee. His hangover hurt like hell.

Jody followed him into the kitchen and sat in a high-backed wooden chair, her legs tucked beneath her. She was wearing a silk pajama top that was his, and nothing beneath it. The material clung to her despite its too large size.

"I want to talk about last night," she said.

Women always wanted to talk about last night, Alex thought. Or last week, or last year.

"Sure," he said, taking a heavy hit on his coffee.

"And I want to talk about us," she said. "About why I can't seem to make you happy."

"You do make me happy," he said. "You make me happier than any woman ever has."

It was a lie, but he wanted it to be true. His wife, Stephanie, had brought him the most happiness he had known. And also the greatest unhappiness. Stephanie, who had rotted and withered in her grave without even the benefit of revenge.

"I want to believe that," Jody said. "I know I'm good for you. I know I make you happy in bed, and I know I can make you laugh, and that you can relax with me." She hesitated. "Sometimes." She looked down at her hands in her lap, then hugged herself. "But there are other times, and then I think, I can't help him because he's as afraid of happiness as he is of unhappiness. He doesn't trust it. He thinks it will betray him. He thinks that everyone, and everything, at any level, will betray him someday. And what I'm trying to tell you is that I won't."

Alex looked around the kitchen, trying to ignore Jody's words. It was warm and comfortable, just like the rest of the small house. He had bought it four years ago, when he had finally realized they had lied to him, that the promises they had made to him would never be kept. That this was it. This was what his life was and would be, and he had better adjust to it. But he couldn't.

"Talk to me, Alex."

He wished he could. He placed the coffee cup on the counter, and placed his hands on either side of her face. She was beautiful. And lovely. She was just like Stephanie had been when he had first met her, even the same age. What was it now? Fifteen years ago. And she was right. He didn't trust the happiness she made him feel. He knew it would evaporate one day, all in one, sudden moment that was just somewhere down the road, waiting.

"The poet says that nothing is forever," he said. He smiled at her.

"The poet's full of shit, Alex. They always are. It's what they do. They put things on paper and make us believe they're real. But the only thing that's real is what's right here in front of us. What's in our lives." She looked up at him, and he could feel the tenderness, the caring come off of her.

"I can't promise you it's forever. That's something you have to work at. Something you have to struggle to keep getting, to keep giving. But I can promise you I'll never take you for granted. I'll never say to myself, Oh, that's just Alex, and I belong to him, and he belongs to me, and he'll always be here when I want him or need him. And I'll never decide you're not exciting to me anymore just because you're always here. And I won't con myself into believing that someone else can give me the excitement I stopped letting myself have with you. Do you understand what I'm trying to say?"

He nodded. He didn't believe it, but he nodded. He understood how she wanted it to be.

He also understood he was fucking up her life. He didn't think he had with the others. He had been a fling with them, even if they hadn't realized it at the start. He had been an exciting, romantic tryst with a professor. With what they themselves wanted to be.

And he had used them too, until they had grown tried of him and decided to get on with their lives.

And he was using Jody as well, even if he loved her. But he wasn't in love with her. It was impossible not to love her. But it was also impossible to be in love with her. At least for him.

"I don't know if I can give you what you want, Jody. I just don't know. I want to. But there are . . ." He shook his head. "There are things that have happened in my life I just can't shake. It's not you. It's me."

"Tell me about them. Talk to me about them."

"It doesn't work that way." He tried to smile again, but could not. "You can understand events in people's lives, and you can try to understand what it was like. But the best you can do is understand what it would have been like for you if it had happened to you. And that's not the same. It's never the same for two people. It just can't be."

"But at least I'd know. And that would be something."

She was right. He owed her that much. And so he told her. Standing there in the kitchen, in a silly, quaint, little Vermont house, he told her everything. And it must have had as much reality for her as if he'd told her he'd come from another galaxy.

When he finished, she just stared at him.

"And you still want to kill this man," she said.

He shook his head. "No. I still *have* to kill him."

She looked down at her hands. They were back in her lap now, and they felt as though they were trembling, but they weren't.

"I believed what you said. About your wife being killed in an accident. I didn't know."

"I wasn't lying to you. I just couldn't tell you the truth," he said. "There's not much difference. But there is a difference." He looked around the room again. "I don't want you to tell anyone about this. It's not that I care what these assholes around here think. It's just that you don't break agreements with these people. Even if they break them with you. They don't forgive that. And they don't forget. They come after you, and they punish you." He noted the concern on her face. "I don't mean with a gun. There are a lot of other ways they can screw up your life. And they're happy to do it."

"I won't tell anyone." Her voice was soft, quiet. He could barely hear her. Just.

She looked up at him. Hopeful. "But if they don't help you, you can't do it, can you?"

"No, I can't."

Jody stared at her hands again. And so you keep dying inside because you can't do what you believe you have to do. And if you do it, you die outside. Dammit, you're not a young man, Alex, she told herself. You're a middle-aged professor of English, no matter what you were ten years ago. And you can't go off hunting killers and expect to survive. And you don't believe you can survive if you don't. But you're wrong. I know you're wrong.

"You were right. I can't feel anything you feel inside. I wish I could, but I can't. But I'm glad you can't go." She stared at him. "Don't hate me for that, Alex. I can't help it."

He took her face in his hands again. "I don't."

She smiled. "You know, I wanted to make love to you when I came out here. I wanted to make you happy that way. I still do, and it's not because of what you told me. I just find myself wanting you all the time."

He smiled at her. "I don't know if I can. This is a pretty serious hangover I've given myself. I don't know if the old wizzer will snap to attention. It might just roll over and lay there and say, Go away, leave me alone, let me die in peace."

"No, it won't," she said. "I'm very good at raising the dead." She came to him and placed her mouth against his and allowed her body to melt against him.

She drew her head back and smiled at him. "How's the old wizzer now?" she asked.

"It's a miracle," he said. "It lives yet again."

"I know," Jody said. "It's made its presence known."

CHAPTER

31

Palm Beach, Florida, 1990

They had gathered in a meeting room at The Breakers, the luxurious oceanfront hotel that American robber baron Henry Flagler had built in 1925 in imitation of many of the great palaces of Europe. The meeting room was on the mezzanine and faced the sea, and the design, with its vaulted windows and large murals and ceiling panels, made it seem like the well-preserved chamber of a Renaissance palace. It was, in fact, an exact copy of a room in the Ducal Palace in Venice. A room stolen and duplicated by the New York architect Leonard Schultze, on direct orders from old Flagler himself. The entire hotel, in fact, was one great theft of brilliance—exact copies of various rooms in numerous palaces —from the finest minds of Renaissance architecture.

Piers Moran sat at the head of a long, narrow table, the windows and sea at his back. The room had been swept only an hour earlier by CIA technicians, and had been deemed secure from any monitoring devices.

"The Pisani brothers have been virtually stripped of political influence in Marseilles," Piers said. "It's a temporary situation. They simply backed the wrong horse in the recent elections, and they're paying a temporary price for it. They'll recover in time, but that doesn't change the fact, or make them any less vulnerable at the moment."

"So they've got a shooting war on their hands." It was Walter

Hennesey, the man who had replaced Piers as assistant DDO more than ten years before. He spoke in support of Piers, not questioning him, and did it through a cloud of pipe smoke that hovered in front of him like a blue haze.

"Indeed," Piers said. "And they don't have the police as a buffer." He drummed his fingers on the table. He looked down at his hand, noted a liver spot on its back, frowned at it. "Normally, the opposition would be picked up upon entering the city, or if not, harassed unmercifully once they were there. As we all know, it's impossible for an invading force to operate on foreign soil without some local cooperation." He pursed his lips. "In this case, the police are simply turning a blind eye, and the Pisanis find themselves under attack for the first time in almost twenty years."

"Certainly they have the manpower to handle it." It was Hennesey's number two, a man named Batchler, a thin, reedy man with a sharp voice and a coarse manner, whom Piers considered far too sure of his own opinions. "What about the other factions in the *milieu?*" he asked.

"They're being held back by Francisci. He's either allowing the Colombians to do his dirty work for him, or he's joined forces with them," Piers said. "We're simply not certain."

"Who is this Montoya character?" The fourth man was Christopher Baldwin, head of the CIA's French desk.

"He's the top man in the Medellín cartel," Hennesey said. "And he has the personal resources of a small country."

"But if he's like most of these South American greaseball gangsters, he wouldn't know the difference between the Eiffel Tower and the Arc de Triomphe," Baldwin said. "I can't see him understanding the nuances of France well enough to operate there. So he can't be sending in a bunch of greaseball shooters who don't even speak the language. So who's doing it for him? Francisci?"

Piers shook his head. "Francisci's just holding back, waiting. For now anyway." He stared at Baldwin, who was short and overweight and balding, one of the new breed of CIA executives who didn't even bother to keep himself fit anymore, he thought. Soft-minded as well, he suspected. He resented the new blood they had been forced to bring into the operation he had begun forty years ago, but there had been no choice. Especially not now.

"He's got Ernst Ludwig running the European end." He leaned

back in his chair and folded his hands across his hand-tailored suit coat. "Seems the Russians did as we asked ten years ago. They packed Ludwig off to South and Central America and set him up with the sundry revolutionary forces they supported there." He smiled derisively. "Now the Nicaraguans are gone, the Salvadorans are suing for peace, the Chileans were never there in the first place, and old Fidel is sitting at home in Cuba, holding onto his ass and praying he's not next." He tilted his head to one side, indicating a fait accompli. "So Ludwig, being the resourceful bastard he is, has sold his services to Montoya. And Ludwig knows how to operate in Europe better than anyone."

"I don't understand this move into Europe at all," Batchler said. He raised a hand. "I understand the interest in expanding the cocaine market there. It's ripe for it. But why try to push the Pisanis out? Why not simply work through them?"

"That's what the Pisanis thought," Hennesey said through another cloud of smoke. "They simply wanted to share in distribution and get a small import fee as a gesture of respect. It's the way it should have been done." Hennesey gave a few furious puffs on his pipe, sending up a billowing cloud that caused Piers to bat the air in front of his face.

"Sorry," Hennesey said, setting the pipe in an ashtray. "Anyway, Montoya told them to get fucked, that he wanted the entire operation—no share, no respect money, nothing. And the war was on. So far Ludwig has assassinated a half dozen of the Pisanis' top people and they haven't been able to respond in kind in Medellín. *Their* people have been stopped at the airports."

"So what do we have?" Baldwin asked. "One crazy greaseball who has enough money to send an army of shooters to France?" He shook his head. "Doesn't make sense. Somebody's got to be backing him."

"We think so too," Piers said. "And we think it's our own people in Colombia." He leaned forward again. "They've been using Montoya as an asset for years now, providing him protection and reaping some nice political and, we think, personal dividends on the side. We believe they want to expand that role to Europe. Not only for the financial rewards, but for the power it will give them inside the agency."

"So sit on them," Baldwin said.

"That would be difficult," Piers replied. "Almost impossible without exposing what we've been doing for the Pisanis for the past forty years." He sat back again. "And they know that."

"So let's come to some kind of agreement," Baldwin suggested.

"We've tried," Hennesey said. "They're playing dumb. They claim they have no idea what's going on there, that Montoya's just a loose cannon. They claim they've threatened to withdraw their protection, but that he's so powerful now, he can tell them to fuck off as well." Hennesey offered a disbelieving smile. "In short, *they're* telling *us* to fuck off."

"So what are our options?" Baldwin asked. "I lose the Pisanis, and my French network, especially in the south of France, turns to shit."

"We cut the head off the snake Montoya has loosed in France," Piers said. "We take out Ludwig. Then Montoya has no one but his greaseballs, as you so aptly describe them. And they won't last a month without him."

"So who do we use?" Baldwin asked. "The Pisanis haven't been able to do it, and whoever it is has to be someone who knows how Ludwig works, and who can work with the Corsicans. It will have to be someone the Pisanis trust. Christ, I don't have anyone who even knows what Ludwig looks like."

"I think we have a volunteer, although he doesn't know it yet," Hennesey said.

"Who?" Baldwin asked.

"Piers's son, Alex."

Baldwin made a face, mirrored by Batchler. Hennesey hadn't discussed the idea he and Piers had hatched, not even with his number two, who had been foisted upon him through agency politics. He didn't particularly trust the man.

"I remember Alex Moran," Batchler said. "I was new to the agency then, but he caused quite a stir." He turned to Piers. "Sorry, but I have to raise some doubts about him. He was somewhat of a loose cannon himself back then. And this is personal with him, not business." He made a face. "I remember the scuttlebutt about him, after he was cashiered out. Ended up teaching at some small college in New Hampshire, didn't he?"

"Vermont," Piers said. "Middletown College. Quite a good school. Teaches English. It's what he was trained to do."

"Talk was he hit the sauce pretty heavy back then. But I suppose that's understandable," Batchler offered. "Is that under control?"

"Completely," Piers said, a bit stiffly.

Batchler nodded. "It's been ten years, he must be past forty."

"He's forty-three," Piers said, a glint of annoyance in his eyes now.

"A bit long in the tooth for this kind of work," Baldwin chimed in. "Is he in shape for it?"

"We can send him to Bragg and make him fit enough," Hennesey snapped. He too was becoming irritated with the two younger men.

Piers placed his forearms on the table and hunched over them. "He's the only man alive who's seen Ludwig face to face. And the Pisanis are like uncles to him. If you recall, they hid him from us when he was under sanction. Do you have anyone better suited for the job?" There was a hint of sarcasm in Piers's voice, and it was not lost on either of the younger men. Both knew they had no one as good.

Baldwin inclined his head to one side, indicating it was acceptable to him, if for no other reason than the lack of alternatives. "How about the Russians?" he asked. "I recall there was a deal with them to keep Alex out of Europe and away from Ludwig."

"Ludwig doesn't work for the Ruskies anymore," Hennesey said. "He's gone on to greener pastures, and they don't particularly like that he did. As long as Alex leaves their people alone, they won't care that he's back in Europe."

Baldwin nodded. "Yes, I can see that. They've got enough on their plate right now. And we're their new buddies." He said the last with distaste. "I don't think they'll even raise the issue," he said.

"But he'll be free-lance, right?" Batchler said.

"This has to be official," Hennesey said. "Full agency backing. It's the only way we have of protecting ourselves. But we have a perfect right to be going after Ludwig. He's a legitimate target. Moran will be a contract employee. Hired for the one hit, at the going rate. He qualifies because he has expertise none of our people have."

"I'm not crazy about it," Batchler said. "But I don't see as we have a choice." He stared down the table at Piers. "How do you feel about using him this way? Ludwig has stayed in practice. Your son has been busy screwing sophomores."

Piers bristled inwardly at the allusion. The man was a swine. "I promised him ten years ago, he'd have his shot at Ludwig," he said. "I simply did not expect to make good on it."

Baldwin hunched forward, imitating Piers's own position. "Is he stable?" he asked, a demanding edge in his voice.

Piers's mind flashed to a scene four Christmases ago. Alex had come to Palm Beach to attend a family gathering. He had been drunk, and Richard had begun baiting him about life in the backwoods of Vermont.

He had suggested, not too kindly, that Alex should come and work at his bank, where Piers himself was now a director.

"We can always find something to fit your talents," Richard said.

Alex sent the stiffened fingers of one hand snapping into Richard's windpipe. Then, as his older brother gasped for breath, he grabbed his hair and bent his head back over the chair, amid the cries of his mother and Richard's wife.

He leaned close to Richard, bathing him in his boozy breath. "I've always wanted to hurt you, Rich*bird*," he said. "Don't give me an excuse to live out childhood fantasies."

Piers shouted at him, demanding to know if he'd lost his mind.

Alex had turned to him and said: "Years ago, *Dad*." He had spoken the name with sarcasm. Then he had walked out of the house. Piers had not seen him since.

Piers returned from the flash of memory and stared Baldwin in the eye. The years had been kind to Piers. Now, at seventy, he looked no different than he had ten years earlier. He looked lean and sharp and capable.

"He's perfectly stable," he said. "I wouldn't suggest sending him otherwise."

CHAPTER

32

Alex sighted in on the target and squeezed the trigger three times. The Walther jumped in his hands with each shot, was brought back on line smoothly even as the trigger was being squeezed again. The bullets smacked into the silhouette target as if his hand hadn't moved at all.

It was evening, and it was early in May, and warmth and daylight savings time had finally come to Vermont. He was wearing yellow-lensed shooting glasses against the fading light, and it brightened everything to a warm, clear summer day.

He removed the glasses and stared at the target, which was only seven yards away. It was the average distance of most combat situations involving pistols, and the one you were taught to practice at. There were three holes in the target, all in an area the size of his fist.

"Not bad. But not the best shooting I've seen either."

Alex turned toward the voice, blinked, and then smiled. Pat Cisco stood about ten yards behind him. He had put his glasses on to see the target, and now he removed them.

"What the hell are you doing here, General?"

"Would you believe me if I told you I came up to do some fishing? It's trout season, isn't it?"

"Yes, it is. And no, I wouldn't believe it."

"Good," Cisco said. "I think all people who fish are assholes anyway."

He walked to Alex and took his hand. "It's good to see you again," he said. "It's long overdue."

"How'd you find me out here?"

"Beautiful young woman at your house." Cisco raised his eyebrows in approval. "Don't think she wanted to tell me, didn't know if she should. This some kind of sanctuary for you?"

Alex nodded.

"I told her I was an old friend who was just passing through. That I really wanted to see you, and wouldn't be able to wait around. So she gave in. Nice lady," he said. "But I'd never hire her. Too trusting."

"She'd never work for you," Alex said. He grinned at Cisco. "Too smart."

"There should be more people like her," he said.

Alex removed the clip from the automatic and ejected the shell in the chamber.

"You still shoot a lot?" Cisco asked.

"Few times a week. It's a hard habit to break."

Cisco ignored the lie. He glanced at a picnic table behind them. "Can we sit and talk a bit?" he asked.

Alex walked back to a shooting bench, slipped the pistol in its case, then joined Cisco at the table.

"So, what are you really doing here?" he asked.

"Came to see you."

Cisco had aged over the past ten years. His black hair was almost completely gray now, but the riveting blue eyes were still hard and clear, and the stocky body and military bearing still seemed intact. But he seemed tired, weary of the job perhaps, and the once easy laugh that used to embarrass him as out of place with who he was and what he did was now gone.

"Actually, I've been *directed* to see you. Ernst Ludwig is back in Europe."

Alex felt his stomach tighten. "Who directed you?" He knew few in government had that power.

"One of the president's top people." Cisco's jaw tightened. "One who plays flunky for the CIA. So it comes from them."

Alex knew how angry that would make Cisco, being manipulated that way. "I always thought my father would tell me," Alex said.

Cisco nodded. "I spoke to him." He stared at Alex. "I wanted him to urge you to turn them down." He paused. "He said that was up to you. He also said he thought the news should come to you officially."

"We had a falling-out," Alex said.

"I know. He told me. But he said that wasn't the reason. He said it would give you more leverage to deal with them directly. I think they knew that too. That's why they pawned it off on me."

"So what are they offering? And why?"

Cisco explained the Pisani–Montoya drug war and Ludwig's role in it.

"They need the Pisanis. Want to keep them in place. And they figure you've got the clearest shot at getting Ludwig. Because you know what he looks like. That's bullshit, and we both know it."

"My father's just keeping a promise. It's ten years late, but he's doing it."

"Maybe," Cisco said. "But I still think you should turn it down. They want you reinstated in the DIA as a contract employee. Then they want you seconded to CIA. You're official, but you don't have any authority other than what they dole out one piece at a time. And they can always say: Yeah, he worked for us. But he wasn't working for us when this happened. It stinks."

"I don't care," Alex said. "I don't expect them to do anything but screw me if they have to. Or want to. My father will be behind the scenes somewhere. At least I'll have him watching my ass."

"Maybe. Maybe not. I don't like this, Alex. There's something wrong with it. And I haven't the slightest fucking idea what it is. You're too far out of the loop, Alex. You're too old, and you're too out of practice. And I don't care how well you can still use that Walther. Your instincts just aren't there anymore."

"Have you told them all that?"

"Of course I have. I don't want to see you sent into a meat grinder." His jaw tightened. "They want you to do a quick refresher course with Special Forces at Bragg." He shook his head. "Christ, they might kill you there. Then we won't have to worry."

"I've been staying in shape," Alex said.

"There's a big difference between being in shape and keeping up with those crazy fuckers. We send kids there. Kids. And you know what it's like for them."

"I remember." Alex thought about it. "But they said a refresher course, right? Not the whole thing."

"That's right. But you're forty-three years old."

"I'll survive it."

"You think so." Cisco stared at him. "Yeah, you probably will. But I'm damned glad I'm not going with you."

They were silent, then Cisco started again.

"I still say it stinks. We have enough good people. So does CIA."

"The Pisanis won't work with anyone they don't know. CIA knows that. So does my father."

"Yeah, there's that. But I don't like those people. I never have. They're nothing but a pair of sleazy drug pushers and killers. I know how you feel about them. But that's personal. You know what they are too. And that's business."

"I know what they are," Alex said. "I know what we are too. There's not a lot of difference, is there?"

Cisco let out a long breath. "Yeah, I think about that. The older I get, the more I think about it. Conning yourself about God and country only goes so far."

"When do I go to Bragg?" Alex asked.

"They'll be ready for you next week. You won't reconsider?"

"It's the only shot I'm going to have at Ludwig. I could try it alone, but I wouldn't have a chance. I need support and intelligence, and they can give me that." He stared at Cisco, his eyes pleading for understanding. "I have to do this, Pat. I won't be able to live with it if I don't."

Cisco stared at the ground. "Stephanie was a special woman, Alex. But she's dead, and nothing changes that. I don't know if you're going after Ludwig for revenge, or to get answers to questions you didn't get answered before." He looked up. "Maybe you'll get answers, and revenge. I don't know. But I do know it won't make any difference. It won't change anything. Don't do this expecting that it will."

Alex didn't respond, wasn't sure how to.

"And you're wrong about something else too," Cisco said. "Your father won't be the only one watching your ass. I will be too. And you can take that to the bank."

CHAPTER

33

Alex drove along the two-lane rural highway, trying to concentrate on the quaint, bucolic setting he would not see again for many months. Perhaps never again, he thought. To his right, cows dotted a rock-strewn hillside framed by distant mountains. On the other side of the road, Lake Champlain cut a broad swath through a valley several miles wide, it too shimmering in the shadow of yet another line of mountainous peaks. When he had first come to Vermont ten years before, he had laughed about the idyllic vistas that seemed to rise up on command. He told himself then that farmers went out every morning and staked their cows along selected hillsides under orders from the Department of Tourism. That the stark white church steeples that seemed to rise from every valley were nothing more than the empty husks of movie sets, erected every winter before the skiers arrived. But it was all real—or unreal in the context of actual life—and he realized now he had grown accustomed to it, fond even.

But that was past. All that existed for him now was what lay ahead, and the fact that he had left everything behind in as cowardly a fashion as possible. He regretted having done it that way—of leaving Jody with just a note saying he was gone and couldn't be sure when, or if, he'd be back. He'd visited a lawyer and had the house put in her name, and he'd signed over the registration of the Jeep and left an extra set of keys, telling her to pick it up at the airport in Burlington. Christ, he'd even left ten bucks to cover the parking costs. He just hadn't had the courage to face her, to see the hurt in her eyes.

It had been easy with the others. They'd simply grown weary of him—a kind phrase, Alex told himself—and had packed up and left. But Jody had hung on, caring too much to give up. *Yet.* He added the word in a final rebuke. And she had deserved better. Better than Alex Moran, and certainly better than a gently worded note and title to some possessions.

He had lied to himself, of course. It was easy to do. To fall back on the legitimate excuse that he couldn't talk about the assignment, or the agency behind it. But that did not forgive a cowardly way out. He hoped it might help her get on with her life more quickly. But even that hope had the weak ring of yet another excuse, and he wished he'd had the guts to handle it differently.

He hadn't handled it much better with the college either. A simple note tending his resignation. No explanation, no expression of regret. It suited his image, he had told himself, and it satisfactorily burned a bridge he never again wanted to cross.

Back to your Corsican past, he told himself as he entered the built-up environs near the airport. That was the one salvation. How good it would be to return to Marseilles and the two aging Corsicans who had been more of a family to him than his own had ever chosen to be. He had not seen his uncles in ten years. They had spoken often on the telephone, and they had written. But, true to their nature, those conversations and letters had been guarded at best, and he longed to sit with them and hear what had happened in their lives in the past decade. Perhaps, he thought wistfully, they could even go hunting again in Corsica, or sit in a café over a glass of *patis*, or just walk and enjoy the aromatic fragrance of the *maquis*. Wishful thinking, he told himself. First you have to survive Ernst Ludwig and his minions, and possibly even those who were sending you. Oddly, he felt surprisingly calm about the task on which he was embarked. The hatred was still there, burning slowly, as it had for years. But the reality of what he was about to do still seemed distant and uncertain. Reality would come, he knew, when he was back in France, in close proximity to the man he had hated for so long. In the place where it had all happened. Where his life had crumbled in hands too weak to stop it. To stop any of it. Then it would be real and immediate, and he had no doubt the hatred would boil up again and drive him until he reached the man who had dominated his thoughts, his dreams, every unwanted moment when he had freed his mind from everyday events.

It was as his uncles had said. It was the Corsican blood that had somehow been infused in him. But when? And how? Somewhere in his childhood, he thought. And again as a young man. It had come from the affection, the love he had so desperately needed and had found only in two old men who had discovered something in him worthy of endearment. Something his own father had never discovered, or perhaps had never even sought out.

But that was past, he told himself. He smiled as the car turned into the airport. But the past is prologue. And perhaps even doomed to repeat itself. Very trite, he thought. Especially for a professor of English. But also apt. And if that was the way it was to be, so be it.

"So be it," he whispered to himself.

Palm Beach, Florida

Piers Moran's house sat across the narrow coastal highway that hugged the shoreline. There was a tunnel that led under the road to the beach, but Piers seldom used it. The beach and ocean view were a status symbol, an investment. It was not something he personally valued.

Alex had come to see his father before heading for North Carolina and Fort Bragg. He needed information; he needed insight. He hoped his father could and would provide it.

Alex stopped the rental car before the front door and pulled an overnight bag from the trunk. As he mounted the steps the door opened to reveal his mother and an uncertain smile. She was a fragile woman in her late sixties, wearing a flowered print dress that was too young, and her hair was still its old shade of blond, though formulated now by a hairdresser.

"Alex, dear," she said, turning a cheek for him to kiss. She squeezed his arm as he kissed her. "You are going to be a good boy, now, aren't you?" she whispered. "Richard's here. I think he's expecting an apology."

"Of course, Mother," he said. He could live with her choreography. He had never written or called Rich*bird* to offer regrets for the minor battering, probably because he had never felt any. But he could do it now. If a happy family gathering was what she wanted, he could provide it.

"Your father and brother are out by the pool, dear," she said. "Why don't you join them?" She looked at him closely, almost as though inspecting him. "I expect you're off on one of your secret things again. Even after all this time."

Alex stared at her, incredulous at her perception.

"Why do you say that, Mother?"

"Oh, I can always tell when your father's up to something in that vein. He thinks I can't, but it's always rather obvious." She fluttered a hand. "But I don't want to know about it. I learned long ago it was better not to know." She smiled. It was the vacant, practiced smile she had also learned to use, he realized. "And besides, I have to supervise Meloxie's dinner."

Meloxie was the black woman who came to cook and clean for his parents. His mother did neither, had never done in his memory, but on his infrequent visits he had heard her give the woman endless instructions about what she wanted and how she wanted it. He had wondered if Meloxie spat in the soup when his mother left her. Now he wondered if it was just part of his mother's way of hiding. Hiding from the things that had always gone on around her.

He found his father and brother seated by the pool, just as his mother had promised. He had often wondered about pools so close to the ocean. It was as if those who owned them had rejected what nature had provided, convinced they could do it better.

His father and brother were dressed in lightweight suits. He had never seen either without a tie in more than twenty years, and he had never seen his father anywhere near his pool without being fully clothed.

His father came to him as he crossed the patio. He took his hand, then his arm. "Richard's here," he said.

"I see that," Alex answered.

"His wife is not," his father added. "The last time was too much for her, I'm afraid."

"I'll miss seeing her," Alex said.

His father gave him a hard look, but he ignored it and walked over to his brother, who stood as he approached.

He had a sudden impulse to throw him into the pool. He smiled at the thought. "Good to see you, Richard," he said. "I want to apologize about the last time. Blame it on the booze."

Richard was tall and slender, a clone of their father, and he carried his forty-six years well, the touch of gray at his temples providing a perfect banker's look. But then, Richard would have had it no other way, he knew.

He raised his chin slightly with Alex's apology, and nodded. "It's forgotten," he said. "How have you been?"

"Enjoying myself," Alex said. "And how's your wife and children?" For the life of him he could not remember their names. Then he remembered. "Emily, and little Susan and Richard, three," he added.

"Excellent. The kids had an event today, and Emily shepherded them," he lied.

"I'll miss seeing them," Alex lied in return.

They took chairs beside the pool and exchanged family news, or rather, Alex listened to family news. He had none of his own.

His mother joined them, briefly complained about Meloxie's dinner—Alex decided to skip the soup—and launched into the latest gossip about Donald Trump's need to sell the old Post estate up the road, making it clear none of the neighbors would miss him. Alex was certain *The Donald* would be horrified to learn this.

His mother began talking about some of her friends—they all seemed to be named Muffy or Buffy, or Winky or Twinky—and Alex tuned her out, satisfying her with smiles or nods at appropriate moments. He loved her, but had never understood her, and he thought it was because they had been having superficial conversations for forty-three years.

Richard took over with talk of the bank, and told him of their father's "particularly clever handling" of a "delicate matter" at a board meeting the previous week. Alex listened. His mother beamed approval. And his father smiled in a self-deprecating way.

An hour before dinner, Piers suggested a walk along the beach, explaining to Richard that he and Alex had some old business to discuss. Richard seemed relieved, Alex thought.

They came out of the tunnel and began walking north. To their right, the ocean was green and flat, and lapped softly at the beach. Fifty yards out Alex could see the occasional shadow of the old coastal highway that had surrendered to a hurricane years earlier. Parts of it were still there beneath the water, as if expecting a car to come rolling along at any moment. They had built good roads in those days, he thought. They simply built them too close to the sea.

"Your brother is a bit of a twit," his father said, surprising him. "But he's good at what he does. And I'm glad you're in a more tolerant mood this time."

"It was four years ago," Alex said. "Perhaps I've mellowed."

His father glanced at him, taking in the sarcasm, choosing to ignore it.

"I hope not," he said. "You're in for a rough time. I hope you're ready for it."

They walked on in silence. Out over the ocean Alex could see a frigate bird soar and dive, its split tail and long, narrow wings cutting the air like a sleek black jet.

"I need you to tell me what you can about it," Alex said at length. He knew his father was awaiting questions, would offer nothing unless asked. It was the training, he told himself. The years of living a covert life, where nothing was offered up on its own. "I don't trust I'll get the whole picture from CIA," he added unnecessarily.

"You probably won't," Piers agreed. "But that's only because it's the nature of the beast."

Piers recapitulated what Cisco had already explained, adding little that was new other than the Pisanis' desperate situation.

"Ludwig's running circles around them," Piers said. "I don't know if they've just gotten old, or if Ludwig's that much better."

"Someone must be helping him," Alex said, unable to speak the man's name.

"Francisci, we think," Piers said. "But no one can prove it. He's the next power in the *milieu*, just waiting to don the mantle. He could have held back and simply outlived them—although he is fairly close in age—but I think the years of subservience made him want a chance to savor the victory while he still had time."

"Why haven't Antoine and Meme simply hit him?" Alex asked.

"Just not done that way. They have their own rules in the *milieu*, although no one short of God can understand them. But once Ludwig is gone, they can handle Francisci. They're just getting hit from too many sides now, and their political protection is at an all-time low." He seemed to think about that a moment, then added: "It's all just come together at once, and it's left them vulnerable."

"That's too much coincidence," Alex said.

"Yes, it is," Piers agreed. "But I can't enlighten you on that. I'm too far out of the loop. I had to satisfy myself with keeping a long-overdue promise."

They turned and started back toward the tunnel and the house beyond. Before they reached it, Piers stopped and turned to face his son. The sun was behind Piers, and it cast a glow about his head. It was almost saintly, Alex thought.

"Between the Pisanis and the agency, you'll find the bastard," he said. "There's a man named Wheelwright in Marseilles. He's CIA's station chief there, and he'll help you. He'll be ordered to. They've promised me that. And Antoine and Meme know you're coming." He laughed. "When I spoke to him on the phone, Antoine told me he was going to take you boar hunting. He said to tell the pants pisser to bring an extra pair." He shook his head. "The man's bravado knows no bounds. He's up to his ass in bullets and blood, and he makes jokes."

Alex smiled and looked away from the sun. His father's voice brought him back.

"Kill the bastard at distance, Alex," he said. "I know you'll want him close. You'll want to look in his eyes when you do it. But that won't help Stephanie, and it won't make it any better for you." He took Alex's arm and squeezed it. "Get him and get out of there alive. The people with him aren't professionals, but they're good at killing. So don't underestimate them." He squeezed Alex's arm again. "Kill him at distance," he said.

CHAPTER

34

Alex spent the night in the guest room, window open, listening to the sound of the ocean. It felt strange, almost hostile, sleeping in his father's home. It had felt that way ever since he had become an adult.

He always thought of it as his father's home, not his mother's, not theirs together. He wasn't certain why. Perhaps it was because his mother just seemed to flit about the place, never doing anything but making sure things were as she thought his father would like them. His father was the presence about which everything revolved, and his mother had always concentrated on him and his needs, leaving her children to the care of a string of nurses and nannies from Aix-en-Provence to Paris to Chevy Chase.

Alex had not thought about it until years later, when he had seen how "families" lived. And he had realized then, he had never been part of a family, but simply a part of his father's household. But he had been an adult by then, with the opportunity to have a family of his own. Now, at forty-three, he had never achieved that goal, and he was back again, a stranger in his father's house.

He breakfasted with his mother—his father had a breakfast meeting at the Everglades Club, and had said he would see him in Washington in three weeks. His mother talked about everything, except where he was going and what he was about to do. She knew something was up, and knew that *something*—with both him and his father—had always involved the intelligence work she had always despised.

But perhaps *despised* was too strong a word. She had never understood it, had not wanted to because of the danger involved. It had upset the order that had always been so necessary to her life. So she had ignored it.

She bade him farewell at the door, offering her cheek again, and he left without ever telling her what he was about to do, or why. And he wondered if she would think about it, if she would worry about his safety. He wanted to believe that she would.

He drove north toward the Florida–Georgia line. It would be a long drive to Bragg, which was in south-central North Carolina, northwest of Fayetteville. But he had two days before he was due, so the pace could be leisurely.

Special Forces had changed since his initial DIA training in 1969. Congress had put it under a Special Operations Command three years before. Now headquartered at McDill Air Force Base in Florida, it included the Green Berets, Navy Seals, Delta Force, and other elite units, all trained to combat terrorism and Third World insurgencies and to conduct drug interdictions and hostage rescues. And in its wisdom Congress had given oversight for these clandestine activities, at least in part, to the Central Intelligence Agency.

Alex had thought it madness when he read about it. Already the new command was embroiled in a running battle, claiming it was being hamstrung by CIA, while Congress insisted it was merely trying to avoid oversight by Defense, CIA, and Capitol Hill, and threatened to withhold appointment of its new commanding general.

The retiring general had testified before Congress that the elite unit simply wanted to escape CIA's natural tendency to withhold needed intelligence, along with the morass of interagency bureaucracy that had caused delays of up to seventy days in ongoing operations. He pointed out that during its recent invasion of Panama, U.S. forces had been denied intelligence by CIA that would have allowed the capture of Manuel Noriega during the early hours of the strike. Congress, incredibly, took umbrage with the suggestion, with one particularly moronic senator insisting the Central Intelligence Agency would never take such a position.

Alex had laughed when he read accounts of the hearings in the *Washington Post*. But he wasn't laughing now. Here he was, headed for the Green Beret training camp at the Special Warfare Center at Fort Bragg—a DIA agent seconded to CIA. And you'll be about as welcome as a hooker at a Fundamentalist church service, he told himself.

But at least it would only be a three-week reindoctrination, not the three-month course he had endured in 1969. He still shuddered at the memory of that training. It had begun with jump school at Fort Benning, then on to night drops into the snake-infested Green Beret camps in the swamps of South Carolina. But now, he had read, they had even added some new wrinkles. There was something called HALO-SCUBA infiltration. High Altitude, Low Opening parachute jumps, where the jumper exited a plane at twenty thousand feet, over water, executed a horizontal, vertical freefall to fifteen hundred feet or less, then splashed down, sank, and continued his infiltration using breathing apparatus. The mere thought of his forty-three-year-old body attempting that sent a shiver up his spine.

But what he was in for would be bad enough. He had exercised, kept reasonably fit, but nothing like the level required of these troops. And the booze and the good food had taken its toll, and he knew if they didn't like him—which they would not—he'd be in for three weeks of hell on earth. He thought about that and decided if he found himself faced with the same instructor he had had in 1969—even if the sonofabitch was now gray-haired, toothless, and in a wheelchair—he'd head straight for Marseille and take his chances at survival there.

Alex arrived at the John F. Kennedy Special Warfare Center at 8:00 A.M. as ordered, and was ushered into the office of a light colonel, who regarded him like a snake that had just crawled under his door. He was a lean, hard, unpleasant-looking man about Alex's size and age. But all similarity ended there, and Alex knew he would never want to meet the man in a dark alley, or even a very bright one.

The colonel, whose name was Hugh Donlon, directed him to sit, then opened a red CIA folder stamped "EYES ONLY," the highest classification used in the military. Donlon read it, then sat back and stared across his desk.

"You know, Moran, we get people your age"—he smiled—"our age, who come in here from time to time. But they're usually officers from first-class line units. Rangers, Airborne, Pathfinders, guys like that. And they're not desk jockeys. They've been out in the field, facedown in the mud with the grunts." He nodded toward Alex's folder. "I've got a ten-year gap on you in here. And twenty-one years since you had our kind of training. You mind telling me what you've been doing?"

Alex swallowed. "Teaching English at a college in Vermont," he said.

Donlon stared at him, his hard blue eyes losing their edge. He almost smiled. "Anything physical, besides fucking coeds?" he asked.

"Some of those coeds were pretty athletic," Alex said. He shrugged. "Look, Donlon—"

"Colonel Donlon, asshole!" Donlon snapped. "You forget it again, and I'll kick your ass from here to Fayetteville, CIA or no CIA."

Alex's left eye narrowed, and he leaned forward in his chair. "You call me asshole again, and you're going to have to, *Colonel*," he said.

A start of a smile flickered to Donlon's lips, then was scotched before it could form.

"I know I've been out of the loop for a long time," Alex said. "And I know I'm worse off than I was when I came here as a shit-green kid in sixty-nine. What you don't know is that I don't *want* to be here. And I sure as hell don't want to be working for those clowns in CIA any more than you do."

"Then why are you here?" Donlon snapped. "Your brethren at Langley didn't bother to explain." He offered Alex a cold stare. "And I suppose you're going to tell me you can't either."

"I'm here because I want to kill somebody, Colonel. And the man I want to kill murdered my wife ten years ago. And *he* hasn't been out of the loop all these years. He's been practicing. And he was better at it than I ever was to start with." Alex offered a cold smile. "So if you can help me, I'd appreciate it. But don't stick your CIA hard-on up my ass. It doesn't belong there."

Donlon sat back and shook his head. "So CIA sends an out-of-shape college professor to hit a working pro, while I sit here with a few hundred trained killers who could do the job and be back home having a beer in forty-eight hours." He tapped his fingers on Alex's folder. "You want it, Moran. You got it." He reached out and pressed an intercom button on his desk. "Send Gunderson in here," he snapped.

The door opened within seconds, and a sergeant who looked like an NFL linebacker marched in, snapped to attention, then fell to parade rest.

"At ease, Sergeant," Dolon ordered. He jabbed a finger toward Alex, and the sergeant turned and stared at him. He was not the kindest or friendliest man Alex had ever seen.

"This is Mr. Moran, Sergeant," Donlon said. He handed Gunderson a sheaf of bound papers. "And this is the course of instruction I want him to follow." Donlon allowed himself his first real smile of the interview. He directed it solely at Gunderson. "And he doesn't like being called asshole," he added.

"Sir, I wouldn't think of calling this asshole an asshole," Gunderson said.

"Good," Donlon snapped. "Now, work him."

Alex got his gear from the quartermaster and lugged it back to an otherwise empty barracks normally reserved for special trainees. It was a long, narrow, single-story building graced only with individual metal-framed bunks, footlockers, and metal clothes cabinets lined along each wall.

When he had stowed his gear, he sat on the edge of the bed he had chosen, and waited for the next shoe to drop. It took about thirty seconds, then the door opened and Gunderson, dressed now in battle fatigues and "Green Beanie," as the distinctive berets were termed, walked smartly across the immaculate painted floor and stopped before his bunk. Alex remained seated.

Gunderson stared at him, from what seemed, to Alex, a great height.

The man was easily six-foot-four and filled out his fatigues with what had to be 235 pounds of lean, hard muscle. There was a jagged scar on his exposed left forearm and another along the side of his neck. His eyes were a cold gray, and his nearly shaved head bristled along the sides of the beret. Alex stared at the beret's flash above Gunderson's left eye, and noted it marked him as a member of 1st Special Forces Group out of Okinawa. He had obviously been recently returned to Bragg himself.

Gunderson smiled at him with uneven, nicotine-stained teeth. His head was square, almost box-like, and the smile made it look like a death's head.

"As far as I know, *Mister* Moran, we are not related," he began, his voice almost soft. "I will therefore not be giving you the normal treatment I reserve for members of my family." His voice changed to a roar. "So get your fucking ass off that bunk and snap to. Now!"

Alex jumped up, the psychology of where he was and what was in store for him kicking in. He felt immediately foolish, but snapped to attention and held it.

Gunderson's voice turned soft again. It was an almost mocking lilt. "Now, if you would be kind enough to change your clothing to full battle dress, complete with unloaded AR-15, I would appreciate it if you would meet me outside in thirty seconds." His gray eyes practically glittered. "There we will begin a four-mile run through the lovely North Carolina countryside, so I can evaluate"—again his voice changed, this time to sneering growl— "just what kind of overaged, fucking inept piece of shit I have to deal with." He paused a beat, then snapped: "Do it!" and turned smartly and marched out of the building.

Alex joined him four and a half minutes later, dressed in full battle gear, his AR-15 held at port arms. Denied the Green Beret he had earned twenty years earlier, he was wearing a camouflage jungle hat.

"You are very slow, *Mister* Moran," Gunderson said. "When I come for you at oh-five hundred tomorrow morning, I do not intend to be kept waiting. I want you to be out here, having taken your full ration of Geritol, and ready for a fun day in the sun. Is that fully understood?"

"Yes, Sergeant," Moran snapped out.

"That is outstanding, *Mister* Moran," Gunderson said. "Now, if you are sure you are ready, we will begin our run. You will keep up with me, or you will die trying, *Mister* Moran. If you die, or appear to have died, I will leave you where you fall. Unplanned death is not on your training schedule, so please try to avoid it. It would definitely put an unfavorable mark on my record. And I very much want to avoid that."

"I will do my best not to die, Sergeant," Alex said.

"I would greatly appreciate that, *Mister* Moran," Gunderson said. "Everyone here would be greatly disappointed in me if you did." He smiled, his eyes narrowing to almost a squint. "Now, if you are ready, we will begin." With that he turned and began a slow, steady run, and Alex scrambled forward and fell in on his right rear.

Alex, despite his exercise regimen, had never included jogging in his daily routine. He hated running, and had always regarded those who did it as mindless fanatics. He looked upon the emaciated bodies they struggled to achieve with disdain, telling himself they all looked like recent escapees from autopsy tables.

They ran steadily, the North Carolina sun beating down and quickly producing a heavy coating of sweat that soaked through clothing, and seemed to carry an airborne filth that coated the body with grime. Alex handled the first mile with a reasonable, tolerable discomfort. The pain began in the second mile, and before it was half over, the heavy jump boots he wore had begun to feel like lead weights strapped to his already hurting feet.

"You are breathing very hard, *Mister* Moran," Gunderson observed without looking back at him. "I see from your file that you're a straight leg, and therefore have not had the benefit of the excellent conditioning they provide at Fort Benning."

"I did my jump training first time around, Sergeant," Alex wheezed.

"Oh, I'm aware of that, *Mister* Moran. But I'm not interested in what you did twenty years ago. And that includes getting your cock sucked by some teenage, mutant cheerleader in the backseat of your car. In fact, you sound like you're doing that right now, with all that heavy breathing. Is this little run arousing you, *Mister* Moran?"

"Yes, it is, Sergeant," Alex wheezed. "I'm feeling very erect."

"Well, be careful, *Mister* Moran. We wouldn't want you to fall and impale some innocent forest creature."

They continued on, with Alex growing more certain with each stride that Gunderson had mapped out a course that included every hill North Carolina could provide. By the third mile he felt as though he would vomit, and before it was over, he was afraid he would not. The ugly black AR-15 he still carried at port arms, diagonally across his chest, had begun to weigh thirty pounds, and his shoulders and arms were fighting with his back and legs and neck to see which could provide more concentrated pain.

They turned down a narrow but well-used trail that led back to the camp, and a four-foot snake slithered across the path in front of them. Gunderson simply stomped on the reptile and continued on, leaving the snake writhing and thrashing on the ground. Alex gave it wide berth, staggering slightly as he moved to avoid it. The snake was thick-bodied and a mottled brown color, and he wasn't certain what kind it was. But as the snake snapped its head toward its injured body, he was certain he could see two small fangs in its open mouth.

"Shit," he muttered, forcing his pace to regain the ground he had lost avoiding the snake.

Gunderson pulled to a stop before a small square cinder-block building with black painted windows, and Alex fought to stay erect against the cramping muscles in his stomach. The run would be a daily routine, he told himself, and he would have to live with it every morning until his body adjusted. You can survive that, he told himself. But just.

Gunderson stood before him, offering a smile that did not carry to his gray eyes. "Delightful, wasn't it?" he asked.

"Pure pleasure," Alex huffed.

"I'm glad you feel that way, *Mister* Moran, because we will repeat it again at seventeen-hundred. And tomorrow at oh-five hundred we will do five miles, and repeat *that* at seventeen-hundred." He jerked his head toward the bunker-like building behind them. "Inside this building you will find an assortment of weapons, which you will study and field strip over the next thirty minutes. I will return then, and you will tell me about them. Then you will strip and reassemble them blindfolded. Is that clear?"

"Yes, Sergeant," Alex said.

"Gooood," Gunderson offered. "I myself am in need of some liquid refreshment. So you'll excuse me, please." He turned and started to leave, then snapped his head back toward Alex.

Alex was still standing in the same spot, trying to *think* his legs into action.

"Snap to, mister!" Gunderson growled.

Alex snapped to.

The weapons included a Russian AK-47, an Uzi, and an assortment of Swedish, East German, and Czech assault rifles and pistols currently favored by terrorists and guerrilla fighters, along with the Glock and Berreta replacements of the old Army Colt .45. Alex managed most of them reasonably well, except the Glock, which was new to him. Gunderson only sneered and assured him he would have ample opportunity to improve on his ineptness over the next three weeks.

"Every day, *Mister* Moran," he said. "Every single motherfucking day. Until they replace pussy in your nightly nightmares."

They left the block house and double-timed to a large gymnasium complex—Alex still lugging the AR-15 at port arms—where Gunderson suggested that his body odor was becoming a problem, and ordered him to shower before dressing in the karate clothing he had been given. Gunderson himself had changed into crisply pressed fatigues.

"We like our people to be clean, *Mister* Moran," he said. "Clean and competent. I'll work to help you meet our standards in both areas."

"Thank you, Sergeant," Alex said, momentarily hoping the upcoming workout would be *with* Gunderson, then thinking better of the idea.

But the workout was not with Gunderson. It was with a small, wiry Hispanic who Alex gratefully noted was about half Gunderson's size. Gunderson introduced him as Sergeant Mercurio, then grinned, and took a seat off to one side.

Mercurio led him to a large matted area in the center of the gymnasium. He motioned him to sit cross-legged, then sat opposite.

"I'm told it's been twenty years since your initial training," Mercurio said. "Have you kept current? Practiced the techniques you were taught on any regular basis?" He waited as Alex admitted he had not. "Then you'll be instructed as if this was a first lesson," he said.

Mercurio had soft, almost kind brown eyes and short-cropped wiry hair that indicated some African ancestry. His features seemed soft too, except for the remnants of a once broken nose, and his skin was a smooth, nearly hairless olive tone.

"The fighting technique we teach in Special Forces has no formal name," he began. "Although those who learn it call it many things during instruction." He almost smiled, as if recalling some of the names the training had been called in the past. "We simply call it hand-to-hand, and, as you may recall, it is a combination of judo, karate, wrestling, and boxing. But it is basically close-in, barehanded fighting, and its object is a thirty-second kill, no longer, not under any circumstances. If you cannot kill your opponent in thirty seconds, the chances are you yourself will be killed."

He paused to allow his words to sink in. "We don't teach you to incapacitate, or simply to maim an opponent. These things are possible if you stop at a given point, but we do *not* teach you to stop. Once you begin, the training teaches you to carry through until the opponent is dead. The techniques are taught over and over again until they are automatic, and you are a machine performing a function. If you are taught properly, you will not even think of stopping."

He paused again. "Now, this is dangerous in civilian life, so you are also taught never to attack unless you intend to kill. Do you understand me?"

Alex simply nodded.

"Good," Mecurio said. "We begin." He rose from the cross-legged position with his hands never touching the floor, and motioned Alex up.

They faced each other across the mat. "The first technique I will teach you is a variation of what the Japanese karate masters call the *kata dan'te*, the dance of death." He reached behind him and withdrew a combat knife from the back of his black belt and tossed it to Alex. "You may kill me now," he said.

Alex gripped the knife loosely in his right hand, the flat of the blade parallel to the ground so the thrust would pass through the ribs without jamming. Knife fighting was something that, once learned, was never forgotten. From that point it was a matter of reflexes and will. Alex knew the will was still there.

He circled slowly, feinting once, twice, then came in low with an upward thrust.

Mercurio moved to his right, coming inside the thrust, blocking the attack with his left hand and guiding it away, then chopping the wrist with his right and sending the knife harmlessly to the mat.

"Disarm," Mercurio whispered, almost to himself, then continued up with the right hand, brushing Alex's lips and nose, a blow if carried an inch closer, Alex knew, would have smashed his teeth and crushed the nasal cartilage and bone. "Stun," Mercurio hissed.

The small Hispanic's hand continued in a circular motion, the fingers forming a claw, ripping a fraction of an inch from Alex's eyes. "Blind," Mercurio said, his voice gaining in excitement as the hand continued its circle, the palm slamming into Alex's temple with minimal force. "Unbalance," Mercurio offered. Again the right hand continued its circle, moving down this time, the fingers again a claw as the left hand thrust out in a short, open hook to the throat. "Deflate," Mercurio said, the fingers of the left hand barely brushing Alex's windpipe.

The right hand, still continuing its flowing circle, had reached its low point and now started up, striking the groin in an open-hand slap, the fingers momentarily closing on the testicles, then releasing, the hand shooting up in a sharp, jerking motion.

Alex bent forward, part from instinct, part from the slight pain the pulled blow had caused. "Your balls are now in my hand," Mercurio whispered. "And you are on your knees." The right hand chopped down, where the back of Alex's neck would have been. "And death," Mercurio snapped.

He straightened, looked Alex in the eye. "The dance is ended," he said, smirking. "Now you try."

Alex repeated the technique, badly, then with some improvement over a dozen attempts. Mercurio stepped back and nodded.

"It will get better in time," he said. "Now, something less exotic." He squared himself on Alex. "Now I attack you," he said.

Immediately his right hand, fingers rigid, struck out, snake-like, tapping the small curvature of bone at the base of the throat. "A quarter of an inch higher in battle," he offered. His hand dropped as the other came up, both grabbing the front of Alex's shirt and pulling him forward. Mercurio dropped his chin to his chest and thrust his head forward in a butt to Alex's nose, stopping just short of contact. "Full force," he said. "The nose and teeth are shattered." He dropped his hands to his sides, then brought them up, each in a wide circle, the open, cupped palms stopping in a simultaneous strike just before crashing into Alex's ears. "Your eardrums have burst," Mercurio said. "The pain is unbearable."

He took a quick step back, his right foot shooting up and out to Alex's groin. "You go to your knees." He jerked Alex to a kneeling position, and his left hand grabbed Alex's hair, jerking the head down as his left knee came up to meet his face.

He pushed Alex back, simulating the way his body would have been forced by the blow, then grabbed his right wrist and straightened the arm, bringing the other knee into the elbow. "Your arm is gone," he hissed, stepping to Alex's side and driving a fist into one kidney, "and you bleed internally."

He stepped behind Alex, both arms wrapping about his head, one forearm just beneath the chin. He jerked and twisted the head, stopping just short of a broken neck, Alex realized. "And you die," Mercurio said.

The small Hispanic glanced toward Gunderson, who was holding a stopwatch. "Time," he snapped.

"Nineteen seconds," Gunderson called back.

Mercurio faced Alex again. "Now you," he commanded.

Alex felt bruised and battered by the time he left Mercurio's two-hour workout. By the end of the week, he had been warned, he would begin contact work with other students, and he knew their blows would not be pulled, as Mercurio's had been. He also knew his body was not yet hard enough to take many of them.

They broke for a half hour for lunch, then moved on to demolition. There the instructor was a sergeant named Wisnewski, a man of average size with steely blue eyes that spoke of someone who knew a mistake could send him to kingdom come in a flash of heat and light.

Wisnewski was balding, about forty, with a flat, expressionless face and thin lips that seemed to form a rigid line. He spoke in a monotone, pausing for emphasis, or, Alex thought, to await an explosion.

The initial part of the instruction centered on Czech plastique, the type favored by terrorists and Third World guerrillas, and various detonation devices, the emphasis heavily weighted on defusing discovered booby traps. Wisnewski also gave a half-hour lecture on the use of explosives in cover areas that might be used by an enemy under fire, such as ditches along a roadway.

"The point of ambush is the target area," he explained. "But laying down a killing field of fire is only half of what's needed. Their people—those who survive the initial burst of fire—will move to the nearest cover. And you want them there. Providing your explosives are waiting for them." He grinned. "It beats hell out of sending in people with grenades to dislodge them."

The final phase of the instruction involved the use of common household articles to create explosives. With deft hands Wisnewski blended various brand-name substances into a vile, greenish, glue-like liquid, and spread it on a sheet of linoleum flooring with a paint brush. Again he grinned. Stepping back, he stooped to pick up a rock and tossed it onto the linoleum. The greenish, now invisible paste burst into a roar of flame. Wisnewski's grin widened. "Home-made napalm," he said. "A fucking fly will set it off, and there's no odor, no coloring to give an enemy any warning.

"One more item," Wisnewski said, "then I'll want you to repeat what you've been taught a few hundred times." There was no grin this time. The man was deadly serious.

Wisnewski withdrew a small gelatin capsule from his fatigues and held it up between his thumb and index finger. "Women take these to strengthen their nails," he said. "You can buy them in most grocery and drugstores."

He broke the capsule open and emptied it. "The capsule dissolves with heat over time," he explained. "The body heat in the stomach is sufficient to do it."

He pointed to a bowl on a nearby table, then walked to it and began filling the capsule with a white power. "The basic ingredient is sodium," he explained, then rattled off the other ingredients, which, again, could be easily purchased in various commercial establishments.

When the capsule was put together again, he walked Alex to a large gasoline can fitted by a long pipe to a small engine. He inserted the capsule into the gas can, then walked over and started the engine.

Taking Alex's arm, he marched him two hundred feet away and stood, waiting.

"It's a simulated automobile," he said. "The gasoline will heat up as the engine runs. If it was a car, it would have traveled about four or five blocks before the gas was hot enough. Or idled about four or five minutes."

As he finished speaking the gas tank erupted in a ball of flame.

"Beauty of it," Wisnewski said, "is that it leaves no traces. No remnants of detonators or anything. Only drawback is you can't determine where it will go off, so there's always the risk of collateral damage." He shrugged, as if the vision of innocent victims who had happened into the wrong place at the wrong time was simply a question of choice, not substance. And Alex knew in the real world of terrorism and counter-terrorism, it was just that.

Alex was taken next to a basic obstacle course, and put through his paces by Gunderson. He was beat and battered, and he dragged himself through in record poor time, as Gunderson was quick to point out.

Next came another obstacle course, this one a mock city block —a type of Hogan's Alley course used by police—only set not only with jump-up targets, but with mock flash explosives simulating booby traps. Live rounds were used in the various weapons he was handed. And Alex "died" fourteen times before he finished the two-hour session.

"You're the easiest KIA I've ever seen," Gunderson told him. "I hope whoever you're going after is old and blind and feeble enough to need a fucking wheelchair." He glared at him. "Otherwise you're going to fucking well disgrace me."

They ended the day with their second four-mile run, a coup de grace that left Alex too weary to even contemplate dinner. But Gunderson marched him to the mess hall anyway, then seated him at a corner table away from the other men.

"You haven't earned the right to eat with troops yet," he snapped. "It would be insulting to them."

Alex looked up at the sergeant, the words *fuck you* forming on his lips. Gunderson stood, waiting for them to be uttered, and when they were not, smiled, and reminded Alex to be "up and out" by 0500 the next morning. Then he turned on his heel and left.

Alex struggled to put a forkful of white mush into his mouth.

As the third week drew to a close, Alex knew he was fitter than he had been in years. His reflexes were honed and as sharp as his forty-three years would allow, and the inch of flab that had circled his waist for over a decade was gone, the years of booze and rich food purged from his system.

Gunderson came to him the night before he was scheduled to leave. He was dressed in civvies, and, impossibly, looked even larger and more threatening than he did in battle dress.

"Thought I'd take you out for a beer," he said. "If you can stand to drink with somebody who's broken your balls for three weeks."

"You are a ballbreaker," Alex said. "One of the best I've ever had the displeasure to meet." He grinned at the bigger man. "And I'd be damned pleased to have a beer with you," he added.

The bar was just outside of Fayetteville, a large, rough, shabby place filled with a mixture of GIs and local boys who could handle mingling with the occasional black face. Not that they had a choice, Alex knew. The military was far from perfect in race relations, but those who were part of it—especially those in elite units like Special Forces or Airborne—didn't take kindly to one of their own being shat upon by anyone. And it didn't matter how big the asshole was, or how many of his friends stood behind him. And Alex was certain it was a lesson that had been learned well and often in this establishment and a host of others that dotted the South.

They stood at the end of the bar, large beers before them, the twang of a country singer blaring from a jukebox.

"So when do you pull out?" Gunderson asked. "If you can say," he added.

"Have to make a brief stop in D.C.," Alex said. "Then I'm leaving. Whether they want me to or not."

"Don't sound like you care for those boys at the big L too much."

"I just don't plan on getting tied into their endless bullshit," Alex said. "I did that for too many years. And I also have some personal reasons."

"Yeah," Gunderson said. "Colonel mentioned that."

"You headed out anywhere soon?" Alex asked, both out of interest and to change the subject.

"Afraid I'm stuck playing nursemaid for a bit," Gunderson said. "Then, who knows? Depends on who needs killing, I guess."

Nursemaid, Alex thought. Not exactly a fucking Mary Poppins. He smiled, wishing he had the nerve to speak the thought aloud.

A large, hard body banged into Alex's side, almost knocking the beer from his hand.

"Shove down, old man," a voice snapped.

Alex turned and found himself staring at a red-faced, redheaded behemoth about three inches taller and twenty pounds heavier than he. The man was staring at the bartender, but there was a smirk on his face, just waiting to become a smile. *After* he had battered Alex into the floor.

"Sure," Alex said. He and Gunderson took two steps to their right.

Alex lifted his beer again, but felt a jab in his shoulder before it reached his mouth. The finger felt like a steel rod.

"Maybe I'd like it better if you found a table," the behemoth said. "Maybe a table in another bar."

Alex's jaw tightened, and his left eye narrowed almost imperceptively. "Sure. I'll just finish this beer."

"Maybe you already finished it."

A flash of movement caught his eye even before the behemoth finished the sentence, and Alex took a quick step back and dropped one shoulder, allowing the beer mug the behemoth had swung at his head to pass harmlessly by and smash into the bar in a shower of broken glass.

His own beer mug, still in his hand, shot out and crashed into the behemoth's face. His knee followed, finding the man's groin, feeling the satisfying softness of the solid hit, seeing him sag, knees buckling, then grabbing his ears, and driving the knee up again, this time into the man's blood-soaked face.

Two massive arms encircled his own, and he felt himself being lifted off the ground.

"Enough. Enough," Gunderson said. His voice was soft and soothing, and Alex couldn't understand what in hell he was doing. The behemoth was pulling himself up, and if Gunderson didn't let him go, the man would drive one of those massive hams he called fists right through his head.

"Let go, dammit," he snapped, fighting to twist away from Gunderson's grasp.

"Easy, boy," Gunderson cooed, apparently oblivious to the red-headed hulk who stood before Alex now, wiping blood from his eyes.

"Let me introduce you to Sergeant Macrae," Gunderson said. "He's one of ours. But it seems this ol' boy could use a refresher course himself."

Gunderson released Alex, letting him drop back to the floor.

"Jesus Christ," Macrae said. "You teachin' these boys too good. Goddamned instructor could get himself killed around here."

Macrae shook his head, sending a few drops of blood flying off into space. Then he extended his hand. "Nice to meet you, Moran," he said. "Not bad for an out-of-shape, over-the-hill asshole. What was your next move gonna be? My nose into my brain?"

"I was thinking about it," Alex said. "Sorry."

"Ain't nothin'," Macrae said. "Couple of days in the sack, I'll be fine." He laughed through blood-coated teeth that Alex was pleased to see were still all where they should be.

Alex turned to Gunderson and drew a long breath. "One final bit of ballbreaking?" he asked.

Gunderson inclined his head to one side and grinned. "Hard to get out of the habit," he said. "Besides, had to find out if you really learned all that shit we taught you."

Gunderson marched him smartly across the parade ground and into Colonel Hugh Donlon's office, saying only he wished they had more time to "get him up," but that "those fucking assholes at Langley said three weeks, no more, no less."

Donlon stood as they entered, returned Gunderson's salute, and nodded to Alex, who was again dressed in civvies and not expected to offer or receive military courtesy.

"Gunderson tells me you're ready," Donlon said. He reached down to his desk, picked up a "Green Beanie," and tossed it to Alex. "He also tells me you earned this. I agree."

"Thank you, Colonel," Alex said.

Donlon grinned. "Hugh's good enough," he said.

"Thank you again, Hugh," Alex said.

Donlon extended his hand, and they shook.

"Go get that fucker," Donlon said.

Alex nodded, then turned to Gunderson. "Thank you, Sergeant," he said.

Gunderson smiled. "Kill the fuck quick and come back for a beer," he said.

"I'll do both with pleasure," Alex said. "And I won't disgrace you."

"I know *that*, sir," Gunderson said. He snapped Alex a casual salute.

Alex arrived at CIA headquarters at nine the following day, cleared security, and was ushered to Walter Hennesey's fourth-floor office.

He had not seen the man since he had accompanied Alex and his father home from Marseilles aboard a U.S. government jet after Alex had agreed to leave the Pisani stronghold in Cervione. He had hated and distrusted the man then, and his feelings had not mellowed in the intervening years.

Hennesey sat behind his highly polished desk, partially hidden behind a blue cloud sent up from his pipe.

"You look as fit as they tell me you are," he said. "So I guess you're ready and anxious to get on with it."

Alex nodded. "The only question is how *you* think we'll play it," he said.

Hennesey picked up on the unspoken threat and chose to ignore it. He briefed Alex on the current situation in Marseilles. Two more Pisani men had been killed in a bomb blast.

"I'll want you to report to our station chief in Marseilles, Jim Wheelwright. He works out of the consulate there, and he has all our updated information on Ludwig." Hennesey paused. "Everything but where he is. We're told he moves back and forth to Colombia—I suppose to confer with his drug boss, Montoya—but he doesn't seem to be out of France more than a week at a time."

"Is he there now?" Alex asked.

"We think so. But if not, he'll be back shortly. And, of course, he won't know you're there hunting him."

"Yes, he will," Alex said. "I intend to make sure he knows. I want to see if he'll come for me. Force him to, if I can."

"He's not that stupid," Hennesey said. "Why wouldn't he just send someone else—one of his greaseball hitmen? Or all of them."

"His supply's not unlimited," Alex said.

Hennesey stared at him. "You know the man," he said at length. "Do whatever you think will work. Wheelwright's there to help in any way he can. He can provide people too."

"I'll use Pisani people," Alex said. "I trust them, and they're better."

Hennesey bristled at the slap, but again said nothing. "As you wish." He drew heavily on his pipe, sending up another plume of blue smoke. "You'll tell Wheelwright as little as possible, and report only to me," he said. "You'll be a bit out of the loop, but we need deniability here."

Alarm bells went off in Alex's brain. Deniability meant only one thing. They could sell you out at their pleasure. "Fuck deniability," he snapped. "You want that, I go without you and work directly with the Pisanis and no one else."

Hennesey leaned forward, his eyes hard. "You try that, we stop you," he said. Alex had no doubt he was serious.

"Good luck," he snapped back.

Hennesey sat back in his chair and stepped on a floor button beneath his desk. The door to Alex's right, to an adjoining office, opened, and his father walked into the room.

"We have a problem," Hennesey said. "Alex doesn't like the deniability aspect of the plan, and has suggested I contemplate having intercourse with myself."

Piers looked down at his son and smiled. "I've suggested the same thing to Walter on numerous occasions," he said. "But this should not be one of them."

Piers took a chair next to his son, and reached out and squeezed his arm. "It's good to see you, Alex," he said. "You look appropriately fit."

"Cut the bullshit, Dad," Alex said. "Let's stick with deniability."

Piers pursed his lips in rebuke but said nothing. He had seen the slight narrowing of Alex's left eye, and knew from years of experience it meant he was ready and willing to go to war. Men who had ignored that telltale sign—either out of ignorance or folly—had wished they had not.

"This is the only way—and the best way—to get to Ludwig," Piers said. "We want you to be able to hit anyone you need to hit. That means French nationals, in the case of any opposition from within the *milieu*, any French government officials—cops or whoever—who get in your way, and, of course, Ludwig and his people. You can use a CIA cover until the killing starts. Then you cannot. At that point you're strictly free-lance—somebody we hired who has gone off on his own." He stared hard at Alex. "There is no other way. You have to trust me on that. And, it's best for you. I say that as your father."

Alex eased back in his chair, nodded to his father, then looked across at Hennesey. "I'll do it your way," he said. "But you fuck me this time, and you better have them kill me. Because Ludwig won't be my last stop."

Hennesey glared at him, then looked away. He wasn't the least bit concerned. He did not expect Alex to survive the mission, and he wondered if Piers had deluded himself into thinking he would.

"I understand you, Alex," Hennesey said. "And I'm not concerned."

He stood and walked around his desk. "I want to walk you down to Supply," he said. "We have some things for you that will be sent on ahead, but I want to make sure you're familiar with them."

"What things?" Alex asked.

"The main item is a KL-43 secure phone transmitter. It's new since your time. And, as I said, I want you reporting directly to me. Without anyone listening in. You'll like it. It's an interesting toy."

"I shan't go with you," Piers said. "I've seen all Walter's toys.

But I'd like it very much if we could have dinner together. I'm staying at the Hay-Adams, as usual. Could you meet me around seven?"

"I'll be there," Alex said.

"Well then, come," Hennesey said. "It's not exactly a James Bond laboratory headed by some truculent man named Q, but I think you'll find our toy department interesting."

CHAPTER

(35)

Medellín, Colombia

Ernst Ludwig sat by the edge of the reflecting pool and studied his image in the water. It was like a mirror; not a hint of a breeze stirred its surface. It was three o'clock and the hot South American sun beat down on the back of his head, and he wished he was inside, sitting in the shade under a moving fan, a cool drink in hand.

But Montoya liked to spend the middle and late afternoons in the garden at the rear of his house, sitting behind the great twelve-foot wall that surrounded the property, basking in the elaborate, carefully tended beds of plants and flowers, staring with personal satisfaction at the cheap imitations of ancient sculpture that rose from the flora like ridiculous specters. But they weren't cheap, or rather, it was an imprecise description. They were expensive cheap imitations, Ludwig told himself.

He stared across the reflecting pool to the place where Venus de Milo stood, staring across a flower bed at a massive marble David. One of Montoya's men had once suggested that David should have an erection as he stared back at Venus's tits, and Montoya had thrown a drink in his face and shouted that he was a crude peasant who didn't understand great art. Later, the man had been found dead. Montoya had feared he had injured the man's sense of machismo, and could therefore no longer trust him.

Ludwig looked to his left, where a bust of Adolf Hitler stood before a backdrop of hibiscus. Montoya worshiped the man, spoke endlessly about how he would have dealt with various situations. It was the way the man had mesmerized a nation, controlled all who surrounded him with an iron will. Montoya liked to think he too possessed the same malevolent charisma, Ludwig believed. And, he also believed, it was the reason he had hired a German to lead his narcotics blitzkrieg of Europe. Ludwig shook his head. The man had even had a Nazi death's head tattooed to the back of his left hand.

He looked back into the reflecting pool and studied the scar on his cheek. He had grown used to it, fond even. It had the look of an old dueling scar, now so highly favored among certain aristocratic young Germans. He turned his head to one side, then the other, searching out the gray hairs that had begun to appear over the past five years. He had colored them, but they had returned and multiplied, and it had proven a regular monthly battle. He had won that fight, but not the one with the faint lines that had begun to appear at the corners of his eyes and mouth. He had been unable to do anything about it—or the scar—to place himself under a surgeon's blade, to lay unconscious before a stranger with a knife. He dismissed the thought, and his gaze returned to the scar, and the memory of how he had received it. But now repayments were being made. The Pisanis, who had helped Alex Moran hunt him, were being slowly decimated, tortured into nonexistence. He had thought of going after Moran himself, but had decided against it. Better to let the man live out his life in the misery that had been created for him, he had concluded.

The sound of leather heels clicking across a stone walkway brought him back, and he turned to see Montoya approaching, a self-satisfied smile spread across his face. The man was dressed, as always, in a light-colored Armani suit—an off-white today—a bright pink shirt, open at the collar to reveal a heavy gold chain, and highly polished, custom-made loafers. He looked like a pimp, Ludwig thought. And he had the mentality of one as well.

Ludwig had nothing but contempt for the man, but not his money. When the Russian bastards had sent him to South and Central America ten years before, he had viewed it as a journey to virgin territory—and himself as a German Guevara. But he had found little more than well-financed rabble, with grasping leaders, many of whom could not read or write their own language. And they had crumbled like what they were, the Nicaraguans most sadly of all, while the great Cubans had sat cowering in a corner, salting away money for the day their own revolution would fall.

He had wanted to go back to Europe then, but there was nothing to which he could return. Eastern Europe had been vaporized by its own hand, with the help of the now self-devouring Russians, and the *Stazi*, once the protector of revolutionaries throughout Europe, had quickly sold out the very men and women they had trained and financed for decades. So he had found himself a Guevara without a revolution, a guerrilla without protection, with no place to hide. Oh, there were the Arabs—the Palestinians and the Islamic madmen who did the bidding of Iran—but their vision of the world was worse than the capitalists, and even Montoya had been better than that.

And Montoya's money.

Ludwig made no excuses for the money. The revolution had failed, and there would be no socialist fighters sitting at the heads of new governments. Those that were there now—even in such bastions as China and Romania—were hanging on by the barest of threads. No, money would rule. And, after all, the results for those who had it would be the same. Privilege and power were the ultimate goals—along with whatever good was possible for the masses—and each could be achieved through either money or politics. He had simply chosen politics, and it had proven the wrong path at this point in history.

"So, how was your flight?" Montoya asked as he came to a halt at the reflecting pool. Twenty steps behind him was his ever present bodyguard, Hector, a short, slender ferret of a man who carried an Uzi at all times, even here behind the twelve-foot walls of Montoya's garden.

"It is a long flight. Always tiring," Ludwig said in Spanish.

Montoya allowed his thick lower lip to protrude and wagged his head from side to side in a gesture that both sympathized with and ridiculed the complaint.

"Telephones and the mails are not for us," he said. "Besides, I like to see your handsome German face, and hear how you are destroying my enemies."

Montoya was a small man, little more than a fifty-year-old bantamweight, with an oversized nose and capped teeth that had somehow managed to remain crooked despite the painstaking dental work. He had jet black hair and brown eyes that always seemed to dart from one place to another. He reminded Ludwig of a fox who always believed the dogs were close at hand.

Montoya, Ludwig knew, thought of himself as a sophisticate in the European tradition—a laughable idea for a shrewd, brutal, sociopathic peasant, all dressed up like a bad Hollywood version of a gangster. But it was what he wanted to think, how he believed others viewed him, and Ludwig knew it was a scenario that played well for him. Two "Europeans" directing their Colombian peasant army on the continent.

"Your enemies are being destroyed at a steady pace," Ludwig said.

"But too slow," Montoya said. "It should go faster, no?"

Ludwig stood so he would have the benefit of towering over the five-foot, five-inch drug czar, something he knew Montoya hated.

"No," he said. "Too much violence would bring unwanted attention. Marseilles has just been scandalized by a very public murder that involved two city councilmen, who were also doctors and who were involved in a battle over control of health clinics." He shrugged. "A certain amount or killing is expected, and tolerated, but open warfare would shine a light on us. And it could bring the Americans in, if only to protect their assets in the *milieu*."

Montoya waved a disparaging hand. "The Americans," he spat. "They are fools who don't know what they want. Their people spend forty billion a year on our product, while their government wages its ridiculous war on us. And at the same time, its chemical companies ship us everything we need for manufacture. If the Americans were serious they would go to Dow and tell them to keep their chemicals at home."

"There is a difference between their government and the people who run their country," Ludwig said.

Montoya's face turned to a scowl. "The difference is that we are losing money," he snapped. "I want the Pisanis dead, and I want them dead now." He was raging, and he glanced quickly behind him to make sure Hector was there. He had a fear of Ludwig, and Ludwig understood it. He was not used to dealing with intelligent killers, and the reality made him nervous.

Montoya flashed a smile, his mood changing in another erratic swing. "Europe is gold," he said, his eyes glittering now. "Almost as much gold as America. Maybe more someday, as one goes up and the other goes down. And when you see gold you must mine it quickly. With a machine gun."

Montoya paused to laugh at his joke, then beckoned Ludwig to some chairs off to the left of his bust of Hitler. When they were seated he gestured toward the bust. "He understood," he said. "Overwhelm your enemy with your power. It is the only way."

Ludwig nodded. And then shoot yourself in your bunker, he thought. But by then I'll be gone, he told himself. And what would happen to Montoya would be a fait accompli. Europeans would never deal with South American filth. They would be offended by them, and even their money would not wash away the stench. Europeans preferred their own thieves and killers. They did not offend their sensibilities, and their money was just as good, perhaps better.

"We will do it however you want," Ludwig said. "I can only offer advice."

Montoya raised a hand. "And it is good. But you are too cautious." He offered his uneven capped teeth—a gesture of friendship and tolerance. "In a few weeks I will join you in France. I want to meet with this man Francisci, and I want to enjoy the death of my enemies."

"I will find a place for you," Ludwig said.

Montoya waved a hand around his garden. "Something suitable," he said, his thick lips forming a pout.

Of course, Ludwig thought. And we will put up a sign announcing your presence.

"There is a villa outside Aix-en-Provence that Francisci owns," Ludwig said. "I am sure he'll make it available."

"Suitable?" Montoya asked, waving his hand about his garden again.

Ludwig smiled. "Not as grand as your own home, but then, the Europeans are not as rich. But it is old and dignified and very European. I think it will suit you."

Montoya nodded. He liked the answer.

Raphael Rivera joined them for dinner. He was an impeccably dressed man, no more than forty, who spoke flawless Spanish, although with what Ludwig detected as a distinctly American accent.

Montoya treated him like visiting royalty, although Hector still remained close at hand, and Ludwig was not sure if it was because of his own presence or Rivera's as well.

Rivera had been introduced as a businessman from Bogotá, but Ludwig thought he had the smell of CIA about him, and he wondered if his old enemies had decided to switch sides and drop their longtime assets, the Pisanis, into the slaughterhouse. It would explain Montoya's sudden machine-gun bravado, he decided.

"Our friend here is buying some points in our European enterprise," Montoya explained. "And he agrees with me that we should move quickly against these Corsicans."

Rivera gestured with his manicured hands in what could only be described as halfhearted agreement. Ludwig noticed that Montoya was rubbing the death's head tattoo on the back of his left hand, something he did only when agitated.

"What do you think of the timing?" Rivera asked. He was tall for a Hispanic, nearly six feet, and he had the slender, well-conditioned, straight-backed bearing of someone who had spent time in the military. But there was a slippery sense to him as well. He had the narrow, pointed face of a thief, and dark, close-set eyes that spoke of someone who would pick your pocket or slit your throat, if either proved convenient.

"The timing, in France, is not good," Ludwig said, noting the angry glare from Montoya. He ignored it, but not completely. There was money at stake here. "If we can take out the Pisanis themselves, I think their faction will fold, and our friend Francisci will simply swallow what is left into his own group. If it's a protracted bloodbath, I think it will hurt us." He paused, gauging the man he was now certain was an American. "My worry is what the Americans will do. If they will send support to their old friends."

"What if I told you they were already doing so?" Rivera asked.

"Then I would say we should move quickly, before they're in place." He stared at Rivera. "Who, and how many are they sending?" Ludwig asked.

Rivera smiled. He was like a cat watching a bird with a broken wing, Ludwig thought.

"Someone you know," Rivera said. "A man named Alex Moran. And he should arrive quite soon."

Ludwig's eyes hardened, then his mouth broke into a slow smile. "Then they know I am there," he said.

"Oh, yes," Rivera said. "They know."

"Then I think we should move very quickly indeed," Ludwig said. "And I think we should add my old friend Alex to our list."

"Or make it appear he's behind any bloodbath that is forced on us," Rivera said. "*Before* we kill him," he added, almost as an afterthought.

"Yes," Ludwig said, nodding. "Although it's always regrettable to postpone pleasure."

CHAPTER

36

Marseilles

The drive from the airport brought back a flood of memories, some pleasant, others that served only to fuel his anger and self-contempt. Alex was surprised how being back in Marseilles had intensified his feelings. As the taxi passed the Vieux Port and turned toward the Corniche Kennedy, he glanced toward the battered roofs of the old quarter, and the vision of Stephanie's body flew at him, taking him back to the Street of Pistols and the blood-soaked squalor of the tenement basement.

He avoided looking at their old apartment building as the taxi passed it, staring instead out at the sea, only to find himself recalling the view from their windows and the day he had stared out at the deep blue of the Mediterranean as Stephanie acknowledged her affair.

No, the memories here were not good, would never be, and he realized Marseilles was a city to which he would never have returned had it not been for the chance to kill Ernst Ludwig.

He thought about Ludwig now, wondering if he were here. Wondering how many he had killed in the intervening ten years. And whose conscience carried those lives.

The man's face was still vivid in his mind. The vision of him crouched and firing; young, foolish Blount, his body flying back into a doorway. Dead before he hit the ground. And of Ludwig turning, the weapon seeking out a new target—himself this time

—the eyes clear and sharp with the will to kill again, the hint of a smile—although the last might be imagination, he told himself, forged out of time and hatred. But the face was burned in his mind. He would not forget it. And he wanted to see it again—and the smile, if it existed then, now—and he wanted it all just before the man died.

But more than the face, he remembered the voice. The cruel, mocking tone as he described Stephanie's sexual attributes, praised her talents, told him what she had done to him, with him. Conversations that had replayed again and again, and had left him trembling, still left him that way.

And then he had killed her. Butchered her and left her body as a vile, battered message. And he had robbed him not just of the woman, but of the chance of ever knowing if they could have survived what had happened between them. Kept him from knowing if what Ludwig had said was true. If they had been together for months or, if not, if they could overcome her affair with Morganthau. If she had wanted them to.

The thought of Morganthau brought him back to his last dinner with his father. He had asked him why it had taken so long. Why the promises made years before in Cervione had never been kept.

Morganthau, his father had said. What had happened to him had angered people. Made them believe he was too unstable.

"What about Morganthau?" he asked, bewildered.

"You didn't know?" His father stared at him. "No, you didn't, did you?"

"Tell me!" he demanded.

His father shook his head. "The man was beaten. Very badly, very professionally. In a way you could have done, or had done."

He said the man had fled the service, run away in terror. And that those in power in the agency had used it against him.

It was a lie, of course. An excuse to escape their promise. He knew that, but he had kept silent. Alex only hoped his father had not been part of it.

And he knew who had had Morganthau beaten and terrorized. And in a strange way he was grateful for it. At least one old account—deserving or not—had been settled.

The car pulled to a halt, bringing him back, and he found himself at the gates of the Pisani estate. There were four men at the gate now, and two more off at a distance whom he could see. The brothers were on a war footing and taking no chances. He glanced up toward the house, at the corner balconies that had been reinforced to give and repel heavy-weapons fire. They had never been manned to his knowledge, but now they were. The Pisani brothers were afraid. And he had never witnessed that before.

Alex and his driver were searched and questioned, the trunk and front and rear seats inspected. The taxi driver, a man from Marseilles, took it all well, as something to be expected, and tonight, Alex knew, he would tell of it gleefully in his favorite café. And he would be the envy of his friends.

When the taxi pulled before the front door, Antoine did not come bounding down the front steps. Instead two more men descended, and searched and questioned him again. Then they walked him— still watching—to the old, remembered study, where he found his uncles sitting before the unlit fire, awaiting him. It was as it had been ten years ago, and it was not.

"Donkey," Antoine shouted, rising from his chair, embracing him, squeezing the air from him in a huge hug. He kissed him ferociously on both cheeks, only to be followed by Meme, who did it all again but with less strength, less vigor.

Alex stared at them, pleased to see them, to be with them again. And he saw they had become old men and was surprised he had not expected it.

He thought about it and realized Antoine must now be seventy, Meme sixty-nine. And the gray had come heavily to them, and the lines in their faces, and a certain frailty that had never been there before. It will be hard for them to survive this, he told himself. And then he dismissed it. He would never want to confront them, he knew. Not even old and frail as they seemed.

"Come, sit. Tell us everything," Antoine bellowed, gesturing toward a chair by the fireplace.

"How have you been?" Alex asked, taking his appointed chair.

"I have been well," Meme said. "Antoine grows worse by the day. The older he gets, the more aggravation he brings to my life. I have even thought of killing him just to put him out of his misery."

Antoine snorted and waved a hand in disgust. "He could not find enough help to do it, or he would have tried," he said. He hooked his fingers along either side of his mouth. "He is like an old pig who has lost its tusks." He winked at Alex. "You remember the pigs, eh? You old pants pisser?"

"I never did. Your mind is failing you," Alex said. He was smiling, couldn't help himself.

"I have lost many things," Antoine said. "My dick mostly. But my mind remembers everything."

"Don't tell us what your mind remembers or your dick has forgotten, you old fool," Meme snapped. "I want to hear about our nephew, and how his life has been the past ten years." He raised a finger to Alex. "You should have visited us. I am very upset with you."

"I wrote," Alex said. His face hardened. "Europe was forbidden to me."

Antoine grunted. "We have been surrounded by dunces," he said. "But tell us. We want to know of your life."

Alex told them. He ended it with the visit from Cisco, and the training at Bragg, and finally the meeting with Hennesey and his father.

"I need you to help me," he said. "And I need the use of your men."

"You don't trust the help they offer you," Meme said. It was not a question and was not spoken as one. He watched Alex nod that it was so. "You are wise," he said. "I do not trust them either, even though we have little choice."

"Tell me what has happened," Alex said. They were speaking French as they always had, and the sentence structure of the language—which he had not used much in the intervening years —seemed strangely formal to him. "I have heard their version. Now I need to know yours."

"Much," Antoine said. And he explained the war that had been launched against them by Montoya and Ludwig.

"They have been killing our men at will," Antoine said. He glowered. "We have struck back. But we have not been able to do so with the force that is needed."

"Why?" Alex asked. "Is the *milieu* not behind you?"

"It is not the *milieu*," Meme said. "Although there are enemies there as well." He shrugged. "Francisci and some others would like to see us fall. As you know, in the *milieu* the leader of a faction does not have the authority to choose an heir. If he dies, or loses power, each lieutenant has the right to break away to join another group or start his own faction. So it is in the interests of the other factions for us to fall. They would no longer have to deal with our

power, and what we have would be there for the taking." He offered
Alex a face filled with contempt. "But that is a problem we have
always faced. It is not what is hurting us. Now it is politics more
than anything. We lack the influence we once had there."

"I don't understand," Alex said. "What caused it to disappear?"

"Fate," Antoine said.

"More than fate," Meme countered. "Madness as well."

Alex waited, and Meme drew a long breath, then explained.

"Old Gaston died in 1986, and there was a grasping for the power
that had been his for more than thirty years. At first the Socialists
could not agree on a candidate, which was to be expected after so
many years of Gaston's iron rule. Robert Vigouroux, a surgeon,
stepped in after Gaston died, and wanted to run for a full term as
mayor. We were never close to him, so we did not support him."
Meme raised a finger. "But we did not oppose him. We supported
no one." He shrugged. "Then there was Michel Pizet, a longtime
activist in the local Socialist organization, and Bernard Tapie, a
businessman, who owned a soccer team, and they both wanted to
keep the Socialist nomination from Vigouroux." He waved his
hand. "If it had been the *milieu*, blood would have flowed in the
streets, the fight was so bitter.

"Then there was Jean-Claude Gaudin, the neo-Gaullist, and
the Communists as well, all seeing a chance to seize City Hall from
the Socialists at long last, along with all the political wealth and
power it holds."

He raised a finger again, wagging it. "But it was Jean-Marie Le
Pen who turned it all to true madness. The man is a fascist, although
he claims he is not, and his National Front Party made the im-
migrants their battle cry. France for the French. It was shit, but
people listened."

"And Corsicans were suddenly viewed as foreigners," Antoine
added. "Because of the great separatist movement at home on our
island."

"And the others—the Socialists, all of them—were suddenly
fearful that association with the *milieu* would be the kiss of death,"
Meme said. He shook his head sadly.

"So we had waited to see who would come out of it strongest.
And suddenly no one wanted us. It was as though we were diseased.
So we supported no one, and when Vigouroux won, he owed us
nothing. And he has given it to us."

"Then the other madness started," Antoine said. "Suddenly the people of Marseilles became offended by their image. They did not want to be known as a place of criminals and thieves. They pointed to Paris and the fact that its crime rate was higher than Marseilles." He beat a hand against his chest. "And who made it that way? We did. It was our power that stopped the fighting within the *milieu*. We have given them peace, and they give us shit."

"And now there is this new organization," Meme said. "They call it: *A New Outlook on Marseille*. It is filled with businessmen and doctors and politicians and lawyers, and they even threaten to sue the newspapers if they say anything bad about the city. They even threaten to sue individual citizens who say the city is corrupt." He raised his hands to the heavens. "My God, they are all mad." He let his hands fall to his lap. "But *we* are now like shit on the street. And they are pleased when they hear another Corsican has been murdered. They are delighted. It is the elimination of a plague to them."

"And the police—the bastards—they have picked up on it," Antoine said. "And we can count on them for nothing, except to raid our businesses and hound us. And this, after all the money we have paid them all these years." He waved both hands. "We can survive that. These men could not find their dicks in their own pants. But they do not interfere with our enemies. We do not get the help we once got. And that has left us exposed as we have not been in years."

"And if we fight back too hard, they will hound us even more," Meme concluded. "So we have kept the killing outside the city. But we cannot continue it. Not if we want to survive."

"Don't they see the danger of the drugs?" Alex asked. "The cocaine and the South Americans, all the killing it has brought with it everywhere it has gone?"

Meme snorted. "They do not want to know about it. Vigouroux visited Panama four years ago, right after Gaston died. He went there, he said, to urge the Panamanians to give a contract to a local company. And then he entertained Noriega here in Marseilles." He offered a ferret's smile. "It was before anyone knew about Noriega's drug business. But now they know, and they are pointing back to it, and all the politicians are hiding. 'What drugs?' they are saying. 'There are no drugs in Marseilles. We have never heard of such a thing.' " He used a high-pitched, little girl's voice, mocking them.

"And when anyone even suggests the Colombians are moving in, they tuck their heads under their arms and make believe they are like little ducks, just sleeping in the sunshine." He turned and spat into the fireplace, unable to control the need.

"And every time *our* names come up in the bastard newspapers, they talk about *The French Connection*," Antoine snapped. "Shit, that was decades ago. And was anyone ever arrested? Did we spend one day in jail? It is we who should sue." He forced himself to calm down, then almost smiled. "Except everyone would laugh at us."

"I am glad to hear I won't be limited where I work," Alex said. "But if you think it is better without your men—"

"No, no," Meme said. "We want to end this. You must kill the bastards where you find them. And our men will help you."

"Do you know where Ludwig is?"

Antoine snorted. "If I knew, I would be able to take you to his grave and help you piss on it." His face grew red, angry. "He is like a phantom. We only see him when he kills us. And when we kill his men, others arrive within days."

"I'll find him," Alex said. "I have a need to."

"And we have someone who will help you," Meme said. "She has a need as well."

"She?" Alex questioned.

"It is someone you know," Meme said. "Her husband was killed by Ludwig." He shook his head. "He was an accountant, nothing more. He was not truly part of us. He should not have died." Meme was silent for a moment. As was Antoine. It was as though they couldn't bring themselves to speak the rest.

"And her son," Meme finally added. "Only three years old. Blown up in the same car."

"Who is this woman?" Alex asked.

"Michelle Cabarini," Antoine said. "The young girl you knew as Michelle Sabitini, whose family you lived with in Cervione." He paused, as though the words left a taste in his mouth. "She works for us now. She manages export sales for our vineyards. And she too has a need to kill Ludwig."

Michelle arrived after lunch. She entered the study, much the same as Alex had remembered her, only older, more womanly, and with a look of deep sadness about her eyes.

"Hello, Alex," she said, extending her hand, then thinking better of it and reaching out to embrace him. She felt soft and warm in his arms, and he recalled the beauty and innocence he had come to know in Cervione so many years before. The beauty was still there, even more so, he thought. But there was something hard there as well, and it was something he understood and appreciated.

"I am sorry about your husband and your son," he said. "Deeply sorry for you."

"It has been almost a year," she said. "And the pain is not as strong."

Alex knew it was a lie, or rather, something she wished to be true.

He stood looking at her. She was exceptionally beautiful, even through the deep sorrow that lay beneath the surface. Perhaps even more so because of it. She was wearing heels now, and was taller than the five foot, seven inches he remembered, and she was wearing a silk business suit that flattered her figure, a far cry from the young woman who had dressed so demurely in Cervione. But the soft brown eyes and the lustrous dark hair were as he remembered them, along with the delicate Mediterranean features that had once tempted him to forget she was little more than a child.

"It's odd to meet you grown." He stumbled over the next words. "To see you not . . . as a child," he said.

"I was not a child then," she said, smiling. "And I did not think of you as older, really. But now I know you were. If not in years, then in life. It is a sad truth I have learned."

"Cervione was a protected place," Alex said.

"Yes. I should have stayed there. But I was ambitious. The years at the Sorbonne made me so." She hesitated, looking toward Antoine and Meme, smiling at them. She looked back at Alex. "You remember the great lecture I gave you about the evils of vengeance?" she asked.

He nodded. "I remember. We were in the old graveyard."

"Then I suppose I was a child," she said. "Intellectually. And I spoke with all the naivete of a child." Her eyes were suddenly very hard.

It saddened Alex to see it. But he understood.

They sat before the fireplace talking, the four of them. Several hours passed, and they reviewed in detail every attack Ludwig had made, the methods used, the weapons, the number of men, and how they had been deployed. Antoine and Meme skipped the attack against Michelle's husband and child. But she added it to the conversation, telling it completely despite the pain it obviously caused.

He learned more of Michelle's role in the Pisani vineyards. Meme had been modest. She was chief executive of that legal enterprise, although it was clear it had some illegal aspects as well, notably the smuggling of wine out of Corsica in violation of French law. And Alex knew it was unusual for a faction of the *milieu* to trust a woman with such authority. Chauvinism was deeply rooted and unending. So she had to be a woman of high business acumen. And she had to be someone who would not speak beyond the walls of a Pisani stronghold. And now she had indicated she was ready—no, anxious—to kill a man to avenge her husband and child. He had no doubt she would try. He had not known how Corsican she truly was.

"Michelle can provide you with a believable cover," Meme said. "She often deals with representatives of foreign vineyards who want to buy cuttings for transplantation." He waved his hand in a circle. "It is a common thing, and these people often spend considerable time with her. You could be a representative from a vineyard in California. They are common here now."

Alex nodded. "I'll use it with the police if necessary."

The telephone rang, and Antoine moved to get it.

"It would be good to keep your presence hidden from Ludwig as well," Meme said.

"I am not sure I want that," Alex said.

Meme stared at him through narrowed eyes, and Alex caught a look of surprise from Michelle as well.

"The telephone. It is for you, Alex." Antoine too looked surprised, but about the call. It was on a private line few people had, and one only the Pisanis themselves answered. "Someone knows you are here?" he asked, cupping the mouthpiece with his hand to hide his words.

"No one should," Alex said.

He walked to the telephone. "Yes," he said.

"It is good to hear your voice again, Alex Moran," another voice replied.

Alex stood listening as the voice continued.

"Yes, I know," he said at length. His left eye had narrowed, and his jaw had become tight, the muscles dancing beneath the skin. Several moments passed.

"I will see you soon," he said, then replaced the receiver.

He turned to face the others. "We don't have to worry about that other matter," he said. "That was Ernst Ludwig on the phone."

CHAPTER

37

The telephone call played out in Alex's mind. It had done so throughout the night, and had continued into the morning.

"It's so good to hear your voice again, Alex Moran." The same sneering contempt, the same overriding superiority, met now only with silence.

"Do you know who this is, Alex?"

"Yes, I know."

"I thought you would remember me. Recall the sound of my voice. It *has* been ten years. But I am told people have a tendency not to forget me." A laugh. Soft but filled with ridicule.

Again silence.

"I remember *you* very well. And I remember your wife, although for the life of me, I can't seem to recall her name." The soft laughter again. "But then, I am like that. I have this difficulty for names." More soft laughter. "But I never forget what certain individuals do. There my memory is always excellent. Especially if what they do is pleasurable." Alex could feel him grinning. "Have you brought me a new woman, Alex? It will be so nice if you have."

Silence from Ludwig now, awaiting some reply.

"I will see you soon."

"Oh, yes, Alex Moran. Yes, you will." The final words coming as Alex lowered the receiver.

His hands tightened on the steering wheel, and the traffic ahead became a momentary blur. He was driving to the U.S. consulate in a car the Pisanis had given him. There was another car behind

Alex, filled with Pisani men who were shepherding him through the city. His uncles had been concerned that Ludwig had found him the very day he had arrived, had traced him to their home within hours.

It was obvious to Alex that someone had leaked his arrival. The idea that Ludwig might have people watching the airport and that they would be able to identify him from a ten-year-old description was not plausible. Ludwig himself might have, of course. But the man would not expose himself that way. And he was not a watcher. He was a killer, and a director of killers. And his ego would never allow him to take on such a subservient role.

No, Alex told himself. It was possible someone with access to CIA information was helping him. And it meant that someone was helping Montoya. It also meant he would have to be careful dealing with Wheelwright, the CIA station chief he was on his way to see.

Of course, it could have been someone within the Pisani faction. Traitors were not unknown to the *milieu*. He had mentioned that, as gently as possible, to his uncles, and the idea did not seem to surprise them. It was obviously something they had considered, had been worried about. So they had chosen men to protect him whom they considered beyond suspicion. Alex wondered if anyone truly fitted that category.

And then there was Michelle. Concern had flooded her face when she learned it was Ludwig on the telephone. Then her eyes had glittered with hatred and anticipation at the thought it might bring the man to Alex. And therefore to her. He had thought then that the look in her eyes was not dissimilar to that of the boar he had seen so many years ago. The look just before it charged. Pure, naked malevolence. A hatred that could only be satisfied by death. And he had instantly known that Michelle would never betray him, unless it was to bring Ludwig close. And that was a betrayal he would gladly live with.

So there were three people he could trust. His uncles and Michelle. His father flashed to mind, and he instinctively wanted to include him. But he was too removed from the action. He was inconsequential.

Alex left the car in front of the U.S. consulate, and quickly moved to the reception area, getting himself off the street.

The interior of the building hit him at once. It had not changed—not even the furnishings, he thought—since Stephanie had moved through its rooms every day. Stephanie and Morganthau, the secret lovers playing out their clandestine romance. He hated the building, hated being there. It was stupid, absurd, but he knew he would always feel that way. It made him think of his last days with her, his final memories, much as his telephone conversation with Ludwig had. Perhaps if he destroyed Ludwig *and* the building, he would be able to forget. Perhaps.

Michelle moved about her apartment, dressed only in a short black silk robe. The apartment was on the broad hill that rose on the south side of the city's center, not far from the Basilica of Notre Dame-de-la-Garde, and it looked down on the distant quaintness of the Vieux Port. But Michelle ignored the view. She ignored everything but her own agitation—and her unsuccessful attempt to control it.

The man was close. For the first time in almost a year, the man who had killed her husband and her little Pierre was coming close. Close enough . . . She allowed the thought to die, but just barely. Rene and Pierre. How much the thought of them made her ache, tore at her in a way she had never dreamed possible. And Alex would bring the pig who had killed them to her, give her the chance she had sworn to have, even at the cost of her own life.

And what if it cost him his? she thought. What then? Was it worth her need for vengeance? No, he was risking his life for his own vengeance. Would do so no matter what she did.

She felt a stirring for him, one that brought her back ten years, to the time when she had first known him in Corsica. The naive young woman so taken with the man and his pain. And the pain was still there, she told herself, after ten long years it was still there inside him. She wondered if her own pain would still gnaw at her ten years from now. Yes, she told herself. And even more so if Ludwig was still alive.

She lit a cigarette, but ground it out almost immediately. She had begun smoking years before while a student in Paris, and then she had given it up, banished it from her life. She didn't need it, she told herself now, and immediately lit another. Alex would be coming to her later. After his meeting with the American who ran the CIA office here. And she told herself she must find a way to remain close to him so she would be there when Ludwig made his assault. What an innocent word, she thought. Assault, instead of the brutal killing he would attempt. Perhaps even with the same pleasure he had taken when he had killed Alex's wife.

But this time it would be different. This time she would help him, and Ludwig would be the one who would be trapped. She only had to make sure Alex did not keep her from him. Try to keep her away from the danger: keep her safe. She had no need of safety. Only of revenge. She wondered if little Pierre, and gentle, oh so gentle Rene, would have understood.

Alex was ushered into James Wheelwright's office. The man remained behind his desk, his eyes red with lack of sleep, or something. He gestured toward a chair, and Alex sat. He stood then and walked to his suit coat, hanging on a hat tree in one corner, and removed a pack of cigarettes. He was of average height, average appearance, seeming more like a salesman than a spy, with thinning, mousy brown hair that was overwhelmed with dandruff. And he was slightly overweight. Alex guessed his age at about forty-five as he lit a cigarette and perched on the edge of his desk.

"This is a great pain in the ass for me, Moran. And I'm not even sure how much I can help you." He drew on the cigarette, but even behind the smoke Alex could smell the previous night's booze waft off his body.

"I'm not sure how much you can either," Alex said. "But since Ludwig already knows I'm here, somebody sure as hell seems to be able to help him."

"What do you mean, he knows?" Wheelwright said.

"He telephoned me yesterday. At the Pisanis' house."

"Shit," Wheelwright snapped. "Then we better not talk here. We better go to a more secure room."

"What is it, Wheelwright? You think Montoya's got you bugged? Or don't you trust your own people?"

Wheelwright glared at him. "I don't trust anybody anymore, Moran. Not even you. There's so much drug money floating around, I don't know who's been bought, and what's been sold." He glared at Alex. "And I don't like being told to jump for some rogue agent just so he can help a bunch of greaseball drug dealers save their asses. Understood?"

"Yeah, I understand," Alex said. "And fuck you too."

Wheelwright stared at him, and for a moment Alex thought the man might take a swing at him. Then he walked past him. "Follow me, big shot," he snapped, and headed out of the room.

Wheelwright took Alex into the building's basement, through a security checkpoint manned by a Marine guard, and into the Bubble Room. Alex had read about the new secure rooms, developed since he had left the service to counteract new Russian listening devices.

The room was literally a room within a room, with two doors leading inside and a gap of several inches between exterior and interior walls. The exterior walls were lined with four inches of acoustic dampening materials so nothing could be heard inside. Any listening device would have to be planted inside the dampening materials on the interior walls, and those walls, built inches away from the others, were made of Plexiglas, so any listening device secreted there would be visible to those inside. It was like being inside a windowless, glass-walled cocoon.

There was a long table surrounded by chairs, and they took seats across from each other.

"Sometimes I wonder if these rooms are to protect us from ourselves or our enemies," Wheelwright said. "Or if we even know the difference anymore." He tapped his fingers on the highly polished wood. "What do you want to know, and what help do you expect?" he asked.

"I want to know everything you know about Ludwig and Montoya, and I want access to any new intelligence that comes in. As soon as it comes in," Alex said.

"What about men?"

"I don't need any help there."

"Prefer your greaseball gangsters, huh?"

"That's right. They're better than the clowns you have on the street."

Wheelwright stared at him. "Remember what you said to me upstairs?" He offered a cold smile. "Well, fuck you too."

"Good," Alex said. "Now we have that out of the way. So tell me what you know."

Wheelwright continued to stare at him, then snorted, and finally smiled. "You're every bit as much of a prick as they said you'd be, Moran. But they told me to do what I could to help keep you alive. At least until you killed this terrorist cocksucker. So I will."

"Thank you," Alex said.

"You're welcome."

Wheelwright leaned back in his chair and rubbed his bloodshot eyes.

"We *think* the center of activity is somewhere up around Aix. But that's mainly because Francisci operates out of there, and some South Americans have been seen with his people. There are about fifty South Americans, as best as we can estimate, but they're kept pretty much under wraps, so they have to be stashed somewhere. Little fuckers don't speak anything but Spanish, so they stick out everywhere but the Spanish quarter of Marseilles. And we know they're not living there. Our guess is that Ludwig has one or two locations outside the city, where he's got them holed up, and only brings them out when he's going to hit somebody, or to give them a little R & R. We think Francisci sends in hookers to clean their pipes, but frankly, I haven't had enough men to put a tail on all his *poules* to find out."

"I can arrange that," Alex said.

"I'm sure you can," Wheelwright said. "The Pisanis probably know about every hooker within a one-hundred-mile radius. It is their business."

"One of them," Alex said.

"Yeah," Wheelwright added. "Probably the cleanest one they have."

"What about political contacts?" Alex asked. "Through Francisci or Ludwig?"

"We don't see any other than what Francisci has always had. But that doesn't mean shit. It could be through the cops, but, Christ, the Marseilles police will deal with anybody who's got the bucks."

"Except the Pisanis."

"If you say so," Wheelwright said. "I've never been allowed to work them. They've always been controlled out of Langley."

Alex was surprised to hear that, but kept it to himself. "You know I'll be reporting directly to Hennesey? It was his idea, not mine," Alex said.

"Yeah, I know," Wheelwright said. "I'm not happy with it, but that doesn't mean shit either. I'd be appreciative if you could keep me as informed as you can. Just so I don't look like a complete asshole."

"I'll do what I can. Did they send the KL-43 I'm supposed to use to contact Langley?"

"I've got it here," Wheelwright said. "I'll run through it with you again, and I'll arrange for you to come and go as you need to. So you can come here and use it anytime. Night or day."

"I have to use it here? Hennesey didn't say anything about that."

"Those are my instructions," Wheelwright said. He had placed a small attaché-like case on top of the table. It looked like a cross between a briefcase and small portable typewriter case.

"These babies are all owned by NSA [National Security Agency], and they're one of the most classified pieces of equipment we have. They don't go outside secure buildings, for obvious reasons. And if we're ever overrun, our instructions are to destroy this first. Even before classified documents. So I can't let you walk around with it. Even Hennesey can't okay that."

Wheelwright noted the concern on Alex's face and decided to ease it. Otherwise he'd never use the damned thing, and Langley —being the pricks they were—would blame him for scaring the man off.

"Look," he said, "this fucking thing is completely secure. And I mean completely. There is no way anybody can tap into it while you're using it. Even if they tap into the telephone you're using, all they get is scrambled crap, and even that's in code." He tapped the top of the box, then began to open it. "And after you're finished, everything you've put into it is automatically erased. And if anyone tampers with the machine, tries to cut off the automatic erase or anything else, the little bugger is programed to shut itself down to the point it can't be started up again. It's like an ultimate computer virus."

The KL-43 lay open between them now, and Wheelwright began to explain it. Alex had been briefed at Langley, but decided to hear Wheelwright out just to see if the instructions varied in any way.

"Here you have a small computer with a liquid-crystal diode screen. The phone cable is unhooked from the back of any regular telephone and plugged into one cable of a Y cord." He held up the cord. "That plugs into the computer, and back into the phone." He held up a small cassette. "This tape cassette holds the transmission code, and it slips into this slot on the side of the computer." He gestured with both hands. "That's all the assembly required.

From that point you just type in your message on the keyboard. All conversations are typed, transmitted automatically in code, and automatically decoded by the receiving machine before they appear on the receiving screen. Hennesey's machine is kept in his office. So the only way your message can reach anyone but him is if he chooses to give it out. Even if someone had the code, it wouldn't do any good. Not unless they had the machine too. And as I said, they all belong to NSA, and they know who has them, and check daily to make sure they're all where they're supposed to be."

"So why make a portable transmitter that can't leave a secure location?" Alex asked.

Wheelwright gestured helplessly with his hands again. "Hey, you think maybe engineering and security don't talk to each other." He grinned. "Or maybe engineering did its job so well it made security shit when they saw it. It's chicken and egg, my friend. Like everything else in this business. And we end up with a portable transmitter that an agent could take anyplace, and transmit from any regular telephone he can find. Except he can't, because it's not allowed. So he has to travel to a secure building. Maybe from someplace out in the boonies, or some fucking jungle, and intelligence that's urgent enough to go out on this little sweetheart is delayed a day, two days, a whole fucking week. You explain it to me. We developed it, then cut its effectiveness in half. For the guy in the field, he might as well use smoke signals, for all the good this does him."

Alex stared at the machine, then at Wheelwright, but said nothing.

"What else do you need?" Wheelwright asked.

"Some new documents," Alex said. "In the name of Owen Morris, and identifying me as a buyer for a California vineyard. They'll replace what Langley gave me, which doesn't fit with what the Pisanis have in mind."

"They'll be ready by the end of the day," Wheelwright said.

"I'll pick them up," Alex said.

Wheelwright nodded. "Where can I reach you if any new intelligence about Ludwig comes in?"

"Contact the Pisanis," Alex said. "They'll find me. Anything else I should know?"

"Just one thing," Wheelwright said. "Your old friend Bugayev is back in Marseilles." He watched Alex's eyes, saw the interest there he couldn't mask. "I don't know if it means anything or not," he added. "He was shipped out to Afghanistan about a year after you left the service. Now he's back. And so's Ludwig. We haven't seen any contact, and it could be coincidence, but who the fuck knows?"

Alex slipped into the passenger seat of his car, leaving the driving to the Pisani man who had taken the wheel while he was inside. It was the same man he had met in Cervione ten years ago. Jo-Jo Valeria, the Pisani *casseur* who had waylaid the Russian hit team that had come for him then.

"You drive," Alex said. "I'm going to Michelle Cabarini's apartment."

Valeria nodded. He had aged well over the past ten years, only a hint of gray hair acknowledging his thirty-five or so years. He had grown a thin line of mustache, but otherwise still had the same lean, hard good looks and intelligent eyes that Alex remembered. The mustache made him look like a pimp, but perhaps that was what he wanted, Alex told himself.

"I will have you there in five minutes," Valeria said. "Will you be long?"

"I don't know," Alex said. "I've got to learn something about the wine business."

"That could take years," Valeria said, smiling. "I'll let my men take lunch, one man at a time. It's early, but I like to keep them fed." He grinned again. "There's a café on the corner."

"That's fine," Alex said. "Just don't hold me up when I'm ready to leave. There's an old friend I want to look up."

As the car pulled out into traffic, he thought about Sergei Bugayev. He didn't believe in coincidence, and if Bugayev hadn't lost his love of bouillabaisse, he knew where to find him.

Michelle opened the door of her apartment and greeted Alex with a warm smile. She was dressed in a simple blouse and full skirt, reminiscent of the young girl-woman he had first known in Cervione. He wondered if she had intended it.

He returned the smile. "Seeing you dressed that way, I feel we should take a walk along the *maquis*," he said.

"You remember our walks," she said.

"What man could forget walks with a beautiful and innocent young woman?" he said.

"I was not so innocent," she said. "I was very infatuated with you. And I dreamed of more than our walks together." She looked at him steadily as she spoke, and there was no hint of flirtation in her voice or her eyes.

She turned and moved toward the kitchen. "Can I offer you a coffee?" she asked.

"I'd love it," he said.

"Good. Then we can talk about wine. And I would like to do it in English. I get little chance to practice it, and it is good for me."

They sat in the spacious living room, Michelle on a large white sofa, Alex in a carved wooden chair opposite, a silver coffee service on the low table between them. Large windows opened on to the Vieux Port, and Alex thought of the quayside restaurant where Bugayev had always gone to take his bouillabaisse. He would be there, he told himself, half listening as Michelle explained what he would have to know to be a believable buyer of vine cuttings. He was sure that couscous had not replaced Bugayev's love of French food during his years in Afghanistan.

"I do not think you will have to know much more," Michelle said at last. "Frenchmen know their wine, but only from the drinking of it. Few understand the process of transplantation and the soil comparisons needed to make it work. And most will be satisfied to regard you with disdain, thinking only of an American coming to buy their cuttings in an attempt to imitate French wines. Allow their egos to satisfy them, and I think you will be safe," she said. "I have drawn up a letter, dated many months ago, which appears to answer a request from you to come and meet with me. I have used the name we discussed yesterday."

"That should do fine," he said. "I doubt I'll ever need it—I intend to avoid the police—but it will cover me, at least temporarily."

Michelle sat quietly for a moment, then leaned forward. "Tell me about Ludwig," she said. "How you plan to take him."

"I intend to make him come to me. If I can," he added.

"I want to be with you when he comes." Michelle noted the objection that came immediately to his eyes and hurried on. "It isn't necessary that I kill him," she lied. "But I want to be there when he dies. I want to see it."

"I can't promise you that. I don't know when or how or even if he will come."

"Just let me be with you whenever you can," she said. "The Pisanis have given you a large apartment. Let me stay there with you." She stared at him. "I am not trying to seduce you, Alex. To change anything you have in your life now. It is for my dead husband and for my little Pierre. He was only three, Alex. Only three."

He thought she was about to cry, was sure of it. But somehow she fought it back and continued to stare at him. He wondered how he could say no to her. Her family had sheltered him ten years before, and he thought of old Grand-père, of Madame, who had lost a great-grandchild, and of Michelle's parents, and of Michelle herself. How could he say no?

"It will be dangerous," he said. "And you will have to do exactly as I say."

"I will," Michelle said. "And I will be a help to you. You will see that."

She hesitated, as though deciding if she should push it further. "What did he say to you yesterday? That you did not tell us?"

"How did you know there was more?" he asked.

"It was there in your face," she said.

He nodded. "He spoke about my wife. Just to remind me about our conversations ten years ago, when she was his captive. Back then he would tell me what he was doing to her. And what she was doing to him. And he claimed they had been seeing each other for months." Alex's left eye had narrowed, and the muscles along his jaw were doing a rapid dance. "Last night he said he couldn't remember her name. He could only remember the pleasure she had given him."

Michelle closed her eyes. She wondered if Ludwig remembered the names of her husband and of her sweet, dead child. Her hands began to tremble.

"I don't want to talk about him anymore. I want to talk about something pleasant." She smiled weakly. "It is still hard for me thinking about him." Her eyes darkened. "Even though I do it every day."

Alex nodded. He more than understood. He reached out and took Michelle's hand and smiled.

"I'd like to go back to Corsica when this is finished," he said. "It's been a long time since I've been there."

"Nothing much has changed," Michelle said. "Corsica always remains Corsica. It is beautiful and peaceful." She hesitated. "And home."

"Will you go there with me?" Alex asked.

The telephone rang before she could respond, and she went to it.

"It is for you," she said. "A man." Something about the way she said it made Alex realize who it was. He thought Michelle instinctively knew as well. Her eyes were frightened and angry.

He took the phone and spoke a terse "Yes."

"Alex, you lied to me," Ludwig's voice purred across the line. "I asked you if you had brought me another woman, and you never admitted that you had."

Alex replaced the receiver and stood staring at it.

"It was him, wasn't it?" Michelle asked.

He turned to her and nodded. "There was one other thing he said last night that I didn't mention."

"What?" she asked.

"He asked me if I had brought him another woman."

Michelle felt a chill creep up her spine and willed it away.

"Then I can definitely help you," she said.

"Not as bait," Alex said. "Never that way."

"That will not be for me to choose," she said. "Ludwig will decide that for us."

Alex looked away from her.

"You had better go and pack," he said. "I don't want you here any longer. We'll go to my apartment now."

"And I will be with you when you go out? When you do what you must do?"

"Yes, you'll be with me," Alex said. He had no intention of letting this woman out of his sight.

CHAPTER

udwig replaced the receiver and smiled. Moran and the
woman had arrived at the apartment the Pisanis had given
him. The smile broadened. He had taken the woman with
him, had run like a frightened rabbit to his hole. Yes, he was
frightened for himself *and* for her. He feared for her safety—that
was obvious—and for his own, and it would distract him, keep him
on edge, watching over her, while trying to remain alive himself.

He thought of his telephone call to the woman's apartment and
how it had so shocked Moran. He had simply hung up and run for
cover. The mention of the *new woman*, right on top of the earlier
conversation, when he had spoken about his wife. The two together
must have been devastating for him, Ludwig told himself.

Now he must be certain the same horror awaited him, a reprise
of unforgotten terror, that would force him to relive the past in
more than memory. And then to die himself, unavenged.

No, you'll be safe there, frightened Alex, he told himself. For a
short time. The apartment—the entire building in the Opera
district—was a fortress. All the other apartments and the street
itself were manned by Pisani men. It would take an army to get to
you there. He laughed softly. But I don't need to reach you there.
I don't want you anywhere right now. You will come later. Once
I've finished my work for Montoya. And I will know where you
are every minute. And when I choose—yes, *when I choose*—then
you will die. And the woman too. Just for the joy of it. And perhaps
I will let you watch. Before you die. Just to help you remember.

He turned back to the other men in the room, still smiling.

"You seem pleased, my friend. I hope the news is worthy of your pleasure." Marcel Francisci smiled back at Ludwig, but his always cunning eyes searched for any hint that what pleased the man was not something that would prove a disadvantage to his own interests.

"It always pleases me to see an enemy run for cover," Ludwig said.

"And your old enemy is running?" Francisci asked.

"As quickly as he can," Ludwig said.

"Then it is good news. A man cannot hunt when he is hiding. And you know where his hole is?" Francisci asked, still probing.

"Yes, I know."

"And will you kill him there?"

"He is not of consequence right now," Ludwig said. "First the Pisani brothers will die. Then, when we control Marseilles and Alex Moran is stripped of all his protection, then I will kill him. At my leisure. So I have time to enjoy it."

"He will still have his government's protection," Francisci cautioned.

"Do you think so?" Ludwig asked. The smile had returned again. "Perhaps I have another surprise for you," he said. He took pleasure in Francisci's questioning look. "But that will have to wait for another time."

Francisci inclined his head to one side, indicating he was willing to wait for more pleasant news. "My main concern is the Pisanis, as you know. The sooner they are eliminated, the faster our power will grow."

"I agree, my friend. So let us do it now."

Francisci raised his eyebrows, questioning the obvious bravado. "What makes you feel we are ready?" he asked. "Assassinating a *paceri* in the *milieu* is something that must be carefully planned. To attempt it and fail would only make other factions believe the Pisanis are still too strong to be attacked. They might abandon their decision to sit back and watch, especially if Antoine and Meme call for their help."

Ludwig turned and walked across the large sitting room in which they had gathered. He was annoyed by the questions, by the obvious doubt. They were in a secluded house deep in the countryside outside Aix-en-Provence, one of Francisci's many hideaways, and one only a select handful of his men even knew existed. It was an ideal place, but the isolation, and the inactivity it necessitated, were eating at him. He turned back to face the *milieu* leader. "The intelligence we have now makes failure improbable," he said. "And Montoya arrives within days. I want a body to greet him with. A Pisani body."

Francisci shrugged. "Nothing would give me greater pleasure, my friend. How will you do it?"

Ludwig offered him a contemptuous smile. The man was telling him the assassination would be his task and his alone. Francisci had no intention of involving himself in anything that might place his faction at risk if it failed.

He glanced at the other men in the room—two of Francisci's lieutenants and one of his own South Americans, the latter sitting like a lump of stone, listening to a language he did not understand.

"My men and I will move into Marseilles to be ready at the first opportunity. We know the various routes the Pisanis take from their home."

"They never move together," Francisci cautioned.

"I am aware of that," Ludwig snapped. "I will hit whichever one moves first. And I will kill him personally and leave his body gutted in the street. I will leave it as a symbol to all of what is left of the Pisani faction." He smiled at each man in turn. "Then the other will have to seek vengeance, and he will have to come out of his hole to do it. His men will expect him to take a personal hand in avenging his brother, will they not?" He watched the Corsicans nod agreement, but did not miss the doubt on their faces.

"And then he too will die."

Francisci turned to one of his lieutenants, a middle-aged, bulky man with a face that looked as though someone had stepped on it, repeatedly.

"What do you think, Louis?" he asked the man.

"I would kill whatever brother it is at distance," Louis said. "And I would use automatic weapons. They are old, these Pisanis, but they are dangerous men. And they have survived many years because they are not easy to kill."

Ludwig glared at the man. "I appreciate your concern," he said, emphasizing the final word. "But killing is not something about which I need instruction." He forced himself to smile, to soften the rebuke. "And I have a personal debt to the Pisanis, one that goes back ten years." His mind flashed back to the time he himself had been forced to run like a frightened rabbit, the only time in his life he had been made to do so. "And I want to kill them close at hand. I want them to know the debt is being repaid."

"You will have backup to assure success?" Francisci asked.

Ludwig's eyes flashed anger at the suggestion he might not survive the attack. "I will have support both from without and within the Pisani faction," he snapped. "Does that satisfy your concerns?"

Francisci's eyebrows rose again, and he inclined his head again to acknowledge both his surprise and satisfaction. "I did not know you had achieved so much," he said. "I compliment you."

Francisci pushed himself up from his chair with surprising agility. He was a man of the Pisanis' generation, but looked and moved like a man many years their junior. He seemed more like a fit fifty-year-old than a man in his late sixties. He crossed the room and placed a hand on Ludwig's shoulder.

"Do not be impatient with us, my friend," he said. "We have opposed the Pisanis for many years, and we have survived it. There are no others who can say this."

"Sometimes caution can go too far," Ludwig said.

"Yes, you are right," Francisci agreed. "And I have no doubt you will succeed. My only concern is your safety in that success."

Ludwig almost laughed at the lie, but thought better of it.

"I too have survived many years," he said. "And I have always done it at the killing end of a weapon."

"And you will do so again," Francisci assured him. "Especially if you have truly penetrated the Pisani armor, as you say."

Ludwig knew Francisci was awaiting some assurance, some information about how, and through whom, such a penetration had taken place. It was something he would not get. Not now. Not ever. Promises had been made to that person that the Pisani faction would be theirs, and that was something Francisci would not be pleased to hear.

"All is in readiness," he said, noting the momentary look of disappointment and concern in Francisci's eyes. You know, don't you? he thought. You know I can take away what you want at will. But I won't do that. I will only force you to share it. It won't make you happy, but it will make you even richer and more powerful than you are. And that will soothe the blow to your ego. Money and power always have that effect.

Francisci slipped an arm around Ludwig's shoulders and walked him to the French doors that led to a sprawling garden of wildflowers outside. Ludwig knew the man would just as happily slip a knife between his ribs if it proved in his interests.

"You and your men should relax now," he said. "I have some women coming to you who I think will please your South Americans."

"And do you have one for me as well?" Ludwig asked.

"But of course," Francisci said. "A very special one." He stopped and turned to Ludwig, a look of reproach in his eyes. "But send this one back intact. Please."

Ludwig laughed. "I did not know you had such personal concern for your *poules*," he said.

Francisci shrugged. "It is like lending a man several automobiles," he said. "When they keep coming back damaged, the owner becomes concerned about the cost."

Ludwig laughed again, and this time Francisci joined him. But Francisci's laugh lacked sincerity. He hated waste, especially when it was needless.

Francisci's car pulled out of the long, wooded drive and out onto the rural highway. He was seated in back, Louis and the driver in front. Francisci drummed the fingers of one hand on his knee. Ludwig's spy in the Pisani faction was a danger to him, and he knew that danger had to be eliminated. A Byzantine plot was forming in his mind, and it brought an eventual smile to his lips.

"Louis," he said, forcing the man to turn to face him. "I want you to sit on our friend Ludwig. And I want you to learn who the traitor is in the Pisani nest."

"Do you want him killed?" Louis asked.

"No," Francisci said. "He is too valuable to die now. That will happen later, and we will let someone else do it for us."

"I will find out," Louis said. "It will not be hard now that we know he exists."

Francisci nodded. "Yes, our friend Ludwig should never have told us that. Sometimes his ego gets in the way of his judgment. He has too great a belief in his own power." He smiled. "Men who take themselves too seriously always place themselves at risk." The smile broadened. "You must try to remember that, Louis. It is a great lesson in life."

———

The woman walked across the bedroom, allowing her movements and the erotic costume she wore to evoke the fantasy she hoped to create. She was dressed in a flimsy silk top cut low to expose her ample breasts and ending just above her pubic mound, which was covered in a G-string emblazoned with a single embroidered rose.

It was all done in a deep whore's red, Ludwig thought as he watched her, naked, from the bed. Even the stockings and garter belt were in that bright, lascivious color. It had a touch of the ridiculous about it, and he wanted to laugh at her, but decided he would save that for later. After he had finished with her.

The woman stopped at the foot of the bed and smiled at him. It was a coy, whorish smile, and he liked that. It suited her; it suited the moment. She was tall and beautifully proportioned, with long, slender legs that rose up to a tight, well-rounded bottom. She was no more than nineteen, he guessed, and her face—even though it was the face of a whore—still held a certain innocence that he found appealing. And he liked the way her long blond hair hung down over both shoulders, just caressing the sides of her breasts.

"Do you have something special for me?" he asked.

She looked down at his erect penis and smiled. "I see you have something special for me," she said. She knelt on the bed and began to crawl slowly, erotically toward him.

Sitting with his back against the headboard, he extended one hand to her, and when she reached it, she began to lick his fingers. He liked that too. Perhaps he would not hurt this one. Perhaps he would want her back again. He would have to see. It would depend on just how much she pleased him.

His other hand was under the pillow at his side, and he allowed his fingers to play over the handle of the stiletto he had hidden there. He wanted to use the knife. It always gave him pleasure to use it with a woman. But perhaps he wouldn't cut her, as he had the others.

He always found the faint, razor-like cuts arousing. The sight of blood always had that effect on him. Yet he wasn't sure if it was the blood or the terror in their eyes when they saw it. He liked the terror. That was the best part of it for him. He liked them to know he could do what he wanted. Go to any length.

But perhaps he wouldn't cut this one. A thought came to him, and his smile widened. Perhaps he would shave this one. Tie her to the bed and shave her. Watch her eyes as the knife flicked away the pubic hair, wondering all the time if his hand would falter, cut her in a way that would go beyond her worst nightmares.

He liked the thought of it. He liked the idea of producing dreams that made someone wake, screaming in their bed. His father had made him dream like that as a child. Awaken in fear and terror of the beatings that would come when he failed to satisfy his expectations. The man had loved to beat him. Beat him like some animal.

His hand began to tremble at the memory, and the woman reached out and began to stroke it, as though she were soothing his fear.

He glared at her, then forced his face to soften, replacing his anger with a smile.

"Lie down," he said. "I want to tie you. And then I have something very special for you."

"Oh, I like that," she said. "I like special things in bed."

"Then you shall have it," he said. And we shall see how much you like it, he added to himself.

CHAPTER

39

Sergei Bugayev sat at the small, front-window table in the quayside restaurant he favored, awaiting the arrival of his bouillabaisse. Normally it was a pleasant experience, anticipating the pleasure about to be his. But today it was not. Alex Moran sat beside him, holding a pistol under the table, the barrel pointed at Bugayev's balls. He had intended to find Bugayev the day before. But Ludwig's call to Michelle's apartment had forced him to change those plans. It had forced him to run instead. Now the running was over.

"Are we to meet like this every ten years, my friend? With me at the unpleasant end of a gun?"

"Let us hope not, Sergei," Alex said. "And let us also hope you have all of your parts the next time we do meet."

"Oh, Alex, I assure you I share that thought," Bugayev said. "But the last time, you were much kinder. You allowed me to enjoy my lunch before you assaulted me."

"I have no intention of assaulting you, Sergei. I simply want you to tell me all you know about Ludwig. Primarily where he is and how I can get to him."

"And the gun, my dear Alex?"

"Merely a precaution, Sergei. For my own protection, *and* to let you know how seriously I take this matter."

Bugayev's eyes became sorrowful, so much so it surprised Alex. "Put the gun away, Alex. And we shall talk as friends. Ludwig does not work for us. Has not for more than a year now. And I would like to help you. Nothing would make me happier than to see him dead. Except, perhaps, to do it myself."

Alex slipped the pistol into his belt and sat back in his chair. "I wish you had felt that way ten years ago," he said.

"I did, my friend. But it was something I could not act upon then." He hesitated, then pushed on. "The KGB knew nothing of his plan to kill your beautiful Stephanie, Alex. If we had known— if I had known—I would have killed him then and suffered the consequences." He drew another breath. "I learned you were here the day you arrived, Alex." He shrugged. "The KGB is still efficient enough to note the movement of agents. You were seen going into Langley, as we watch anyone who enters there, and the old photograph we had of you was circulated to our watchers at various airports. If you had not come to me, I would have sought you out to offer my help."

"And you didn't advise Ludwig I was here? He called me that same day, Sergei."

"Never," Bugayev said. "If I had, I would not have told you now that we had spotted you."

"And why would you offer your help? He was yours. Still is, for all I know."

"He is not ours, Alex. Not for more than a year, as I said. He is a pig, doing a pig's work now. I assume you know what that is. And that you're here to protect the CIA's assets, which he now threatens."

Alex bristled inwardly at the suggestion of doing the work of his CIA masters, but he knew it was true. "I'm here to kill him. Whatever other good or bad it accomplishes doesn't concern me."

Bugayev nodded at the suspected lie. He believed Alex would do all he could to protect the Pisanis, his "uncles." He certainly owed them a personal debt.

"And why would you or the KGB want to help me?" Alex asked.

"*Glasnost* is real, my friend," Bugayev said. "The South Americans will only destabilize the French economy. And that no longer holds any interest for us. We want the French economy strong. Both to hopefully lend us money and to buy our goods someday. We want to be part of this united Europe. We are all budding capitalists now." Bugayev's sudden smile faded. "And it is a matter of personal honor for me," he said. "Even though we had no part in his actions ten years ago, we created the monster." He looked down at the table, then back at Alex. "And I protected him, rescued him from you and the Pisanis."

Alex stared at him, hating him at that moment. "Then help me now," he said. "Tell me where the sonofabitch is and how I can reach him."

"I don't know where he is," Bugayev said. He leaned forward, holding Alex's gaze. "But we know one of Montoya's men purchased an airline ticket in Bogotá a few days ago. And we also know a limousine has been rented in that man's name in Marseilles the day he is due to arrive. We suspect it is Montoya who is coming, using his lieutenant's name." He smiled at the foolishness of the man. "The limousine is a white Mercedes, one of the ridiculously long ones favored by your movie stars and rock musicians. The idiot might as well be leaving a trail of bread crumbs." His eyes hardened. "Find him and follow him, and I expect Ludwig won't be far behind."

"When is the plane due to arrive?" Alex asked.

"In four days," Bugayev said. Then he gave him the name of the airline and the flight number.

Michelle was waiting in the car when Alex came out of the restaurant. A second car, holding the Pisani men, was parked behind her, and the two men who had been stationed at the front of the restaurant now climbed into the rear of Alex's car.

"The man at the window? That was the Russian you told me about?" Michelle asked.

"That was him."

"I am disappointed," she said. "He didn't look nearly as dangerous as I expected."

"That's why he's dangerous," Alex said.

Michelle thought about that and nodded. "Did you learn what you hoped?" she asked.

"Some of it."

"And what do we do now?"

"We go to see Meme and Antoine, and tell them what we've learned."

"Will you tell your people as well?"

"No. Not yet."

"You do not trust them, do you?"

"Not for a minute," Alex said.

"If it is a limousine, then he is going out of the city," Meme said, when Alex had told him what he had learned. "The man could not be fool enough to call attention to himself that way if he was staying in Marseilles. Right in our own nest. And if he goes to Aix, then we know it is Francisci who is helping him, and we will hit him with everything we have."

"As long as we hit Ludwig as well," Alex said.

"If it is Francisci and we cut off his head, then we cut off Ludwig's protection. After that he will not be hard to find," Meme said.

"We will not disappoint you, Alex." It was Antoine, and his eyes glittered with anger. "We have not forgotten the Street of Pistols, and the infamy we found there ten years ago."

"I know you haven't, Uncle. I just don't want him to have a chance to run again."

"He will not run," Meme said. "He will die here in France. He has spilled too much of our blood here." He looked at Michelle, nodded to her. "I promise you both this. No matter what it costs me."

"Just leave Ludwig for me," Alex said.

"Only if I don't reach him first," Michelle said.

Alex looked at her, then nodded himself. He intended to see that did not happen. But he could not argue with the woman's intent.

They were in the Pisani study, and the tension in the room seemed palpable, almost like another person seated among them.

"I will go to the club and prepare things," Antoine said. "I want men at the airport and all along the roads to Aix. We will take no chances with this."

Antoine walked to his desk and pressed a buzzer. The door to the study opened almost immediately, and Jo-Jo Valeria stepped inside.

"Yes, *Padrone*," he said.

"Get a car ready for me," Antoine snapped. "I want to go to Club Paradise. Call ahead and tell the men I am coming, and that I have work for them. I want three men with me now. We have weapons to bring the others, and I want all of you with me to be well armed," he added.

"I will go with you myself, *Padrone*," Jo-Jo said. He seemed excited by the prospect.

Meme stared at his brother. "Be careful," he said. "Take the bullet-proof car."

Antoine grunted.

When they returned to the apartment in the Opera district, Michelle could still feel the tension that had permeated their meeting with the brothers. It had confused her then, but she thought she understood it now. It was the cold, merciless planning that went into death delivered on a large scale. They wouldn't just be killing the man who had murdered her husband and child. They would be killing everyone who was with him, anyone who had or would try to help him. And no one who got in the way would be left untouched. And the people who would do most of the killing—the Pisani men—wouldn't even have a reason, other than it was expected of them. She felt a shiver go through her. When they left, Antoine had been headed into the basement, where she knew a hidden room held an arsenal of weapons. To bring them to his men, she told herself. To get them ready for all the killing.

They were going to war, and it was something she had never experienced before. It frightened and repulsed her. And still, she wanted it. And perhaps that frightened her most of all.

She went to the window and stared down into the street. The Opera district, a place visitors to Marseilles found so curious and titillating. A place filled with whores and thieves and people who would cut your throat if told to do so. And now they were out there—many of them—watching so she and Alex could do their killing, and so that no one could get to them before they did. She watched a young woman swaying her hips as she walked along the street, trying to attract attention, because that was how she earned her living. How she was allowed to do it, told to.

And how different are you? she wondered. And is this the final memory you're to have of your beautiful child?

"Are you all right?" Alex asked. He had taken off his suit coat, thrown it on a chair, and begun mixing them both a drink.

She turned to face him "Yes, I'm fine," she said. Then she looked at him and smiled. "No, I'm not fine. But I will be." It's too late, she told herself. Much too late to go back.

"It takes time," he said. "To get used to it, I mean."

"You mean to get ready to kill someone?"

"Yes."

"It's not that," she said. "I'm ready to kill him. I've been ready for it for almost a year. I'm just not ready for all the other killing it seems it will involve. I hadn't expected that. Hadn't thought of it that way."

"No one ever does," Alex said. He stared at her, wanting to make his words gentle. "Do you remember what you told me in Cervione? How the vengeance always seemed to get out of hand? Kept on, even though people didn't really want it to?" He watched her nod her head. "It's like that now, Michelle. And you can't change it. Just remember, the others all played a part in what Ludwig did. And they did it because they wanted to, because it was in their interests to do it. Try to to think of it that way."

"And will it be that way for us?" she asked. A hint of fear had returned to her eyes. "When we kill him, will there be a price for us to pay? Will it go on and on for us too?"

"It could," he said. "It could turn out like that for us too. We'll have to deal with that when it happens. If it happens." He stared at her, then started forward, their drinks in his hands. "You can leave it, you know. Let me do it for you."

She shook her head. "No, I can't," she said. "The hatred's too much a part of me. I've made it that way." She took the drink he handed her, her fingers trembling as they touched the cold glass. The drink slipped from her hand and fell to the floor.

"Oh, God," she said.

Alex put his own drink on the table and reached out and drew her to him. She felt soft and warm, and she rested her head in the hollow of his shoulder. He slipped his arms around her and ran his hands gently along her back.

"It will be all right," he said. "We'll survive it, and then we'll walk away from it."

"I want that, Alex," she said. "I want it to be over. I want to leave it and never have to go back to it."

He stepped back and took her face between his hands. "It's what I want too," he said. "If I could leave it now, I would. I just can't."

She nodded, her face moving against his hands.

He smiled at her, then leaned forward and kissed away a tear that was moving along her cheek. She was that young, innocent girl again. The one he had known in Corsica. And all the feelings he had felt then—feelings he had forced down and hidden—came back to him now. He moved his lips to her mouth and kissed her softly. Her arms slid up behind him, and he could feel a sudden heat come off her body.

After a time, she pulled her head back and looked at him.

"I want you, Alex," she said. "I wanted you as a girl in Cervione, and I want you now, as a woman."

He smiled at her again, telling her with his eyes, it was the same for him. Then he drew her to him again.

CHAPTER

Antoine's car moved through narrow streets, weaving its way to Club Paradise in an intricate backtracking route. Antoine was in the back, Jo-Jo Valeria beside him. Two others were in the front, the one in the passenger seat armed with an Uzi already set on full automatic and capable of spitting out two hundred rounds a minute. The trunk of the car held an arsenal of shotguns, pistols, and assault rifles, along with a sealed box of hand grenades stolen from the French Army.

"Why are we going this way?" Antoine snapped. "I want to get there. I don't want a fucking tour of the city."

"It is my fault," Jo-Jo said. "It's easier to see someone behind us on these narrow streets. I'm sorry, *Padrone*. It is for your safety."

Antoine slapped Jo-Jo's knee. "You're like an old woman sometimes," he said. He snorted. "And I'm like an old bull who thinks it may be his last time to fuck a cow."

Antoine stared out the window, watching the quiet residential dwellings roll past. There were a few young children playing on the sidewalks as their mothers watched over them. A simple life, he told himself. With a husband and father who came home from work and took pleasure in his family. Something you have never known, except from a distance.

He felt the bulk of the old Colt .45 automatic stuck in his waistband, the barrel digging at his groin. It was the same weapon Piers had given him years ago. And he had used it then, and since. And, God willing, he told himself, he would use it again now. It's the life you have chosen for yourself, and, God help you, you have enjoyed it.

The car pulled up at a stop sign, leading into a larger road. There was no traffic moving along the one-way street, and Antoine wondered at that, given the time of day. He leaned forward and looked to the side from which traffic should be coming. The police had set up a barricade, and there was a truck with workers in the middle of the road, looking as though they were preparing to dig. Just leaning on their shovels, he told himself. Lazy French bastards.

"Do we have enough room to get around?" he asked the driver.

The man pointed to an abondoned gas station. "I can cut through there," he said. "Then we'll be clear, *Padrone.*"

Antoine sat back, grunting his annoyance. No one worked in Marseilles anymore. They were all a bunch of fucking communists who expected everything to be given to them.

The car pulled out and swung wide, around the truck and the workers, cutting toward the abandoned gas station. A burst of automatic-weapon fire raked the front and rear tires on the driver's side, shredding them and sending the wheel covers flying into the street. The driver fought for control as the car rocked and skidded, the right front fender smashing into the gas pumps, jolting the car to a halt.

"Out," Antoine shouted. "Get the bastards." He was seated on the rear passenger side, shielded by the car, and he flung open the door, the old Colt already in his hand, and threw his bulky body to the pavement.

The driver started out, but was thrown back by a fusillade of bullets, his body rag-like, spraying blood across the interior of the car, dead before he hit the seat.

The man on the passenger side was out and firing his Uzi over the top of the car, the weapon cutting an arc through the attacking force.

Jo-Jo tumbled out behind Antoine, his own automatic in his hand. "Fucker," he mumbled, then turned and fired two rounds into the side of the man with the Uzi.

Antoine turned with the sound and swung his pistol into Jo-Jo's head, knocking him to the ground.

"You fucking whore," he roared. He leveled the pistol and fired just as a four-round burst slammed into his side. His bullet struck

Jo-Jo in the arm, smashing the bone and almost severing it from his body.

Antoine struggled to his knees and emptied his automatic at the man coming toward him, a Mach 10 in his hands. The man's body spun and flew off to the side.

Two more bullets struck Antoine in the chest, knocking him back to a sitting position. He looked up and saw a blond man coming toward him, a long stiletto flashing in his hand. He struggled back to his knees, blood pouring from his mouth now, knowing who the man was and wanting him before he died.

As Ludwig reached him, Antoine threw his body forward, his bear-like arms snapping about the younger man's waist, pinning his hands to his sides. He stood, lifting Ludwig with him, squeezing his midsection with all his strength, praying he would have enough to break his spine.

Ludwig howled in pain, his feet kicking in the air, his knees fighting to find the old man's groin. But still Antoine held on, squeezing, his face pressed into Ludwig's chest.

"Die, you Nazi cunt," he growled, drawing in a breath and squeezing harder. "Come to hell with me, you bastard," he managed once more.

A .32-caliber bullet smashed into the right side of Antoine's head, blowing a massive chunk of bone and brain and blood out the left. His hulking old body crumbled to the ground, dropping Ludwig beside him.

Jo-Jo stared down at his dead *Padrone*. "Old pig," he hissed, his wounded arm hanging at his side, pouring blood, his other still holding a .32-caliber Berreta outstretched.

Ludwig struggled to his feet and kicked Antoine's lifeless body. "You old bastard," he snarled. "You fucking old bastard."

He glared at Jo-Jo, offering no thanks, nothing. "You stay here," he snapped. "You survived the attack. Understand?"

Jo-Jo nodded, momentarily wanting to blow the man's face off.

Ludwig knelt and turned Antoine's body onto its back. The stiletto flashed in his hand.

"Now, you old pig. I'll leave a present for your fucking brother."

Michelle lay against him, her head against Alex's shoulder, her fingers tracing through the hair on his chest. He felt so good to her, as she had known he would, the flash of guilt she had felt at first gone now. Dismissed as the foolishness it was.

She had not been with another man since her husband's death. She had felt the physical need, but had not wanted to share it. Now it was different, and she understood why.

He had been as gentle, as tender as she knew he would be. He had been patient with her, had felt her momentary reluctance, and had given her time to decide. Just stroking her, petting her like a child who needed comfort, reassurance.

And the fire had come to her, just as she had known it would. She had wanted him with such intensity she could hardly wait. She could barely control herself to give him the pleasure she wanted him to feel. With her. This first time between them.

He had seemed to sense it then, and he entered her, filled her with himself, the sensation of it after so long driving her to a frenzy. They had made love a second time later. Long and slow and languorous love. And then she had given him the pleasure she had wanted him to have, thinking how much better it was now. Now that she was a woman and knew what she could give and how to give it.

"Did you think of making love to me in Cervione?" she asked, her fingers still toying with the hair on his chest.

"At least once a day," he said. He wondered if that were really true. He knew he had thought of her that way, couldn't help himself. But he thought he had dismissed it. His mind too turbulent, too filled with rage to sustain anything else. He stroked her back, feeling the soft skin that was damp now with the heat of their lovemaking.

"Perhaps you should have," she said.

"I would have been killed," he said. "The entire village would have hung me from a tree."

She laughed, pressing her face into his chest. "Yes, that is likely. But because you were under the Pisanis' protection, perhaps they would only have cut certain parts from you."

Alex grunted. "Thank God for powerful relatives," he said.

"I am glad you did not," she said.

"Oh?"

"I think it is better now. I had no knowledge of men then. I think I would have been clumsy and foolish." She listened to his silence, knowing he did not know how to respond. "Did you know my mother knew how I felt? How much I cared for you?"

"Did it upset her?"

"No. I think she understood. She told me you would have to leave. That it was good how I felt, but that there would be someone else for me to love."

"She was right," Alex said, stroking her back again, knowing the memory of the man she had found would cause her pain.

"Yes," Michelle said. She was quiet for several moments. "She was right about that," she said at length. "It was right for me to wait."

"Remember the good things you had with him," he said. "Don't let the rest replace it."

She stroked his chest, harder this time, as though making sure he was truly there. "Can you do that, Alex? Can you remember your wife that way?"

"No," he said. "There was too much other pain before she died."

"And yet you still want to avenge her death." It was not a question, not offered as one.

"Yes. Don't ask me to explain. I don't think I could. Maybe it's just hating the man who did it." He drew a long breath. "I don't just want to kill him. I need to."

The telephone rang before she could respond, and Alex freed his arm from around her and swung his legs out of the bed.

She listened to his voice, soft at first, then crisp and brittle, and she could feel the pain coming from him. Her heart began to beat faster.

He replaced the receiver, but didn't turn to face her.

"I have to leave," he said.

"What happened? Tell me."

"They killed Antoine," he said. "I have to go there."

She felt her breath catch, felt the tears filling her eyes. She didn't think she would be able to speak.

"I'm coming with you," she said. Then she began to sob.

Antoine's body lay under a blanket to shield his gutted corpse from the morbidly curious throng that had gathered behind the cordon of police who had sealed off the area. Alex and Michelle pushed past the police, guided by two of Meme's men, who ex-

346 / WILLIAM HEFFERNAN

plained they were relatives who had been called for by the *Padrone*. There was only one now, Alex thought as he made his way to Meme's side. One *Padrone*. One *Patriarche*. One *Paceri*. All the various titles given to the men who carried the gold medallion of the *milieu*, marking them to its members as *Un Vrai Monsieur*, a man of honor. And one uncle, Alex told himself. It was the only title he had ever cared about.

"They have slaughtered him," Meme said, his face a mixture of tears and rage. "They have slaughtered your Uncle Antoine."

Alex wanted to place his arms around the man, but instinctively knew he should not. He understood that Meme could not be allowed to appear weak. Not in front of his men. Not before the public or the police. His tears were acceptable, as was his rage. But his power and his authority must not appear to be diminished.

Michelle rushed to him and was comforted by Meme. He stroked her hair and spoke softly to her. "You should not be here," he said. "This horror is not for your eyes."

"I want to be with you," she said. "As you and Antoine were once with me."

He nodded, but his eyes were distant. He continued to stroke Michelle's hair.

"I would like you to call Cervione," he whispered. "Call the priest at the cathedral. And call Colette. Tell them we will bring Antoine home to them tomorrow."

Michelle nodded her head against his shoulder, but found she could say nothing.

Meme beckoned to one of his men with his head. "Take her to my house," he said. "Take men with you, and stay with her." His eyes bored into the man, telling him that no further harm must come to his family.

The look in the man's eyes told Alex that would not happen.

Meme took Alex's arm and led him toward the body. The police moved aside. There was little to investigate. What had happened had occurred many times in the past. The weapons in the car had been discovered and had been seized. But charges could only be made against those who were already beyond punishment. Jo-Jo Valeria had been taken to a hospital, and he had told the police he had been walking along the street and had been hit by a stray bullet. There were no witnesses to prove the lie.

Meme lifted the sheet and revealed his brother's mutilated body. Alex stared at it, then looked away.

"It was the German," Meme said, his voice barely under control. "Jo-Jo told us. He was badly hurt and could do nothing." He looked away himself, allowing the sheet to fall back. "He said Antoine fought to the end. That he almost killed the *Boche* bastard with his bare hands. But that someone else killed him and saved the German pig." He turned to Alex, his eyes filled with a perverse pride. "The police said he was shot eleven times, and still he fought. My brother was a *dur* to the very end of his life."

Alex could say nothing. His lips moved, but his mouth felt numb, useless.

"Tomorrow I will take him home to Cervione," Meme said. "Home to Corsica, where he belongs now." He stared at Alex, his eyes glittering, black as coal. "Do not fear, Alex," he said. "We will not forget this Montoya bastard. My men will be there awaiting him, following him, seeing where he goes and who he is with. And when I have buried my brother I will go after them all. I will paint France with their blood if I have to." His entire face seemed to glow with hatred now. "And I will not forget the one who betrayed my brother. That one will die at my own hand. And he will wish, with his last thought, that his mother had never conceived him."

CHAPTER

41

Cervione

The music rose in the small cathedral, filling every corner, the sweet soprano voices of the village children floating from the choir in the rich, melodic language of the island. The priest, old and weathered, sat in a side chair, alb and surplice folded about him, biretta atop his head, eyes closed, listening to the voices of the children, perhaps even praying.

Placed before the steps leading up to the altar, the bronze casket that held Antoine Pisani lay atop a funeral bier, the lower half covered with the flowers of the *maquis*, the upper half open, revealing the peaceful, cosmetic repose achieved by a Bastia mortician.

The cathedral was full, with many standing in the rear, others spilling out into the small village square. The men who had hunted with Antoine were seated directly behind the family—Meme, Michelle, Alex, and Colette—followed by men of the Pisani faction. On the opposite side were others of the village, seated ahead of myriad factions within the *milieu*, whose members had traveled from Bastia and Ajaccio and Marseilles, men who shed no tears but who sat and calculated what advantage, if any, the funeral they were attending might bring.

Meme sat stoically, his eyes hard on his brother's remains. His men had been ordered to carry no weapons, to do so openly, blatantly, in a gesture of defiance that spoke of his power and the unassailability of his surviving family. But few doubted there were those at hand prepared to slaughter any attackers before they could leave the mountain village.

Michelle held Meme's hand, stroking it, as much to comfort herself as him. Colette, older than Alex remembered, her ruined face hidden behind a veil, clutched Alex's arm, her occasional gasps and sighs speaking of the loss she felt for the man she had harangued through much of her life.

It was an unaffected ceremony, lacking any grandiloquence, and it spoke of power born of simple origins that had not been forgotten. Alex thought his uncle would have liked it, and he recalled the day he had brought him to this same church and roared with laughter as a village ancient, knife in hand, had chased two French fools and their stupid dog into the street. The gentle, and brutal, giant of a man who could soothe a child's fears and cut a throat all on the same day and see no conflict in his mind, nor feel one in his soul. It had created an imbalance in his own mind that Alex knew he would never resolve, and had long before decided he would never attempt.

Piers Moran had not come, nor had any member of the American intelligence community, all sending telegrams instead, expressing their sympathy and pleading the speed of the funeral as their excuse. The older politicians of Marseilles had sent representatives and an abundance of flowers, uncertain of the Pisani power now but still not wishing to offend, yet remaining away themselves, unwilling to be tarnished by men whose money and muscle they had accepted throughout the years. But they were not missed, Alex thought— except perhaps his father. Antoine himself would have preferred a gathering of old hunting companions, and the people of the village who had called him *Patriarche*, and the children, and those of his faction who had shared the violence that was so much a part of his life.

And he would have liked Ludwig's head sitting atop a stake outside the church, Alex told himself.

The priest spoke briefly in the rolling, rhythmic Corsican language, and celebrated the Mass for the Dead, and those present filed quietly past the open coffin, leaving the family behind to watch the lid lowered one final time and to follow it into the street.

There was no hearse, no cortege of cars. Antoine was carried on the shoulders of men with whom he had drunk and laughed, out through the village and along the dusty road that ran above the *maquis*, and finally to the vault on the sprawling grounds of the Pisani Cervione home.

Michelle walked ahead, holding Meme's arm, Alex and Colette behind them, Alex unsure who was supporting whom as the veiled older woman marched on ageless legs along the road she traveled every day to tend to the needs of the Pisani household.

He had not seen her since childhood—he had been told to stay away from the Pisani house for his own safety when he had hidden in the mountain village years before. She was in her early sixties now, and seemed much more frail than he remembered. And he wondered if she still tended her garden—sure she would have fought giving it up—and he remembered their game of hide and go seek, and of the vague and disturbing words she had spoken to him when he had left her that last time.

He recalled his father's nervousness whenever she was near, and he thought he understood it now. She had been his father's lover during his halcyon days in Marseilles, and the thought both surprised and pleased him, leaving only the question of why his father had abandoned her in her disfigurement, offering neither solace nor emotional support. But it fit his father's nature, he knew. To reject that which was not as perfect as he would have it. But it was something Alex would rather not accept about his father.

They stopped at the large stone burial vault, the line of mourners gathering across the casket from them, and the priest gave a final blessing, sprinkling the bronze coffin with holy water. The sun was steady and hard, but the breeze that came up from the *maquis* pushed the heat away, bringing with it the scents of juniper and buckthorn, lavender and wild thyme, and it reminded Alex of his walks with Michelle, who stood beside him now, and of his boyhood hunt with his uncle and the great pig they had killed together.

Alex felt his throat catch with the loss of the man, but he fought it back, telling himself he would not be a "pants pisser" at Antoine's funeral. The memory of the words brought a faint smile to his lips, and he knew he would remember him for that, and for the affection and friendship he had showered on him, and would dismiss the other parts of his life to the realm of ignored reality.

The casket was carried through the solid iron doors of the vault and placed on a stone bier to one side. Alex allowed his eyes to remain on the coffin until the heavy doors were swung shut, closing Antoine away.

As the doors closed, Alex felt Colette squeeze his hand, still watching as a key was turned in the lock.

"You will not have to fear this place as you did as a child," she whispered. "Antoine is here to guard it now."

Somehow the thought of that gave him peace of mind.

Meme received his guests in the house, providing food and drink for those who had come to offer respect to his brother. He sat alone on one side of the vast sitting room that faced the sea, and others remained far away so those who chose to—both villagers and members of the *milieu*—could have a private word with him to offer their support and regret.

Marcel Francisci was among the mourners, and he went to Meme, sitting in a chair provided, and spoke with him for several minutes. Meme's face remained impassive throughout the conversation, and Alex marveled at both men's composure, playing out their separate roles in a morality play headed for future violence.

Later, after the last of those who wished to speak with Meme had moved away, Alex went to his uncle and asked what Francisci had said.

Meme's face showed nothing as he spoke, only the coal black of his eyes hinted at the hatred that simmered inside.

"He wanted me to know the loss he felt," Meme said. "He told me the years of rivalry meant nothing when a great man of the *milieu* was lost to all." A small smile played on Meme's lips. "And he warned me he thought Antoine had been betrayed, and that the one who had done it was still among us." The smile disappeared. "He said he told me this as a gesture of friendship and respect."

"Did he give you a name?" Alex asked.

"Oh, yes," Meme said. "He gave me the name I already knew. He is throwing the betrayer to the wolves to be eaten."

"Why?" Alex asked. "Is he afraid you will trace the man back to him?"

"No. I doubt he has ever spoken with him. This was Ludwig's man. And Montoya's. It is because he fears Ludwig and Montoya will give this pig our faction as payment for his treachery. And it is something he wants for himself."

"So if you kill the traitor, you serve his ends," Alex said.

Meme nodded. "And Francisci can take that victory to his grave with him."

Alex did not ask who the traitor was. He knew his uncle would tell him when it was necessary that he know.

"When will you kill him?" Alex asked.

Meme looked toward the windows and the sea.

"He is being prepared for death even as we speak," he said.

Marseilles

The two ambulance attendants presented the transfer papers to the head nurse. They were signed by the hospital administrator, although the man had never seen them, and explained that Jo-Jo Valeria was to be taken to a special orthopedic clinic outside Nice. The two men, both members of the Pisani faction, were from Paris, and were not known to Valeria, and when they placed him on the gurney, he was smugly gratified at Meme's concern for his well-being.

That sense of satisfaction ended when the ambulance pulled into the long drive of the Pisanis' Marseilles home, and Valeria found himself staring into the barrel of an automatic pistol.

"What is this? Where are you taking me?" he demanded.

The man with the gun said nothing. He simply leaned forward and spat in Valeria's face.

When the ambulance stopped, the driver came to the back door and opened it, then yanked Valeria off the stretcher, oblivious to the pain it caused.

"Walk, pig," he snapped.

Valeria grimaced, then stared up at the Pisani house, and his expression gradually changed to one of terror.

"Where am I going?" he tried again.

"Into the basement," the driver said. "You can wait there for your *Padrone*. And you can think about how you are going to die."

Cervione

Alex walked about the grounds with Colette. Most of the guests had gone now, and she had told him she wanted to show him the many flowers she had planted since he had last been there.

"Antoine and I fought about the flowers every time he saw them," she said. "He used to tell me there were enough flowers in the *maquis*, and that they were more beautiful than these 'French flowers' I was bringing to his garden." She laughed, and the sound was light and gay, making her seem like a young girl, Alex thought.

"I think if I did not plant the flowers, he would have complained about that. It was his nature to fight with everyone. Especially me. And I loved to give it back to him. It made me feel less like what I am: a woman who cares for others because there is nothing else for her to do."

"I think he did it because he loved you," Alex said. "It was the only way he could express it."

Colette nodded her head slowly, digesting his words. "Yes, and I loved him. I loved both of them. They made me as a sister to them. An old, spinster sister who cared for them." She laughed again, at herself this time.

Alex guided her to a bench and they sat facing each other.

"You loved my father too, didn't you?" Alex asked. He was not sure why, but felt the moment was right for it.

Colette looked at him for several moments. It was impossible to read the reaction on her two-sided face, but her eyes seemed to grow distant for a moment, he thought.

"Yes, I loved him," she finally said. "But you must not think badly of him for that. It was a strange time then, right after the war ended."

Alex knew she was saying those words for him, not to excuse his father, and he felt great affection for her, for her gentleness.

"I was a *poule*, you know, back in those days." She had said it suddenly, almost as though she were afraid she might not if she waited. She shrugged. "I was very young, and I came from a hard family, and I thought it was a way to escape them and to get money for myself. To have a life I wanted to be very exciting. Like in the movies, you know? Fine clothes. Fine restaurants. Handsome men." She laughed again, softer this time. "The young innocent girl led into a life of sin. It is like that old cliché, eh? The whore with the heart of gold." She wagged a finger at him. "But it was not like that. Oh, I stole from the *mecs* every chance I got. Just like all of us did. And if there was a scheme to make money, we were all the first in line. But those were the old days, and they were what they were. I make no excuses for myself."

She offered a crooked smile, and reached out and stroked his hand. "But I have dignity now. I work hard, and my work is appreciated for what it is. And I care for two of the most powerful men in France." She lowered her eyes. "One now," she said. She drew a breath, gathering herself. "And they always listened to me," she added. "I wish I had found this life earlier." She reached up and brushed a hand against her ruined cheek. "Even if it still meant this. But I don't regret the old days. I learned from them." She touched her cheek again. "I only wish I could have learned another way."

"And my father?" Alex probed. His voice was gentle.

She looked away toward some flowers, then back at him, her ruined face offering a jagged smile, her eyes soft. In remembrance, Alex thought.

"He was very handsome, and very . . . personable then," she said. "He was like no man I had ever met." Her eyes became firm. "And he was good to me during those years. He wanted me to have my little dreams of being the *petit bourgeoise*. And I wanted to be with him." She lowered her eyes. "No matter the circumstances."

"But then he abandoned you," Alex said. He said it as gently as he could.

Colette waved a hand. "It was his way," she said. "I do not excuse him, but I understand. I do not think he had ever been loved passionately before," she said. She looked at him, as if afraid he would misunderstand. "I do not say this as anything against your mama," she added. "I do not think it was something he ever permitted, that he ever allowed to happen to him. Do you understand what I mean?"

"Yes, I do," Alex said.

Colette reached out and placed a hand under his, then placed the other on top.

"I fear for you, my little Alex," she said. "Oh, I know what you are doing. I know more than anyone here thinks I do." She hesitated, then went on. "Is your father involved in this thing you do?"

"Yes, he is," Alex said.

Her eyes grew sad, and she looked away for a moment, then back at him, as if taking time to choose her words.

"Do not trust him, Alex. I do not say this because he does not love you. I know that he does." She pressed his hand between her own. "I say it because he only knows one way to live. And it is a way that excludes everyone. Even the people he loves."

Meme left for Marseilles that evening, off to do his personal bit of killing, Alex knew. He remained behind with Michelle, to give her time to visit with her family, with whom she would stay, then to go on to Marseilles the following evening. It was like a respite, he told himself. Before the serious killing would begin.

The next morning, she took him down the steep path into the Valle di Compoloro, to the old Romanesque Chapel of St. Christine, where she had gone to pray as a young girl. He stood behind her, watching her pray, kneeling on the stone floor, her head bowed and covered with a scarf. And he understood that he loved her— not just as he had loved her as a young woman, enchanted by her innocence and beauty—but as an equal who had been hardened by life but who had not surrendered her loveliness.

They left the chapel, hands joined, and walked into a field of flowers that rose almost to their waists. Michelle turned to him and slid the scarf from her head, allowing the sun to play against the dark, shining beauty of her hair.

"Make love to me, Alex," she said. "Here in this field. It is an important place for me, this valley, and I want to love you here."

She knelt, hidden from other eyes by the flowers, and began unbuttoning her blouse. Alex understood what she was saying: how she wanted this innocence to their lovemaking now, before they returned to Marseilles and began what they had chosen to do. It was as though she thought they would never have the opportunity again.

He knelt beside her and began removing his own clothing, then leaned forward, and kissed her face and lips. She drew him down to her, pressing her cheek against his.

"Make love to me as though I were the young girl you wanted years ago but could not have," she whispered. "Make love to me gently, because I am innocent and unsure of what I must do," she said. "And allow me to surprise you with how deeply I love you."

He lay beside her and brought her gently against him.

"It is the way I shall always think of you," he said. And he wondered if the days ahead would change that forever.

Meme entered the basement room alone, leaving his men upstairs. He wanted the pleasure of killing the man by himself, with only his brother's spirit with him. And, he believed, Antoine would be there, the old Corsican superstitions still holding sway for him. And he also believed Antoine would never rest, would never allow either of them a moment's peace, until his murder was avenged. It was foolishness, and instinctively Meme understood that. But he believed it anyway.

Valeria lay on a massive table, his arms and legs spread and tied. He was naked, and he was shivering in the damp basement, both with cold and with fear. He stared at Meme as he walked slowly toward him, his eyes wide, and suddenly he was sweating despite the cold.

"*Padrone*, you must listen to me. I had nothing to do with your brother's death. I swear to God, and on the heads of my family."

He tried to twist against the ropes to gain a better look at Meme's eyes, hoping they would tell him he was believed. The pain in his shattered arm surged and forced him to fall back with a gasp.

"You not only were part of it, you told them how to do it," Meme said. His voice was a low hiss, and he stood above Valeria, staring into his face.

"You think I forget how you work? How you favor using the fake *flic*, with the barricade and the workers digging in the road?" His lips broke into a horrific smile, and Valeria began to tremble again.

"How many times did you do that for me over the years, Jo-Jo? How many times did we laugh at the fools who fell for it?" He leaned his face closer. "Did you use it this time out of contempt for me and my brother?" he asked. "Did you think we were too old and foolish to remember?"

Valeria began to stutter, fighting for words of denial. The sharp click of Meme's stiletto snapping open froze him, and he knew the words would be wasted.

"Please, *Padrone*. Do not kill me this way. I will help you find them. I will do anything you ask of me."

"My brother asked for your loyalty, and he gave you his trust," Meme said. "Was that not enough?"

"Oh, please. Please. Not this way."

"Yes. This way. Only this way."

Meme reached down and grasped Valeria's penis in his hand, pulling it roughly. Then he placed the blade of the stiletto against it as the man's body bucked against him, oblivious now to the pain from his arm. The blade sliced quickly, severing the member, as blood spurted in a fountain, washing across his legs. He screamed, his eyes riveted on the now grotesque part of his body as Meme impaled it on the end of the blade.

Meme's hand shot out, pressing against his jaw, holding his mouth open, then forcing the severed penis into his mouth and down his throat.

Valeria gagged, thrashing his head from side to side. Meme worked quickly, wanting him to feel all of it before he lost consciousness. He grasped his testicles and cut them free, then placed his thumb at the base of one eye socket and popped the orb free, leaving it dangling on Valeria's cheek on thread-like tissues. Quickly he inserted one of the testicles, then paused to allow Valeria to see his face one last time.

"Pig," he hissed.

Then he did the same to the second eye.

He waited, watching Valeria die, listening to his muffled screams. Then he dropped the knife to the floor and slowly stripped off his clothing. They had the man's blood on them. They were tainted and vile to his mind. And he never wanted to use them again.

Then he turned and walked out of the basement, his body naked, looking strangely old and frail, the splashes of blood the only indication of what he had just done.

CHAPTER

42

Washington, D.C.

The large suite in the Hay-Adams Hotel looked out across Lafayette Park at the impressive facade of the White House. That was the place where the American people—*all the bumpkins*—believed the major decisions of their government were made, Piers Moran thought as he stared out the tall window before which he stood. But they were not, of course. The decisions were made elsewhere, often in rooms like this, and then affirmed in the great white building, based on information provided by those who had already made them. Oh, there were times when a decision was rejected, but that happened rarely. And then it was merely a question of accomplishing the desired ends in a more covert way. It was the same in all governments, Piers knew. Decisions made by men whose names the masses never heard. It was a fact of life both for the men who made those decisions and the people whom these strangers ruled.

Piers turned back to face the others in the room. The ad hoc committee on narcotics, as he liked to think of them, plus one other, with whom he now had to deal.

He looked at Raphael Rivera, the CIA station chief for Bogotá, and offered the "swarthy little bastard"—as he thought of him—a cold smile that would not be missed by the others, the true committee members.

They were scattered about the large room in chairs and sofas, waiting to see how much of their lives would be changed by what would now be decided.

Walter Hennesey was there, chugging on his pipe. So was Christopher Baldwin, overweight and balding, and John Batchler, reedy thin and coarse as ever—the same group who had met only months before at The Breakers in Palm Beach, when all this madness had begun.

"So it would seem your operation—your little grab for power—has run into difficulty," Piers said, his cold smile still radiating at Rivera.

"Not so much it can't be corrected," Rivera said. He had ignored the smile and the sarcasm, sitting pat with his hand—which was far from pat, Piers told himself.

"If that were the case, you wouldn't be here," Piers said, softening his tone and his manner. "So let's talk about the deal we have to strike to make *everything* work, and place all the bravado where it belongs."

Rivera offered a helpless gesture with his hands. "I'm not here to fight," he said. "Only to be fair." He smiled. It was an oily smile, Piers thought. Just like the man. "So long as that fairness extends to everyone."

"And just what is your idea of fairness?" Hennesey asked.

Piers raised a hand. "Let's recapitulate first," he said. "Just to get everything clear, before we begin speaking about what's fair." He nodded to Rivera, then added: "For everyone."

Piers walked to a chair that made him the center of the discussion and sat.

"It would seem your people—Montoya and Ludwig—aren't following the game plan very well, and now find themselves facing a very determined faction of the *milieu*," Piers said.

"A mistake," Rivera said. "They were told—or rather, Ludwig was told—to be sure to take out *both* the Pisani brothers at the same time," he lied. "It seems Montoya, greedy little shit that he is, was hungry for action, and that pressured Ludwig to get what he could to keep Montoya off his back." Rivera shrugged. "But the other brother is a doddering old fool, and I don't expect Ludwig will have any trouble getting to him."

Piers leaned forward, angered by the terminology used for a member of his own generation but hiding it as best he could.

"Meme Pisani is the most lethal 'doddering old fool' you will ever meet," Piers snapped. "If the two of you were alone together in a room, there would be no question in my mind who would come out alive."

Rivera sneered at him.

Piers smiled. "Because the fucking floor would fall out from under you, if that was what it took," he snapped. "Don't sell the man short, my bright young friend. You won't survive if you do."

The others in the room smiled, unaccustomed to hearing Piers use profanity.

"I thought Antoine was the tough old bird," Rivera said, still sneering but changing his language to soothe the old man. "Ludwig didn't seem to have much trouble with him."

"Antoine is tough—was tough in the same way an uncaged gorilla is," Piers said, still finding it hard to think of his old friend dead. "And it still took a small army and a traitor from within his own faction to get to him." He leaned forward in his chair, his eyes filled with malevolent pleasure. "And have you heard what happened to that traitor?" he asked.

Rivera shook his head. "No, I haven't."

"He was found last night. With his penis in his mouth, and his testicles where his eyes should have been. And he was found in Aix-en-Provence, Mr. Francisci's home base, and the very place from which your man Ludwig is believed to be operating." He sat back again, looking pleased. "*That* is the work of Meme Pisani. And I would be amazed if the doddering old fool hadn't done the cutting himself."

"So, you see," Hennesey interjected, "your people are about to be hit very hard. And there won't be much left"—he waved his hand, indicating everyone in the room—"for any one of us when it's all finished."

"The French won't stand for this kind of bloodbath." It was Baldwin this time. Head of the CIA French desk. "They're used to their own killings. A half-dozen Corsicans knocking each other off now and then, as happened in the so-called 'Lemonade War' a while back. But when they see South Americans are involved, and that it's all about who's going to control narcotics in France, those large frog noses are going to be very much out of joint."

Rivera raised his hands. "I never said there weren't problems." His eyes became cunning, feral. "But I assume you can control *your* man, get him to back off."

Piers let out a long breath. "No, we cannot. It's already been suggested, and now Meme won't even accept contact from us." He leveled his gaze at Rivera. "Would you expect him to? It would be suicide for him—not to avenge his own brother."

"But you can call your son off. Right?" Rivera was almost smiling now, cutting to the root of the opposition's dilemma.

"Pisani won't let us reach him," Piers said. It was a weak excuse and he knew it.

"And he wouldn't listen if you could," Rivera said. "Let's be honest about this, shall we?"

"All right." It was Batchler, Hennesey's number two this time. "We've got a loose cannon on our hands and we know it. Some of us have suspected it from the start." Piers began to object, but Batchler cut him off. "He's severed all contact with Walter," he said, staring Piers down. "Shit, he never made contact in the first place short of a quickie visit to the consulate."

"So that's the problem," Rivera said. "I believe I can get *my* people back under control. You know you can't. At least not until we have a bloodbath that's going to hurt all of us." He smiled. "That *is* the bottom line, isn't it?"

"The bottom line," Piers snapped, "is your incursion into Europe. And your decision to attack Company assets."

"I thought we were putting bravado aside," Rivera shot back. "The bottom line is that my 'incursion,' as you put it, threatens the drug profits you gentlemen have been squirreling away for years now."

"That is a concern," Hennesey conceded. "But we are not, repeat, *not* going to surrender Company assets to a cabal of agents stationed in South America who are supposed to be working for the Company first."

Rivera raised his hands in a gesture of surrender that was nothing of the sort, Piers decided.

"I can concede that," Rivera said. "As long as these new profits are shared." He stared at Piers. "That's what I mean by fairness to everyone."

Piers stared to speak, but Rivera shook his head, stopping him. It seemed everyone was shutting him down, Piers thought.

"The real question is who the assets in France should be," he continued. "The way I see it, you can't call off Pisani because he can hit back. He's got enough information on all of you—and probably years of records to go along with it—to kick up a scandal that would bring everyone down. Probably the agency itself."

"And your people wouldn't?" Piers demanded.

"In time," Rivera said. "But I don't propose leaving them in place that long. I envision a regular process of attrition, with replacement drug lords that we"—he imitated Hennesey's gesture, taking them all in with a sweep of his hand—"*all of us*, can control." He offered an apologetic shrug. "Your mistake, as I see it, gentlemen, was leaving your asset in place too long."

"So what you're proposing," Hennesey said, "is cutting you in on the proceeds, while we take over control of Montoya and Ludwig?"

"In Europe," Rivera corrected. "We maintain control in South America. In other words, we control the product. *And* we cut you in on profits outside Europe."

The members of what Piers thought of as the ad hoc committee glanced at one another, none indicating any objection to the proposal. The swelling of their bank accounts seemed obvious under Rivera's proposal.

"And Pisani?" Piers asked, his tone friendlier now.

"He's got to go," Rivera said. "I can't replace Montoya and Ludwig that quickly. It could take years to set up this deal again." He smiled. "Years of some very nice profits that don't exist in Europe right now."

"And if we stand by Pisani, *someone* just might leak information about our long-term connection with his faction," Hennesey said.

Rivera raised his eyebrows. "Let's not even discuss that kind of unpleasantness." He rubbed his thumb and index finger together. "That's in no one's real interest."

"So, how do you see the current situation?" Hennesey asked.

Rivera leaned forward, now taking center stage. "We let Pisani go ahead, but we pull Montoya and Ludwig and as many of their people out as we can. So the only target left for Pisani is Francisci, and whatever South Americans get stuck in the cross fire. Without an acknowledged drug boss in the body count, it will just look like Francisci was doing a deal with South Americans, and Pisani took offense."

"And then?" Piers asked.

"Then, with Company help, we hit Pisani, either set him up for the cops or kill him. Whichever works. And we strike a deal with another faction in the *milieu* for a piece of the action. With Pisani and Francisci both gone, the others will all be looking for their shot at the top spot. It'll be 1945 all over again."

"Could work," Batchler said.

The others nodded. Piers twisted nervously in his chair.

"And what about Alex?" he asked.

"If you can call him off, fine. If not"—he gave Piers as sympathetic a look as he could manage—"well, then I'm truly sorry, Piers."

"He'll have to be sanctioned," Baldwin said. "You know it, Piers, and so do we all."

Hennesey leaned forward, his pipe held out before him. "Look at it this way, Piers. This should have happened ten years ago. If it wasn't for you, he'd be long dead. My God, man, you bought him all that time."

Piers stared at the floor, realizing there was no choice, no card he could play. He felt suddenly nauseous at what he was being asked to condone.

"But we shall try to reach out to him," he said.

"Of course," Hennesey said. "But we cannot tip our hand about the move against Meme Pisani."

Piers thought about his old friends, Meme and Antoine. He regretted what would happen, what had already happened. But it was like being told an old friend had cancer. One could sympathize, even agonize, but there was really nothing one could do. He only hoped the same was not true of Alex. He looked at Hennesey.

"That's understood," he said.

Marseilles

"Montoya went to Aix," Meme said. "He's rented a house there, or rather someone has rented it for him."

"Was Ludwig there?" Alex asked.

"There was no way to tell. Not without making our own presence known. But we will find out," Meme said.

They were in the small office at the rear of Club Paradise—Alex, Meme, and Michelle—and when Alex had arrived, he had noticed the entire Opera district was on a war footing. Pisani men were everywhere. The old battlements had been raised, he told himself.

"And what's your plan?" Alex asked.

"I want to hit them within days," Meme said. "All of them, Francisci included. We will find out where they will be at a given hour, and we will hit them all at the same moment." His eyes, coal black now, stared at a blank wall. "There will be no one left to respond."

"Will the CIA be involved?" Alex asked.

"Fuck the CIA," Meme snapped. He realized what he had said, and in front of whom, and offered Michelle a pained look. Then he turned to Alex and explained the directive that had come from Hennesey.

"He told you to back off." Alex was incredulous. "The bastards are selling us out."

"If they try, it will cost them everything they have," Meme said. "I will see to it."

"When it is over they won't be able to do anything, will they?" Michelle asked. She was suddenly shocked by her own acceptance of the mass murder they were discussing. It has come this far, she told herself.

"No," Meme said. "They are very good at accepting the fait accompli. It is their nature to do so."

"Don't count on it," Alex said. "It will depend on what deals they have made."

"We will face that when it happens," Meme said. "Killing these pigs is the only concern we have now."

"I don't want Michelle there," Alex said. "We don't need her to do this."

"I am going!" Michelle snapped back. "You cannot stop me. It would not be just."

"No!" Alex said.

Meme grabbed him by the shirt front. It was the first time his uncle had laid a hand on him in anger.

"She is Corsican," he said. "Her need for their blood is as strong as ours. You will not interfere." His eyes and voice softened. "I love you, Alex. You are truly my nephew, just as you were Antoine's. But this is not for you to decide."

The telephone call came an hour later, as they were still going over plans for the needed surveillance in Aix. Meme handled the call tersely with a cold dispassion, then turned to Alex when he had finished.

"It was Wheelwright, the CIA station chief here," he said. "He wants you to know that a man named Baldwin, who he says heads something called the French desk, will be here tomorrow and wants to meet with you at the consulate."

"The hell with him," Alex said.

"I think you should meet him," Meme said. "It is good to know what is on the minds of people you no longer trust."

Alex nodded. "If you want. But not at the consulate. I'll meet him in a place I choose. And I'll want him alone."

"I will have men there," Meme said. "They can assure your meeting will be a private one."

"Good," Alex said. His face broke into a slow smile. "Then I hope he brings someone. Your men will set a nice tone for him."

Alex chose an apartment in a building Meme owned in the city's old quarter, and insisted Baldwin walk there so he could be certain he was not being followed. Pisani men picked off Baldwin's three bodyguards two blocks from the building, and prodded Baldwin on, alone, at the point of pistols. The building was on a narrow street called the Street of Refuge, and the apartment was on the third floor, reached only by a narrow, winding staircase. Alex did not know Baldwin at all, did not know he was overweight and long out of shape, and like most men of that ilk hated exercise. Had he known, he would have chosen an apartment on a higher floor.

Baldwin was red-faced and breathing heavily when Alex opened the door.

"Think I was a fucking mountain goat?" Baldwin snapped as he pushed past and entered the shabbily furnished apartment. He stared at a battered, overstuffed chair, as if weighing what it would do to his suit, then finally sat, too weary to resist.

"You know who I am?" Baldwin asked. His voice was decidedly unfriendly, arrogant even, for a man sitting in a building he would leave only at someone else's pleasure. He was a fool, Alex decided.

"Wheelwright said you were head of the Company's French desk," Alex said.

"That's right. Walter Hennesey asked me to stop and see you on my way to Paris." His eyes narrowed. "He's not at all pleased with you. Says you've broken contact." He paused. "Shit. Says you never *made* contact with him, despite your orders."

"Things have been a bit hectic," Alex said. He kept his voice even, playing Baldwin out.

"Well, he wants you back at Langley. Says you've got to see him, straighten this thing out."

"Tell him I'll ring him up on the KL-43."

Alex could see Baldwin's mind working. Figuring how they might grab him at the consulate, then wondering if they'd be able to get him out of the building, out of Marseilles.

"That's not good enough," he said. "He needs a personal briefing."

"I'll give it to you. You can give it to him," Alex said.

"You think I'm your messenger boy, Moran? You'll do as you're told. Just like we all do."

Alex pulled up a wooden chair, placed it before Baldwin, and sat. "I think you're a fat little shit. And I think you run a terrible con." He paused to smile at Baldwin's reddening face. "And I think I'm going to slap that sneer off your face if your tone of voice doesn't change quickly."

His voice had been soft and even, guessing that Baldwin was the type who liked to shout and snarl at those over whom he held power. Men like that, he knew, were unnerved by those who had no need of such tactics.

"Are you threatening me?" It was a moderate shout, a last gasp for control.

"Yes," Alex said.

Baldwin twisted in his chair, as if suddenly understanding his position. Then he caught himself, recognizing he must not let that weakness show.

"I don't believe this," he said. "You work for us, and you're threatening me."

"No, I don't work for you," Alex said.

"Since when?"

"Since Hennesey, my father, whoever's involved in this, decided to sell the operation out."

"That's bullshit," Baldwin snapped. "Nobody's selling anything out. You're screwing it up."

His voice had risen again, sharp, snappy. Alex's foot shot out, catching Baldwin just below the knee. His eyes widened with the sudden pain, and he let out a small, girlish cry.

"You kicked me," he said, incredulous.

"Very observant. Next time I'll stand up. And you won't. Not for a long time." Alex's voice was still soft, almost a purr.

"I'm getting out of here," Baldwin said, starting to push himself up.

"Not walking," Alex said. "Not until I say so."

Baldwin fell back into the chair. His eyes were fearful now.

"I want to know the deal. I want to know why," Alex said. "Tell me."

"I don't make policy."

"Bullshit."

"They want you out. That's all I know."

Alex shook his head, almost sadly. "Maybe you'd rather talk to my uncle," he said. "Maybe you've heard about the last person who sold him out. Maybe they'll find you in Aix tonight—with your dick in your mouth."

It was all said softly, almost gently, and the juxtaposition of the words and the reality made Baldwin's eyes widen.

"We're on the same side," Baldwin said, incredulous again.

"Uh-uh. Never have been. I'm here to kill Ludwig. You guys? Who the hell knows why you're in this." He inclined his head to one side. "But I'll find out."

Baldwin looked like a cornered animal—an overfed rat, Alex decided.

"Look, they made a deal. That's all I know. The government's interests change. You were in the business long enough to know that."

"The government's, or Hennesey's?"

"Hey, you're talking over my head now. I'm just carrying a message."

Alex knew he could force the information out of the man. But it would only send them after him faster, harder. If it was a private deal, they'd have to find an excuse to send men after him. They'd have to cover their asses. A battered Baldwin would be enough of an excuse. Otherwise, it would take time to manufacture one. And he needed that time.

"Go home, Baldwin. Tell them I'm going to finish what they sent me here to finish."

"You're crazy," Baldwin said. "Your father knows about this.

He agrees. He wants you out. Call him if you don't believe me. He'll tell you. Christ, you're choosing sides against your own government. What do you think that's going to do for you?"

Alex smiled at him. "It will make me feel safer. I'll know where the knives are coming from." He took time to let the words sink in. "And tell my father I'm disappointed. Next time he should do his own dirty work."

"I can't believe you're doing this," Baldwin said. "You're kissing your ass good-bye."

"Be careful going down the stairs, and out in the street," Alex said. "It's a rough neighborhood."

CHAPTER

43

Aix-en-Provence, 8:00 A.M.

It was a small, charming city, with ancient chestnut trees lining the main street, set in the Rhône delta, with the steep hills Cézanne had loved to paint rising from its eastern suburbs. The twelfth-century capital of the counts of Provence, Aix had become the home of one of France's finer universities, and its quiet, narrow, womb-like streets were dotted with book shops and quaint cafés dominated by students.

It was also the base of operation of Marcel Francisci, a darker side of the city that the *milieu* leader seldom allowed to show. As one of France's favorite tourist attractions, he understood, wisely, it was best not to tarnish her image.

James Wheelwright met Montoya and Ludwig in a small chalet —a CIA safe house—in what the locals called the Cézanne hills on the outskirts of the city.

Montoya had been brought out from the massive country home he had rented by a CIA team that had entered by way of a thick wood. They had evacuated Montoya by the same route, and when he reached the chalet, the white linen suit he was wearing was tattered and dirt-stained, and he was not a happy man.

Ludwig had come on his own, from a still unknown location, after a telephone call was made from Montoya's house. He had been told to send as many of his men as he could to Marseilles, to hole up there with others in rented apartments scattered throughout the city.

Wheelwright was accompanied by Raphael Rivera, who had flown in from Langley the previous day. Hennesey's preceding KL-43 message had been clear. Montoya and his men were assets, and the Pisani faction was on a rampage over their injection into France. He was to assist Rivera in guaranteeing their safety until the matter could be dealt with. Alex Moran was also out of the game, the message had said. CIA protection for him had been canceled. The whole thing smelled, and Wheelwright thought he understood the odor. And he was sure the message was only a prelude to a sanction against Moran. As the agent in place, he had seen no reason for that to happen.

Rivera had met with Montoya and Ludwig alone, another strong indication that the game was not official, at least not yet. When they emerged from the room they had used, Ludwig was clearly not pleased, and Montoya had the look of a man who did not want to be where he was.

"Señor Montoya will remain here," Rivera said. "He'll be guarded until the storm's over in this locale, then he'll be taken to an airport for a flight out of the country."

"What about our other friend?" Wheelwright asked. He indicated Ludwig with a curt nod. Ludwig had not been identified by his correct name. But Wheelwright knew who he was. The description he had been given earlier of the man fit too well.

"He's to be taken into Marseilles. Covertly, of course. You'll drop him off wherever he wants, and he'll go the rest of the way on his own. He'll be picking up his operation again once we have the Pisani faction under control."

Wheelwright bristled at the orders. Ludwig was being hidden away, even from CIA, Marseilles. Just in case we decide to question the orders, or ignore them, he told himself. The stink was getting stronger.

"You don't want us to provide the gentleman with cover in Marseilles?" he asked.

Rivera gave him a cold look. Wheelwright knew who Rivera was, just as he knew who all the station chiefs were. The man was out of Bogotá, and his presence in France made no sense even if he'd been running Montoya in Colombia.

"I think the orders are clear," Rivera said. "If you have any questions, Hennesey will confirm."

Wheelwright bit down on it. He wouldn't question anything. Not yet. He'd wait and watch, give them the benefit of the doubt. It was possible Montoya had been an asset in Colombia, had over-extended himself, and that the Company had agreed to go along with him. And pigs could fly, Wheelwright told himself. If a sanction came down on Moran, he'd know the operation was bogus. Until then he'd cover his ass, as he'd learned to over the years.

9:30

Ludwig sat in the rear of a closed van on a bench seat across from Wheelwright. Two other men sat beside each of them, both armed with automatic weapons, as were the two men in the front seat. He was running again, for only the second time in his life. And again Alex Moran was the cause of it.

Rivera had promised Moran would be taken out. But Ludwig didn't want that. He wanted the man himself. He wanted the personal pleasure of seeing him die at his own hand. And he wanted the woman who was now with him, whoever she was.

It was the only thing that would satisfy the humiliation of it. Erase the failure he felt in his gut.

He could not understand where it had gone wrong. He had been certain the Pisani faction would crumble with the assault on Antoine, that others within the *milieu* would swoop down on what remained like the vultures they were. Francisci had promised as much. But it had not happened. Valeria's body had been virtually dropped on their doorstep, and now they were running for cover, all of them. Meme Pisani had proved as tough an old bastard as his brother had been. And Francisci had underestimated him. Both of them.

He thought about Antoine, the way the old bastard had come after him. It still chilled him, it had been that close. The old man had been hit enough times to stop an elephant, and still he hadn't been ready to lie down and die. He had grabbed him and had almost squeezed the life from him, had left him shaking like a coward. Like a fucking child. No one had frightened him like that since his father. No one had left him shaking that way, feeling so stripped of strength and power.

"You don't seem happy."

The voice snapped him back, and Ludwig stared across the van at the speaker, the one they called Wheelwright. The man's eyes were filled with contempt, hatred. The man knew who he was, who he was being forced to protect. But of course he would, no matter how cleverly his masters had tried to keep it from him. And they hadn't been very clever, had they? They had been their usual inept selves, scrambling to recover from one disaster while they tried to prevent yet another. Just as he had seen them do time and again in the past. He forced a smile at Wheelwright, hoping to cut him with it.

"I am quite content," he said. "I have you to protect me."

Wheelwright's eyes glittered, and his jaw tightened. He is thinking of all the fools you have killed, Ludwig told himself. All those he counted among his own.

"Think how the others feel," Wheelwright said. "The ones who have to wait for old Meme to hit them. And Moran too." He shook his head. "It's personal for them. And with Moran, it's been brewing a long time." He leaned back against the side of the truck, looking self-satisfied, Ludwig thought. "People like that, they don't worry about covering their own asses. They just come at you," he added.

"And then they die," Ludwig said. He was sneering. But it was forced, and he could feel it in his gut.

"Yeah," Wheelwright said, nodding. "Sometimes that happens."

Ludwig held the sneer, then looked away. He no longer cared what happened to Montoya or his cocaine operation. He had enough money salted away to ensure a comfortable life. He just wanted Moran dead. Then he could disappear and never concern himself about when the man might reappear again.

"Does it bother you? Having the CIA cover your ass this way? You must be at least a bit amazed after all the years they hunted you."

It was Wheelwright again, still trying to bait him.

Ludwig smiled again, wanting to cut the man badly this time. Force the words down his throat.

"It is amazing"—he gave Wheelwright a wink—"what people

will do for this foolish white powder." The smile widened. "And, of course, the money and the power it brings."

He watched Wheelwright stiffen in his seat. Good, he thought. Enjoy that little bit of information. Savor it.

10:00

Pierre LeBrec sat in his bathtub, enjoying the ministrations of one of the Francisci faction's finer *poules*. The woman had spent the night with him, and was now making sure his day began pleasurably. As the faction's second in command, it was one of the benefits of his power, earned through years of loyal service and not a small amount of danger.

The danger had left its mark on him. Even in the safety of his own home, and with the Pisani faction badly battered, he still kept a 9 mm. Beretta close at hand. Right now it lay on a small table within easy reach from the tub.

The *poule*, who was young and dark and heavy-breasted—all the things LeBrec liked in a woman—was washing his groin softly, lasciviously, and it was quickly making him hard. He knew what he wanted from her, and he wanted it quickly.

LeBrec placed his hand on the back of the woman's head and pushed it down toward his rather large penis, which was protruding from the water. His action, his greed for her mouth, probably saved the *poule*'s life. When the bathroom door burst open under a heavy kick, LeBrec pushed her head down farther, using it to gain purchase so he could reach his pistol, and the twin shotgun blasts that severed his head from his shoulders never touched the woman.

When the *poule* rose from the water, gagging and fighting for breath, she was confronted by what remained of LeBrec's head, splattered across the bathroom tiles.

Her screams filled the small room. She shrank back, then scuttled along the floor to escape the horror. She never saw the two Pisani men standing in the doorway. Never saw them smile at each other as they took time to appraise her naked, blood-spattered body. And never saw them turn and leave, sparing her life.

She did hear one of their voices as they retreated down the hall: "Poor bastard, he never did get his cock sucked this morning."

10:10

Andre Bastini sauntered along the tree-lined street, his iridescent gray suit sending off sparks of light as the morning sun filtered through the branches and caught snatches of the material as he walked. Bastini reached the large outdoor café and nodded to the four men he was meeting with an air of importance. He was a lieutenant in the Francisci faction, and the men members of the group he headed and, as such, fully subservient to him.

Bastini had come up through the ranks, as all members of the *milieu* did, doing his share of "shit work," as he now thought of it, and scratching out what he could for himself as the steady flow of illegal money trickled slowly from the upper ranks of the faction. But it was as it should be, he believed. A man of the *milieu* earned his bread as best he could, and gathered the rewards of that hardship later in life. Bastini was now fifty-five years old.

He took a seat at a large corner table, his back to the wall of the café and away from the drove of always curious students, making sure his conversation could not be overheard.

"What is happening with old man Pisani?" one of his men asked.

Bastini affected a bored expression. The dropping of Valeria's mutilated body in the heart of Aix had caused a stir of admiration and concern among his men. At first they had anticipated an attack by the Pisani faction, but it had not come. Now it was viewed as a warning to the Francisci group, to whom, it was assumed, Valeria had sold his services. But there must not have been proof, they said among themselves. Otherwise the Pisani group would have had no choice but to attack. But without it, they would have risked alienating all other factions throughout France. Old man Francisci had just been too clever for them, they had agreed.

"Why do you ask about that old fuck Pisani?" Bastini asked. "Does he make your balls tighten up?" He laughed, jabbing a finger of ridicule at the man.

"I am just curious," the man said defensively. He was no more than twenty-five, and the ridicule of his superior fueled his natural sense of insecurity.

"He sits at home with his wrinkled old prick in his hand," Bastini said. "What else can he do?"

He had given an elaborate gesture with the words, and the theatrical movement had caused him to look toward the street. A car had just pulled up there, and two men emerged from the passenger and rear seats. They were wearing long coats, and it struck him immediately that it was inappropriate in the morning heat.

The alarm bells came slowly, far slower than they should have, and the two men had already withdrawn Mach 10's from beneath their coats and leveled them at the table before he could react. By then it was too late, but the look on his face had already caused the young man he had ridiculed to reach inside his coat for a hidden pistol and to turn smartly toward the street. Bastini felt admiration for the man's intuitive sense of survival and his youthful agility. It was the final thought of his life.

The two Pisani men opened fire, spraying the corner of the café with a five-second burst that shredded the walls, the table, the chairs, and sent the five Francisci men bouncing about like rag dolls. Only when the echoes of the gunfire had died were they able to hear the screams of the other patrons. But it did not concern them. They had done as they were instructed, and—as ordered— no innocents had gotten in the way.

The two men turned dispassionately, climbed back into the car, and were driven away.

10:12

Louis Calabristi was newly arrived from Calvi, the small city on Corsica's west coast where Christopher Columbus was said to have been born. Throughout his youth he had dreamed of becoming a man of the *milieu*, and had saved his money from hard manual labor and emigrated to Marseilles. There, a chance meeting with a man of the Francisci faction had provided his long hoped-for opportunity, and he had joined the faction at its lowest level, grateful to be there at all.

Calabristi parked his old Renault a half block from the Francisci clubhouse on an unusually wide side street in Marseilles's old quarter. It was the solitary bastion of Francisci power in the port city, and the bulk of Francisci forces had gathered there every morning to await orders about a possible attack by the Pisani faction, which most now believed would never come.

The young man, who was only twenty-two, was late arriving, as he always seemed to be. It was his greatest failing, and one he had been warned by his lieutenant that would cost him dearly one day. He locked his car and started for the clubhouse, sure he had parked far enough away so he wouldn't show disrespect for any higher-ranking member who might want one of the spaces closer to the building. He knew his place, and hoped his sense of subservience would make up for his seeming inability to get out of bed every morning. There was much to keep in mind if one was to survive and prosper in the *milieu*, which was all he wanted in life.

The flash of light was followed by a billowing fireball, then the concussion and the sound of the blast. The force of the explosion knocked Calabristi to the ground, even though he was still a quarter of a block away, and sent much of the exterior of the old building out into the street.

As he struggled to his feet, bewildered and terrified, Calibristi knew that all inside the clubhouse, at least thirty-five men, were dead, torn to burning shreds by the massive blast, which had broken windows throughout the block. Surprisingly, the street appeared empty, with no sign of injured innocents, and he instinctively knew the bomb had been detonated by a remote device, which meant the killers were not far away. He turned, still staggering from the concussion, and watched a black Citreön make a slow U-turn in the street behind him. The driver looked at him closely, as though appraising who he might be. Calibristi froze in place, wondering if his slothfulness might have provided only temporary survival. The car continued its turn and drove slowly away, and Calibristi made up his mind that he would return to his native Calvi that very afternoon. And he would sleep late for the rest of his life. Only a fool questioned the will of God.

10:15

Marcel Francisci took his breakfast in the sun-drenched garden at the rear of his large stone house, which offered a pleasing view of the Cézanne hills in the distance. Inside the house, a Cézanne hung on one of the walls. He had owned others—but only temporarily—the result of various art thefts he had masterminded over the years, and he fancied himself a true lover of the arts, in the tradition of France itself.

Francisci was a dedicated Francophile, something uncommon for a Corsican, even among those who preferred the idea of Corsica as a part of the French nation. But he also understood that his Corsican roots were indispensable for his position in the *milieu*, and so he only made a show of his "Frenchness" among certain friends and in the isolation of his modest estate. Even the men he chose to guard him—there were six this very day—were selected with care, and with consideration heavily weighted on their ability to keep their mouths shut.

Francisci bit into a brioche, preferring them to the more traditional croissant, and washed it down with a sip of rich coffee. He dabbed his mouth fastidiously with a linen napkin, and gazed out toward the hills.

All was going well. He had met with his primary contact within the Marseilles police department the previous evening, and had fingered Meme Pisani in the Valeria murder. The *flic*, a fat and greedy chief inspector, had assured him Meme would be arrested after a search of his home produced necessary evidence—planted if needed—and that a warrant would be obtained tomorrow, Monday, from the appropriate judge. With Pisani in jail on a murder charge, Francisci believed, his faction would be vulnerable from all sides as never before. The thought of it—a long hoped-for opportunity—brought a smile to Francisci's lips. The only thing that would give him more pleasure would be to kill his old rival personally. But life could not always be ideal, he told himself.

Alex slipped soundlessly through the large ornamental shrubs that grew fifty yards from the west side of the house. One of Francisci's six guards was beside an ancient chestnut tree. He was smoking a cigarette as he watched the long drive that led up to the house.

Alex had run a silent reconnaissance an hour earlier, and had pinpointed the location of each man. He had selected three—the most difficult to reach—for himself, and left two others for the Pisani men with him. The final guard, the one who remained at Francisci's side, would be the last to die. Meme had insisted it be that way, and when Alex objected, his uncle had only glared at him. Francisci would die at his hand, he said. He had no intention of allowing anyone else the pleasure of the man's death.

It was an interesting image, Alex thought. One seventy-year-old man sitting patiently in a car, awaiting word that he could come and kill another seventy-year-old who was having a quiet breakfast in his garden.

Alex tensed as the guard watching the drive stretched and yawned. It was the moment he had been awaiting—sound and movement by the target that would cover a fast assault from the rear.

The man's arms had just fallen to his sides when the wire of the garotte dropped over his head and around his neck. Alex's arms had been crossed as he slipped the wire into place. He snapped them apart now, and the wire sliced into the guard's throat, cutting both his flesh and air supply, as Alex's knee slammed into his back and held him firmly.

There are only two ways to survive a garotte. One is to get one's hand between the wire and one's throat. The other is to be able to turn and face one's attacker. When both were denied, the victim lost physical control within seconds; pain and panic overwhelmed him; he lost consciousness thirty seconds later, and was dead two minutes after the attack was begun.

It was an ugly way to die, and an unpleasant way to kill. But it was quiet and efficient, and many professionals preferred it to a knife, insisting it offered less risk of missing its mark.

Alex left the garotte in place and dragged the guard's body back into the bushes. The second man was just to the right of the front door, his back to the wall of the house, his body all but hidden by a large stone lion. Alex took a .22-caliber High Standard automatic from his belt and attached a long, thick silencer to the barrel. He rested one arm against the side of a tree, using it, and both hands to steady the weapon. Sighting carefully, he squeezed the trigger. The hollow-point bullet took the man in the left temple, dropping him without a sound. Alex moved quickly across the front lawn to the east side of the house.

The third man was the most difficult because he continued to move, walking along a predetermined stretch of ground again and again. The movement had two effects. It made him an easy target for an open assault by heavy weapons, but a difficult one for a single, silenced shot. For a quiet kill one would have to get close, and then preferably use knife or garotte to do the job rather than risk any shot on a moving target. Despite the image portrayed in film and television, a pistol and a moving target seldom produce the desired result.

Alex wondered if Francisci knew this, and had ordered the man to patrol in exactly that way, using him to draw fatal attention to any attack.

Alex slipped into a line of trees the man would pass, then dropped to the ground and watched him approach. He had a Steinkin submachine gun slung across his chest, and Alex saw that the selector switch was forward, placing the weapon on full automatic.

Alex removed a short, thick-bladed knife from a sheath at his back, and turned the blade so it was horizontal to the ground, thus eliminating the chance it might jam between two ribs. Alex knew —had been trained to know—that no vital organ in the human body was more than four inches from the surface of the skin. So a long-bladed knife was superfluous. What was needed was something thick and sturdy and easily concealed, something that would not snap if it struck bone, and would not prove too unwieldy for use at close quarters.

He had chosen the place where the man normally turned and started back, and as he did so this time, Alex rose and came up behind him, the knife in his left hand. Alex's right hand circled the man's right side, pinning the arm, his hand slapping across the trigger guard of the submachine gun, preventing it from being fired. In the same motion he plunged the knife into the man's back, just to the left of the spine, and into his heart. The man's body bucked momentarily, and he let out a short grunt. Then his body sagged back, and Alex lowered it slowly to the ground.

He checked his watch. It was 10:25. It had taken ten minutes to take out the three guards, and by now the Pisani men were to have eliminated the other two.

He moved up along the line of trees until he could see to the rear of the property where the other two guards had been stationed. One of the Pisani men stepped from behind a tree some fifty yards distant, and nodded that all had gone as planned. Alex then took a hand-held radio from his belt and pressed the transmitter button twice, sending two blasts of static to the radio in Meme's car. A few minutes later the car moved slowly up the drive and stopped in front of the house.

"He's in back," Alex said as he approached his uncle. "He's having breakfast, and there's one guard with him."

"Kill the guard as soon as he sees us," Meme snapped. "Leave Francisci to me."

As they rounded the corner of the house and came into view, the guard immediately went for the pistol hidden beneath his coat. Six rapid shots from Alex's High Standard sent three bullets into his face and head, and dropped the man in place before the weapon cleared its holster.

Francisci jumped up from his chair, saw Alex, Meme, and the four men emerging from the rear of his property, and immediately slumped back into his chair. He smiled at Meme, inclining his head to one side.

"This is not what I had planned," he said. "Is there anything to discuss?"

"Little," Meme said. "You can die easily if you tell me where I can find Ludwig. Less pleasantly if you make me force the information from you."

"And what can I offer you to remain alive?" Francisci asked.

"That day is long past," Meme said. His eyes were cold and hard, but his voice held no audible anger.

Francisci nodded and glanced toward the Cézanne hills, thinking how much he would miss them. He shrugged. "It's been a good life, and a long one," he said. "We did not do badly for two young boys from Corsica, eh?"

"You should have remained there," Meme said.

"No," Francisci said. "You should have stayed in Cervione." He laughed, but there was a touch of fear in his eyes. "It would have made my life easier. And longer," he said.

Meme took the High Standard and a fresh clip from Alex, and walked to the table and sat across from his old rival. "Tell me. Now," he said.

Francisci drew a breath and gave directions to the small farmhouse where Ludwig and his men were staying.

"He could be in Marseilles, but I doubt it," he said. "But who ever knows what a German will do."

Meme nodded and raised the pistol, leveling it at Francisci's forehead. Fear flickered through the man's eyes, then disappeared, as though he had willed it to be gone. Meme squeezed the trigger, sending a round into Francisci's head.

He stood and handed the weapon back to Alex. "He was a bastard, but he was a *dur*," he said. "Right to the end."

Alex noted approval in his uncle's eyes.

———

Michelle had waited in Meme's car, but she refused to wait behind when they hit the old farmhouse on the outskirts of the city. She was armed with a Glock automatic, its partial porcelain body making it light enough for her to handle easily, and its 9 mm. firepower guaranteed that anyone she hit would fall, no matter where the bullet struck. She had a look of fear and anticipation mixed in her eyes, and when they found the farmhouse empty, that look changed to one of relief and disappointment. Alex wished she had not come. Wished she did not feel the need to kill the man. He wasn't certain if he felt that for her sake, or simply because he did not want to be robbed of the pleasure himself. It made him think of Meme's need to horde the pleasure of Francisci's death, and he realized he found the similarity disturbing.

"Montoya's house was found empty as well," Meme said. "The men who went there just called in by radio."

"They're running," Alex snapped, fearful he would once again lose Ludwig.

"No," Meme said. "They're being hidden. Kept safe until we can be stopped."

Alex knew who Meme was speaking about, and he wondered if he included his father among those who had betrayed him.

"He'll be in Marseilles, then," Alex said. "And Wheelwright will know where." He turned and headed for one of the cars.

"I'm going with you," Michelle said.

"It will not be safe to stay in the apartment you were using," Meme called after them.

"I'll let you know where we are," Alex said. "Watch out for old friends," he called back. He thought Meme would know exactly who he meant.

Jean Paul Benot, the police inspector with whom Francisci had spoken, heard the radio report about the slaughter of the Francisci faction as he drove his wife and daughter to a Sunday picnic. The report disturbed him, not as a police officer but as a businessman. Francisci's death would mean a sharp reduction in his income. But it would only be temporary, he told himself. Someone else would take Francisci's place, and he too would be willing to pay for services rendered.

And it also meant he would not have to see a judge about a search warrant the following morning. There was no longer any profit in arresting Meme Pisani. After all, he might very well be the next man to pay him.

"This is an outrage," Benot's fat wife said as she too listened to the report. "These Corsicans, they are nothing but animals. They should go back to their ridiculous island and kill each other there."

Benot grunted agreement. But not too many of them, he thought. Or else his wife would not enjoy the comforts she considered her right. And then she would be even more unpleasant to live with. He glanced at the woman, noting the sour look on her once pretty face, and he wondered if that were possible.

The black Citroën forced Alex's car to the edge of the road five miles outside of Aix, and before he could bring a weapon to bear and open fire, he saw Sergei Bugayev's smiling face emerge from the rear seat. Bugayev was unarmed.

"You will never know what pleasure it gives me to attack *you* for a change," Bugayev said as he reached the open driver's window.

"You came very close to having your head blown off, Sergei." Alex's hand still held the pistol, still uncertain what was happening.

"We Russians are the only ones expected to have a sense of humor in these matters, eh, my friend?" Bugayev said. "But this is serious. You and the lovely lady must come in my car, and I will explain. One of my men will follow with yours."

In the rear of the Citroën, Alex introduced Michelle, who permitted Bugayev to kiss her hand. The gesture surprised Alex. It was a side of the fat little Russian he had not seen. It seemed he fancied himself a bit of a lady's man.

"Your friend Wheelwright came to me," Bugayev said, turning serious. "It seems his people monitored our previous meeting, and he thought I might know how to reach you. I was noncommittal, of course." He inclined his head to one side. "Anyway, he wants you to know an order of sanction has come down against you. The cable arrived early this morning."

Alex was surprised, both by the speed of the sanction and by Bugayev's ability to find him so quickly.

"Wheelwright told you this? And somehow you knew where I could be found?"

"Wheelwright told me, yes," Bugayev said. "And, yes, *I* knew where to find you. Let us say I have been monitoring certain activities that you were a part of."

"I'd like to know the why of both," Alex said, still suspicious. "Tell me about the sanction first."

Bugayev drew a long breath. "It is an involved story. In fact, it goes back to the 1950s. But the short of it is that certain individuals in the CIA—including your father and Walter Hennesey—have been sharing in the Pisani brothers' rather lucrative drug operations for many years." He made a circular gesture with his hand. "They provided protection and certain technical advantages, and the Pisanis provided money." He watched for Alex's reaction—saw none—and continued. "Now this Montoya moves in, wanting to push the Pisanis out—to expand his own activities—and your father and his partners learn that he is being backed by a similar but less influential CIA group in Bogotá, who want to see their own little bit of profiteering expand into Europe." Bugayev shrugged. "As you can imagine, this will provide them several advantages, not the least of which would be to add to their own strength in the agency by having one of their major assets become a power in Europe as well. And then, of course, there is the money.

"Then they learn Montoya and his CIA friends are using Ernst Ludwig to lead their assault in Europe, and they see a way of stopping Montoya officially without having it appear they are simply fighting to save the Pisani drug empire. And they have the perfect tool to do that."

"Me," Alex said. His left eye had narrowed. "Yes, I can see that."

"But suddenly something unexpected happens. Ludwig makes a mistake. He is supposed to eliminate both Pisani brothers, but he gets only one—Antoine. Now there will be open warfare that cannot be controlled by Montoya's friends in the *milieu*. So the Bogotá group offers a deal—a sharing of the new profits, so to speak. But it will require calling you off, because without Ludwig, Montoya's chances of success drop significantly. But you won't give up your chance at Ludwig. So . . ."

"I can buy most of it," Alex said. "But not my father's involvement."

"Regretfully, it is true," Bugayev said. "I know it from personal experience."

He went on to explain how he and his superior had been offered a share in the profits ten years before as the price of freeing Alex from the earlier Soviet sanction.

"And we have kept track of the situation since," he said. "My superior, being the good communist that he is, had the profits monitored quite closely." He smiled. "To be sure we were not being cheated. For years now, your father has been laundering those funds through your brother's bank in Florida. I can assure you, it can be proven. And I believe your uncle will confirm what I have told you." Bugayev smiled again, a bit sadly this time. "It is also the reason we have been monitoring yours and Meme's activities. We were not certain how this new arrangement might affect our own little deal."

"And the reason they're giving for the sanction—my father and his friends?"

Alex's voice had become chillingly cold, and Bugayev decided he would not wish to be Piers Moran at the moment he had to face his son again.

"You've gone rogue again," he said. "Joined up with criminal elements in order to secure some drug profits for yourself. You know the CIA has never acknowledged the Pisani involvement with narcotics. Now they're doing so. But they are claiming it is something new for them—and quite unacceptable to the agency, of course."

"So they'll be going after Meme as well," Alex said.

"No, they want Ludwig to do that bit of dirty work for them. Or the police. They don't want to find themselves facing the entire *milieu* if things go wrong. They might not be able to reestablish themselves with a new faction if they do that. And if Montoya loses as well, they could end up with nothing. Personally or professionally."

Alex turned and stared out the window. He felt Michelle's hand on his, wanting to offer comfort but not knowing how.

"So I'm the linchpin," Alex said, still looking away. "And Wheelwright has guessed at least part of what's going on and wants to stop it."

"So it would seem," Bugayev said.

Alex turned hard eyes on Bugayev. "And what's in it for you, Sergei? Saving your own profits?"

"Alex!" Michelle said. "He is trying to help us."

Bugayev waved a dismissing hand. "I am afraid those will be lost in any event, Alex. If the Pisani faction wins this little fight, they will not forget this betrayal. Your father's group will be out. And us with it, of course. And if Montoya wins"—he shrugged—"well, we will be out anyway.

"No, Alex. For me this is personal. I owe you a debt from ten years ago. For something I did not do then. Let us just say I am trying to repay it."

He shook his head. "I also took their dirty money years ago, and was happy to have it." He laughed. "After all, I was only being a good communist, helping the West corrupt itself. It was a very convenient rationalization at the time. And it gave us a rather nice bit of leverage against our enemies." He offered another rueful smile. "Of course, we could never use it—then or now—without exposing our own venality to some rather dour old men in the Politburo."

"Why would they turn against the Pisani faction after all these years?" It was Michelle. She seemed overwhelmed by the information, by the convoluted nature of the betrayal.

"Money," Bugayev said. "But also, they didn't believe Meme would survive. Not after Antoine was killed. And even if he did manage to beat back Montoya, he would be so weakened, another leader would soon take his place. Meme suddenly became quite expendable. And he didn't appear to have much to offer for the future." He paused. "He still doesn't, I'm afraid. Not even with what he has done this day." He smiled again. "But it will scare the hell out of them, and I would not be surprised if our friends in Washington sent an emissary to see him."

"There is only one man he would see," Alex said. He was staring out the window again, and Michelle and Bugayev could see the muscle dancing along his jaw.

"Yes, I think you are right."

"Meme might very well kill him," Michelle said, suddenly frightened by what it would all mean if he did.

"No," Alex said. "He'll let him play out his game. And then he'll cut his balls off. Later. *Then*, when he's done that," he nodded to himself, "then he might kill him."

"Don't underestimate your father, Alex," Bugayev warned. "He can be a very persuasive man."

"Yes, he can," Alex said. "But this time Meme will know what to expect. I'll see to it he does."

"And what of Ludwig?" Bugayev asked.

Alex turned to him and smiled. It was not the most pleasant sight Bugayev had ever seen.

"I'm going to kill him," Alex said. He glanced at Michelle and corrected himself. *"We're* going to kill him. And then I'm going to pay back a few other debts."

CHAPTER

44

"Why aren't your father and the others afraid Meme will expose them—tell what they've been doing all these years."

Michelle was staring at Alex, still trying to understand the plot in which she found herself embroiled.

They were in a Russian safe house on the outskirts of Marseilles, one Bugayev had guaranteed his American friends had not yet discovered.

"For the same reason they knew Bugayev would never blow the whistle," Alex said. "Meme would have to acknowledge his own involvement. And besides, it's not the way he does business. He repays his debts in his own way."

"Are you afraid for your father?" she asked. She hoped he would say that he was.

"He's a big boy, and he's on his own." He looked away, then back at her. "He's sold me out one too many times. He started ten years ago, when he chose not to back me up." He stared at her, his eyes hard. "And he had the power to do it then. It would seem he controlled the purse strings of a very lucrative deal that involved people he could have forced to back me up. But he took the easy way out. He paid off the Russians and maintained the status quo. You see, my father likes the status quo. It makes him feel comfortable. And sending his son into exile, and just a touch of personal torment for all those years, was worth the price to have it."

"But he wanted to save your life," Michelle argued, not sure why she was defending the man.

"Bless his heart for that," Alex said. "But I didn't ask to be saved. I asked for his help. The only help I got was from Meme and Antoine. And they risked *their* very lucrative deal to do it.

"No, my father just wanted the easy way out. He was perfectly willing to send me into a dangerous situation now, ten years later. And he was willing to do it because it suited his needs. And only because it did."

He shook his head and walked to a window that looked out across a street at a row of quiet, unassuming houses. Surprisingly, he found he didn't hate his father. He simply found him despicable. And he wondered if that meant he had surrendered his need of the man. No, he told himself. You can't lose what you never had.

"You spoke to Meme earlier," Michelle said. "Did you tell him?"

Alex had called Meme from a telephone booth, to avoid any possible trace. He had told his uncle he would leave a message with one of his men whom he would find at random and would give him the address of the safe house, plus "some other information" Meme would need. He turned back to face Michelle.

"Yes, I told him," he said. "It's not revenge, Michelle. I owed my uncle that. I'm not going to allow my father to set him up as well out of some misplaced sense of loyalty."

Michelle stared at him, realizing how truly alone the man was, wondering how she would feel if she discovered her own family had betrayed her. The thought was inconceivable to her. She walked to him and slipped her arms around him.

"I love you, Alex," she said. "And I want to be with you in this."

"I know you do," he said. "But we'll be hunted now, and I can't be sure how long we can count on Bugayev. If his Russian masters get wind of what he's doing, his help could stop rather abruptly."

"I like the idea of being hunted with you," she said. "I like the sense of romance it gives us."

He pulled away from her and held her at arm's length. There was a touch of incredulity in his eyes.

"I assure you, it won't be romantic," he said.

She pulled him back to her again. "I assure you it will," she said.

———

They made love slowly, gently, taking time to explore each other's bodies as though it were their first time together.

Alex ran his mouth along the length of her body, treating each part as though it were something new and wondrous and just discovered. He felt her body arch and heard her moan softly as the caresses became more erotic, the stimulation more intense.

She took his hair in her fingers and pulled him gently to her, and he kissed and ran his tongue along her thighs, and gently brushed her vagina with his lips, filling himself with the smell and taste of her.

As Michelle's hips rose from the bed, her head arched back, and a high, breathless cry called out her pleasure. Her body began to shudder in uncontrollable waves, until she fell limp and panting, wanting him inside her, quickly, so she could feel even more of him.

She pulled him up to her, her eyes telling him what she wanted, all the need and love she felt for him, and he felt it himself and entered her quickly, eagerly, only aware of her internal muscles seizing him, drawing him more deeply inside her. They writhed and thrust against each other, each movement finding another avenue of pleasure, unable to control themselves now, not wanting to, content and eager in the giving and taking of new sensations, finding new heights with every movement.

And then they fell against each other, exhausted, fully spent, and clung to each other as though making sure neither would pull away, attempt to leave what had been so satisfying, and thereby diminish it.

"Oh, God, Alex. You've made me feel so whole again," Michelle whispered, pressing her head into his shoulder. "I wish we could just have this, just each other, and not the rest of it."

He knew what she was talking about. About chasing Ludwig down or waiting for him to come for them. About the killing that still lay ahead.

"You could go back to Corsica and wait for me," he offered. "I'd come to you when it was over."

"If I could, I would do that," she said. "But I cannot walk away from it. From you. From the need I feel. And still I know I wish it wasn't there. It's like a madness inside me."

"But there's a cure for the madness," he said.

"If it ends with it."

"It will," he said. "For you it will end as soon as he's dead."

"And for you?"

"Soon after that."

She understood what he meant, but didn't want any elaboration, could not deal with it if it were given.

"What will we do next?" she asked.

"We'll go to Wheelwright without letting him know we're coming. And we'll put him in a position that he has to tell us what he knows about Ludwig. Then we'll go after him, or find a way to make the bastard come to us. On our terms."

Michelle could feel his body tense as he spoke; she could almost feel the anger and the hatred roll from his skin. Juxtaposed with their so recent lovemaking it seemed harsh and unreal, and she wished it was not there. But it would be there, she knew, until they had done what they had to do. She prayed then it would disappear. But she also knew that might never be possible.

James Wheelwright walked from his office and headed for an American-style bar in a nearby hotel. It was 9:00 P.M., and he hadn't had a drink since lunch, and was badly in need of one. He entered the bar and took a table in the far corner, as was his custom. With the end to East–West tensions, the only danger that remained for a CIA station chief was the threat of Arab terrorism, and that threat seemed pretty much scotched for the moment. At least in Marseilles.

Wheelwright was staring into his drink, thinking about his evening conversation with Walter Hennesey, and his inattention left him no opportunity to act when Alex and Michelle took seats on either side of him, with Alex taking pains to show him the small Walther automatic in his hand.

"Looks like your old service weapon," Wheelwright said, nodding toward the pistol. "I assure you, you won't need it."

"I'm happy to hear it," Alex said. "But I may *want* it."

"You don't have to threaten me, Moran. I'm on your side. And you can make book on that." He snorted derisively. "I just got off the horn with that thieving asshole Hennesey, after listening to him accuse me of hiding you out."

"What did you say?"

"I told him I wasn't, but would if I knew where you were."

"That must have thrilled him," Alex said.

"A lot of things are thrilling old Walter these days. Mainly his inability to find you."

"You could make yourself a hero," Alex suggested.

"I don't think Walter is going to be in a position to hand out any medals when this is all over."

"Don't count him out."

"I know," Wheelwright said. "Never count them out. Take them out instead." He drew a breath and looked at the pistol again. "What can I do for you?" he asked, smiling now. "Since you have me at the point of a gun."

"Tell me where I can find Ludwig."

"If I knew, I would." He offered a look of regret. "But I *can* tell you where to find Montoya. Maybe Ludwig will be with him."

"Where?" Alex asked, unable to keep the eagerness from his voice.

"He'll be headed for the airport tomorrow morning. Driving in from a small village outside Aix." He gave Alex the route the car would take.

"Your people will be guarding him?"

"Supposedly," Wheelwright said. "But I wouldn't be surprised if the trail car managed to get lost somewhere along the way."

"How come?" Alex asked, still suspicious of the man.

"I've been told to keep hands off Montoya because he's a Company asset. And to leave Ludwig alone because he works for him." He took time to sip his drink, then smiled. "If Montoya didn't exist anymore—and they tell me that happens to drug bosses all the time—well, then I wouldn't consider Ludwig as working for anybody. And I doubt certain people at Langley would have the balls"—he glanced at Michelle—"sorry," he said. "I don't think they'd dare complain about me going after a terrorist who's killed so many of our people."

"What about helping me? I understand there's a sanction out now."

Wheelwright grinned. "I almost forgot to tell you. That's been put on hold. Seems your old boss, Pat Cisco, got wind of it, and raised hell in a hand basket. Our orders are to sit tight and wait."

"That's interesting," Alex said.

"It's got them a little uptight at Langley. In certain quarters anyway." He paused, choosing his words. "So much so, I understand your father's on his way here. Wants to set up a meet with Meme Pisani."

"How delightful," Alex said. "The man does love to travel."

"Yeah," Wheelwright said. "We'll be picking him up at the airport day after tomorrow. You have any message for him?"

"Not now," Alex said. "I'll have one for him later."

CHAPTER

45

Montoya was raving. He marched back and forth across the sitting room of the CIA safe house, his short, stocky body dressed in a white Armani suit, his arms flailing flamboyantly, all of it making him seem like some sallow-complected ghost bent on intimidating a mortal who had crossed his path.

In fact, he was trying to intimidate Ernst Ludwig, who sat in a chair watching the spectacle, his eyes going occasionally to Raphael Rivera, who stood stoically across the room. Rivera avoided Ludwig's gaze after the first few times. The eyes were laden with contempt. It was as though they said: You created this fool, now control him. And do it before I cut his throat.

But no one was going to cut Montoya's throat. Two of his bodyguards, as always, were standing within easy reach of any attacker. They were hard, flat-faced men—part Indian, Rivera thought—who looked as though they would kill with the dispassion of one insect eating another. Rivera closed his eyes for a moment and questioned why he was even there. This was not what you had in mind when you graduated from Dartmouth, Rivera told himself.

"We are not attacking, we are sitting, playing with our pricks, and waiting for this old *miracon* to come at us," Montoya was raging in Spanish. He turned and glared at Ludwig. "It's not what I pay you for. You're supposed to be a fucking killer. So go kill the old bastard. Show me you have the balls of a bull, not some fucking chihuahua."

Montoya had stopped his pacing, and stood now rubbing the

death's head tattoo on the back of his hand. Ludwig could imagine him at a Nazi death camp, raging at the guards because the Jews weren't dying quickly enough.

Ludwig stared up at Montoya, his face one large sneer. One of the bodyguards took a step forward, watching him. He knows, Rivera thought. He knows how close his boss is to getting his head blown off.

"Answer me!" Montoya shouted. He seemed to suddenly catch the look in Ludwig's eyes, and he turned and walked quickly away. "I must know what your plans are before I leave," he added, his voice softer, more controlled.

Ludwig scares him, Rivera thought. Even with his bodyguards standing here, the man makes him nervous.

"First I am going to kill Alex Moran—"

"But that is just to protect yourself," Montoya snapped, cutting him off. "I want the Pisani faction wiped out. Then you can kill anyone you want. But first Pisani and all his fucking men. They attacked me." He jabbed a finger in his chest. "Me! Who the fuck they think they are?"

"Ludwig's right," Rivera said, causing Montoya's head to snap toward him. He doesn't like being contradicted, Rivera thought, and he held up both palms, begging patience.

"Moran's a professional. Just like your man is." He nodded toward Ludwig. "And if we hadn't been able to cut Moran off, he could have called in a lot of resources to put against us." He gestured with his hands again, begging more time. "But even without them, he's more dangerous than Pisani right now. He knows if he kills Ludwig, your operation stops until you can replace him. He knows you need someone like Ludwig to run things here. And he knows if he kills you"—he watched Montoya's eyes glitter at the suggestion—"the whole operation is dead, because there's nobody to run it."

Rivera knew he was weaving a texture of lies, but he also understood they would play well off Montoya's own beliefs. He believed he needed Ludwig, even though he could hire a half-dozen European killers to do the same job—at first, anyway. And he believed no one could run his operation but himself, even though Rivera's CIA group was essentially running it for him. And Rivera also understood that Moran didn't give a rat's ass about Montoya. He just wanted Ludwig dead. If Montoya's death made Ludwig more vulnerable, all well and good. If not, he wouldn't waste his time on the man.

"What we have to do is cut off the head and watch the body die," Rivera said. "The French police wouldn't tolerate all-out warfare on the streets of their second largest city. Especially when it involves foreigners going against—"

"But Pisani's the head, not this fucking Moran," Montoya interrupted, shouting again. He watched Rivera wave for patience.

"There are better ways to cut off a head," Rivera said. "Moran's considered part of Pisani's family. And the old man can't afford to have another member of his family hit like his brother was. He'd look too vulnerable to the rest of the *milieu*, and they'd make a move on him." He nodded, as much to himself as to Montoya. "Get Moran and the others will take care of Pisani for us." The nod changed to a reassuring smile. "And then they'll come to you for a piece of the operation."

It was all hypothetical, and Rivera knew it. But he also knew he needed Moran dead. By now he would have learned about the long-standing drug deal between Pisani and the others. Pisani certainly would have told him, pissed as he must be—as he should be—at the way he had been hung out to dry. And that was the biggest danger everyone faced right now. A loose cannon like Moran, who knew more than he ever should have.

And Rivera didn't have any faith in the plan to placate Pisani. The time for that was long past, and he was certain Piers Moran's upcoming attempt at doing so would prove a wasted effort. The others were just pissing in the wind, and hoping nothing would splash back on their shoes.

Montoya had turned back to Ludwig. He was rising and falling on the balls of his feet, like some little shit of an emperor, Ludwig thought. Some South American Napoleon who never should have been allowed out of the dusty, heat-baked hole of a village from which he had crawled.

"So you kill Moran," Montoya snapped. "You don't wait, you kill him." He had digested what Rivera had told him, and had adopted it as his own idea.

"Soon," Ludwig said, his voice as cold as his eyes.

"What is soon? Now!"

"I have to find him first," Ludwig said. He smiled for the first time. "Or let him find me."

"So do it!"

Ludwig had come to the safe house at Montoya's order. To see the man before he boarded a plane and got himself safely away. He knew what he wanted to tell the man, but it wasn't time yet. That would come later. And perhaps Montoya would find himself looking down the barrel of a gun when he finally did. The thought was pleasing.

"He'll be dead before the week is out," Ludwig said. He wished he could walk out, and leave the little fool to do his own killing. If he could. But the only protection he had was from the CIA, and without it he'd be far too vulnerable. Alex Moran would remain alive and would never stop coming for him. And if he walked away now, the CIA would sell him quickly. They'd buy Moran off with his body, serve it up to him on a platter.

"Everything takes a week here," Montoya complained. "In Bogotá, I want a man dead, the mortician is dusting off the coffin the second I snap my finger."

Ludwig nodded toward one of the bodyguards. "You think *your* men can do it faster. . . ." He shrugged and let the sentence die. He smiled at the smaller man. "While you are burying them, I will go about my business and kill Moran my way."

The two bodyguards bristled at the insult, which had been spoken in Spanish, but Montoya did not. He was still intimidated by Europe, the little he had seen of it. Things were not as he had expected. There seemed even to be rules for killing people here. Fucking rules! he raged inwardly. At home he could order a judge killed, a police chief, the fucking president of the country, and no one would expect any less. Here he couldn't kill a fucking gangster the way he should be able to. Only local gangsters could do that. But not him, not his men. It was because they were foreigners, and the killing of locals would give offense. It was like some kind of discrimination, he told himself.

And his men, they were useless here. They couldn't even speak the language. They couldn't find a place to shit without help. And Ludwig knew it. He knows you need him. And so he pisses on you. Challenges your orders in front of your own men.

Montoya drew himself up, becoming as imperious as he knew how. He squared himself on Ludwig, who was standing now, making him feel physically small.

"You have him by the end of the week," he said. He waved his hand in a gesture of benevolence, entirely for the consumption of his men. "You understand this country, so I give you the leeway to do this the way you think best." He forced a smile and raised a cautioning finger. He was the patron lecturing a minion. "But only a week. No more."

Rivera thought Ludwig would fly across the room and seize the man by the throat. But instead he smiled. It was a chilling sight, Rivera thought. They'd have to get rid of Ludwig when his part in all this was over, he told himself. Otherwise Montoya would find himself dead, and they'd have to start again, breaking in another South American punk with a fancy tailor.

"I assure you, Rudolfo. It will be done," Ludwig said. "He is number one on my list."

Montoya missed the hidden message. He turned from one man to the other, making sure he included his bodyguards, and gestured and nodded his head, indicating his approval.

"When I come back," he said, opening his hand and holding his palm like a cup, "then we will have this country here." He nodded his head again. "The whole continent will be here." He turned to Rivera and offered him a sly look. "And we will make much money eh, my friend? Much, much money."

Montoya rode in the rear of the long black Mercedes. He was annoyed that he had been denied the limousine that had been rented for his arrival. It made him feel as though his stature had somehow been diminished. But he had no choice, and, to a degree, he understood it. And at least it was still a Mercedes.

The car moved along an open stretch of highway winding through the French countryside. It was pretty here, he supposed. But it lacked the lushness of his own country, Montoya told himself. But it was old. As old as the Aztecs, from whom—he liked to tell people—he had descended. It wasn't true. At least he didn't know if it was or not. But he liked the idea. And so he made it true.

His thoughts turned back to Ludwig, as they had repeatedly over the months he had used him. The man was dangerous. Too dangerous to remain alive. But there was no choice for the time being. But later it would be different.

Most of the men who worked for him were from his own region in Colombia. Either that, or relatives, or the husbands of relatives. You couldn't trust people who weren't bound to you by blood, or close to blood. Or the sanctity of your own part of the world. The others he used, he got rid of when he no longer needed them. It would be the same with Ludwig. He'd use him until he could replace him with one of his own. Already he had told some of them to start learning the French language. They had looked at him like he was crazy, but they were doing it. His people always did what they were told.

His man in the passenger seat had turned and spoken to him, but he had not heard what he said.

"What is it?" he snapped. The man should not have interrupted his thoughts. It was disrespectful.

"The CIA car," the man said, his tone more subservient. "It is not behind us."

Montoya turned and looked out the rear window. The road behind was empty.

The fools had probably had a flat tire, or had gotten themselves lost in the last village they had passed through. He glanced at his $7,000 Rolex. There wasn't time to look for them. They had timed his arrival for the plane so there would be no waiting, no unnecessary exposure. He waved a dismissive hand toward the man. The two bodyguards were well armed, and it was only a short distance now.

The roadblock came into view as Montoya's car rounded a sudden bend in the road. He stared at it, momentarily concerned, then dismissed the worry when he saw it was manned by only two gendarmes, one of whom was apparently a woman. The bodyguard in the passenger seat chambered a round in his weapon, and Montoya snapped at him, ordering him to place it under his seat. The last thing he wanted was a confrontation with French police. While the CIA might be able to resolve any dispute, it would undoubtedly cause him to miss his plane, especially now that his CIA escort had managed to get themselves lost or broken down.

The car pulled up in front of the makeshift barrier, and one of the gendarmes—the man—came to the driver's window. He had a submachine gun slung from his shoulder, but he wore it casually, as though unconcerned about its possible use. The other—the woman—wore a holstered automatic. She stood back at the barrier, watching the car. Montoya thought she looked nervous.

The gendarme at the window asked a rapid question, and the driver shrugged helplessly, indicating he could not understand French. The gendarme gave him a disdainful look, then glanced at the other bodyguard and then Montoya, and received the same response.

He motioned to the driver curtly, indicating the rear of the car. He wanted to inspect the trunk, Montoya knew. The CIA had warned him there might be occasional roadblocks in France, making routine checks for weapons and explosives. They had cautioned him against carrying any weapons in the trunk of a car, since it was the place most often checked by police.

The driver opened the trunk, and the gendarme looked inside, then raised the lid of the well that housed the spare tire. Satisfied, he nodded to the driver and walked slowly back to the barricade, while the woman waved the car around it.

"And have a nice day," Alex said as he watched the car drive off.

He turned to Michelle. "Flashy-looking little guy, this Montoya," he said.

"I had hoped Ludwig would be with him," she answered.

Alex grunted. He understood what she meant. It would be over then. At least for her.

He reached into his pocket and withdrew an electronic detonator that Pisani had provided, then turned to watch the car as it drew farther away. The road ahead was clearly visible for a long stretch, and he wanted to be sure no innocents would stray past.

The image of Montoya came back to him. He had been hard-eyed and had seemed tense sitting in the rear seat, and there had been a look of avariciousness about the man that seemed to go with his chosen occupation.

He stared at the car for several seconds more, then depressed the red button on the detonator. The explosive he had planted in the tire well went off after a one-second delay, sending a ball of flame and debris into the air, part of which, he knew, were the remains of the three men in the car.

He had chosen the false police barricade because that had been the way they had killed Antoine. It was a personal form of revenge and he thought his uncle would have appreciated it.

He picked up the barricade and tossed it to the side of the road, choosing not to look at Michelle. He didn't want to see her eyes, afraid of what might be there.

Ludwig was alone now. Cut off and on his own. Montoya's men would scatter with their boss blown to bits. There was nothing left for them, no profit to be had. The CIA might hang in with Ludwig until Montoya was replaced. But that would take time, and time was one thing Ludwig didn't have. And he would know it, and he would strike back to protect himself. He would know Meme would seal off the city—the whole of France, if necessary—to stop his escape. It was ten years ago all over again, and Ludwig would know he had no other choice but attack. Because this time Alex would pursue him. And there would be no place to hide where Alex could not follow. No protection against it. And that was just the way Alex wanted it.

CHAPTER

46

Piers Moran was ushered into the rear office of Club Paradise, and was immediately struck by the fact that it had changed so little in the years since he had been there last. But there was one significant difference. Meme was seated behind the desk, as he always had been. But Antoine no longer occupied the heavy, old, overstuffed chair that sat beside it. Piers sincerely regretted his absence. But that had been a matter of business, and business, he understood, often involved a certain amount of unpleasantness.

"My old friend," Piers said, extending a hand to Meme. It was something he truly felt, and it hurt him when Meme simply pointed to a chair opposite and did not take his hand. But it did not surprise him.

"First," Piers said as he lowered himself into the chair. He paused, drawing a breath. "First, I want you to know I had nothing to do with the absurd decision to remove CIA support over the past few weeks." He shook his head. "I was kept completely out of the picture, was never even consulted. I suppose it was because they knew I'd raise holy hell, if for no other reason than it also placed Alex at jeopardy."

Meme nodded but said nothing, waiting for Piers to continue.

Piers shifted in his chair. There was no way for Meme to know the truth, no way for him to know he had played any role in the decision to back Antoine's killers. *If he had, you'd be dead already,* he told himself. *Or dying in some way only Meme could devise.*

He had learned of Montoya's assassination before he had left

Washington. And he had known immediately who had done it. It clearly bore the mark of the training Alex had undergone.

Hennesey had brought the news to the airport himself. And he had known as well. But Alex was only part of the problem they faced. They had to smooth things over with Pisani, find their way back into his good graces. And even failing that, they had to make sure Alex was brought back under control. Or stopped permanently if he had learned about the long-standing drug deal with the brothers. It was purely a question of survival. Piers had fought that part of the plan, but was reluctantly forced to accept it. But he had forced one concession. If Alex didn't know, they'd allow him to take care of Ludwig, even help him, and put an end to the whole mess that damned Bogotá group had initiated. And then send that bastard Rivera back to his hellhole with his tail between his legs.

"Meme, I assure you, I have gotten things back on track. If I'd been part of it, if I'd had any voice in the decision, I assure you this never would have happened."

Meme sat forward, his forearms on the desk. He looked old and frail to Piers, and very, very tired.

"Why should I believe you, Piers?" he asked. Even his voice sounded tired, Piers thought. Or perhaps it was just sad.

"Because we are old friends," Piers said. "And we have been through much together."

Meme squeezed his eyes with his thumb and index finger, then looked up at the man he had first met in 1947. They had been very different then, yet alike in many ways. It had not changed over the years.

"Yes, it has been a long time," he said. He sat back in his chair. "Tell me, Piers." He stopped a moment. Not really gathering his thoughts. More trying to control them. And his words, Piers thought.

"These associates of yours. Who we've dealt with for so many years. Did you not wonder what their plans were when Antoine was killed? Did you not question what action they would take to help us avenge him?"

Piers began to speak, but Meme's eyes stopped him. He understood he could not make believable the lie that he had simply assumed the right thing would be done.

"And when they decided to issue a sanction order against your son. Did these men, who you know so much about, did they not fear what you might do if they ordered him killed?" Meme shook his head. "A man in such a position might do anything, eh? He might even forsake whatever price he himself might have to pay out of the need to avenge his son's death."

Piers shifted his weight in the chair. "You don't understand how these things are done," he said.

"I don't understand?" Meme's eyes rose in mock surprise. He looked away for a moment, then back. "I understand that you made these men very wealthy. I understand that you have the power"— he held his thumb and index finger an inch apart—"and all the little bits of information, gathered over the years, to take that wealth away. And to destroy them." Meme nodded, more to himself than to Piers. He wanted him to understand that he too had such information. "I would think these men would be very careful about offending you."

Piers rubbed his palms together. They were sweating, and he worried that he would be unable to keep the tension he felt from his voice.

"They knew I would never use that information," he said. "That I could not."

Meme smiled for the first time. "Ah, truth. At last." He leaned forward again. "You see, I do understand, Piers. Because I am the man who made *you* wealthy." He waved his hand as though dismissing an unspoken objection. "Oh, I know you brought Luciano to me. But I took the deal because I knew you would live up to your word, and provide the protection we needed to make it work. And I knew you would, because I knew you were greedy for money. And that your greed would not go away over time." He stared at Piers for a moment, still smiling.

"I don't say that as an insult," he said. "I believe in greed. It is one of the factors in life that drive men to do great things." He waved a hand. "Build railroads. Transform whole continents. Conquer nations." He let out a laugh that held no warmth, no pleasure. "You see I am not the ignorant Corsican you thought you had met in 1947." His fists tightened on the desk. "And I was not ignorant then. I saw you and I understood you. I saw a man who was pleased that his somewhat foolish wife had a considerable amount of money. And I also saw a man who regretted that money was not his own." He unclenched his fists and let them lie, palms down, on the desk.

"And I understood that this man, if he got the chance to have money for himself, would take it and would do whatever was necessary to keep it." Meme's eyes darkened, and he glared across the desk at Piers. "But I didn't think he would go so far as to betray his true friends—and his own son." He sat back; his face had gone suddenly slack. "So I failed you there, Piers. I failed us all. Because I never understood how truly great your greed was."

Piers felt defeated, more so than ever before in his life. It was as if all the juice and air had been sucked from his body. He knew he could not lie to the man, and it left him feeling robbed of his only weapon. And it made him angry. "I find it amusing to be lectured by you about greed," he said.

Meme laughed, and the laughter was directed at Piers. "Yes, I have known greed all my life. I had greed for money and for power ever since I was a small boy. And once I had those things, I had the greed to keep them." His eyes hardened. "But never at the cost of my friends and my family. It is the difference between us." He held up his thumb and index finger, again showing that small inch of space between them. "I had that small amount of honor. And that is something you have never known."

Piers sneered at him, unable to control his anger at being preached at. "Your belief in honor among thieves, eh?"

"No. Never among thieves. Among friends, and among family."

"So what will you do now? Use the information you have to destroy us?" He leaned forward and stared at his old friend. "Don't forget it will destroy you as well," he snapped.

Meme shook his head. "I will not have to destroy you."

"What, then? Kill us? Kill all of us?" There was a sneer in his voice. He was suddenly not afraid of the man any longer.

Meme smiled. It was cold and hard and certain. "I think I will let Alex do that," he said.

This time it was Piers's eyes that shot up in mock surprise. "Alex would never kill his own father," he said. He seemed amused by the suggestion.

"Oh, yes, Piers. He will kill you. But perhaps he will do it in a way you will never understand."

"So he knows. You've told him everything."

"I've told him nothing. I simply confirmed what he already knew. And now he knows all there is to know about his father."

"And you think that will make him kill me?" Piers's voice was laden with contempt. "You don't know my son," he said.

Meme sat back in his chair. The faint trace of a smile was still on his lips.

"No, Piers. It is you who have never known your son. Never."

Wheelwright was reluctant to provide Piers with any information. But Piers had the power of the Company behind him, and he was able to force the information from the man, and from his records.

He had already known where to find Ludwig. Rivera had provided that. And as he had made his way up the battered old staircase that led to Ludwig's seedy hole, Piers felt a great weight at what he was doing. But he was able to push it aside.

Ludwig threw back his head and laughed. They were seated in the small front room of the decrepit apartment in the city's old quarter, and Piers had remained perched on the edge of his chair. But not out of nervousness. Rather out of concern that the grime that seemed to be everywhere would get on his clothing.

"So you come to tell me I must kill your son," Ludwig said. He leaned forward, his face mocking his visitor. "But you see, I already know that."

"I'm here to tell you how you can do it. And how you can do it quickly," Piers snapped.

He felt nothing but contempt for the man. For what he was, for what he had been all his life. It made him feel dirty to be dealing with him. As dirty as the apartment in which they sat. Piers also despised what he himself was doing. But he understood he had no choice.

"I am always willing to accept advice from a man of such experience," Ludwig said. He was laughing again, but only with his eyes. "So tell me. Where is your son?"

"I can't tell you that."

Ludwig laughed out loud this time.

"Bugayev is hiding him," Piers continued, ignoring the contemptuous laughter. "And Alex is with a woman named Michelle Cabarini."

Ludwig thought he recognized the name, but could not place it. "How do you know these things?" he asked.

"Through the agency," Piers said. "You can find him through those people."

"Bugayev." Ludwig spoke the name with open contempt. "I should have known that Russian bastard would get his filthy hands in this." He smiled. "It will give me pleasure to cut his throat."

"After you find Alex," Piers said. "Then you can kill whomever you wish."

"Ah, fatherhood," Ludwig said. "It is such a wonderful thing. In the whole animal kingdom it is always the father of whom the children must be wary. They are the ones who eat their young." He smiled at Piers. "You would have liked my father. You had much in common. Except your politics," he added.

"Don't be smart with me, young man," Piers snapped. "Just do your job. Do what you're being paid to do."

Ludwig smiled at the contempt in the old man's voice. Such a moralist, he thought. He wanted value for value received. He was so typical.

"Don't worry, old man," he said. "I will kill your son for you. I must admit, I am curious about why you want him dead. But not that curious." He sat forward in his chair and smiled. "Would you like to know how I shall do it? Do you have any interest in the pain your little Alex will have?"

He watched Piers's face pale, his jaw tighten. And he laughed again.

"I see." He stood and walked across the room. For dramatic effect, Piers thought. Then he turned. He was smiling again.

"Be assured it won't be quick. I don't really enjoy it when it is. I always found all those bombs I planted so depressing."

"You are perhaps the lowest form of life I have ever met," Piers said.

Ludwig threw back his head, and his laughter filled the room. Piers got up and walked quickly to the door. Ludwig's words chased him into the foul-smelling hall.

"Look in the mirror, old man. Look very closely in the mirror."

CHAPTER

47

Wheelwright found Alex through Bugayev. But he was not taken to the Russian safe house. Instead he was picked up by two of Meme Pisani's men and brought to a small park in the northern end of the city. There he found Alex, Michelle, Bugayev, and Pisani. The park was ringed with enough armed men to repel a small invasion.

"Very impressive," he said as he joined them at a large picnic table. "It would seem the lines of battle are pretty clearly drawn." He glanced at each one in turn—the communist, the gangster, the defrocked spy, and the widow. "Strange bedfellows, as they say. But then, the other side is rather interesting too."

"Spare us the philosophy, Wheelwright," Alex said. "You had something for me. What is it?"

"Don't even like your friends in the agency anymore, eh, Moran?" He nodded. "But that's okay. I don't much like mine either. Just so you know who your friends are." He pulled out a cigarette and lit it with an old Zippo lighter. "Your father's in town," he said through a stream of smoke.

"I know," Alex said. "He's been to see my uncle."

"He's been to see me too," Wheelwright said. "Asking a lot of questions about you. Questions that if I were you would make me very nervous about what his intentions were."

"I know what his intentions are," Alex said. His voice was cold and flat. It was as though he were speaking about someone long dead.

Wheelwright raised his eyebrows, asking what those intentions were.

"He wants me dead," Alex said. "No." He shook his head. "He needs me dead. There's a difference."

"What did you tell him?" It was Michelle, her voice charged with emotion, accusation.

"Just about everything he wanted to know," Wheelwright said. "It was all in reports anyway. And I couldn't keep them from him. I was ordered to show him anything he wanted to see." He smiled. "But they forgot to order me not to tell you."

"So he knows *merde*," Meme said. "Because that is all you know."

Wheelwright winced and glanced across the table at Bugayev.

"Don't feel bad," Bugayev said. "He has already given me his opinion about my beloved KGB. Unfortunately, his views were quite accurate."

"Where do you think he went with that information?" Alex asked.

"Ludwig would be my guess." Wheelwright offered Alex a look of regret. It was not a pleasant thing to hear about your own father. "He's the only shooter he's got left right now. He knows he can't count on my people. And Pat Cisco's got them tied in knots where any official sanction is concerned." He watched Alex stare off into space. "If you want to pay him a visit, I know where he's staying," Wheelwright added. He looked at Meme. "Or if you do."

"Not yet," Alex said. He turned back to face the CIA station chief. "Exactly what does he know?" he asked.

"He knows the young lady is with you. He knows our KGB friend is hiding you out. And he knows you offed Montoya, and that Ludwig's next on your list."

"And he knows that Alex has learned about his involvement in narcotics," Meme said. "It is why Alex must be killed."

"You told him that?" Wheelwright asked.

Meme said nothing.

"You kind of put our boy here on the hot seat by doing that," Wheelwright said.

Again Meme did not respond.

"What he did sent my father to Ludwig. That's what it was supposed to do," Alex said.

Wheelwright smiled and nodded. "So your uncle fed him what you wanted him to know. And he fed it to Ludwig." He thought about that a moment. "So now Ludwig knows where to look if he wants to find you. And he'll come to you."

"It's easier than finding him," Alex said.

"Why didn't you just have the old boy followed? Get to Ludwig that way?"

"He would have spotted the tail," Alex said. "He's been a pro for a long time. He might have decided to just step back and let Ludwig work it out himself. It wasn't worth the risk."

"There's another way to stop him," Wheelwright said. "And to get to Ludwig. With our help this time."

Alex just stared at him, sensing what the offer would involve. Wheelwright took in the look, but pushed on anyway.

"Tell me everything you know about the narcotics deal this group of his has been working. And give me some evidence to prove it, or at least a starting point of where to look." He tossed his cigarette out onto the grass. "I'll take the evidence over their heads, and I'll bring enough heat down to stop them. And, I promise you, I'll get you enough help to nail Ludwig. No matter where he runs."

Alex continued to stare at him, as though thinking the offer over. "Not yet," he said at length.

The CIA man began drumming his fingers on the tabletop. "Yeah, somehow I didn't think you'd buy that." He looked at his hands, kept staring at them as he asked his final question.

"What are you going to do about him? Your father? When all this is over?"

This time Alex remained silent.

Alex and Michelle returned to the Russian safe house, driven by two of Meme's men, who had been ordered to remain with them. Alex had rejected both Bugayev's and Meme's offer of additional bodyguards. He didn't fully trust the KGB officer, and he believed any more of Meme's hard-looking Corsicans would only attract undue attention.

It was Saturday afternoon, a bright, sunny day so typical of the south of France, and the neighboring yards were filled with children playing under the lazy watchfulness of their parents.

Michelle stood at the sliding glass doors that led to a rear patio and watched the family next door. There was one child, a boy about five years old, she thought, and he was building bucket-shaped mounds of dirt in a sandbox, then running to his mother when each construction was completed to accept her expected admiration and approval. The father sat in a chaise, reading a newspaper, but his eyes drifted from the newsprint repeatedly, and Michelle could see a small smile play across his lips as he watched his son.

It was a painful sight for her, a painting in which she could have been a figure had not Rene and little Pierre been murdered. And she realized with a cold, hurtful stab that she would never know what her child would have been like at five or beyond. He would remain a three-year-old forever, with her final memory of him being the still horrific sight of his tiny white coffin, looking so desolate and alone, as she was taken from the graveyard where he was buried.

She turned away from the window and fought for composure. All the conflicting horror she had felt about searching out and killing her son's murderer—about the deaths of the others who had helped him—seemed suddenly absurd. Life was precious, the life of a young child the most precious of all, and those who denied it, who stole it on a whim, had no right to it themselves. It was not a question of vengeance. That would not ease her pain, or give back an hour of what had been taken from her child. It was a matter of punishment. And that was something, she believed, that was worthy of pursuit.

Alex had been watching her from a chair across the room. He heard the voices of children filtering in from outside, and he understood the scenario that must be playing out in her mind.

"Is it hard for you here?" he asked. "In this neighborhood of families and children."

She looked across the room at him, as though momentarily confused by where his voice had come from.

"Yes," she said. The line of her mouth hardened. "And it offends me too."

"How so?"

"Having this—this safe house here. It isn't safe at all, is it? It's a place where people are hidden from others who want to do them harm." Her eyes bored into him, as though he were somehow responsible. Perhaps because he had done the same himself in the past.

"And these people don't know." She waved her arm, taking in the room, but really the neighborhood. "And if violence comes, they'll be part of it. And they won't have done anything to deserve it."

"It's what makes it hard to find," Alex said. "It's what makes it safe."

"But it's wrong."

"Yes, it is."

Michelle's eyes momentarily filled with tears. "It is what it was like for my husband and my child," she said. "I heard the police talking about it. They said they were just targets of opportunity." She shook her head. "Such a cold phrase for what happened." She stared at him. "You see, my husband never had anything to do with what they are fighting about. The drugs. He was just working for the wrong people in the wrong place at the wrong time. And my child was with him." She waved her hand toward the window. "Just like these people."

Michelle stared at the floor, wondering why she was even speaking about it. She was dressed in a brightly colored blouse and a full summer skirt that had large, deep pockets. She reached into one and withdrew a slender object, then pressed a button on the handle and watched as the long, thin blade of the stiletto snapped into place.

"Look at what Meme gave me at the park," she said. "He said it was better than a gun because it was easily hidden, and because no one would look for it on a woman." She stared at the knife. "He said it was his and that he wanted me to have it. I wonder how many people he's killed with it."

"He just wants you to be able to protect yourself," Alex said. The words were lame, but they were the only ones he could think to say.

"He said you'd teach me how to use it," she said. She looked at him again. Her eyes seemed filled with accusation, as if simply knowing how to use a knife was a confirmation of past guilt, a condemnation. Watching him kill Montoya and his men had altered her feelings, Alex thought. It was difficult to watch someone kill others and feel the same as one had before.

"Do you want me to show you?" he asked.

"Yes." Her voice was firm; there was no hesitation in it.

Standing, Alex walked to her and took the knife from her hand. He stepped to one side and ran his hand over her upper body, front and back, lightly touching several places so she would remember them. Then he explained how the knife should be held for different killing thrusts.

He watched her jaw tighten, her eyes blink at the thought. He closed the knife and handed it to her, then turned and walked back across the room.

"Would you like a drink?" he asked.

"No," she said. "I want to go out. I want to get away from here for a while. Perhaps go to the cemetery and visit my son's grave." She shook her head. "I don't know, just do something . . . normal."

He had turned back to her, concerned. "I don't think that's wise," he said.

"I'll be all right."

He nodded. Not certain she would be, but knowing there was nothing he could do to dissuade her. "I'll go with you."

"No." She tried to smile. "I just need some time alone. Alone with my son."

Alex felt helpless. How could he stop her? How could he ask her not to go?

"You'll have to take Meme's men with you," he said. "I can't let you go alone."

"I'll take one of them. It will be enough."

"Take both," he said. "Just for my peace of mind."

"All right."

Michelle walked across the room and rested her head against his chest. She did not place her arms around him, or touch him in any other way.

"I love you, Alex," she said. "It's just hard for me now. Please understand."

"I know it is," he said. He wondered if it would ever be easy for her again.

The cemetery was on a hill overlooking the sea. Little Pierre was buried here in France, not at home in Corsica. There had been so little left of his small body after the explosion, she had not had the strength to take what remained across the sea, to carry his torn and dismembered body home.

The thought of it came back to her now, standing before his grave, and the pain surged in her stomach, doubling her over, and she sank to her knees and began to sob.

The two Pisani men stood far back, glancing at each other nervously, not certain what they should do.

Michelle reached down and stroked the new grass that covered the grave. Oh, my Pierre, she thought. How I miss you. How I long to hold you again and feel you against me. How I wish I could die and be with you now.

She drew a deep breath, feeling it catch in her throat. But not before I find him. Not before I can look into the eyes of the man who killed you. Not before . . . She straightened and drew another breath, fighting for composure. She could not speak to her dead child of what she must do. She could not defile his memory that way. But she would do what must be done, and she would do it coldly, with calculation, and she would see that man die. And if her own life ended doing it, that would be all to the good. Her God would understand. She believed that with all her heart. And He would bring her to her little baby, and they would be together again.

She stroked the grass again, then rose—surprisingly composed now—and turned to her bodyguards. Tears still stained her cheeks, but her eyes were cold and hard, and it seemed to make the men nervous.

"I want to go to my office now," she said, her tone offering no room for objection. She received none. "It will only be for a minute," she said as she marched past them.

I will do something normal, she thought as she moved toward the car. If nothing else, I will read my mail and pretend my life is simple and clean and . . . yes, and human again.

Michelle's office was in a baroque building with a caged elevator that held two comfortably, three intimately, and four with a sense of the obscene. But few people ever came to the building in numbers, and on Saturday it had an abandoned, almost lonely quality about it.

But she had loved it from the first time she had seen it. The building had charm and grace to it, and she had often wished she had known something about its history, and had promised herself that one day she would look into its past, discover who had worked there, and for what purpose it had originally been built. But that would be for another time. When her life was sane again.

She opened the office door, the two Pisani men behind her, and entered the bright, spacious outer room where her small staff worked. She moved past the empty desks and into her own office. It too was large and gracious, and flooded with light from two floor-to-ceiling windows. And it had the added luxury of a private bath.

She went to her desk and picked up the stack of mail her secretary had left there awaiting her return. It was all mundane and unimportant, but it gave her a sense of normalcy she had not felt in several weeks. She seated herself behind the desk and began opening the mail.

"I won't be long," she said, glancing up at the two Corsican bodyguards. They were young and looked fit and strong. And they had that air of invincibility about them so common to young men who had no sense of their mortality.

But they must be quite competent, she told herself. Otherwise Meme would never have used them this way.

Michelle returned to the mail; she never heard or saw the bathroom door inch open. The two bodyguards remained equally ignorant. They had seated themselves on a large, overstuffed sofa, and they never noticed the thick cylinder of the silencer inch into the opening.

The single short burst from the silenced Uzi sounded like nothing more than the quiet thumping of an old fan. The sound didn't startle Michelle. At first she thought it some foolish noise made by one of the two men. And when she looked up from the mail, her initial reaction was disbelief at the sight of the bloody bodies of the two young men sprawled grotesquely across the sofa.

Her eyes, wide with terror, shifted to a movement at the bathroom door, and she watched the slender, blond man come slowly into view, his small, ugly, still smoking weapon now pointed at her. There was a sneering grin on his face, and she thought, absurdly, that he was about to laugh.

"That old bastard Pisani should hire better men," Ludwig said. "Or at least train them to check out a room before they curl up for a nap." His smile widened at his own joke.

He stopped in front of her desk and gave a short, Aryan bow, adding a soft click of his heels. The gesture seemed to amuse him even more.

"Ernst Ludwig, here to serve you, *Mademoiselle*," he said. His face took on a look of concern at having made some faux pas. "But I see from your mail, it is *Madame*, is it not? So I must wonder, where is your husband while you are off fucking my good friend Alex Moran?"

Michelle glared at him. He didn't even know who she was. Didn't even recognize her as a woman whose husband and child he had murdered. She was just a woman, any woman, whom he wished to humiliate.

"Answer me!" he snapped. "Where is your husband?"

"He is dead," Michelle said.

Ludwig's face broke into a grin again. "How convenient for you," he said. "And for dear Alex." His eyes hardened. "If you don't wish to join him, do everything I say."

Michelle wanted to throw herself at him, find some way to tear at his face, his eyes. To kill him with her hands if she could. But the Uzi made it impossible. And she didn't want to throw her life away without the satisfaction of taking him with her.

"Stand up!" he snapped. He watched her rise obediently. "Are you armed?"

"There is a pistol in my purse," Michelle said, nodding toward the large straw bag on her desk.

Ludwig dumped out the contents, picked up the Glock automatic, smiled at it and Michelle in turn, then tucked it into his belt.

"Anything else?" he asked.

He watched as she shook her head, then came around the desk and placed the barrel of the Uzi lightly against her jaw. Slowly, pleasurably, he ran his hands along her body, lingering over her breasts and inner thighs, the smile growing as he did. In his effort to humiliate her, to enjoy her body, his hand never touched the stiletto in the pocket of her wide, full skirt. She had forgotten it was there herself, and she vowed now to use it as soon as she could.

Ludwig stepped back and perched on the edge of the desk so their eyes were at the same level.

"Where is Alex Moran?" he asked. His voice seemed soft, relaxed, as though the killing he had just done, and the bodies behind him, were all part of some other time and place.

"I don't know," Michelle said.

His hand shot out, catching her solidly on the side of the jaw, and she staggered back, almost falling against the large window behind her desk. She felt her jaw swelling, but she willed the pain away and glared at him.

"Tell me the truth!" Ludwig snapped.

Michelle's mind began clicking into gear, and she recalled Wheelwright telling them that Alex's father had undoubtedly met with

Ludwig, and had told him about her, about Bugayev, and about the unknown safe house.

"A man named Bugayev—a Russian, I think—has hidden him somewhere. They did not tell me where," she said.

Ludwig's eyes narrowed, then became suddenly playful. He ran his hand gently along her cheek, allowing the fingers to linger at the corner of her mouth. "Then how does he reach you when his cock gets hard, and he wants to use your beautiful mouth?" he asked.

Michelle jerked her head away from his touch.

"Or how do you reach him when you want it?" he said. His voice had remained soft, but his hand snapped out, grabbing her cheeks between his fingers and squeezing tightly.

"Tell me!" he demanded.

She fought his hand, then gave up. "One of Bugayev's men contacts me," she said.

He nodded and released her.

"Bugayev," he said. "Don't you find him an exceptionally ugly little man?" he asked. His eyes hardened again. "Where is the car you came in?" he demanded.

"In front of the building," Michelle said.

"Are there other men there?"

She shook her head.

"If there are, I will kill them. And you," he warned.

"There is no one else."

Ludwig smiled, his eyebrows rising slightly. "We shall see," he said. He nodded toward the bodies behind him. "One of them has the keys?" he asked.

"Yes."

"Good," he said, his voice almost a purr. "Go and get them!" he snapped.

Ludwig stood quietly, watching with obvious pleasure as Michelle moved reluctantly toward the bodies, and began searching the pockets of one of the men. Her face was a mixture of revulsion and horror, and the sight of it gave him a sense of delight. When she turned to face him, keys in hand, his eyes were glittering. His pleasure seemed almost sexual, she suddenly thought.

The call came into Bugayev's office at three, as he was finishing a report for Moscow Center on the assassination of the South American drug boss.

"Bugayev, my old friend. Are you still as ugly as I remember you?" the caller began.

He recognized the voice immediately, could almost visualize the self-satisfied sneer he had not seen in ten years.

"Ernst, my good friend," Bugayev responded, keeping his voice light and friendly. "You sound as though you must be standing before a mirror, as you so often did in the old days. Tell me, did you ever have that nasty scar repaired? The one that swine—oh, what was his name, now? Oh, yes. Alex Moran. The one he gave you so long ago. It must have been so upsetting to all your women. You were such a handsome man in those days."

There was silence on the other end of the line, then, finally, soft laughter. Bugayev thought it sounded forced.

"It is my good friend Alex I am calling about," Ludwig said. "I have something he will want. The Cabarini woman. I would like you to get a message to him."

"But how would I know where to reach him?" Bugayev asked. "And how would I know what I was telling him was the truth? You always had a nasty habit of lying to me, Ernst."

"Would you prefer I just kill her and send you her body for delivery instead?" Ludwig asked.

He sounded confident, almost playfully so, and it immediately angered Bugayev that he had not killed the man long ago.

"Ernst." He made a clucking sound. "If you want to kill her, it doesn't concern me. After all, one less capitalist in the world, what would it matter? And I also know you have already decided if she will live or die. Whatever I do will have no effect on anything."

"Just do it, my fat, ugly little friend. I don't think Moran would forgive you if another of his sleeping partners died because of what you did, or didn't do." He laughed. "And he seems to have developed an unpleasant disposition these days, hasn't he?"

Bugayev let out a heavy sigh for Ludwig's benefit. He wanted to give Alex options, an excuse for delay if he chose to use it.

"I will see what I can do," Bugayev said. "But I can promise nothing."

"The woman will die at seven o'clock if he does not call this number at exactly six-forty-five," Ludwig said. He rattled off the number.

He is too clever, Bugayev thought. He allows no leeway. But perhaps this time he has miscalculated.

"I will be happy to oblige you, Ernst," he said. "Oh, and Ernst, you should know that things are much the same as they were ten years ago. Only perhaps a bit worse this time. This time Alex Moran is hunting you with the Pisani faction *and* the KGB. I only hope I can be there when you die, Ernst. It would give me so much pleasure."

"Perhaps I will let you see me. Before I leave. Just for old time's sake," Ludwig said. Bugayev heard him laugh again before the line went dead.

"You must calm yourself," Bugayev said. "I believe he has made a mistake this time. And I think it will allow us to get to him."

They were at the KGB safe house, and Alex was pacing the front room like a caged cat. His fists, held rigidly at his sides, opened and closed, and Bugayev thought he might lash out at anyone who came too close.

"Ludwig doesn't make mistakes," Alex snapped. "He only makes it appear that he has."

"Perhaps," Bugayev conceded. "But we have nothing to lose in seeing if he has. My men are already working on it."

Alex stopped pacing and turned to face him. "What mistake?" he asked.

"He has given us a telephone number, and time to find its location. I have already confirmed it is not a public booth. It is a private line, in a house or apartment here in Marseilles." He watched Alex begin to pace again. "We can hit it, before six-forty-five, and then we will know."

"He'll kill her," Alex said.

"Yes," Bugayev agreed. "I think he will. No matter what we do or do not do." He gave Alex time to digest that. "I will do whatever you think best," he said at length.

Alex stopped and stared through the doorway that led to the rear room, and the sliding glass doors at which Michelle had stood only hours before. Watching the family next door, she had been thinking of her own dead child, and he remembered the pain that had been etched on her face. All she would want was Ludwig dead, he told himself. Nothing else would matter to her. But it did to him.

"We'll do as you suggest," he finally said. "But I want my uncle's men involved too. They're better at moving around the city unnoticed." He stared at Bugayev. "And I want you to do one other thing for me, Sergei."

"What is that?" the Russian asked.

"I want you to contact Wheelwright and find out where my father is. And then watch him. If Michelle dies, I'll want to get to him quickly," Alex said.

Bugayev nodded, but the request sent a shiver through his body.

The apartment was located in an empty building which was undergoing extensive renovations, in a block behind the Basilica of Notre-Dame-de-la-Garde. Alex, together with five Pisani men and three KGB agents, hit it at six-thirty-five, using blue-light stun grenades to immobilize anyone inside. The precaution proved unnecessary. Neither Ludwig nor Michelle were there. The telephone, which Ludwig had obviously rigged himself, was connected to an answering machine, on which a recorded message had been left. Alex played the message and heard a voice other than the one he had expected.

"You must go to a telephone located in a café on the corner of La Canebière and rue de Rome," Michelle's voice said. "From there you must call this number."

Alex listened as the number was given. Hearing her voice, doing Ludwig's bidding, he could hardly breathe.

"Alex," the message continued, then paused before going on, "Ludwig wants you to know you will be watched when you go there. He said to tell you, he assumes you are standing in the apartment now, listening to this recording. He said he is sorry you wasted your time. He also says you will be watched as you complete the next instruction. And he wants me to tell you . . ." There was a pause, then a voice in the background before she continued. Alex could not hear what the voice had said.

"He wants you to remember what happened ten years ago, when you did not do as he said. And he wants you to remember what happened with your wife before she died. He said those things can happen again. He said to tell you he knows you will understand. That he just can't help himself."

The recording ended, and the machine automatically began to rewind. Alex stood staring at it, the whirring sound of the machine assaulting his mind. There had been an obvious tremor in Michelle's voice, but he hadn't been able to tell if it had come from fear or barely controlled rage. And he wondered if she had understood what Ludwig had meant when he alluded to Stephanie. If Ludwig had described in vivid detail what he had done to Stephanie. Done with her, before he had taken her life. He knew personally how much the man enjoyed telling it.

"What will you do?" Bugayev asked. He had entered the apartment immediately after the raid and stood next to Alex, listening to the message.

"I'll do as he says," Alex said. "I'll do everything exactly as he wants it done." He turned to Bugayev, and his eyes were like nothing the Russian had ever seen before. "And then I'll do what I've been waiting to do for ten years," he said.

"You did extremely well," Ludwig said as he removed the headphones he had been wearing. They were fed by the small microphone he had secreted in the apartment, and he had just listened to Michelle's recording and the reaction it had produced from Alex.

Michelle sat before him, her body trembling with rage. She had been forced to help this man cause Alex even more pain. And then to spy on him. To give him an advantage that would help end Alex's life. She twisted against the ropes that bound her wrists behind her back. The effort brought a smile to Ludwig's lips. He glanced across the room.

"Don't you think she did extremely well?" he asked. His voice was mocking, filled with an elated assurance about what would follow.

Raphael Rivera turned from the window. He had been watching Alex and the others leave the empty building across the street.

"They're leaving now," Rivera said, ignoring Ludwig's question.

"Is Moran taking anyone with him?"

Rivera turned back to the window. "No, he's leaving in a car by himself. The others are just standing around, trying to decide what to do next."

"And your man is stationed near the telephone at the café?"

"Just as we planned," Rivera said.

Ludwig turned back to Michelle and stroked her cheek. She jerked her head away from him. He looked down at her and laughed.

"Make sure your men are well stationed around the final location," Ludwig said, his eyes still on the woman. "I want to be sure any help that follows Moran is well taken care of."

"We know our job," Rivera said. "You just make sure you do your part as we planned it."

Ludwig's head snapped toward Rivera, his eyes glaring at the implied rebuke. Rivera softened his tone.

"I don't want her killed until Moran gets there. I don't want it screwed up because he failed to show." He walked toward Ludwig, trying with his eyes and expression to mollify the man.

"It has to look like they killed each other in some dispute over drugs," Rivera said. "I don't want anybody back in Washington drumming up sympathy for Moran and forcing an investigation. That won't help any of us."

Ludwig turned back to Michelle and reached out to her face again, taking it between his fingers this time and forcing her to look at him.

"Don't worry," Ludwig said. "I have no intention of killing her too soon." He smiled down at her. "And perhaps she won't have to die at all." His smile widened, became even more mocking. "Not if she's especially good to me."

Rivera had returned to the window and was looking down into the street.

"The others are leaving now," he said. "As soon as we get the next phone call, we can head for the next location."

"I can't wait," Ludwig said. He was still holding Michelle's face, still forcing her to look up at him. "I imagine you're anxious to get there too," he said to her. His smile had grown grotesquely sexual. "It will be very nice indeed," he said. "You will see how wonderful it will be."

CHAPTER

48

A lex punched a button on the visor and disconnected the car telephone. It was a new design that did not require the user to hold it and therefore avoided any unwanted attention.

His uncle had responded tersely to the call, his voice filled with the cold dispassion that seemed to mark everything the man did. It was just the way Alex wanted it. Cold and hard and lacking emotion. Ludwig had manipulated his emotions ten years earlier, had kept him stumbling along blindly, terrified at every turn. But not this time. This time he would play it like one of the Special Forces exercises he had run. He would play it coldly and professionally. Not give the bastard any edge he could use.

Michelle forced her way into his thoughts, and he pushed her away. It would do no good to think about her, about what might be happening to her even now. He could help her only by getting to Ludwig quickly and killing him before he could harm her. It was the only thing he would allow himself to think about. Just get to the bastard. Get to him fast.

He pulled the car into an illegal space in front of the café at La Canebière and rue du Rome. It was eight o'clock on Saturday, and the café was alive with couples enjoying a light evening meal.

He made his way to the telephone and found it in use. A young woman was speaking excitedly, angrily at times. To a boyfriend, he supposed. One who had failed to show up as expected. He waited, not allowing the delay to reach him.

The CIA man—one of Rivera's people, who had been flown in

from Bogotá—watched Alex from a nearby table, making it seem he too was observing the antics of the woman.

The target looked too calm, the man thought. Too loose and controlled. Not at all the way he would have wanted him if he were running this hunt. If a target had to know you were after him, he preferred them jittery and tight. They made mistakes that way, and they didn't watch their surroundings as they should.

The man returned to the omelet he had ordered, not wanting to make his observations too obvious. It would have made him stick out not to have had his attention drawn to the woman's anger. But too much curiosity, he knew, would be just as bad.

He mouthed a forkful of cheese-drenched egg. He didn't understand why they just didn't hit the bastard now and have done with it. Take him on the street and let the French police work it out. Christ, the man's connections with the French underworld should provide enough reasons for anyone. But Rivera wanted it to look like a drug deal—was insistent about it—and that just seemed like one helluva lot of overkill to him.

But, shit, what did he care? The team would do its job and be on their way back to sunny South America the next day. Back to all those lovely señoritas who liked to sweat when they did it. He smiled to himself. Life was good there. And it held the promise of getting even better.

The woman hung up the phone and stormed across the room. Alex took her place, keeping himself cold and relaxed, telling himself the delay had proved beneficial. He had spotted the watcher three tables away. The man's movements had been good; he had been well schooled. But that was all, and whoever had picked him had done it badly. The man was too big, too bulky to pass as a Frenchman. And the clothing was wrong. It was the wrong style for a continental European, and too formal for an American or British tourist. And the man held his fork in his right hand, something a non-American would never do.

He had committed the man's features and clothing to memory, and one phone call from the car would have two Pisani men on him as soon as he left. If he simply followed, he'd be taken out of the game. If they were lucky, he'd head to the final destination. Then they'd have Ludwig pinned, and the real game could begin.

The phone rang four times before Ludwig answered, just as Alex knew it would. Part of Ludwig's plan to raise the level of tension.

"It is déjà vu, Alex, is it not?" Ludwig began without preamble.

"Does seem that way," Alex said. "Are you ready for me, Ernst?"

"Oh, yes, Alex. And by the way, don't waste your time tracing these calls. They are being automatically transferred to another location. It is amazing, is it not, how science has improved our lives." He laughed. "Oh, and your choice in women, it has improved over the years as well. I compliment you. This new one, she is exquisite."

Alex forced down the rage, allowing it to flow from his body in a momentary pause.

"It's just your age, Ernst," he said. "You've come to appreciate them more."

The pause came from Ludwig now. The unexpected calm, the token insult, had thrown him off.

"I hope it won't be necessary to hurt this one, Alex," he said. "I hope you've overcome your tendency not to do as you are told."

"Come, Ernst. Let's not play games. You've killed her already."

"No, no, Alex. I have not. I am saving her. She is quite special."

"Let's get on to something important," Alex said. "Like where I'll find you."

Ludwig paused again, hesitant now, uncertain. Moran seemed not to care about the woman, and that didn't play into the expected scenario.

"You don't believe me, Alex," he said, probing. "That hurts me. I like to be thought of as a man of my word." He hesitated a beat. "Would you like to speak to her?" He paused again, then hurried on before Alex could answer. "Of course you would. But understand if she is a bit breathless. She has been very busy."

Alex's hand tightened on the receiver, and he felt the rush of his heart rate, and he forced himself to breathe evenly. It was the only game he had thought possible with Ludwig. Make him wonder if the woman really mattered to him. But just enough doubt. Enough to make him keep her alive, so he could see at the very end. Retain that final bit of perverted pleasure for the last.

"Alex. Don't come, Alex. He's—" The phone was pulled away, and the last he heard of her was a small cry of surprise and anger. Her voice had sounded strained, and there had been an edge of fear in it, but he could tell she was fighting it. Ludwig's voice purred back across the line:

"I think she wants more time with me, Alex," he said. "And, I must confess, I would like that as well. Your Stephanie had a lovely mouth—oh, I learned that so well over all the months we had together. And I have not yet had time to explore this one's talents in that area." He laughed softly. "But I will, Alex. I will take the time."

Alex remained silent.

"Am I boring you, Alex?" The laughter again. "No, I think not. I think you are just jealous of the pleasure I will have. But enough of that." He rattled off another telephone number. "You will go to a telephone booth in the parking lot nearest the labor exchange. You have ten minutes, Alex. More time than you need. But I need time to have you watched." He paused. "Oh, and you will not be speaking to me when you call." Again the laughter. "I expect to be busy. But the instructions you receive will be mine. See that you follow them precisely."

The disconnecting buzz hummed in his ear, and Alex replaced the receiver carefully, almost as though it were made of porcelain and might break in his hand. He turned and wound his way through the tables, passing close to the watcher, resisting a primal urge to smash his fist into his face, and headed out to his car.

Thoughts of Michelle were flooding his mind again, and this time he could not push them away. But she was alive. And that was more than anyone—excluding himself—had hoped for. Now, if only he could keep it that way. Just for a while longer. Just a little longer this time.

He punched out Meme's number on the visor phone as he pulled away from the curb, and immediately heard his soft, cold voice over the speaker. He gave him the description of the watcher and the location to which he was headed.

"My men are outside as we speak," Meme said. "I too am leaving. But I will have a man here to relay your messages."

Alex understood. Ludwig had killed Antoine, and Meme wanted to be there when he died, wanted to see his body, even have the satisfaction of killing him if he could. There are too many people after you, Ernst, he told himself as he disconnected the car phone. Too many people with too good a reason to want you dead. He wondered if the man understood that. Wondered if his vanity made him feel secure with the men who were covering his back. I hope so, Ernst, he thought. I truly hope you do.

———

Ludwig pushed Michelle down the darkened corridor ahead of him and into the large, open room that would be his killing ground. There was a certain poetry to the place he had chosen, and he liked that. Liked the final effect it was sure to have on Moran, the final edge it would put on his nerves before he killed him.

Michelle stumbled and fell, and she floundered, trying to right herself, her hands still bound behind her back, making it difficult. Ludwig pulled her roughly to her feet and turned her toward him.

Immediately her knee shot up, striking for his groin, but he turned his hips and easily warded off the blow. His hand lashed out, slapping the side of her face, and the force of it knocked her to the floor again and loosed a thin line of blood from the corner of her mouth.

He grabbed his crotch and squeezed it provocatively, his eyes glaring down at her.

"Is this what you want?" he hissed. "I will let you have it. I will let you have all of it you can stand." He stepped forward and used the barrel of the Uzi to spread the opening in her blouse, forcing one button loose, then a second.

Michelle scuttled back along the floor, and he stepped with her, toying with her inept attempt at flight.

"It is too bad I can't untie your hands," he said, his voice soft, the terrifying purr back in it now.

"Are you afraid what I might do with them?" Michelle snapped, fighting her fear, struggling for some obscure, unattainable degree of dignity.

Ludwig laughed, thoroughly enjoying himself.

"You are a silly bitch," he said. "Why not enjoy your final minutes? You would be amazed at the pleasure I could give you." He laughed again. "Even more than you would get by killing me. Of course, maybe you are the type who has an orgasm when you kill. Is that it?" His face settled into a leering grin. "I can understand that. It has happened that way for me." He rubbed his crotch in a grotesque mockery of sex. "It makes me hard here, the way women like me to be. Even when they're dead." The grin returned. "Perhaps it will again."

Michelle cringed at the sound of his laughter, fought off the shudder she felt coursing through her body. She could play up to him, get him to untie her hands, she told herself. Give herself a chance to get to the knife in the pocket of her skirt. But the thought revolted her: The idea of his hands touching her, for whatever purpose, was more than she could bear.

Ludwig knelt beside her, keeping to the side of her leg, out of range of any blow. He reached inside her open blouse and cupped her breast in his hand. Michelle began to pull away, but he squeezed her breast and pulled her toward him, causing her to cry out in pain.

"Ah, a cry of passion," he purred. "I do so like to hear that in a lover." He laughed again and mocked her with his eyes. "Tears of joy. They so become you," he said.

He reached up to wipe away a tear moving slowly down her cheek. Michelle's head snapped to his hand, and her teeth clamped down, and she let out a cry of rage as she bit through the flesh, feeling his blood in her mouth, tasting it.

Ludwig howled in pain and surprise, and he reared back and sent the Uzi crashing into the side of her head. Michelle's body fell back; her head hit the floor with a loud crack, and her eyelids momentarily fluttered as she lost consciousness.

Ludwig raised the Uzi, preparing to bring it down in a crushing blow to her skull. His eyes were filled with rage and pain, and his mouth twisted into an obscene mask. Then he grew suddenly calm. Staring at the woman, he sucked on the wound to his hand. He would wait, he told himself. Keep her alive until the end. Then kill her with all the misery he could give her. He looked at the wound, at the trickle of blood that had started up again, and his eyes flared. Then he leaned forward and spat in her face.

Alex placed the phone call and listened to an American-accented voice speak to him in French. He was given another location, another telephone number to call. Another ten minutes to do it.

"And Ludwig wants you to know he's fucking her now," the voice added.

"Your French stinks," Alex said, and hung up the phone.

He returned to the car, punched out Meme's number, and passed on the new location.

"The man from the café," the voice said. "He did not follow you." He gave Alex the location to which the CIA man had been followed.

Alex's hands tightened on the steering wheel. You should have known, he told himself. You should have known where he would go to do his killing. He snapped out instructions to the man, then checked the rearview mirror to reassure himself he wasn't being followed, and spun the car into a sharp right turn into a narrow side street. He pressed the accelerator to the floor.

Michelle regained consciousness slowly, the pain in her head throbbing, bringing a new rush of tears to her eyes. She fought back a moan as she turned to see where Ludwig was. He was across the room, his back to her, and he was fixing a rope to the ceiling, giving the task his full attention.

Michelle twisted her body, moving the side of her full skirt under her so her bound hands could reach the knife. She slid it clumsily from the pocket, brought it behind her back, then pressed the button and snapped the blade into place. Slowly, awkwardly, she struggled to bring its razor edge against the ropes that held her wrists.

The figure approached the telephone booth and dialed the number, then listened to the American-accented voice rattle off yet another, and give directions to a third location some fifteen minutes away. Another obscene message followed, but the caller only grunted in response, then replaced the receiver and returned to the car, which was identical to the other Pisani-owned vehicle Alex had been driving.

The man's name was Michel Bonaventura, and he had worked for the Pisani faction for more than twenty years. He was the same height and weight and age as Alex, and had dressed earlier in clothing identical to that which Alex was wearing. From a distance there was no way to tell he was not the man he was portraying.

Alex walked along the Street of Refuge, barely feeling the worn cobblestones beneath his feet, more than aware of the thick film of sweat forming beneath his clothing. Despite the planning, despite the cold deliberation he had imposed upon himself, Ludwig had reached him. Meme's men had followed the CIA agent who had watched Alex in the rue de Rome café to a building on the Street of Pistols. Ludwig had set their final reckoning in the basement where Alex had found Stephanie's body ten years earlier.

Alex entered the dark alley where Meme and five of his men waited. To the west, at the other end of the block-long Street of

Pistols, a half dozen more of Meme's men cut off that route of escape. Bugayev, who had insisted on lending his support, had stationed men along the outside perimeter of the area, out of range of any armed conflict with CIA agents aiding Ludwig but effectively eliminating any routes of escape by means of the labyrinthine tunnels that crisscrossed the old quarter of the city. Everything—every detail of the plan they had meticulously prepared to trap Ludwig —was now in place. Everything was ready except the main ingredient. Alex Moran himself.

"The man from the café went inside the building," Meme said. "First he met with others, who later took up positions in buildings across the street. We know where each of them are, and can get to them before you move."

"And the man inside?" Alex asked.

"It will be hard to reach him without alerting Ludwig," Meme said. "Ludwig will not escape in any event, but—"

"He'll kill Michelle," Alex said, finishing the sentence.

"I do not want her killed," Meme said. There was no accusation in his words, just a simple statement of fact. "So there seems only one solution."

"Let the man inside take me," Alex said.

"He may kill you before you have a chance to kill him," Meme said.

"No. Ludwig wants that for himself. The man will disarm me and take me to him. It will give Ludwig time to do it pleasurably. He never had that chance ten years ago. He only had time to leave me a gift. I think he felt cheated."

Meme watched his nephew and knew he was fighting back the image of that time, the memory of the failure he had felt then. There was a line of sweat on Alex's forehead, and his eyes held a look of uncertainty Meme had seldom seen there before.

"You must do this thing," Meme said. "I will send men into the tunnels to be as close to you as possible, but men coming in with you would be heard. If this pig knows more than two men are approaching, he may panic, kill Michelle, and run."

Alex nodded and turned to go. Meme grasped his arm.

"I have something for you," he said. He nodded to one of his men, who began removing a thin, brightly braided rope from around his neck. It looked like a decorative necklace beneath the open collar of his shirt.

"What is it?" Alex asked.

"An old Corsican weapon," Meme said. He took the braided necklace from the man and held it up in the dim light. Attached to the back was a small sheath fitted with a short-bladed combat-style knife.

"It goes around the neck, under the shirt," Meme said. "The knife hangs between the shoulder blades, high up near the back of the neck. When you are searched, clasp your hands behind your head, then lean your head forward. The knife will rise up under your collar close enough to your hands to reach it."

Alex removed the knife from the sheath. It was flat and compact, and even the handle was no more than a quarter of an inch wide. The blade was four inches, just long enough for a kill, and razor sharp.

"It will kill quickly," Meme said. "It is best to face your enemy after you are disarmed, with your hands still behind your head. Then strike while he is confident he has removed all threat."

Alex nodded and fitted the thick braid around his neck, then practiced the technique several times. The weapon was beautifully balanced and far more concealable than any of the small combat knives used by the military. But then, they were seldom searched as the Corsicans were.

"Will you kill him before he takes you to Ludwig?" Meme asked.

"If he gives me the opportunity," Alex said.

Meme's eyes hardened, turning coal black and gleaming in the dim light.

"Take your time with Ludwig," he said. "Kill him slowly. Let him feel his death coming for a long time. Do it for Stephanie, and for Antoine, and for Michelle's husband and baby." He clasped Alex's arm with surprising strength. "And do it for me," he said.

Alex nodded, not knowing how to respond to this old man he had known and cared for since childhood. But he knew, after this day, he would never feel the same about him again.

The Corsicans moved into the buildings where the CIA team had stationed itself. Each man was armed with a silenced weapon, and each penetrated the buildings through the basement tunnels that had been known and used by the *milieu* for decades.

The CIA men never had a chance to defend themselves. All died quickly, never understanding how they had been found, never able to give a warning of the Corsicans' attack.

The Corsicans left the bodies where they fell and re-entered the tunnels, making their way to the building across the street, ordered to remain far enough back to avoid alerting Ludwig of their presence. They were there to kill him if Alex failed. It was their only purpose. Alex was now on his own. They were simply a final fail-safe device for Meme's brand of Corsican justice.

Alex turned into the Street of Pistols, his mind racing with the same walk he had taken ten years before. Then he had been looking for a small mark on one of the doors, and he had been sweating and frightened and uncertain what he would face. This time there was no mark, no question what awaited him. But the other feelings were the same. He knew only he had to survive long enough to see Ludwig dead. That, and to keep Michelle from his butcher's hands.

Ludwig turned and caught her watching him. Michelle's immediate impulse was to feign unconsciousness again, but she instinctively knew it was too late, that it would only provoke him, perhaps even arouse his curiosity and make him search her again. And she couldn't afford that. The knife had not yet finished its work; the rope still held her wrists.

She looked past him, to the heavier rope that hung from the rafters. He followed her gaze, then looked back at her. The hate-filled smile had returned.

"It is where his wife was when he found her," Ludwig said. "Of course, she was quite dead." He walked slowly forward, then knelt at her side. "I never had the pleasure of seeing his face then. It was most disappointing." The smile widened. He was choosing not to say why the rope was there again, but Michelle had no illusions about that.

"It was a shame," Ludwig said. He reached out and stroked her cheek. This time she did not pull away, and it seemed to surprise him.

"Being forced to kill the woman, I mean." He ran his finger along her blouse, near the unbuttoned portion above her breasts. "She was wonderful, sexually. A very giving, passionate woman. Alex must have enjoyed her favors immensely." He raised his eyebrows lasciviously. "Of course, she did like to spread them around a bit. But I'm sure it was better than being with a frigid French bitch." He ran his hand along the top of her breast. Michelle ignored it.

"I am not French," she said. "I am Corsican." She twisted her wrists, praying it would force the final strands of rope to give way. It made her move closer to his hand.

"Well, then perhaps I was wrong about you." Ludwig cupped her breast, believing the movement he had just felt was intended for his hand. His eyes glittered. He was convinced now he would have everything he had intended. Michelle's jaw tightened, and she fought off the scream of rage she felt building inside. These were the same hands that had killed her child, her husband. And now they were touching her.

"Why did you kill her if she was so good to you?" she asked, buying time, praying her hands would become free. She could see his mind work quickly, searching out a facile lie.

He offered a faint, regretful shrug. His hand was working at her breast now, one finger lightly brushing the nipple, and she saw pleasure come to his eyes. She twisted her wrists again. Still nothing.

"There was no choice," he said. "I couldn't get to him. He was too well protected by your fellow Corsicans. And I had to make him pay, don't you see? And, unfortunately, she was the only means I had."

He shook his head in mock regret. Her nipple between his fingers was erect from the stimulation, and he was rubbing it more roughly, convinced he had finally aroused a sexual need.

"It is different this time," he said. He nodded toward the rope hanging from the rafters. "There is no need for that, if I choose." He looked at her eyes, wanting to be certain she understood. "I wish the same had been true for her, for Alex's wife." He closed his eyes momentarily, as if recalling the pleasure the woman had given him. "Her mouth. It was exquisite what she could do with it."

The thought came to Michelle in a sudden, revolting rush. He would give her the same opportunity, and he would do it eagerly. She could take him in her mouth, and she could bite down with all the ferocity she felt. She could severe his member from his body, leave him screaming in pain as the blood gushed from his body, unable to be stopped. He would kill her, but he would die as well. She pressed against his hand, intentionally this time.

"I am told I do that better than anyone," she said. She pushed away all doubt, all the revulsion she felt, and forced her eyes to become coy. "But I don't know. I only know it is something that has always given me pleasure." She smiled. "Since I was a young girl." She could feel his fingers tighten on her nipple, and she felt a strange sense of arousal now, with the knowledge that she might soon be able to kill him.

Ludwig placed the Uzi beside him, his hand moving to the zipper on his trousers, the other still working her breast—more feverishly, urgently. Michelle twisted her wrists again. Again, nothing.

Ludwig reached inside his pants, then froze. The other hand pulled away from her breast. His eyes searched her face, then seemed to reach a conclusion.

"You're a clever bitch," he said. "But what if I said I just wanted to fuck you? Would you spread your legs for me?" He sneered at her, defying her to make his words false.

"I would be disappointed not to have the other first," she said. She fought to keep the coy look in her eyes, parted her lips slightly to make her mouth more alluring.

Ludwig shook his head. His eyes were sly and knowing.

"I don't think so," he said. "Suddenly I don't trust your mouth. But your cunt, I trust that." He reached under her skirt and began to pull roughly at her pants.

Michelle pushed away, forcing herself back along the filthy floor. Her eyes filled with the rage she had held in check.

"You never had the woman, did you?" she baited. "You only said it to cause Alex pain." Her mouth twisted with the overwhelming hate she felt. "But what woman would want a pig like you?" she snapped. "I'll bet you tried with his wife, and you made her sick. It's probably why you killed her. Because you couldn't stand her being sick at the sight of you."

Ludwig drew back his fist and sent it crashing into her cheek. The blow snapped Michelle's head back, and her mind instantly clouded, only the faint sensation of pain fighting through. Her head began to clear, and she felt both his hands beneath her skirt, pulling viciously at her pants. She drew her knees up and began kicking wildly, not directing the blows, striking out at any part of him within reach.

A foot connected with Ludwig's groin, and he gasped and doubled over in pain. Then his rage swelled up again, and he threw himself on top of her, one hand seizing her throat, the other, in a fist now, crashing into her face again and again.

Michelle's consciousness began to fade under the pain and the repeated concussions. Ludwig's face began to spin in front of her, and it seemed to move farther and farther away as she gradually weakened and finally lost consciousness. The last thing that registered in her head was the snapping of the rope that held her wrists.

Alex moved up the stairs he had climbed ten years earlier, feeling the same sensation of cold and sweat and terror he had felt then. It was as though nothing had changed; the intervening years had never occurred, and he had simply chosen to relive a horror that would repeat itself again and again and again.

He reached out and took hold of the doorknob, feeling the cold metal against the wetness of his hand, and he pushed the door open and stepped slowly inside. His hands were empty, the Walther automatic still tucked into the waistband of his trousers at the small of his back. He moved into the darkened hall, and it seemed the same cooking smells, the same dankness, still permeated the walls, and he saw the same small shaft of light coming from the stairwell that led to the basement.

Ten years ago he had heard a man cough, and the sound of it had terrified him, sent him flat against the wall, pistol raised and ready to kill. Now there was nothing, not the faintest hint of life, and the silence somehow seemed ominous, more threatening.

He stepped toward the basement stairwell, knowing he would be stopped soon, fighting not to anticipate where the man would come from. He wanted the man confident in his element of surprise. He wanted him to feel a sense of satisfaction at his own deftness, his ability to lure a target in and take him easily, almost effortlessly. He wanted him cocky, self-assured.

He felt the cold, hard pressure behind his right ear as he reached the basement door. The voice was equally cold, but there was also a degree of pleasure in it.

"I don't want to kill you, Moran," the man said. "It would upset your buddy downstairs if I did. But if I have to, I don't much give a shit about upsetting him. Understand?"

Alex raised his hands slowly, cautiously, knowing it was what the man would want, and placed them on the back of his head.

"It's in the waistband, at the back," he said.

The man went for the pistol and tucked it into his own belt, then began to run his hands along Alex's chest and waist, then arms and legs and sides.

"Just to be sure," he said, pressing the barrel of his gun even more firmly against Alex's head, then moving it down along his neck and back as he continued the search.

"You're early," the man said. "How come?"

"I remembered this place. Thought I'd check it out."

"Remembered it?"

"Ludwig killed my wife here. Ten years ago. But he was just a common-variety terrorist then. And I was just a poor slob station chief." Alex paused a beat. "How does it feel? Helping scum like that against one of your own, you fuck?"

The man jammed the gun harder into Alex's back, making it arch with pain.

"You're the fuck, Moran," he snapped. "You should have followed the Company line or kept your fucking nose out of it. Not play the rogue bastard you've always been." He pressed the pistol in again. "But you don't have your big boss daddy to save your ass this time. Your daddy's playing with the A-team. And you're just an over-the-hill clown who can't even walk into a building without getting himself nailed. Now move your ass down those stairs."

"Wait. Listen," Alex said. "There's got to be a deal here somewhere." He began to turn slowly, cautiously, and the man stepped back, the barrel of the pistol rising toward Alex's chin, the hammer cocked, ready to fire. Alex's hands were still behind his head, and his eyes seemed to be pleading.

"No deals, Moran. Nothing."

Alex bent his head forward, as if begging with it. "Just listen to me?" he urged.

The thin handle of the knife came up and his hand slipped around it, then continued in a smooth arching motion while the other hand snapped down at the same time, the soft, meaty flesh between the thumb and index finger jamming inside the hammer, blocking the pistol's firing pin.

Alex felt the hammer slam into his flesh as the man instinctively pulled the trigger, and his hand closed around the ejection chamber as the knife in his other hand slashed into the man's neck, cutting deep, severing veins and arteries and muscle, and sending a spurting plume of blood out across the darkened hall.

The man's body began to convulse, and Alex felt him pulling the trigger again and again. He pulled back the knife, then jammed it forward into the man's eye and twisted it, slicing as much brain as the four-inch blade would allow.

The pistol dropped from the man's hand, and his body convulsed again, the muscles losing all control; the legs kicked out, and he began to fall. Alex caught him and eased him to the floor. He smelled the urine and feces as the man who wanted to help him die gave up the last his own life had to offer.

Alex hovered over the man, crouched in the darkness like an animal, his body shaking uncontrollably, his breath jagged and rasping, as he struggled to hear any sound from the basement, any sign that the man's death had given him away.

Ludwig froze with the sharp sound that seemed to come from above and behind him. His fist was still poised to smash again into Michelle's face. He looked at her quickly and lowered his hand. There was no need to hit her again. Her face was battered pulp, covered in blood. She was unconscious, possibly even dead. He swung his leg from on top of her and picked up the discarded Uzi, quickly chambering a round and snapping the selector switch to full automatic. Then he remained still, listening, holding his breath so he could hear every sound.

He heard a faint creak, on what could have been the stairs, and he rose slowly to his feet. Moran, he thought. He shouldn't be here yet, but he could be—he could have figured it out and gambled on finding him. But where were the others, the ones who were supposed to stop him, then bring him down here to die?

He grabbed Michelle by the hair and yanked her to a sitting position, his legs astride her so that her head was below and between his legs. He lowered the barrel of the Uzi to the top of her head and watched the entrance to the stairs. He never saw her hands flop free as he lifted her between his legs.

Alex descended the stairs, close to the wall, the Walther he had retrieved from the dead CIA agent held in both hands, the barrel along his face, almost touching the side of his head. The short hall ahead, the turn into the large basement room, all came back to him, and he felt his heart pounding in his chest, just as he had ten years earlier. You're going to die, Ludwig, he told himself. No matter what else happens, today you're going to die.

He edged his way along the dimly lit hall, fighting to control his breath, wanting it steady and even so he could draw one final deep breath, let it partially out, then hold it just as he swung into the room and opened fire. There was no sound coming from the open, dirty basement, just as there had been nothing all those years before when he had entered it, ready to kill the same man, only to find his wife hanging there, butchered like an animal.

His heart began to pound even faster, and his breath seemed to come in gasps as he thought of finding Michelle there dead and butchered, left by Ludwig as some perversely repeated joke.

He took the final three steps, knowing he should hesitate, wait for some sound of movement, some indication of direction to which he should turn. But he couldn't, and he spun into the room, the Walther out before him now, both eyes open, sighting down the barrel.

"Don't, Moran, or she's dead."

Alex stared at Ludwig's face, at Michelle's bloodied features, held between his legs. He saw the Uzi against her skull, Ludwig's finger on the trigger, seeming larger than life. It all came in flashes, more images being added each mini-second, as if his brain were shorting out, suddenly operating in fast forward and fighting to keep up with the information.

Ludwig's filthy smile came to him. Then the contrasting hard eyes. Then finally his voice, as everything began to slow, return to normal speed. The pistol in his hand began to waver; the hand itself began to tremble, and he struggled to steady it.

"You figured it out," Ludwig said. "I hadn't counted on that. Didn't give you that much credit." He moved the Uzi slightly, making sure Alex's eyes were drawn to it. "I can kill her even if you fire. It's set on full automatic, and you know what it will do, even on reflex. It will send her head all over the room." The filthy smile widened and the eyes glittered madly. "Put the gun down, Alex. *Put . . . it . . . down!*"

The Walther wavered in his hand and slowly began to fall to his side. Alex's eyes were fixed on Ludwig's, knowing he would see it there first, when he began to move the Uzi to swing it in his direction. He caught the faintest of movements between Ludwig's legs, but didn't dare look to see what it was.

Ludwig didn't see it either. His eyes were fixed on Alex, looking for the opening he wanted, the chance to kill him quickly and cleanly.

Michelle's hands moved along the floor, fumbling, finally finding the handle of the stiletto and bringing it in front of her. She grasped it with both hands and raised her eyes, barely able to see through the blood that covered her face. But she could see enough. She could see what she wanted. And she could hear his voice, floating down to her.

She thrust the knife up just as Ludwig began to swing the Uzi up and away. She used both hands, almost raising her body from the floor, as she plunged the blade into his groin. Then a second time. Then a third.

Alex watched Ludwig's eyes snap open in horror—his mouth formed a silent scream—as the slender blade stabbed into his crotch. He swung the Walther up as the blade struck again, bringing a wail of agony from Ludwig's lips. The Uzi fired a long, deafening burst as Ludwig squeezed the trigger reflexively, and bits of the ceiling rained down as Alex fired three rounds into his chest.

The Walther's 9 mm. bullets lifted Ludwig up and threw him back like a discarded doll, sending the Uzi flying off to one side.

Alex stepped toward Michelle, but before he could move farther, she had spun around and was scuttling back along the floor, chasing after the fallen body, the stiletto still in her hand, a cry of pure animal rage pouring from her mouth.

She was on him in seconds, and the knife plunged down into Ludwig's chest again and again and again.

Alex came up behind her and pinned her arms to her sides.

"It's all right," he said. "It's over. It's over. It's over."

Michelle stared down at Ludwig's body, and Alex felt her muscles begin to shake violently. Then she fell back against him and her body went suddenly slack; she began to sob.

CHAPTER

iers Moran paced the living room of the luxurious suite he had occupied for the past five days. The hotel—one of the finest in Marseilles—was located on the Corniche President Kennedy, and all of its rooms opened onto the Mediterranean. Piers had spent the first two days staring at the sea. The next two were spent pacing the room. Now, on the fifth day, he had added drinking to his cat-like prowl.

He had left repeated messages for James Wheelwright at the consulate, but each call had gone unanswered. Then in desperation he had telephoned Walter Hennesey in Washington, and had been assured he would "get on Wheelwright's ass" and have him call back immediately. That had been three days ago, and now Hennesey too was among the missing.

The newspapers had carried accounts of shootings in the old quarter, but the details had been sketchy, and he had thought about contacting Raphael Rivera, or the other members of the "ad hoc committee." But he wasn't certain his calls weren't being monitored just to see who he did call. So he had waited.

He walked to a small side table and replenished his long-stemmed glass from a martini pitcher. Then he opened the French doors that led to the balcony. The fresh sea air hit him immediately, ruffling his hair and making him feel slightly unsteady, and he reached out for the stone balustrade to support himself. He was dressed in the same shirt and trousers he had worn the day before, and his tie was missing, and he had not shaved or even brushed his teeth. He was coming apart, and there was nothing he could do about it.

In the old days, if he had needed to know something, he had simply called Meme Pisani, and within hours he had that information. But that was no longer possible. Marseilles was no longer the friendly city it had been. And he was no longer a man of power here.

It was ridiculous. He could remember it all so clearly—it seemed no more than a year or so ago—when he and Meme and Antoine and Colette had stood on that sea wall, watching hundreds of French children waving tiny American flags as a train filled with food pulled into the station. Now *that* had been power. In those days a man could bend an entire city to his will, an entire nation. Today his government—the most powerful nation on earth—was lucky if it could get some shitpot dictator like Noriega to take its money without adding a dozen outrageous conditions to every deal.

He drew a deep breath, filling his lungs with sea air, as the wind battered his hair again. He turned and walked back into the living room, then suddenly froze. The long-stemmed glass fell from his hand, splashing his drink over the carpet. Alex stood across the room staring at him, his eyes flat and cold and dispassionate.

Piers bent and picked up the glass, then looked around for something with which to clean up the spilled drink, not certain why he was doing so.

"How did you get in here?" he asked, not certain why he had said that either.

"Old intelligence trick," Alex said. "Opening locked doors. I'm sure you remember." He walked to a chair and sat, then pointed to the sofa. "Sit down," he said. Piers did as he was told.

"It's good to see you," he said. "It's good to see you well." He was truly pleased that Alex had survived. But he didn't think the boy would understand that.

"Let's cut the crap," Alex said. He did not seem angry, but more like a man who was doing something he had to do, something which he found distasteful.

"Ludwig's dead," he said. "And Walter Hennesey's on a medical leave. So are Baldwin and Batchler. Seems there's something contagious going around Langley."

"So you turned over the documentation of our little arrangement with the Pisani brothers," Piers said.

"No, I gave the information to Wheelwright. I owed him a favor. The documention's in the safe of a Zurich attorney. To be released to the French media in the event of my untimely death. Langley wasn't pleased to hear that. But they were content that the information wouldn't turn up, by way of France, on the pages of the *Washington Post*."

"So it's over for us," Piers said.

"I would think so."

"Pity."

"You had a long, profitable run," Alex said.

Piers stared at him. "It was more than that, you know. It helped us control France. We accomplished a great deal for the country. *Our* country."

"I'm not interested in your reasons. Or excuses."

Piers nodded. "What will happen to the others?" he asked. Alex noted he seemed to harbor no concern for himself.

"I don't know. You'd know the answer to that better than I. But I doubt the government will issue sanctions against so many ranking intelligence officers. It might look odd, having that many people fall off boats, or crash cars, or commit suicide, don't you think?"

Piers ran his hand through his wind-blown hair, straightening it. He realized how he must look to his son, and it distressed him.

"Meme said you'd come to kill me," he said. "Is that why you're here?"

There was a slight slur in his father's voice, and Alex realized he was drunk.

"No, I think there's been enough attempted murder in our family. It's starting to feel like a Shakespearean play." He paused. "If Michelle had died, I would have. But she didn't. Besides, I think Uncle Meme will take care of that."

"He said not."

Alex leaned forward and interlaced the fingers of his hands, his forearms resting on his knees. "He lied to you. We wanted you to go to Ludwig, just as you did."

Pier's eyebrows rose in disbelief. "You followed me?"

"No. I had too much respect for your skills. We wanted you to get Ludwig to come for me. Use you as a sort of a Judas goat. Somehow it seemed appropriate."

Piers bristled, sat straighter in his seat.

"Don't be impertinent," he snapped. "This wasn't personal. This was a business matter. You were in the game long enough. I thought you'd understand that. It's why I directed you into the business in the first place. You were the best of the brood."

Alex laughed. "Oh, come, Father. Let's not add one lie to the other. Old *Richbird* was always the paternal favorite. We both know that. I was always the son you didn't quite know what to do with."

Piers stood and began pacing the room again. Then he turned and faced his son. He was pleased Alex was alive, and he even felt a grudging admiration for what he had done.

"Richard was always an adequate man, of a sort," he said. "And I loved him. Just as I loved you. But in intelligence he wouldn't have been able to find his dick with both hands, as our Corsican friends are wont to say. You, however. Well, you've shown what you can do. It's why we had to do what *we* did. You were simply too good to risk gambling on."

Alex laughed and sat back in his chair. "You truly amaze me, Father. But then, I suppose you always have. Yes, I'm sure old Richard would have been very offended if you had tried to have him killed." He shook his head, still staring at his father, who suddenly seemed very old. "You are an incredible old shit," he said.

Piers's eyes narrowed, and his lips formed a thin, disapproving line. Alex thought he looked like a schoolmaster displeased with an errant student.

"And you are still a man who has a penchant for tilting at windmills," Piers said. "Always looking for a dragon to slay."

"There seem to be a lot of them around, don't you think?"

"Is that what you'll do now? Go after the others?"

"Perhaps." Alex stood and looked at his father for what he knew would be the last time. "But you're the biggest dragon I know. And Uncle Meme has a bit of a Don Quixote complex himself. I'd be careful if I were you."

"I'll survive Meme," Piers said.

"Perhaps you will."

Alex turned and started for the door, then stopped just as his hand touched the doorknob. "I don't imagine it will be terribly comfortable, though. All the places you'd enjoy, they'll be the ones where Meme will look for you first."

"Perhaps I'll surprise you," Piers said.

"You always have."

Piers realized he would not see his son again. He regretted it. But he knew he'd survive it too.

"I'm glad you killed the bastard," he said. "I'm glad you got to do what you've needed for so long."

"So am I," Alex said. He pulled the door open.

"Do me a favor," Piers said, stopping him again. "Come to my funeral. Just for old time's sake."

"Perhaps I will," Alex said. "If it's convenient."

"I'll try to see that it is," Piers said.

EPILOGUE

Buenos Aires

Raphael Rivera climbed behind the wheel of the gray Lincoln he had imported from the United States, and briefly checked his appearance in the rearview mirror. He was on his way to the club he had joined two months earlier, shortly after he had arrived in the Argentinian capital. There was a particular woman —the rather wayward wife of one of the members—whom he intended to look up today. She had engaged in a casual bit of flirtation the past few weeks, and today he planned to take her up on it and see where it would lead.

Retirement wouldn't be bad, he told himself. He was really too young for it, but the alternative hadn't been all that attractive. And there was enough money to live exceptionally well, and one could do far worse than play out one's days in a beautiful city. Especially one that was filled with lovely Spanish women. He smiled at the thought, but the smile faded quickly. He would miss the power, that was certain. But then, power had a way of returning if you knew where to seek it out. And had the money to pursue it.

He slipped the key into the ignition and prepared to turn the switch. The garotte slipped over his head with a faint whisper, and before Rivera could react, it had snapped tightly around his neck. He arched his back and twisted violently, his arms and legs flailing, his hands reaching for the wire, which had already cut through the skin. The back of his head was pressed against the head rest, and he stretched out his hands, trying to reach the horn on the steering wheel, fighting to send out some kind of alarm that might bring help. But the fingers fell just inches short, and he flailed his arms again, beating against the side window, and kicked with his feet, one finally coming up over the dashboard and against the windshield.

The last thing Rivera saw was his foot smashing the windshield into a spiderweb of cracks, then finally breaking through as one foot emerged into the cool morning air. Then he felt the blood pouring down his shirt front from the severed veins and arteries in his neck, and he died thinking he would never be able to wear the shirt again, and that it was quite new; had been made for him only a month ago.

Chevy Chase, Maryland

John Batchler sat behind the desk in his walnut-paneled study, reviewing the incorporation papers his attorney had just faxed to his home. They were for a new security business he was forming, one specializing in industrial espionage, and taking full advantage of his eighteen years with the Company. He had not intended to take that step for another two years, and then with the advantage of a government pension to help cover the expense. Not cover it financially, but rather do so without dipping into the substantial funds he had secreted away in a Panamanian bank account. Now he would have to worry about those IRS bastards raising questions about where the investment capital had come from, and that was something that always had to be avoided. The last thing he wanted was to end up living on some mosquito-infested island with a bunch of jungle bunnies for neighbors.

But he had to work. He'd go crazy without something to occupy his time. He'd end up sitting at home with his wife, or be off with her—like she was today—to that incredibly boring tennis club where she spent all her time, sitting and chatting with that group of insipid Yuppie wives. Christ, he thought, even a group of jungle bunny neighbors would be better than that.

He stood and stretched, then headed for the kitchen to get himself a sandwich and a cold bottle of beer. He pulled open the refrigerator, then stopped. A faint scratching sound was coming from the adjoining garage, and he walked to the door that led to it, opened it, and reached for the light switch just to the left of the door frame. Nothing. The damned bulb must have died, and now the scratching had stopped. Probably some goddamned vermin that had found its way in and was chewing on something valuable, like his new four hundred dollar fucking golf bag.

He went down the three steps, then stopped to listen again, giving himself time for his eyes to adjust to the dark. He didn't want to open the garage door and let the damned thing escape, so he would have to get the flashlight from the glove compartment of his Mercedes. He stepped toward the car, then stopped, squinting at the door frame. There was heavy duct tape lining the driver's window and covering a hose that had been stuck inside. Sweat began to flood his body as he followed the hose back to the car's tailpipe.

The bastards, he thought. They had assured him no sanction would be issued if he just got out. And now this. Now this.

He turned slowly, expecting to find a pistol leveled at his face, but all he saw was the faint outline of a man standing so close he should have heard him; he couldn't believe he hadn't heard him come up from behind.

The last thing Batchler saw was a flash of movement as the edge of a hand cut the air and crashed into the side of his neck. Then he felt himself falling, but he never felt the floor come up to meet him.

Inside the kitchen, the cold beer remained unopened on the counter top. His wife would wonder later that day why he hadn't drunk it before he had taken his own life.

Georgetown

Christopher Baldwin had decided to get himself into shape, drop the thirty extra pounds he had managed to gain and get back into the size forty-two suit he had not worn in fifteen years. Jogging and diet was the solution, he had decided, and after a thorough physical, to ensure his heart wouldn't burst with the effort, he had begun a daily regimen that had already shed ten pounds of flab in the past month.

He reflected on that success as his Reeboks beat a tattoo on the footpath that ran alongside the Chesapeake & Ohio Canal. It was an easy run—not too many hills, and only a few blocks from his home—and the Washington humidity took care of the needed sweat. And there were also the young lovelies from Georgetown University, up on the hill, to take one's mind off the pain in one's legs.

He rounded a turn and thought about the woman he had met at F. Scotts the night before—the neighborhood watering hole that had become a regular stop since he had left the Company two months before. She had been attracted to him even with twenty pounds yet to go, and they had made a dinner date for the following week. He would not end up like that fool Batchler, he told himself. No one would ever find *him* sucking on an exhaust pipe in *his* garage.

He had just passed the Key Bridge, and he glanced out toward the wide stretch of the Potomac off to his left. It was 6:00 A.M., and the river was free of boats, and even the sounds of traffic along the Whitehurst Freeway and normally frantic M Street were nothing more than a distant hum.

He caught movement some thirty feet ahead of him and looked toward it, then staggered and stumbled to an unsteady halt. The man had stepped out from behind a tree, and he held a silenced automatic in both hands, the barrel level with Baldwin's nose.

"Jesus Christ. Don't!" he stammered.

The man tilted his head to one side, almost in a gesture of resignation. "Your money or your life," he said. But there was no mirth in his voice.

"Come on," Baldwin said. "We can talk about this. We can work something out." He was trembling, his legs shaking so hard, he thought they'd give out on him. His bladder suddenly felt as though it would burst.

"I had nothing to do with it," he rattled on. "It wasn't my—"

The 9 mm. bullet took him in the forehead, just above his left eye, and his body fell like wet laundry, his head just off the path.

The pockets of Baldwin's sweat pants were gone through quickly. His keys were tossed aside, the few dollars he had, removed. Washington had become a dangerous city, a newspaper columnist would write a few days later. Drug addicts were mugging and murdering people every day.

Norfolk, Virginia

The mouth of the James River was smooth as glass as Walter Hennesey pointed his forty-five-foot sloop into the channel that would take him out into the mouth of Chesapeake Bay, past Cape Henry, and into the Atlantic. His last tour of Navy duty, more than twenty years ago now, had been here at Norfolk, and so he had sailed these waters endlessly, knew them, he told himself, like the proverbial back of his hand.

It felt good to be on the water, and in ten minutes, when he had cleared the other boats moored off the marina, he would cut the engine, hoist sail, and enjoy the solitude of the water hissing beneath the hull. It was a great deal of work, running a boat this size single-handed. But it was the way he preferred it, and he hadn't exactly been overwhelmed with offers of companionship when he had moved into a house near the old base a month earlier.

He had taken his Navy retirement. The bastards in the Company hadn't been able to deny him that, although they had certainly tried. But the word had gotten around—as it always seemed to—and his one visit to the base officers' club had made him feel like the pariah he had become.

Fuck them all, he told himself as he watched the gulls circle above the mast. Next week he'd take the boat down the intracoastal to Florida, then over to Bimini, or out to Key West. And then, when things had died down, he'd tap the money that had been accumulating and drawing interest for more than fifteen years, and he'd start his own bloody navy if he chose to.

Piers Moran flashed across his mind, and he wondered where the old francophile had finally holed up. At least *he* didn't have Meme Pisani on his tail. The old greaseball had not taken any offense to his role in the whole fouled-up game. He had had no personal relationship with the brothers, so his actions had been viewed strictly as business. But Piers had been another matter, and he had known it, had gone on the dodge as soon as his feet had touched back down in the States.

Poor bastard, Hennesey told himself. No doubt stuck away in some godforsaken hole, not even able to really enjoy the money he had packed away over all those years. And his snooty old bag of a wife had decided to stay in Palm Beach. Or perhaps Piers had just left her there. He really couldn't be sure. Well, maybe he's found some young thing to keep him happy. It was probably the best he could hope for now.

Hennesey glanced ahead to see how many more boats he had to pass before he could safely cut the engine and set sail. It would be better without the sound of the engine. He liked the quiet. The quiet and a running sea. It was always better then, he told himself.

Alex Moran watched from shore, the field glasses fixed on the retreating forty-five-foot sloop. The gelatin capsule, with its innocent-seeming sodium mixture, would be cooking now, as the fuel was steadily heated by the boat's engine.

He lowered the glasses and kept his eyes fixed on the spot, the boat only a small speck in the distance. When the ball of flame erupted it seemed small and insignificant, as did the rumble of the explosion. Only the following plume of black smoke really indicated that anything truly significant had taken place.

But it happened so often these days. People just couldn't seem to remember to start the blowers on their engines, or to check to make sure the natural gas for the stove was turned off. Then it only took a spark, and all that was left was a burnt-out hull several fathoms beneath the sea.

Pity, Alex told himself, as he turned and headed for his car. He had a flight back to Marseilles that night, and it was still a long drive back to New York.

Cervione

Alex watched as Michelle busied herself about the kitchen, helping Colette put together trays of food to serve their guest. She had not ordered him out of the way yet—nor had Colette—but it would happen soon, he had no doubt of it.

He loved to watch her doing the simple things that had become their daily life together. And he knew the more simple it remained, the more he would enjoy it.

And he loved to look at her as well. The disfigurement to her face, where Ludwig had beaten her so viciously, didn't matter. Everything about her was pleasing to him, and every day he found a new enchantment in her, and anxiously awaited what he might discover next.

The doctors in Marseilles had told her the disfigurement could be corrected, and that only a few small scars would remain. But she had chosen to do nothing about it. Perhaps she still required the wounds, either in repentance for what she had done, or to remind herself that her child's death had finally been avenged. It was her decision, and he knew it was something he would never ask her to change.

He had brought little Pierre's body and that of her late husband back to Corsica, and with Meme's permission he had laid them to rest next to Antoine. He had convinced Michelle it was best that she be close to them, and that, together, they would fulfill the Corsican dictate that flowers be placed on the graves every day.

"Why are you standing there staring at me?" Michelle said, fighting back a smile at the sudden look of guilt that covered his face.

"Yes, why?" It was Colette this time, her voice, and her look, sterner.

"I just like looking at you," he said. He glanced at Colette. "And you," he added.

"Get out!" Michelle said, still fighting the smile, with even more difficulty this time. "Go see to our guest. And make sure he doesn't make you promise to do anything for him."

"I promise you that will never happen," he said. It was a promise, he knew, he very much wanted to keep.

Pat Cisco took in the view from the stone terrace that looked out over the *maquis* to the distant sea. He had flown in from Marseilles that afternoon, unannounced but expected. It had only been a question of time, Alex knew, before Washington sent out a firm warning.

"So Antoine left you this place in his will," Cisco said, openly impressed with Alex's unexpected inheritance.

"Yeah, surprised the hell out of me," Alex said. "It seems Meme owned the house in Marseilles, and this one was Antoine's. The will said he was leaving it to his favorite pants pisser," he added.

"What the hell does that mean?" Cisco asked.

"It's a long story," Alex said. "Someday I'll tell it to you."

"So you've retired to the country life," Cisco said. There was no question in his voice, but his look asked it anyway.

"Completely," Alex said.

"No excursions planned to South America or the States or any other interesting ports of call?"

"None planned, none anticipated," Alex answered. "I don't have any reason to travel."

"And if I tell the boys at Langley that, you won't make a liar out of me?"

"Never happen."

"Good. Then I won't have to deliver their warning."

"That's a shame," Alex said. "I imagine it was an especially awesome one."

"You know the Company. 'Awesome' is their middle name."

"I always thought it was 'clown,' " Alex said.

Cisco smiled and turned back to the view. "They do get a bit belligerent when their people—even their defrocked people—die unexpectedly, and they're forced to answer awkward questions." Cisco turned back to face Alex. "Actually, it's the awkward questions they mind more than the deaths."

"Have some of their friends passed away?" Alex asked. "I haven't kept up with the newspapers."

Cisco smiled at the open innocence Alex projected, caught Alex battling a smile himself.

"Yes. Four to be exact. They had all been forced to resign or retire. Cut off. Just like your father was."

It had been done rather cleverly—especially for Langley. No questions from the press or oversight committees. A minor miracle. Used guises of poor health, time in service, outside business opportunities. And it actually seemed to have worked. No embarrassment for the Company. Then the recently departed all started to really become departed. And they all died in sort of a rush. Quite embarrassing.

"How'd it happen?" Alex asked. His face showed nothing now, not even the previous hint of a smile.

Cisco looked down at his shoes and gave a slight shake of his head. He didn't mind playing the game, would have played it himself had he been on the other side of the conversation.

"Raphael Rivera was the first," he said. "He'd resigned to pursue business interests in Buenos Aires." Cisco smiled. "I suppose he'd accumulated a bit of capital over the years.

"Anyway, seems someone garotted him when he got in his car one morning. Was on his way to a country club he had joined. Wasn't found for several hours. And it was a hot day, and the windows of the car were closed. I doubt it was the way Rivera saw his departure from this veil of tears."

Alex shook his head. "Nasty," he said.

"John Batchler was next," Cisco said. "He'd left the Company to start his own security consulting operation. Something must have gone wrong. They found him inside his Mercedes locked in his garage. The motor was running, and there was a hose going from the tail pipe to the car's interior." Cisco looked back toward the sea. "Funny thing, though. There weren't any fingerprints on the hose. Not even John's."

"He was always a very neat man," Alex said.

"Next came Baldwin. Apparently shot by a mugger while he was out jogging in a park near Georgetown University. Early in the morning. No witnesses, I'm afraid. He'd retired for health reasons. Extreme fatigue. Company had to explain what he was doing jogging. A Company doc told them it was prescribed therapy for a related stress problem."

"Cities are stressful. And they aren't very safe anymore."

"No," Cisco said. "They're not. The *Washington Post* even had an editorial about that.

"Seems boats aren't very safe either. Walter Hennesey—he'd taken early retirement and moved back to the sight of his last naval command, Norfolk—he was out sailing when the engine on his sloop blew up. Burned right to the waterline."

"It's the way he'd like to have gone," Alex said. "Down with his ship."

Cisco drew a deep breath. "So, anyway, the Company decided to find out if there was any connection with all these sudden tragedies. Even questioned Meme Pisani, I understand."

"I heard," Alex said. "But he never said what he told them."

Cisco smiled. "I understand most of it had to be deleted from the report for security reasons—and to avoid offending anyone who might be sensitive about language. But the gist of it was, he was sorry someone else beat him to it."

"That sounds like Uncle Meme."

"Yeah, well, no one came up with any proof of movement by his people to the areas in question anyway."

"So that left me," Alex said. "I'm sorry they think I'm capable of such things."

Cisco fought a smile again. "Oh, I don't think they were terribly sad about the deaths. I think they were a bit miffed that someone from Defense Intelligence might be able to off so many of their people and get away clean. That, and the embarrassment it caused in other ways."

Alex nodded and looked out toward the sea himself. "Well, tell them I'm innocent. That should ease some of their concerns."

"I don't think I'll go that far," Cisco said. "But I will tell them you don't have any future travel plans."

Alex turned back to him and grinned. "I plan to stay right here," he said.

"So what will you do?" Cisco asked.

"The inheritance also included Antoine's share of the Pisani vineyard. We've divided it. Broken it away from Meme's part. Michelle and I are going to make some wine." Alex smiled. "She knows how to make it," he said. "So far I'm just able to drink it."

"The little old wine maker," Cisco said. "Somehow it doesn't quite seem to suit you."

"It will," Alex said. "Given time."

"Speaking of time. How much more do you think your father has?" He watched Alex's eyes, looking for some sign of concern or regret. There was nothing there.

"As much as he wants, I'd guess. As long as he stays holed up in the hills."

"You know where he is?"

"Yes. My mother told me when I stopped to see her." He smiled. "On my *final* visit to the States," he added.

"You don't think Meme will get that out of her?"

He watched Alex shake his head. "It's against the rules. His rules. You don't go near family. Don't involve them."

"Nice custom," Cisco said. "You trust it?"

"Completely," Alex said. "Meme doesn't need any more enemies right now. Even a solitary one like me."

"Yeah, he's under the gun, I hear. Both from the police and the vultures in the *milieu*. It's not as sweet, I guess, without the Company's seal of approval. Who do you think will get him first?"

"I think he'll die of old age," Alex said.

"Your father too?" Cisco asked.

"Probably. The ones who deserve it most always seem to go in their sleep."

Cisco stared at him. "You really feel that way about him?"

"Just being honest," Alex said. "Or trying to be, anyway."

"You know your brother's going to be indicted. For laundering drug money."

"Happens in the best of families," Alex said.

"Your mother will take that hard, I imagine."

"She'll just deny it. She's good at that."

"And your father, you think he'll stay away?"

"He's a pragmatist," Alex said. "Business is business."

Cisco shook his head. He wondered what Alex really felt, but knew he'd never know. He wondered if anyone ever would.

"Would you consider doing a job for me from time to time?" he asked. "Off the books, as they say."

"No, he wouldn't."

They both turned to the sound of Michelle's voice, and watched her coming onto the balcony with a tray of drinks. Colette was behind her, carrying another tray of food, and Cisco was struck by the fact that both women's faces were badly disfigured. Michelle's eventually correctable by surgery, he thought. Colette's never. Alex didn't seem to notice as he kissed Michelle's cheek and smiled affectionately at the older woman.

"You heard the lady," he said. "She intends to keep me tied to her vineyard. Stomping grapes, I think."

"Only for the next twenty years," Michelle said. "Then you can retire and sit in a café and tell lies to the other men."

"Can I go hunting occasionally?" he asked. There was a playful look in his eye, and Cisco suddenly envied him very much. It would be so nice to walk away from it, he thought. So very nice.

"Of course you can go hunting," Michelle said. She glanced toward Cisco. "But not with him."

"I think I'm ready for a café myself," Cisco said. "And I'm very good at telling lies."

Alex smiled at him. He owed the man a great deal. Probably his life. And he knew it would be very hard to turn him down.

"Good," he said. "Come back when you're ready. And we'll sit in a sunny café and show these Corsicans what real liars are."

"It seems you're one of them now," Cisco said.

Alex smiled. "I have been," he said, "for a very long time."